執法英文字彙手冊（三版）

柯慶忠　著

Preface

自序

繼《實用執法英文》出版後，茲再出版《執法英文字彙手冊》一書，將常用的 1300 個常用執法詞彙與 200 則片語動詞進一步整理（按 2016 年 1 月初版為 1200 個詞彙），附注音標、詞性、執法例句，並整合各單字在相關執法領域的運用。其中第 5 頁至 239 頁為共同常用詞彙，第 240 頁至 263 頁為海巡常用詞彙，第 264 頁至 301 頁為再版時續增的片語動詞，謹供讀者參考及對照閱讀。

按專業語言能力的培養，宜講究詞彙、文法及專業知識。英文文法業經語言學家研究徹底；執法專業知識即是我們所修習的各種法規與實務經驗；執法詞彙可能是共同的困難，如何找到這些實用的執法詞彙與片語動詞並加以彙整是重要的，尤其對大學部以下的學生而言，在校時課業與考試繁多，畢業後緊接著忙碌的工作，若要閱讀外文執法書刊，頗感負荷及難以持續。又外文書刊有其專業性，閱讀外文原著究竟是要充實詞彙、文法抑或專業知識，往往難以兼顧，因此，乃參照外文執法書刊，援引執法用語，完成《實用執法英文》與《執法英文字彙手冊》兩書供讀者參考。

感謝您對這本書的興趣，希望本書對您在考試或工作上有所幫助。內容疏漏、錯誤及不周之處，併祈賜教指正。

柯慶忠

2016 年 9 月　於台灣淡水

三版序

　　本書 2016 年初版時以 1200 個詞彙為基礎，並於第二版擴充為 1500 個執法詞彙與片語動詞，今第三版除繼續擴充詞彙及其例句與應用之外，並將原有《消防英文字彙手冊》併入彙整，使本書更臻完整及充實，內容包括常用執法詞彙、海巡詞彙、消防詞彙及片語動詞四大部分，共計 2400 多個詞彙及片語動詞、2000 多個應用組合及 2200 多則例句。

　　按初版自序中提到「專業語言能力的培養宜講究詞彙、文法及專業知識。執法詞彙可能是共同的困難，如何找到這些實用的執法詞彙與片語動詞並加以彙整是重要的」，這有賴於大量閱讀執法相關書籍與文章並觀察用字，固雖然極度專業的法律或執法英文必定艱澀，但其實許多常用執法字彙大家並不陌生，只是還有多一層意義而已，例如 beat 從通常理解的「敲打、心跳」變成「(派出所的)勤區」；examination 從「考試」變成「鑑定、鑑識」或「(法庭上的)詰問」；find 從「找到」變成「裁決、認定、判定」；search 從「尋找」變成「搜索」；sentence 從「句子」變成「宣判、判決」；provide 從「提供」變成「(法條的)規定」；party 從「派對」變成「(訴訟的)一造」；try 從「嘗試」變成「審理、審判」等等。此外本書整理出許多應用組合，目的是讓讀者有素材可以聯想及延伸。總之本書以符合實用為原則，從執法人員的角度將通用且出現頻率高的字詞加以彙整成書。

　　本人曾在警政機關第一線涉外單位服務十餘年，在國內外修讀法律學位稍有基本法律概念，並在警大及警專授課「專業警察英文」，除《實用執法英文》及《執法英文字彙手冊》，另完成《國際刑事合作概論》，將本人在執法英文與國際刑事合作的所學及見聞加以彙整，希望對您在考試或工作上有所幫助。

　　感謝您對這本書的興趣，內容疏漏、錯誤及不周之處，併祈賜教指正。

柯慶忠

2024 年 2 月　於台灣淡水

目錄 CONTENTS

執法英文字彙 6

A 6
B 36
C 50
D 82
E 101
F 118
G 128
H 134
I 140
J 158
K 162
L 162
M 169
N 179
O 182
P 189
Q 211
R 212
S 234
T 261
U 274
V 277
W 280
Y 283

海巡執法英文字彙 285

A 285
B 287
C 287
D 289
E 291
F 291
G 292
H 292
I 293
J 295
L 295
M 295
N 297
O 297
P 299
Q 300
R 300
S 300
T 303
U 303
V 304
W 304

消防相關英文字彙 306

片語動詞與執法應用 322

B...322
C...325
D...328
E...329
F...329
G...331
H...335
K...336

L...338
M..341
P...341
R...345
S...347
T...351
W 354

目錄

執法英文字彙

abandon [əˋbændən]	*vt.*	拋棄，遺棄 According to police, the child was found **abandoned** in a stroller at the parking lot at around 3 a.m. 根據警方所述，該名孩童在清晨 3 點被發現放在嬰兒推車內而遺棄在公園。 A parent is guilty of abandonment of a child when he or she deserts a child in any place with intent to **abandon** such child. 父或母基於遺棄兒童之故意，而拋棄該兒童於任何地方者，犯遺棄兒童罪。
abandonment [əˋbændənmənt]	*n.*	拋棄，遺棄 應用 *abandonment of children* 遺棄兒童 *malicious abandonment* 惡意遺棄
abduct [æbˋdʌkt]	*vt.*	誘拐，綁架 The little girl **was abducted by** a stranger while playing outside her home, police said. 警方說，這個小女孩在她家外面玩的時候被陌生人拐走了。 Authorities have captured the man who **abducted** the little girl. The man's name has not been released. 當局抓到了綁架小女孩的人，該人的名字還沒公開。
abduction [æbˋdʌkʃən]	*n.*	誘拐，綁架 Police are seeking the public's assistance in locating the male believed to be connected to the **abduction** of the little girl. 警方請求大眾協助找尋該名據信與誘拐小女孩有關連的男子。 **Abduction** is the taking away of a person by persuasion or by fraud. Kidnapping is the taking away of a person against his or her will by force or threat. 「誘拐/綁架(abduction)」是以說服或詐欺的方式將人帶走，「擄人(kidnapping)」是以武力或威脅違反他人意願而將人帶走。
abettor [əˋbɛtɚ]	*n.*	【律】教唆犯 Any person who intentionally induces another to intentionally commit an unlawful act is an **abettor** and shall be liable to be sentenced as if he were a principal. 任何人故意引誘他人去故意從事違法行為者，為教唆犯，應如同正犯一樣受到判刑。
abhor	*vt.*	憎惡，痛恨 As a law enfocement officer, I **abhor** crimes and any form of abusive behavior. 身為執法人員，我痛恨犯罪以及任何形式的侮辱行為。

abide [ə`baɪd]	*vi.*	遵守 (+by) Once the prisoner is released on parole, the parolee will be returned to prison if he or she fails to **abide by** the condition of parole. 一旦受刑人被假釋，如果該假釋人未能遵守假釋條件，就會被送回監獄。 Most people are **law-abiding** citizens who never have any problems with the law. 大部分的人都是從來沒有法律麻煩的守法的市民。
ablaze [ə`blez]	*adj.*	燃燒的 The man was caught on a surveillance camera as he fought with the cashier. Suddenly he **set fire to** the store and then **set the car ablaze** with a lighter. 這名男子跟店員打鬥的時後正被監視器拍到，突然間，他就對店家放火，然後用打火機點火燒了汽車。 應用 *to set st. ablaze* 焚燒某物 The arsonist is alleged **to have set** the three vehicles ablaze. 縱火犯涉嫌對這三輛車子放火。
abolish [ə`bɑlɪʃ]	*vt.*	(制度或法律的) 廢止，革除 (+by) Capital punishment **has been abolished by** many countries. Many countries **have abolished** capital punishment either in law or in practice. 死刑已被許多國家廢除了，許多國家不管是法律上或在實務上，廢除了死刑。
abortion [ə`bɔrʃən]	*n.*	墮胎 I believe we can all recognize that **abortion** in many ways represents a sad, even tragic choice to many women. The best way to reduce the number of **abortions** is to reduce the number of unwanted pregnancies in the first place. (from Hillary Clinton) 我相信我們都認同，墮胎從許多方面來看，都是很多婦女的悲傷、甚至是悲劇性的選擇。減少墮胎數目的最好方法就是先減少不想要的懷孕 (希拉蕊)。
abscond [æb`skɑnd]	*vi.*	(為躲避罪責而) 潛逃，逃亡 The suspect **absconded** from jail last week. 嫌犯上星期從看守所逃匿。 He **absconded** from custody while attending the court hearing. 他在參加法院聽證之際，從拘禁中逃匿。 He **absconded** from parole. 他在假釋中潛逃。 He **has absconded** to the US. 他已經潛逃美國。
abstain [əb`sten]	*vi.*	禁絕，戒除，棄權 (+from) You should **abstain from** alcohol if you know you are planning to

drive. Many fatal crashes would not have happened if drivers **had abstained from** alcohol. 如果你知道你將得開車，你應該謝絕飲酒。許多致命的車禍，要是駕駛人早戒除飲酒的話，就不至於會發生了。

abuse [əˋbjus]	*vt.*	濫用，辱罵，虐待，侮辱

Generally speaking, if a woman **is abused by** her husband, her children are also likely **to be abused**. 通常而言，如果一個婦女是被丈夫虐待的話，那她的小孩也可能會被虐待。

If you suspect that a child **is abused**, or if a child tells you he or she **is being abused**, it's time to take action and and call the police. 如果你懷疑有小孩受到虐待，或如果有小孩告訴你他正受到虐待，那就是應採取行動及報警的時候了。

n. 濫用，辱罵，虐待，侮辱

應用

abuse of discretion 裁量的濫用

abuse of power 權力的濫用

abusive behavior 虐待行為

alcohol abuse 酒精濫用

child abuse 兒童虐待

domestic abuse 家暴

drug abuse 毒品濫用

economic abuse 經濟上的虐待

elder abuse 虐待長者

emotional abuse 精神虐待

physical abuse 身體上的虐待

psychological abuse 心理虐待

sex/sexual abuse 性虐待

substance abuse 藥物濫用

verbal abuse 語言辱罵

abuser [əˋbjuzɚ]	*n.*	虐待者，濫用者

abusive [əˋbjusɪv]	*adj.*	濫用的，辱罵的，虐待的

The battered woman said her husband **was abusive**. 受暴婦女說她丈夫愛虐待辱罵。

People who are **abusive** often express anger toward their partner. **Abusive** behavior include harassment, bullying, **verbal abuse, physical abuse**, etc. 會虐待辱罵人通常會對伴侶發怒，侮辱的行為包括騷擾、霸凌、言語辱罵、身體虐待等。

accident [ˋæksədənt]	*n.*	意外事件，事故，災禍

Police are seeking help from the public with any information about the fatal hit-and-run **accident** that occurred Friday. 警方請大眾幫忙提供有關上星期五發生的致命肇事逃逸事故的相關資訊。

應用 *accident scene* 意外事故現場
accident victim 意外事件被害人
car accident 車禍意外事件
cimbing accident (或 *mountain climbing accident*) 登山意外事件
drowning accident 溺斃意外事件
hit-and-run accident 肇事逃逸事件
traffic accident 交通事故

accidental [ˌæksəˈdɛnt!]	*adj.*	偶然的，意外的 Fire, motor vehicle incident, and drowning are major causes of **accidental death**. 火災、車禍及溺斃，是意外死亡的主因。 An officer with the city police department was injured in an **accidental shooting** last Friday. The officer was accidentally shot while he was cleaning his service weapon. 市警局的一位同仁在上星期五的一場槍枝意外走火事件中受傷，該員警在清槍時被意外擊中。
accidentally [ˌæksəˈdɛnt!ɪ]	*adv.*	The pedestrian lost his life after being **accidentally** struck by a motorist. He was **accidentally** hit from behind and tragically killed at the scene. 該行人被開車的人意外撞到之後，失去了生命。他被從後方撞到並不幸當場死亡。
accomplice [əˈkɑmplɪs]	*n.*	共犯，同謀 **Accomplice** is a person who is involved with another in the commission of a crime whether as a principal or as an accessory. Both principals and secondary participants are defined as **accomplices**. Each **accomplice** shall be liable according to the measure of his own guilt and irrespective of the guilt of the others. 共犯，是指一個擔任正犯或從屬犯而與他人涉入犯罪的人，正犯與從犯兩者被定義為共犯(accomplice)，每一個共犯應依自己的罪行負刑事責任，而不論其他人的罪刑是如何。
account [əˈkaʊnt]	*vi.*	解釋，說明 [(+for)] Edward claimed that he was not there that night but was not able **to account for** his whereabouts during the time of the shooting. 愛德華聲稱他當晚沒有在那裡，但無法交代他在槍擊案發生時的行蹤。
	n.	(有關金錢、責任的) 答辯，解釋，說明，理由 The CCTV images can help identify suspects, and verify a

		witness's or suspect's **account**. 閉路影像可以幫助確認嫌犯及確認證人或嫌犯的說詞。
		The suspect gave us a detailed **account** of his modus operandi. 嫌犯給我們詳盡地說明了他的犯罪手法。
	應用	*take account of* 考慮到
		Correctional officials should **take account of** a prisoner's criminal history, and assesses the prisoner's special needs. 矯正官員應考慮受刑人的犯罪紀錄，並評估受刑人的特殊需要。
	n.	帳戶
	應用	*fictitious account* 假帳戶
accountability [ə,kaʊntə`bɪlətɪ]	*n.*	當責
		Accountability is a vital element of policing. **Accountability** includes both what the police do and how they perform. 當責是警政不可或缺的一個要件，當責任包括了「警察的作為」以及「警察如何作為」。
accountable [ə`kaʊntəb!]	*adj.*	(對人或事)應負責任的，(對……)有解釋義務的
		People expect law enforcement authorities to work together to solve crimes and **hold** criminals **accountable for** their offenses. 人們期待執法機關共同合作解決犯罪，並且讓犯罪人為其犯罪負責任。
	應用	*to hold sb. accountable for* 由某人為(某事)負責
		President Barack Obama said the Baltimore riots show that police departments need to hold officers **accountable** for wrongdoing. We must **hold officers accountable** when they break the law. 歐巴馬總統說，巴爾的摩暴動顯示警察部門必須有員警出面為錯誤負責。當員警違法時，我們必須要員警承擔起責任。
accusation [,ækjə`zeʃən]	*n.*	(法律的)控訴，控告，告發
		In the criminal proceedings, when the police have solved a crime and refer the investigation report and evidence to the prosecutor, the prosecutor will make a formal **accusation** against the suspect. 在刑事訴訟中，當警察解決一件犯罪，並移送調查報告及證據給檢察官時，檢察官會對嫌犯做正式的控告。
		They **brought** a false **accusation against** the innocent man. 他們對這名無辜者提起了誣告之訴。
	應用	*false accusation* 又稱 *false allegation*
		false accusation of (+罪) 不實指控……罪
accuse [ə`kjuz]	*vt.*	(法律的)控訴，控告，告發
		The suspect **was accused of** stealing backpacks from the gym.

嫌犯被指控在健身房竊取背包。

He **was accused of** setting a series of blazes at the restaurants near the shopping mall. 他被指控在賣場附近的餐廳放了一連串的火。

accused [əˋkjuzd]	*adj.*	被控告的 At trial, the accused person has the right **to confront** the accuser and the witness. 審判時，被告之人享有與控訴者及證人對質的權利。
	n.	被告 Criminal courts must prove an **accused** guilty beyond a reasonable doubt. 刑事法庭對於被告有罪必須證明至無合理可疑。
accuser [əˋkjuzɚ]	*n.*	原告，提告人
acquit [əˋkwɪt]	*vt.*	宣告……為無罪，無罪釋放[(+of)] The defendant **was acquitted of** murder charges in the criminal trial. He **was acquitted** for lack of evidence. The judge **acquitted him of** all charges. 被告在殺人刑事審判中，被無罪釋放，他因為證據欠缺而被無罪釋放，法官對於他所有控訴的罪行都無罪釋放。 The jury **acquitted** the defendant on all charges against him. He **was acquitted** after the trial. 陪審團對於所有不利被告的指控全都無罪釋放。他在審判後被無罪釋放。 The jury **acquitted** the man accused of setting a car on fire downtown. 陪審團對於在市區對一輛汽車放火的男子予以無罪釋放。
acquittal [əˋkwɪt!]	*n.*	宣告無罪，無罪開釋 O.J. Simpson's **acquittal** continues to be one of the most discussed and debated cases in US history. 辛普森的無罪釋放仍然是美國歷史上最被討論與辯論的案件之一。
act [ækt]	*n.*	作為 The basic elements of a crime consist of intent, conduct, and causation. Conduct means an **act** or omission. 犯罪的基本要素包含犯意、行為及因果關係，行為指的是一項「作為(act)」或「不作為(omission)」。
	n.	法案 The main difference between **act** and **bill** is that a bill a proposed law or a draft that is present to the Parliament for discussion whereas **an act** is a law passed by the government. In this sense,

a bill becomes **an act** when it is passed throught the government. (from eppida.com) 關於 act 與 bill 兩字 (按：中文翻譯都是「法案」)，其分別在於，bill 是提議的法律或草案，而 act 是經過國會通過的法律，按這意思來說，bill 經過國會通過之後就成為 act。

應用 *an act of God*【律】天災，自然災害，不可抗力

The insurance company refused to pay the money because they said that the forest fire was **an act of God**. 保險公司拒絕賠償金錢，因為他們說森林大火是不可抗力。

The earthquake **was an act of god**. It was an unforeseeable **act of god** for which no numan is responsible. 地震是天災，這是無法預見的天災，沒有人必需負責。

---

acting   *adj.*   代理的

[`æktɪŋ]

He will serve as acting police commissioner until the new mayor makes a permanent appointment. The appointment as **acting** chief is effective December 25. 他會擔任代理警察局長的職務一直到新的市長做出長久的任命為止，代理局長的任命於 12 月 25 日生效。

---

action   *n.*   行動，作為

[`ækʃən]

He threatened **to take legal action against** the eyewitness. 她威脅對目擊證人提出法律訴訟。

應用 *to take appropriate action* 採取適當的行動

to take legal action against 對……採取法律行動

to take police action 採取警察行動/作為

n.   訴訟

應用 *action for divorce* 離婚訴訟

civil action 民事告訴

criminal action 刑事告訴

inaction 無所作為，不做任何作為 (刑法的「不作為」是 omission)

【補充說明】action 可指廣義的訴訟，但時至今日多被用來指民事方面的訴訟，刑事方面則用 prosecution 一字。

---

activate   *vt.*   啟動

[`æktə,vet]

Notice! In the event of a fire, **activate** the alarm before leaving. 注意！ 萬一火災時，離開前請啟動警報。

---

activation   *n.*   啟動

[,æktə`veʃən]

The **activation** of the Emergency Operation Center (EOC) is based on the levels of threats and seriousness of the disaster. **Level 1 Activation** is full activation; **Level 2 Activation** is partial activation; **Level 3 Activation** is limited activation. 「緊急應變中心(EOC)」的開設是依據威脅的等級與災害的嚴重性，一級開設是完全開設，二級開設是部分開設，三級開設是有限開設。

---

addict [ə`dɪkt]	*vt.*	沉溺於……

Unfortunately, most individuals who **become addicted to** alcohol and drugs cannot merely discontinue their use. 不幸地，大部分耽溺於酒精及毒品的人就是無法停止他們的吸食。

addict [`ædɪkt]	*n.*	入迷的人，有癮的人

應用 *drug addict* 毒品成癮者

heroin addict 海洛因成癮者

opium addict 鴉片成癮者

sex addict 性成癮者

---

addiction [ə`dɪkʃən]	*n.*	成癮，沉溺，上癮

Drug **addiction** affects our brain and behavior. He spent the next two decades in and out of the drug rehabilitation centers to recover from drug **addiction**. 吸毒成癮會影響我們的腦與行為。他在之後的 20 年進出於毒品勒戒所，為的就是從毒癮恢復。

應用 *drug addiction* 毒品成癮

alcohol addiction 酒精成癮

---

addictive [ə`dɪktɪv]	*adj.*	使成癮的，上癮的

Cocaine is highly addictive and it can be injected, snorted as a powder. 古柯鹼具有高度的成癮性，它可以用注射、以粉末用鼻子吸食。

---

adjourn [ə`dʒɜn]	*vt. &* *vi.*	(法庭、會議) 延期、再擇期

Judge Anderson granted a court order and the murder trial was **adjourned**. 安德森法官當庭喻知擇期再審理殺人案。

adjournment [ə`dʒɜnmənt]	*n.*	(法庭、會議) 延期

Defence advocate requested the **adjournment**, saying his client was not feeling well. 被告律師請求延期延期，他表示他的委託人身體不適。

---

adjudicate [ə`dʒudɪ,ket]	*vt.*	判決，審理

Adam was **adjudicated** guilty of robbery. He was **adjudicated** guilty and sentence to life in prison for the robbery. 亞當獲判強盜有罪。他因為因此一強盜案被判強盜有罪並判處無期徒刑。

All defendants are to be considered innocent until proven or **adjudicated** guilty in court. 所有被告在被法院證明或判決有

罪之前，應被認定無辜。

In the US, a child uder sixteen years of age will be **adjudicated** in a juvenile or family court. 在美國，16 歲以下孩童會由少年或家事法庭審理。

---

administer
[əd`mɪnəstɚ]

vt. 執行，實施，給予，提供

First arriving officer should **administer** medical assistance if required. 最先抵達的員警應於需要時，進行醫療協助。

The nurse **administered** insulin to the clients with diabetes. 護士為糖尿病的患者施打胰島素。

The nurse **administered** the medicine to the sick child. 護士給生病的孩子服藥。

應用 *to administer oxygen to the patient* 供給氧氣予病患
to administer oral glucose to the patient 供給口服葡萄糖予病患

---

admissibility
[əd,mɪsə`bɪlətɪ]

n. 【律】(被接受、被採納的)資格，能力，容許性

The **admissibility** of evidence shall be determined by the court. In other words, the question of **admissibility** of evidence is left to the discretion of the trial court. 證據能力應由法院認定，換言之，證據能力的問題，是留給審理法院裁量。

---

admissible
[əd`mɪsəb!]

adj. 【律】有資格(能力)的，有容許性的

Rules of Evidence provide that relevant evidence is **admissible**; irrelevant evidence is not **admissible**. Hearsay is not **admissible**. 證據法則規定，有關聯性的證據有證據能力；無關聯性的證據無證據能力。傳聞，沒有證據能力。

adj. (移民法上)合於入境的

Any alien who is wanted by the Interpol or foreign judicial authorities is not **admissible** and shall be taken into custody for deportation. 任何受國際刑警組織或外國司法機關通緝的外國人，是不得許可入境的，並且應予拘禁以便遣送。

---

admission
[əd`mɪʃən]

n. 承認，坦白

A false confession is an **admission** of guilt. 不實的自白是有罪的自認。

n. 進入許可

An arriving alien who is a stowaway is not eligible to apply for **admission** or to be admitted and shall be ordered removed upon inspection by an immigration officer. 抵達的外國人為偷渡客時，是沒有資格申請入境許可或被許可入境的，並且在移民官查驗時，將被命令遣返。

Correctional authorities should screen each prisoner upon the prisoner's **admission** to a correctional facility to identify the prisoner's immediate potential security risks. 矯正機關在每一位受刑人到矯正處所報到之時,應過濾該受刑人,以找出受刑人立即潛在的安全風險。

admit [əd`mɪt]	*vt.*	承認 [(+that)] The arsonist **admitted** that he had set the fire at the apartment in an effort to cover up the homicide. 縱火犯坦承他在公寓放火,為的是掩飾殺人案。
	vi.	承認 [(+to ving)] After being arrested, he **admitted to** setting the three fires. 他在被捕之後承認了三件縱火。
	vt.	容許,准許 At trial, the judge may decide to **admit** the defendant to bail or to dismiss the complaint and discharge the defendant. 審判時,法官得決定准予被告交保,或駁回訴狀並釋回被告。
	vt.	准許進入,准許……進入 (加入) [(+into/to)] The gunman opened fire in the shopping mall. 5 people **were admitted to** hospital with multiple gunshot wounds. 持槍歹徒在購物中心開槍,五人住進了醫院,有多重槍傷。 The man **was admitted to** the intensive care unit. 該名男子住進了加護病房。 James **was admitted to** the hospital for food poisoning. 詹姆士因為食物中毒住進了醫院。 An arriving alien who is a stowaway is not eligible **to be admitted** and shall be ordered removed upon inspection by an immigration officer. 抵達的外國人為偷渡客時,不具有被許可入境的資格,並且在移民官查驗時,將會被命令遣返。
adolescent [ˌædḷ`ɛsnt]	*n.* *adj.*	青少年 青春期的,青少年的
adopt [ə`dɑpt]	*vt.*	收養 Once you have **adopted** a child, you would have all of the joys and responsibilities of being a parent. 一旦你收養了一個小孩,你將會擁有當父母的所有喜悅與責任。
	vt.	(法律) 通過,採納 Controlled delivery **was** formally **adopted by** the 1988 United Nations Convention against Illicit Trafficking in Narcotic Drugs and Psychotropic Substances. Since then, The UN encourages Member States to **adopt** national laws and procedures in respect of controlled delivery operations. 控制下交付在 1988 年的「聯

合國禁止非法販運麻醉品和精神藥物公約」正式獲得通過，從那時候開始，聯合國便鼓勵會員國通過有關控制下交付行動的內國法及程序。

adoption [ə`dɑpʃən]	n.	收養

adoptive [ə`dɑptɪv]	adj.	收養的
	應用	*adoptive child* 養子女
		adoptive parent 養父母

adultery [ə`dʌltərɪ]	n.	通姦，通姦行為

Adultery isn't just a crime in the eyes of the spouse. 通姦，在配偶的眼中可不只是犯罪而已。

A person is guilty of **adultery** when he engates in sexual intercourse with another person at a time when he has a living spouse, or the other person has a living spouse. **Adultery** is a class B misdemeanor. (N.Y. Penal Law § 225.17) 任何人與他人從事性交之時，其本人尚存配偶或他方尚存配偶者，犯通姦罪。通姦罪為 B 級輕罪 (紐約州刑法 225.17 條)

adverse [æd`vɝs]	adj.	不利的，有害的，敵對的

The right to cross-examine is the right of **adverse** party. 交互詰問的權利是對造的權利。

	應用	*adverse party* 對造
		adverse effect 負面影響

advise [əd`vaɪz]	vt.	告知 [(+ of)]

Officer **advised** him of his right to remain silent and his right to council. 員警告知他有保持緘默及聘請律師的權利。

In this case, the court found that defendant **had been** fully and completely **advised of** his rights, that the admissions were freely and voluntairy given and that they were admissible at the trial. 本案中，法院認定被告有被完全而整告知權利，且自白的提出是出自於自由及自願，而在法庭有證據能力。

advocate [`ædvəkɪt]	vi.	提倡，擁護，支持，致力促進……(權益)

She **has advocated for** the right of victims of crime. 她一直致力於促進犯罪被害人的權益。

	n.	提倡者，擁護者，支持者，權益促進者，辯護者，律師

Victim advocates are trained to support victims of crime. **Victim advocates** often work with law enforcement officers and meet people at the crime scene, at the hospital, in their homes, or in the police department. 被害人權益促進者是接受訓練去支持犯罪被害人。被害人權益促進者常與執法人員合

作，與這些人在犯罪現場、醫院、家裡或警察局等地方相見。

應用 *domestic violence advocate* 家暴權益促進者

human right advocate 人權倡議者

sexual violence advocate 性侵害權益促進者

social service advocate 社福權益促進者

victim advocate 被害人權益促進者

affect	vt.	影響
[əˋfɛkt]		

Drug **addiction** affects our brain and behavior. 吸毒成癮會影響我們的腦與行為。

He was affected by the use of **intoxicating beverage** at the time of the accident. 車禍的當下，他受到酒精飲料所影響。

vt （疾病的）侵襲，罹患

Doctor confirmed that this patient **was affected with** an unknown disease. 醫生證實，這個病患感染了不明的疾病。

Doctor warned that if wait too long, bacteria can start to grow in the **affected** area. 醫生警告，如果等待太久的話，細菌可能會在被感染的地方開始滋生細菌。

affiliate	vt.	隸屬於……，為……的成員
[əˋfɪlɪɪt]		

Police said the man **is affiliated with** a criminal gang. 警方說男子依附在一個犯罪幫派。

n. 成員，附屬成員，分支，分會

Police requested that the person be designated as a criminal gang **affiliate**. 警方請求將該人認定為犯罪幫派成員。

affirm	vt.	(原判決的) 確認，維持……
[əˋfɝm]		

Based on the evidence presented, the judgment of the district court **is affirmed by** the court of appeals. 依據所提出的證據，地方法院的判決受到上訴法院維持。

【請參看 uphold, vacate, remand】

afford	vt.	(金錢上)買得起……，負擔得起……[+to-v]
[əˋford]		

The mayor urged the City Council to approve the budget for advanced equipments, saying the Fire Department can't **afford to** lose any more firefighters. 市長呼籲市議會通過先進裝備的預算，說消防局無法承受再失去任何消防員。

If you cannot **afford** a lawyer, one will be appointed for you if you so desire.如果你請不起律師，而如果你想的話，法院會為你指派。

against	prep.	反對，不利於
[əˋgɛnst]		

Officers said that Richard's car smelled like marijuana, but they could not **bring** any drug **charges against** Richard because there was no drug found in the car. 員警說,理查的車子聞起來像是大麻,但他們無法針對理查提出毒品的指控,因為沒有毒品被發現在車子內。

The witness identified Richard as the killer and **testified against** him in court. The judge advised Richard that no person shall be compelled in any criminal case **to be a witness against** himself without due process of law. 證人指證理查為殺人犯,並且在法院做不利於他的作證。法官告訴理查說,沒有正當法律程序,任何人均不得被強迫在任何刑事案件中,成為不利於己之證人。

Police confirmed that there were three criminal charges **pending against** the suspect. 警方證實,嫌犯目前還背著三件未結的刑事告訴案件。

The Constitution **protects people against** unreasonable searches and seizures by law enforcement authorities. 憲法保障人民免於受到執法機關不合理的搜索及扣押。

Illegally-seized evidence cannot **be used** as evidence **against** defendants in a criminal prosecution. 非法扣押的證據,不得在刑事起訴中用為不利被告的證據。

If you do say anything, what you say can **be used against** you in a court of law. 如果你說任何話,則你所說的話,可以在法庭中被用來做為對你不利的證供。

Investigators will **enter charges against** a person believed to have violated the law. 偵查人員對於被認為已違法的人,會進行控訴。

In the criminal proceedings, it is the prosecutor that will **make the accusation against** the suspect. 在刑事訴訟中,會對嫌犯做正式控告的是檢察官。

No person shall be compelled in any criminal case **to be a witness against** himself. 任何人均不得被強迫在任何刑事案件中,成為不利於己之證人。

In all criminal prosecutions, the accused shall enjoy the right to be confronted with the witnesses **against** him. 在所有刑事起訴中,被告享有與不利於己之證人對質的權利。

Investigators said that they had gathered enough evidence to **to make a criminal case against** the suspect. 偵查人員說,他們已蒐集了足夠的證據使嫌犯的刑事案件成案。

Confidential informant may choose to cooperate with the law enforcement authorities **to seek revenge against** their enemies. 線民有可能選擇與執法機關合作，來報復他們的敵人。

Police are preparing **to press criminal charges against** the alleged perpetrators of the durg trafficking. 警方準備將對涉嫌毒品販運的犯罪指者提出刑事指控。

The prosecutor reviewed the case and decided that there is enough evidence **to file criminal charges against** the suspect. 檢察官審閱了該案，並且認定有足夠的證據對嫌犯提起刑事告訴。

agency [ˋedʒənsɪ]	*n.*	(專業行政機關) 局，處，署

In the US, there are basically three types of law enforcement **agencies**, local, state, and federal. Local law enforcement **agencies** include police and sheriff departments. State **agencies** include the state police or highway patrol. Federal agencies include the FBI, DEA, US Secret Service, etc. 在美國，基本上執法機關有三種，包括地方、州、聯邦。地方執法機關包括警察(police department)與郡警察(sheriff department)；州執法機關包括州警 (state police) 或高速公路巡邏警察(highway patrol)；聯邦執法機關包括聯邦調查局(FBI)、緝毒局(DEA)、美國秘勤局(US Secret Service)等。

應用　*National Police Agency* 警政署

【補充說明】按我國警政署、日本警察廳及韓國警察廳都使用 National Police Agency 為機關譯名。

agent [ˋedʒənt]	*n.* 應用	(美國聯邦執法機關的) 幹員 *FBI Specail Agent* 聯邦調查局幹員
aggravated [ˋægrə,vetɪd]	*adj.* 應用	(事態等)嚴重化的，加重的 *aggravated assault* 加重傷害 *aggravated larceny* 加重竊盜 *aggravated robbery* 加重強盜 *aggravated offense* 加重之罪 *aggravated crime* 加重的犯罪
aggression [əˋgrɛʃən]	*n.*	侵略罪，侵犯行為，攻擊性格

An officer is permitted to use the amount of force necessary to overcome the resistance or **aggression**. When the resistance or the **aggression** is reduced, the officers must reduce his or her force correspondingly. 員警被容許使用武力的多寡，僅得在壓制抗拒或侵犯的必要程度內，使用之。當抗拒或侵犯降低時，員警必須相對地降低武力。

aggressor	*n.*	侵害者，加害者，挑釁者

[əˋgrɛsə]		You may press criminal charges against the **aggressor** or abuser, but you do not have to press charges in order to get a protective order. 你可以對加害者或虐待者提出刑事告訴，但你不需要為了取得保護令而提出告訴。
agony [ˋægənɪ]	n.	極度痛苦 The suspect fell to the ground and screamed **in agony** after he was hit in the knee during the shootout. 嫌犯在槍戰中被擊中膝蓋後倒地，並極度痛苦地喊叫。 He was **in agony** and was struggling to walk. 他極度痛苦，並且掙扎地走著。
aid [ed]	n.	幫助，援助 應用 *first aid* 急救 *on scene first aid* 現場的急救 *legal aid* 法律扶助
aider [ˋedə]	n.	幫助犯 An **aider** is someone who, knowing that a felon has finished committing a crime, helps the felon avoid arrest or trial. 幫助犯是指一個知悉重罪犯已經完成犯罪，而幫助該重罪犯逃避逮捕或審判的人。
aim [em]	vt.	將……瞄準於……[(+at)] The suspect **aimed** his gun **at** the officer, and the officer fired three times at the suspect, striking him in the right arm. 嫌犯將槍瞄準員警，而員警三度對嫌犯還擊擊中其右手臂。
	phr.v.	致力於……，旨在……[(+at)] The new law **is aimed at** reducing domestic violence against women and child. 這項新的法律旨在減少針對婦女及兒童的家庭暴力。
alarm [əˋlɑrm]	n.	警報，警報器 **Alarms** are intended to alert building occupants that a fire or other life-threatening situation exists. 警報器是用來向建築物的居住者示警有火災或其他有生命威脅的情況存在。 應用 *to give false alarm* 提供假警報、謊報 *burglar alarm* 竊盜警報 *car alarm* 汽車警報 *false alarm* 假警報 *fire alarm* 火災警報 *smoke alarm* 煙霧警報
alcohol [ˋælkəˌhɔl]	n.	含酒精飲料，酒 If the operator has consumed **alcohol**, the police officer may

further request such operator to submit to a one or more of the following tests: breath, blood, urine, or saliva. 如果駕駛人有飲酒，則員警得進一步要求該駕駛人服從以下一項或多項檢測：呼吸、血液、尿液或唾液。

應用 *alcohol breathalyzer* 酒測呼吸器

alcohol screening 酒精篩檢

alcohol treatment 酒精勒戒

alcoholic beverage 酒精飲料

driving under the influence of alcohol (DUI) 受酒精影響之下，酒駕

alcohol abuse 酒精濫用

alcohol addiction 酒精成癮

blood alcohol content / blood alcohol concentration (BAC) 血液酒精濃度

---

alcoholic [ˌælkəˈhɔlɪk]	*adj.*	酒精的，含酒精的，酗酒的
		It is illegal to operate a motor vehicle while under the influence of **alcoholic** beverages. 在酒精飲料的影響下開車是違法的。
		【補充說明】酒精飲料也可以用 intoxicating beverage

---

alert [əˈlɝt]	*n.*	警示，警戒，警報
		Police are warning the public **to be on the alert for** suspicious packages. 警方警告大眾對於可疑的包裹要提高警覺。
	adj.	警覺的，留意的
		Highway patrol officers urged drivers **to stay alert**, buckle up and drive safely. 高速公路巡邏員警呼籲駕駛人要保持警覺、繫上安全帶並小心駕駛。
	vt.	向……報警，使……警覺，使……注意[(+to)]
		Alarms are intended **to alert** building occupants that a fire or other life-threatening situation exists. 警報器是用來警示建築物的居住者有火災或其他有生命威脅的情況存在。

| alias [ˈelɪəs] | *n.* | 化名，別名 |
| | | It is not uncommon for criminal offenders to use **alias**, fraudulent names and false dates of birth. 犯罪者使用別名、假名及不實的出生年月日，這並非不尋常。 |

---

alibi [ˈæləˌbaɪ]	*n.*	【律】不在場證明
		Most alleged persons tend to give false **alibi** to the police to cover up their crimes, unless they are caught red-handed. 大部分的涉嫌人會傾向給警方假的不在場證明，來掩蓋他們的犯罪，除非是他們被當場逮到。
	應用	*false alibi* 不實的不在場證明

		alibi witness 不在場證人
alien	*n.*	外國人
[`elɪən]	*adj.*	外國的，外國人的
	應用	*alien registration* 外僑登記
		Alien Resident Certificate (我國的) 外僑居留證
		alien smuggling 外國人偷渡
		criminal alien 犯罪的外國人
		deportable alien 應遣送之外國人
		illegal alien 非法外國人
		unauthorized employment of alien 未經核准聘雇外國人
		unlawful employment of alien 非法雇用外國人
alive	*adj.*	存活的，活著的
[əˋlaɪv]		The bod who was reported missing over the weekend **has been found alive**. He **was found alive** and was taken to the hospital to be evaluated. 據報周末失蹤的男童被發現還活著，他被發現還活著並被送往醫院接受評估。
allegation	*n.*	指責，指控，辯解，主張
[ˌæləˋgeʃən]		A stranger broke into the school and allegedly molested the victim. Victim's parents called for an investigation of the alleged molestation and criticized the school's response to the **allegation**. 一位陌生人潛入學校並疑似猥褻被害者。被害者的父母要求調查這起疑似猥褻，並抨擊校方對於這項指控的回應。
allege	*vt.*	(無充分證據而)斷言，宣稱；(作為理由或論據而)聲稱，提出
[əˋlɛdʒ]		He **alleged that** police beat him during the arrest and tortured him into a confession. 他指稱警方在逮捕之時毆打他，並且刑求到他自白。
		It is alleged that the suspect knowingly possessed some of the stolen goods, police said. 警方說，推測嫌犯是故意持有一些贓物。
		The suspect **is alleged to** have committed at least five sexual offenses. 嫌犯推測已經犯下至少五起性侵害罪。
		The arsonist **is alleged to** have set the three vehicles ablaze. 縱火犯涉嫌對這三輛車子放火。
alleged	*adj.*	指控的，指涉的，主張的，陳述的
[əˋlɛdʒd]		The suspect was charged with the **alleged** crime of murdering his ex-wife. 嫌犯被控告這起涉嫌謀殺前妻的犯罪。
		Police said that they had arrested the suspect in the **alleged** killing, and ask anyone with information about the **alleged**

homicide to call the CIB detectives at (02) 2766-1919. 警方說，他們已經逮捕到疑似殺人案的嫌犯，並請求有關於這起疑似兇殺案資訊的人，打電話(02)2766-1919給刑事局偵查員。

allegedly [əˋlɛdʒɪdlɪ]	*adv.*	據傳說，據宣稱

The drug ringleader **allegedly** murdered his rival in his home with a gun. Police **alleged** that the suspect murdered the person at his home last Monday. 毒品集團首腦疑似在他家用槍謀殺了他的敵對者，警方推測，該嫌犯上星期一在他家謀殺了這個人。

He **allegedly** set his neighbor's home on fire. 他涉嫌對鄰居的家放火。

allude [əˋlud]	*vi.*	略為提及，暗示，間接提到，拐彎抹角地說道 [(+to)]

The bank clerk said the suspect **alluded to** having a firearm during the robbery but did not brandish the weapon. 銀行行員說，嫌犯在搶劫時暗示有武器，但並未揮動。

alter [ˋɔltɚ]	*vt.*	改變，變樣，變更，變造，修改

Any person who forge, counterfeit, mutilate, or **alter** passport or travel document will be subject to criminal prosecution. 任何作假、偽造、撕掉或變造護照或旅行文件的人，會受到刑事起訴。

ambulance [ˋæmbjələns]	*n.*	救護車

The woman called for an **ambulance** at 9 p.m. fearing that she may have having a stroke. 該名婦女因害怕可能會中風，就打電話呼叫救護車。

When you call emergency center, you will **be sent an ambulance**. 當你打電話給緊急中心時，會有救護車派給你。

ambush [ˋæmbʊʃ]	*vt.*	埋伏，伏擊

Officers must be alert to the possibility that others may be waiting for you to create an **ambush** and try to take your prisoner from you. 員警必須警覺有可能其他人可能製造埋伏正在等著你，並想帶走你的囚犯。

amend [əˋmɛnd]	*vt.*	修訂，修改

Earlier this year, the traffic law **was amended** to permit a police officer to stop a motorist for operating a vehicle while using and portable electronic devices. 今年初，交通法規已被修正，允許員警得將騎車使用行動電子用品的騎士攔下。

amendment [əˋmɛndmənt]	*n.*	修訂，修改

The US Fourth **Amendment** prohibits the government from

conducting unreasonable searches and seizures. 美國憲法第四修正案禁止政府不得進行不合理的搜索及扣押。

analysis [ə`næləsɪs]	n. 應用	分析，分解，解析

computer analysis 電腦分析

computer forensic analysis 電腦鑑識分析

crime analysis 犯罪分析

DNA analysis DNA 分析

drug analysis 毒品分析

handwriting analysis 筆跡分析

image analysis 影像分析

intelligence analysis 情資分析

telephone analysis 通聯分析

telephone toll (record) analysis 通聯紀錄分析

trace analysis 微物分析

voice analysis 聲紋分析

analyst [`æn!ɪst]	n. 應用	分析者，善於分解者

crime analyst 化學分析人員

drug analyst 毒品分析人員

forensic analyst 刑事鑑識人員

analyze [`æn!,aɪz]	vt.	分析，對……進行分析

Forensic scientists **analyze** and interpret evidence found and collected at the crime scenes. Such evidence can include blood, saliva, fibres, trace evidence, explosive residue, etc. 刑事科學鑑識人員分析及解釋在犯罪現場發現及蒐集的證據，這些證據可能包括血液、唾液、組織纖維、微物證據、爆裂物殘跡等。

anonymous [ə`nɑnəməs]	adj.	匿名的，來源不明的

To urge people to tip off police about crime, police will set up an **anonymous** tip line for people to give a clue. 為了呼籲民眾向警方通報犯罪，警方會設置匿名報案專線，讓民眾提供線索。

anti	adj. 應用	反對~

anti-abortion 反墮胎

anti-corruption 反貪腐

anti-socialist 反社會的人

anti-terrorism 反恐怖主義

apologize [ə`pɑlə,dʒaɪz]	vi.	道歉，認錯，賠不是[(+to/for)]

The offender **apologized for** the pains he has caused to the deceased family. 犯罪者為他對死者家屬所造成的痛苦表示道歉。

The offender **apologized to** the victim **for** his wrongdoing, and expected forgiveness of the victim and the victim's family. 犯罪者為他錯誤向被害人道歉，並期望獲得被害人及其家屬的原諒。

apology [əˋpɑlədʒɪ]	*n.*	道歉，認錯，賠不是[(+to/for)]

Researches indicate that not every survivor feels an **apology** is significant to him or her. 研究顯示，並不是每一個生還者認為道歉是有重要意義的。

應用　*to make an apology* 向……道歉
to give an apology 向……道歉
to receive apology 接受道歉
to accept apology 接受道歉

appeal [əˋpil]	*n.*	上訴

The plaintiff decided **to file an appeal**. 被告決定提起上訴。

The case **is on appeal from** the district court. The case **is on appeal to** the court of appeals. 案件正由地方法院上訴中。該案正在向高等法院上訴中。

He **made an appeal to** the court of appeals, claiming that he was merely a courier of the heroin and 15 years sentence was excessive. 他向高等法院提起上訴，聲稱他只是該起海洛因的交通，並且 15 年的徒刑太過高。

The court of appeals agreed **to hear the plaintiff's appeal**. 高等法院同意聽取原告的上訴。

The judge **dismissed his appeal** on the ground that his fingerprints were all over the inside package. 法官駁回了他的上訴，理由是郵包的內部到處都是他的指紋。

vt.　【美】將……上訴，對……上訴

He **appealed** his case to the Supreme Court. 他將案件上訴到了最高法院。

vi.　上訴[(+against)]

The defendant **appealed from** his conviction on firearms charges 被告對於他的槍枝案件的有罪判決提起上訴。

He **appealed against** the two-year sentence he had been given. 他對於被判兩年徒刑提起上訴。

vi.　訴諸，求助[(+to)]

We should not **appeal to** force. 我們不該訴諸武力。

應用　*court of appeals* 上訴法院 (亦稱 *appeal court*、*court of appeal* 或 *appeals court*。在美國，聯邦的上訴法院亦稱為巡迴法院 *circuit court*)。

appear [ə`pɪr]	vi.	出庭，到案 The murder suspect is scheduled to **appear** in court next Monday. 殺人嫌犯預計下星期一出庭。 似乎，看起來好像 The suspect **appeared** to fire randomly. He **appreared to** have no connection with any of the victims. 嫌犯似乎是隨機開槍，他似乎與任何被害人都沒有關聯。
appearance [ə`pɪrəns]	n.	出庭，到案 The suspect is scheduled to make first court **appearance** on shooting charges next Monday. 嫌犯預計在下星期一就槍擊案的指控做第一次出庭。 His next court **appearance** is set for September 18. 他的下次出庭訂於 9 月 18 日。
appease [ə`piz]	vt.	平息，緩和，撫慰 The judge hoped the guilty verdict would **appease** the victim's family. 法官希望這個有罪判決能平復被害者的家人。
appellant [ə`pɛlənt]	n.	上訴人 The **appellant** was charged with two counts of robberies. The legal issue was raised by the **appellant**. 上訴人被指控兩項強盜罪。上訴人提起了法律爭議。

應用　　美國法院判決開頭標題範例

----

902 F.2d 1337 (卷宗號)

United States of America, Appellant (上訴人)

v.

James McFrancis Crumb, Jr., Appellee (被上訴人).

No. 89-1925.

United States Court of Appeals, Eighth Circuit. (法院)

Decided May 9, 1990 (判決日期)

----

appellate [ə`pɛlɪt]	adj.	上訴的，受理上訴的 **Appellate** court is a court with jurisdiction to review decisions of lower courts. An **appellate** court is commonly called an appeal court, court of appeals, court of appeal, or appeals court. 上訴法院是一個具有審理下級法院判決權力的法院。上訴法院通常被稱為 appeal court、court of appeals、court of appeal 或 appeals court。

appellee [ˌæpəˈli]	*n.*	被上訴人，被告

applicable [ˈæplɪkəbl]	*adj.*	可適用的，可實施的 Starting on Jauary 1st, 2024, anyone convicted of operating any type of motor vehicle while intoxicated will lose their driver's licence. The new law is **applicable** to crimes occurring on or after January 1st, 2024. 自 2024 年 1 月 1 日起，任何人因酒醉駕駛任何種類之車輛者，將喪失駕照，新法將對 2024 年 1 月 1 日起之犯罪適用之。

apply [əˈplaɪ]	*vi.*	實施，適用 [(+ to)] The new law **applies to** everyone irrespective of race, religion or color. 新的法律適用於任何人，不無論其種族，宗教或膚色為何。
	vi.	申請 [(+ for)] If you are 18 years old or older, you are eligible **to apply for** a driver's license. Before you can get a license, you must **apply for** a learner permit and take the written test. 發如果你是 18 歲或以上，你有資格申請駕照。在你可以取得駕照之前，你必須申請取得學習駕照並參加筆試。
	vt.	塗，敷，將……鋪在表面[(+to)] The nurse **applied** the ointment to the wound. 護士把藥膏敷到傷口上。 The EMTs **applied** ice packs to his arm to reduce pain and swelling. 緊急救護技術員將冰袋敷在他的手臂以減少疼痛及腫脹。

apprehend [ˌæprɪˈhɛnd]	*vt.*	逮捕 During the highspeed police pursuit, officers must balance the need to immediately **apprehend** the fleeing suspect with public's safety. 在高速警察追逐時，員警必須就「立即逮捕逃逸嫌犯的必要」與「公眾安全」做權衡。 Fire investigators have confirmed that the suspected serial arsonist **was apprehended**. 火災調查員證實，這名連續縱火嫌犯被捕了。

apprehension [ˌæprɪˈhɛnʃən]	*n.*	逮捕 The information provided by the informant has led to the **apprehension** of the criminal suspect. 線民提供的資訊導致了嫌犯的逮捕。

approach	*vt.*	接近，靠近

[əˋprotʃ]		In general, an officer can **approach** a person, stop him and question him even if the officer has no reason to suspect that the person has done anything wrong. 通常，員警可以前往某個人、把他攔下並問他問題，即使員警沒有理由懷疑他有不對的事。
argue [ˋɑrgjʊ]	*vt.*	（法律上）主張，爭論，爭執 At trial, the prosecution **argued that** the evidence proved that the accused was a sexually moviated serial killer. 審理時檢方主張，證據顯被告是一個基於性侵害動機的連續殺人犯。 Defense lawyer **argued that** the evidence is irrelevant and inadmissible. 被告律師主張證據沒有關連性而無證據能力。 The defendant **argued that** his killing of the intruder was justificable. 被告主張他殺了入侵者是正當的。
	vi.	爭執 [(+ with/over/about)] He **argued with** his wife. They **argued about** money. 他與他太太爭執，他們為了錢而起爭執。
arise [əˋraɪz]	*vi.*	出現，產生，形成 [(+ from / out of)] The homicide **arose from** the defendant's desire to protect his family. 這起殺人案起因於被告想著要保護家人。 The car accident **arose from** drunk driving. 這場車禍起因於酒後開車。 The homicide **arose out of** an argument between defendant and the deceased. 這件殺人案起因於被告與死者的一場爭執。
armed [ɑrmd]	*adj.*	武裝的 Officers are allowed to pat the person's outer clothing If they reasonably suspect the person is **armed** and dangerous. Pat down is conducted for the officers' safety, and must be based on a reasonable suspicion that the person **is armed**. 員警如果有合理懷疑某個人攜帶武器而且是危險的，即被容許拍搜他的外部衣服。拍搜是為了員警的安全，並且必須基於該人有攜帶武器的合理懷疑。
	應用	*armed robbery* 攜械強盜 *armed bank robbery* 攜械搶劫銀行
armored patrol car		裝甲巡邏車
armored police vehicle		警用裝甲車
arrest [əˋrɛst]	*vt.*	逮捕 He **was arrested** on charge of murder. 他因謀殺罪的指控而被捕。 James **was arrested** on suspicion of arson, but another arson

suspect is still at large. 詹姆士因涉有縱火之嫌而被捕，但另一名縱火嫌犯仍然在逃。

| | n. | 逮捕 |

The man **was placed under arrest for** stealing a car. 這個人因為偷車而被逮捕。

At this time, I'm **placing you under arrest for** robbery. You have the right to remain silent. 現在，我以強盜罪將你逮捕，你有權保持緘默。

應用　*to avoid arrest* 逃避逮捕

to effect the arrest 實施逮捕

to initiate an arrest 發動逮捕

to justify an arrest 將逮捕正當化

to make an arrest 進行逮捕

to resist an arrest 抗拒逮捕

arrest report 逮捕報告

arrest warrant 逮捕令、通緝書

citizen's arrest 公民扭捕(公民發現罪犯，可自行扭捕送至執法機關，即現行犯的逮捕)

false arrest 錯誤逮捕(又稱 *wrongful arrest*)

lawful arrest 合法逮捕

provisional arrest 暫時逮捕

search incident to arrest 逮捕附帶搜索

warranted arrest 有令狀逮捕

warrantless arrest 無令狀逮捕

| | n. | 【醫】停止 |

應用　*cardiac arrest* 心跳停止

Many people die each year from heart disease. Most of these deaths are caused by sudden **cardiac arrest.** 每年，許多人因為心臟疾病死亡，大多數是因為瞬間心跳停止。

| arrestee | n. | 被捕者 |
| [ə,rɛs`ti] | | |

The arrester must have reasonable cause to believe that **arrestee** has committed a felony. 逮捕者必須有合理事由相信被逮捕之人已犯下重罪。

| arrester | n. | 逮捕者 |
| [ə`rɛstə] | | |

The **arrester** must have reasonable cause to believe that arrestee has committed a felony. 逮捕者必須有合理事由相信被逮捕之人已犯下重罪。

| arson | n. | 縱火(罪)，放火(罪) |
| [`arsn] | | |

Arson is sometimes used to conceal another crime such as murder. 縱火有時候被用來隱藏另一項犯罪，例如謀殺。

應用

arson for profit 為利益而縱火

arson investigator 縱火調查員

attempted arson 縱火未遂

residential arson 住宅縱火

arsonist [ˈɑrsnɪst]	*n.*	縱火者 (參 pyromania 縱火狂)

To seek revenge, an **arsonist** will target the home of someone in retaliation for an actual or perceived injustice against him or her. 為了尋求報復，縱火者會鎖定某個人的家當作目標，以報復一個真正或自我感覺的不公平。

The **arsonist** ignited the fire, ran outside and fled from the scene. 縱火犯引燃火災，跑了出去並逃離現場。

應用

serial arsonist 連續縱火犯

article [ˈɑrtɪk!]	*n.*	(法律條文的) 第……條，條文

He was prosecuted under **Article** 271 of the Penal Code. 他被以刑法第 271 條起訴了。

【補充說明】法律條文的符號是「§」。條號除了用 article 一字之外，也有以"section"作為條號，例如加拿大刑法 (The Criminal Code of Canada) Section 28 指第 28 條。德國司法部官方翻譯的德國刑法(German Criminal Code)也是以"Section"作為條號，例如 Section 1. No punishment without law: An act can only incur a penalty if criminal liability was established by law before the act was committed. 第 1 條，無法律即無處罰：行為受到處罰，以行為前法律已訂有刑事責任。

ASEANAPOL	*abbr.*	東協警察首長協會 ASEAN Chiefs of National Police
assailant [əˈselənt]	*n.*	攻擊者，襲擊者

The **assailant** allegedly approached the woman from behind, displayed a knife and demanded money. 襲擊者涉嫌從後方接近該女子，亮出刀子並且要錢。

assault [əˈsɔlt]	*vt.*	攻擊，襲擊

An officer **was assaulted** in the line of duty, and sustained injuries. 有一位員警在執勤中受到攻擊並且受了傷。

	n.	攻擊，襲擊【律】侵犯人身，【律】施暴

應用

aggravated assault 加重傷害

sexual assault (未經同意而)性交，性的侵犯

assault with a deadly weapon 以致命的武器攻擊

assemble [əˈsɛmb!]	*vi.*	集合，聚集，集會

The **right to assemble** allows people to gather for peaceful and lawful purposes. The police department is the primary law enforcement authority during an unlawful assembly or riot situation. 集會權容許人民基於和平及合法的目的而聚集，在一個非法集會或暴動的情況中，警察局是主要的執法機關。

| assert | vt. | 聲稱，斷言，主張 |
| [əˈsɚt] | | Defendant **asserted** that he was not part of any conspiracy to kill the victim. 被告聲稱他沒有一起共謀殺害被害人。 |

assess	vt.	對……進行估價，評價
[əˈsɛs]		As an EMT, it is important **to assess** a patient's condition at the scene. For example, if a patient has chest pain or discomfort, the EMTs should **assess** the cardiac and respiratory systems. 身為緊急救護技術員，在現場評估患者的狀況，很重要的。例如，如果患者有胸痛或不適，緊急救護技術員應該評估心臟及呼吸系統。
	應用	*to assess the mood of the crowd* 評估群眾的心情
		to assess the credibility of witness 評估證人的可信度
		to assesses the prisoner's special need 評估受刑人的特殊需要

assessment	n.	評估
[əˈsɛsmənt]	應用	*initial assessment* 初步評估
		medical assessment 醫療評估
		patient assessment 患者評估
		risk assessment 風險評估
		trauma assessment 創傷評估
		to conduct assessment 進行評估

| asset | n. | 財產，資產 |
| [ˈæsɛt] | | **Asset forfeiture** laws allow the government to take the ill-gotten gains of drug kingpins and use them to put more cops on the streets. Criminal forfeiture operates as punishment for a crime. (President George Bush) 資產沒收的法律讓政府得以將毒品要角的不法所得拿走，並用來增加路上的警力，刑事沒收是做為對於犯罪的處罰(喬治布希總統)。 |

assign	vt.	派定，指定，選派[(+to/for)]
[əˈsaɪn]		After graduation from the police academy, new sworn officers **are** generally **assigned** to the uniformed patrol unit. 從警察學校畢業之後，新進員警通常會被指派到制服巡邏單位。
		Officer going off duty should not **be assigned to** take crime reports. However, they may **be assigned to** cover in-progress crimes or to standby at the scene. 即將退勤的員警不應再被指派去受理犯罪報案，但可以指派他們去支援進行中的犯罪，或在現場待命。

		Around 50 firefighters **are assigned to** the fire, the Incident Commander said. 事件指揮官說，大約有 50 名消防員被派去這場火災。
assigned counsel		指定辯護人(或稱 *court-appointed attorney; court-appointed counsel; appointed counsel*)
associate [ə`soʃɪt]	*n.*	同夥，交往，夥伴，同事，朋友，合夥人
		Police believed that he was an **associate** of Boston Marathon bombing suspect. 警方相信他是波士頓馬拉松爆炸案嫌犯的同夥。
	vt.	聯想，把……聯想在一起[+with]
		Police arrested a suspect **associated with** the shooting that occurred last Friday. 警方逮捕到一名與上星期五發生的槍擊案有關的嫌犯。
		The FBI released photos of a vehicle that **is associated with** the robbery. 聯邦調查局公布了一張與該件強盜案有關的汽車相片。
	應用	*associate justice* 陪席大法官 *the right to associate* 結社權
association [ə,sosɪ`eʃən]	*n.*	結合，交往 [+(with)]
		The suspect denied any **association with** the defendant. 嫌犯否認與被告有任何關聯。
	應用	*freedom of association* 結社自由
assume [ə`sjum]	*vt.*	以為，假定為，(想當然地) 認為 [+(that)]
		We can't **assume** the suspects to be guilty simply because they've decided to remain silent. 我們不能認定嫌犯有罪，只因為他們決定保持沉默。
		The truck driver mistakenly **assumed that** he had the right of way, and then struck the taxi and seriously injured the occupants. 卡車司機誤認他有路權，並因此撞上計程車並嚴重地導致乘客受傷。
	vt.	承擔
		In general, prosecutors and the investigating officers must **assume** the burden of proving the accused person guilty. 通常而言，檢察官及偵查人員必須承擔被告有罪的舉證負擔。
assumption [ə`sʌmpʃən]	*n.*	假設，假定
	應用	*assumption of innocence* 推定無罪
	n.	承擔
	應用	*assumption of liability* 承擔責任 *assumption of responsibility* 承擔責任

assumption of risk 承擔風險

asylum [ə`saɪləm]	*n.*	庇護，避難，庇護所，避難所

The **asylum seeker** is physically present at the territory of the U.S. He filed a petition for **asylum** and have been granted **asylum** in the United States. 這名尋求庇護者目前人在美國領域內，他提出了庇護的請求，並且已經獲得美國的核准。

應用　*political asylum* 政治庇護

to file a petition for asylum 提起庇護的請求

to grant asylum 同意/准予庇護

to seek asylum 尋求庇護

atone [ə`ton]	*vi.*	補償，彌補 [+(for)]

The offender hopes to be given the opportunity **to stone for** the harm he has caused to the victim. 犯罪者希望獲得機會補償他對於被害人所造成的傷害。

attack [ə`tæk]	*vt.*	襲擊

A male **was attacked** at random by a group of gangsters in the downtown. The victim had severe injuries. 一名男子在市區遭到一群幫派分子隨機攻擊，被害人有嚴重的受傷。

At trial, any party, including the party that called the witness, may **attack** the witness's credibility. 審判時，任何一方，包括傳喚證人的一方，均可攻擊證人的可信度。

n.　進攻，襲擊

The methods of **fire attack** differ depending on the situation. 滅火的方式視狀況而有不同。

The frontage of a building is important to firefighters, since most **attacks** begin from the front. 建築物的正面對消防員而言是重要的，因為大多數的滅火勢是從前面開始。

Street conditions can severely hamper a **fire attack**. 街道的狀況有可能會嚴重阻礙滅火。

When you begin with your **attack**, it is important to ensure that you have enough water and hose to complete the **attack**. 當你開始滅火時，很重要的是確定你有足夠的水及水管，來完成滅火。

n.　(疾病的) 發作

應用　*heart attack* 心臟病發作

asthma attack 氣喘發作

attacker [ə`tækə]	*n.*	襲擊者

The attacker was caught on surveillance video. 襲擊者被監視錄影帶拍到。

attempt	vt.	試圖，企圖，試圖做[+to-v][+v-ing]
[ə`tɛmpt]		Police are on the lookout for a man who **attempted to** rob a convenient store in downtown, but fled empty- handed. 警方正注意找尋意圖在市中心搶奪便利商店但空手而逃的男子。
		The suspect possessed a deadly weapon and **attempted to** escape. 嫌犯持有致命的武器，並企圖逃走。Firefighter said there were several people in the building when the fire alarm went off. They **attempted to** put out the flames. 消防員說，當火災警報響的時候，有很多人在這建築物內，他們試圖滅火。
	n.	嘗試，企圖，未遂
		When someone makes the effort to accomplish something without success, the act is an **attempt**. 當某人努力要完成某件事但沒成功時，這個行為是一項未遂。
	應用	*in an attempt to* 試圖
		with an attempt to 試圖

attempted	adj.	企圖的，未遂的
[ə`tɛmptɪd]		In New York, **attempted** murder is a serious crime which carries a sentence of up to 25 years in prison. 在紐約州，殺人未遂是一項嚴重的犯罪，得處高達 25 年刑期。
	應用	*attempted arson* 縱火未遂
		attempted assault 未遂攻擊
		attempted crime 未遂罪
		attempted robery 強盜未遂
		attempted suicide 自殺未遂

attention	n.	注意，注意力
[ə`tɛnʃən]		The sound of gunshots **drew the attention of** the patrol officers. 槍聲引起了巡邏員警的注意。
		Johnson was a notorious gang member, and thus he had **come to the attention of** the police before he was shot. 強生是一個惡名昭彰的幫派分子，因此在他被開槍之前，就已經被警方注意了。

attest	vi.	證實，證明[(+to)]
[ə`tɛst]		Interrogators must ensure that the suspect has read the written statement in person and understand its contents, and that the suspect **attests to** its accuracy. 偵訊者必須確保嫌犯已親自閱讀筆錄並了解其內容；並且嫌犯確認其正確無訛。

attorney	n.	【美】律師，(根據委任狀的)法定代理人
[ə`tɜnɪ]	應用	*attorney* 律師(又稱 *attorney-at-law*、*counsel* 或 *solicitor*)
		attorney 檢察官(又稱 *public prosecutor* 或 *district attorney*)

Attorney General【美】檢察總長

attorney visit 律師會見

court-appointed attorney 指定辯護人(又稱 *assigned counsel*、
court-appointed counsel 或 *appointed counsel*)

defense attorney 辯護律師

power of attorney 委任狀，授權書

prosecuting attorney 起訴檢察官

authority [ə`θɔrətɪ]	*n.*	權，權力，職權 Officers shall not use their **authority** or position for financial gains. 員警不得使用其權力或職位，來謀取財產上的獲得。
	n.	官方，當局[複數] I want to commend the work of the NYPD, the New York Fire Department, and the FBI, which responded swiftly and aggressively to a dangerous situation. And I also want to commend the vigilant citizens who noticed this suspicious activity and reported it to the **authorities**. (US President Barock Obama) 我要嘉許紐約市警局、消防局及聯邦調查局的工作，迅速而積極回應危險狀況，並且我也要嘉許這些有警戒心的市民，能注意到此一可疑的活動，並向當局報告(美國總統歐巴馬)。 Officers shall not, under color of **authority**, make any public statement that could be reasonably interpreted as having an adverse effect upon department. 員警不得假藉職權，發表任何可被合理解釋為會負面影響警局的公開言論。
	應用	*under color of authority* 假藉職權，以職權為藉口
authorization [,ɔθərə`zeʃən]	*n.*	授權，批准 In general, a search requires prior **authorization**. A search conducted without prior **authorization** is unreasonable. 通常，搜索需要有事先的授權，未經事先授權的搜索是不合理理的。
authorize [`ɔθə,raɪz]	*vt.*	授權，批准 Law enforcement officers **are authorized to** maintain public peace and order, prevent and detect crime, make arrest and enforce the laws. 執法人員被授權維持公共的和平及秩序、預防及發掘犯罪、進行逮捕，以及執法。
autopsy [`ɔtɑpsɪ]	*n.*	【醫】屍體解剖，驗屍 They performed **autopsies** to discover the cause of death. 他們進行驗屍，以找出死亡原因。
	應用	*autopsy report* 驗屍報告 *to perform autopsy* 相驗

		to conduct autopsy 相驗
avoid [ə`vɔɪd]	*vt.*	避免，躲開 [(+v-ing)] The suspect was found using the name of his brother **to avoid** being arrested. 嫌犯被發現使用他弟弟的姓名逃避逮捕。
	應用	*avoid arrest* 躲避逮捕 *avoid being take into custody* 躲避拘禁 *avoid deportation* 躲避遣返 *avoid justice* 逃避司法 *avoid prosecution* 逃避起訴 *avoid using seat belt* 使用安全帶
award [ə`wɔrd]	*n.*	報酬 Payment to confidential informants (CIs) can be divided into two categories – awards and **rewards**. **Awards** may be based on a percentage of the net value of assets seized as a result of information provided by a CI. Unlike **awards**, rewards come directly from an agency's budget. 付給線民的費用可以分為兩類：獎金(award)與報酬(reward)，獎金會是依據線民提供資訊而查扣到的資產淨值的某個比例。報酬則與獎金不同，報酬直接來自於機關的預算。
BAC	*abbr.*	血液酒精濃度(*blood alcohol concentration* 或 *blood alcohol concentration*) In most jurisdictions, if a measurement such as **BAC** is in excess of a specific level, there is no need to prove impairment or being under the influence of alcohol. 在大部分的管轄中，如果像是血液酒精濃度(BAC)的測量超過一定標準時，就沒有必要證明是受酒精干擾或影響。
backfire [`bæk`faɪr]	*n.*	【消防】逆火
back up	*v.*	後退，倒退回去，倒(車) Police have been called to multiple accidents on the westbound lanes. Four lanes are closed at the moment. Vehicles are getting by on the shoulder of the road. Traffic **is backing up**, please try to avoid the area and use an alternate route. 警方已被呼叫前往西向車道的連環車禍，四線車道目前被封閉，車輛目前是由路肩經過，交通正在回堵中，請盡量避開這個區域並且使用替代路線。
	n.	支持，支援 If additional **backup** is needed, our dispatcher is in radio contact with beat officers and is able to call for **backup** instantly. 如果額

外的支援有需要的話，我們的派遣官與勤區員警有無線電聯繫，可以立即請求支援。

The policeman called for **back-up**.　員警呼叫了支援。

	n.	backup [`bæk,ʌp] 後援，備用，備用物，【電腦】備份

background [`bæk,graʊnd]	*n.*	背景，背景資料，出身背景，(包括學歷在內的)經歷 Officers could run a **background** check if they have reason to believe that someone has committed a crime. However, running unauthorized **background** check is an intrusion of privacy.　員警如果有理由相信某人犯罪，就可以做背景清查，然而，進行未經核准的背景清查則是隱私的侵犯。
badge [bædʒ]	*n.*	臂章 Police **badge** is a symbol of public faith.　警察臂章是公眾信賴的象徵。
bail [bel]	*n.*	保釋，保釋金 Due to the seriousness of the crime, the amount of **bail** was very high so that the accused criminal would not **skip bail**.　由於犯罪的嚴重性，交保金額非常高，讓犯罪被告不會棄保。 In some cases, the defendant or his defense attorney can file a motion to the court **to release** the defendant **on bail**. However, courts have power **to deny bail** to protect the victim or to prevent escape.　有些案例，被告或他的辯護律師可以聲請法院將被告交保釋放，然而，法院有權拒絕保釋，以保護被害人或防止逃匿。 If a person who has been **released on bail** jumps bail, the court will declare the **bail** forfeited.　如果一個被交保釋放的人棄保的話，法院會宣告將保釋金沒收。
	vt.	保釋(人)，(法官)將(在押犯)交保釋放 [(+out)] Due to the seriousness of the crime, the judge set the bail at 1 million. However, the detainee's family cannot gather enough funds **to bail him out of jail**.　由於犯罪的嚴重性，法官訂出一百萬元保釋金額，然而，被拘禁人的家屬無法湊足資金將他保出來。
bailsman [`belzmən]	*n.*	保釋保證或提供保釋金的人
bailiff [`belɪf]	*n.*	法警 If there is any disruption during the trial, the **bailiffs** will have the obligation to remove any persons disrupting these proceedings.　如果審判時有任何擾亂，法警會有義務排除任何擾亂程序的人。

ban [bæn]	*n.*	禁止，禁令

Because of the expected typhoon, police announced a parking **ban** will be in effect from Friday at 9 p.m. until noon on Sunday. 由於預期的颱風，警方宣布停車禁令，將從星期五晚上九點生效至星期日中午。

應用 *to lift the ban on* 取消……的禁令
to put a ban on 對於……予以禁止

bar [bɑr]	*vt.*	中止，禁止

If you violate the conditions of your admission, you may be deported from the country and may **be barred from** returning for a certain period of time. 如果你違反入境許可條件，你可能會被遣送出國，並被禁止於一定期間內再來。

應用 *behind bars* 【口】被關押，坐牢，在監獄服刑

If a person is convicted of robbery and sentenced to six years in prison, he or she will **be put behind bars** and serve the jail term. 如果某個人被判強盜罪確定，並判刑 6 年監禁，他就會放被到牢裡服刑。

n. 律師業，司法界(常大寫)

In the United Kingdom, a lawyer who is admitted **to plead at the bar** and who may argue cases in superior courts is called barrister. 在英國，允許在法院辯論及可以在上級法院論告案件的律師稱為 barrister。

應用 *to take/pass bar exam* 參加/通過律師考試

bargain [ˋbɑrgɪn]	*vi.*	(法律上) 協議，提出條件

Defendant attempted **to bargain with** the prosecutor and offed to plea guilty of the robbery. 被告試圖與檢察官協商，並提議就強盜案認罪。

n. (法律上的) 協議

In the U.S., you can ask for a **plea bargain**, but the prosecutor can choose not to **plea bargain** with you. If you agree on a **plea bargain**, it must be approved by the Judge. 在美國，你可以要求認罪協商，但檢察官可以選擇不與你協商。如果你同意認罪協商，該協商必須經過法官准許。

Many people choose a **plea bargain** instead of going to trial because it is much faster and you can be sure of the outcome. 很多人選擇認罪協商而非進入審判，因為認罪協商比較快速而且可以確保結果。

barrel [ˋbærəl]	*n.*	槍管，砲筒 (或稱 *gun barrel*)

應用 *to forge gun barrel* 偽造槍管

to make gun barrel 製造槍管

barricade [`bærə,ked]	*vt.*	阻塞，擋住，在……設置路障，築柵欄防禦 Investigators said that the suspect **barricaded** himself inside the home and refused to come out. SWAT officials and K9 units were called to the scene. 偵查人員說，嫌犯把自己封鎖在家裡，並且拒絕出來，霹靂小組與警犬隊都被呼叫到了現場。
	n.	柵欄，擋牆，障礙物，路障，街壘 Police put up a **barbed wire barricade** to seal off the government building and blocked the protesters' path about two hundred meters from the building. 警方架設了鐵絲網拒馬以封鎖政府大樓，並將抗議者的路徑阻絕於大樓 200 公尺之外。
	應用	*barricade tape* 封鎖線(又稱 *barrier tape，police tape，crime scene safety tape*) *barbed wire barricade* 鐵絲網拒馬 (或稱 *razor wire barrier* 蛇籠鐵絲網)
barrier [`bærɪr]	*n.*	障礙物，路障，柵欄
	應用	*barrier tape* 封鎖線(又稱 *barricade tape; police tape; crime scene safety tape*) *razor wire barrier* 蛇籠鐵絲網
batter [`bætɚ]	*vt.*	連續猛擊 The offender allegedly **battered** his wife with a stick. 該名犯罪者涉嫌用棍子毆打他的妻子。
batterer [`bætɚd]	*adj.*	被打爆的，被痛打的 Prosecutor said that the laws protect **battered** women, and encourages **battered** women to obtain protective orders against the **batterers**. 檢察官說，法律保護受暴婦女，並鼓勵受暴婦女去取得保護令以對抗施暴者。
	應用	*battered child* *battered child syndrome* 受虐兒童症候群
	n.	*battered husband / wife / parent / spouse* 受暴丈夫/妻子/父母/配偶 *battered woman syndrome* 受暴婦女症候群
batterer [`bætərɚ]		施暴者
battle [`bæt!]	*vt.*	與……作戰，與……搏鬥 Firefighters spent three hours **battling** the blaze before they were finally able to get it under control. 消防員花了三小時滅火，才終於將火控制住。 Nearby streets were closed as firefighters **battled** the blaze. 附

近的街道在消防員滅火時，都被關閉了。

baton [bæ`tn]	*n.* 應用	短棒，權杖，警棒 *police baton* 警棍 *baton technique* 警棍技巧 *expandable baton* 伸縮警棍 *illuminated baton* 照明指揮棒

be + at...	*vi.*	be + at 動詞片語 *at large* 逍遙法外，在逃：As of this morning, the suspect in connection to this robbery remains at large. 直到今晨，與這起強盜案有關聯的嫌犯仍然在逃。 *at stake* 處於危險中：The boat stranded in the river and 30 lives were at stake. 船在河中擱淺，30 人命在旦夕。 *at risk* 有風險：Rescuers said the hikers' lives were at risk. 救援人員說登山客性命處於險境。 *at fault* 有過錯：Officers believed that the truck driver was at fault. 員警認為是卡車司機有錯。
be + in...	*vi.*	be + in 動詞片語 *in cardiac arrest* 心跳停止： If you suspect that a person is in cardiac arrest, call the local emergency number immediately. 如果你懷疑某人心跳停止，立刻撥打當地的緊急電話。 *in coma* 昏迷中：She is in a coma, and still hold on to life. 她仍在昏迷中，而且不放棄生命。 *in custody* 受監禁：The suspect is in custody 嫌犯是在拘禁中。 *in distress* 在困境中：The patient appeared to be in distress. 患者顯然還在困境中。 *in labor* 在分娩中：The woman is in labor. 這位婦女在分娩中。 *in progress* 在進行中：Call 1-1-0, if the crime is in-progress. 如果犯罪還在持續中，打電話 110。If CPR is in progress, continue until the AED is turned on. 如果 CPR 在進行中，那就一直持續到 AED 開啟。 *in shock* 休克：If you think a person is in shock, call 911 for immediate medical help. 如果你認為某人呈現休克，撥 911 請求立即的醫療協助。 *in peril* 在險境中；The gunman was shot and his life is in peril. 槍手被擊中而生命垂危。 *in jail* 在押，監禁中：The murderer is in jail. 殺人犯在監獄中。 *in turmoil* 騷擾，混亂中：The city is in turmoil. 城市陷入一

片混亂。

in uniform 穿著制服：A police officer does not have to be in uniform to make an arrest. 警察並不一定要穿制服才能進行逮捕。

in cession 開庭中：The court is in cession. 法庭在開庭中。

in recess 暫時休庭中： The court is in recess. 法庭暫時休庭。

in writing 以書面： Police said that statement must be in writing. 警方說，陳述必須以書面為之。

be + on...　　　　vi.　be + on 動詞片語

on appeal 在上訴中：The case is on appeal. 案件在上訴中。

on bail 在交保中：The accused is on bail. 被告在交保中。

on duty 在執勤中：The police officer is on duty. 員警正在值勤中。

on fire 著火了：The house is on fire. 房子著火了。

on patrol 在巡邏：The police officer is on patrol. 員警正在巡邏中。

on probation 在緩刑中：The offender is on probation. 罪犯正在緩刑期間。

on call 聽候召喚、待命：Officers told Reuters they were on call 24 hours a day. 路透社說他們一天 24 小時都在待命。

on trial 受審：The suspect was on trial for robbery last week. 嫌犯因強盜案在上星期受審。

be + under...　　　vi.　be + under 動詞片語

under arrest 受逮捕：Freeze! You are under arrest. 不要動，你被捕了。

under attack 受到攻擊：Officer said he was under attack and returned fire immediately. 員警說他受到攻擊並立即開槍還擊。

under control 在控制中：Police said the situation was under control. 警方說狀況已經在控制中。

under fire 【比喻】受到嚴厲的批評：The police were under fire for the wrongful arrests and excessive force. 警方因為錯誤的逮捕及武力過當受到批評。

under investigation 受調查中：The cause of the fire was under investigation. 火災的原因還在調查中。

under pressure 受到壓力：The police are under pressure because the suspect is still at large. 由於嫌犯仍然在逃，使警方感到壓力。

under review 審理中：The case is under review by the court.

本案在法院審理中。

under scrutiny 受到高度檢視：Police **are under scrutiny** after CCTV image shows that officers used excessive force against protesters. 由於監視器影像顯示員警對抗議者過度使用武力，警方現正高度受到檢視。

under surveillance 在監控中：The suspect's vehicle was under surveillance. 嫌犯的車子正在監控中

beacon [ˋbikn]	*n.*	警示燈

bear [bɛr]	*v.*	攜帶，運送，佩帶，擁有，具有

The Second Amendment to the U.S. Constitution provides that the right of the people to keep and **bear** arms shall not be infringed. 美國憲法第 2 修正案規定，人民擁有及攜帶武器的權利不得受到侵犯。

The proficiency of the 911 dispatchers directly **bears upon** the safety of every officer in the field. 派遣官的專業直接攸關轄內每一位員警的安全。

|應用| *bear on* 與……有關，對……有影響

beat [bit]	*vt.*	痛打

The gangsters have been charged with murder as they allegedly **beat up** the victim and left him for dead in the park. 幫派分子被指控謀殺，因為他們涉嫌毒打被害人，並將他遺棄在公園而死亡。

|應用| *to beat someone black and blue* 將某人打得瘀青

n. (警察等的)勤區，巡邏路線，負責區域

Normally, **beat officers** handle all cases on their beats. 正常而言，勤區員警要處理勤區內的案件。

There are several types of police patrol. In foot patrol, officers **walk the beat**. 警察的巡邏有數種，在徒步巡邏方面，員警是在勤區內走動。

bigamy [ˋbɪgəmɪ]	*n.*	重婚

The man was arrested on suspicion of **bigamy**. 該男子因涉有重婚之嫌而被逮捕。

binding [ˋbaɪndɪŋ]	*adj.*	有約束力的

The final decisions of the Supreme Court **are binding** on the court of appeals and district courts. 最高法院的終局判決對於上訴法院即地方法院有拘束力。

|應用| *binding force* 拘束力

Basically, international agreements can have the same **binding** force as treaties. 基本上，國際協定與條約有同樣的拘束力。

blackmail [`blæk,mel]	*vt.*	敲詐，勒索，脅迫[(+into)] 【註：以傷害身體、毀損財物或揭露私密等而非法索取錢財的方式】 The girl **was blackmailed into** having sex when she was 18. 她18 歲的時候被脅迫而發生性關係。 The man **was blackmailed for** ten thousand dollars. 男子被勒索 1 萬元。 The ex-boyfriend was accused of trying **to blackmail** the girl for a million dollars after they broke up. He allegedly **blackmailed** her with pictures and videos she feared would ruin her career. 他們分手後，這名前男友被控勒索女子一百萬元，他涉嫌用這些讓她害怕會毀掉她人生的照片與影片進行勒索。
	n.	勒索，敲詐 The **blackmail** happened two weeks ago. 這敲詐勒索發生在兩星期前。
black market		黑市，黑市交易 It is true that the seizure of a very large shipment of heroin does cause a temporary shortage of **black-market** supplies. 查獲非常大量的海洛因運送，確實會造成黑市供應上暫時性短缺。
blame [blem]	*vt.*	責備，指責 ，歸咎於……[(+on/for)] The wife **blamed** her husband **for** her son's injury. 妻子為了兒子受傷一事責備她的丈夫。 Police said Jackson **was to blame** for the offense. 警方說，該項犯罪應歸咎於傑克遜。 Many victims **blame** themselves, feeling embarrassed to come forward and get help. 許多被害人怪罪於自己，覺得出面尋求幫助感到尷尬。
blast [blæst]	*n.*	(一陣) 疾風 (或氣流等)，爆炸，爆破 A man died in the **blast**. Witnesses told fire crews they had smelled what they believed was natural gas near the site of the **blast**. 一名男子在這次爆炸中死亡。證人告訴消防同仁說，他們在靠近爆炸的地點，聞到他們認為是天然氣。 爆炸
	vi.	The fire **blasted up** from the basement of the eight-story apartment building. 這次的火是從這棟八層樓公寓建築的地下室爆炸的。
blaze [blez]	*n.*	火焰，火災 The **blaze** was quickly extinguished. Firefighters say the blaze has left three people dead. 這場火很快地就被撲滅了。消防員

說這場火造成三人死亡。

Several houses had been burnt to the ground when the **blaze** was put out. 大火撲滅時，好幾間房子已經被燒毀。

block	*vt.*	阻塞，阻擋，阻止，封鎖，妨礙，限制
[blɑk]		

Protesters blocked downtown traffic to protest mayor's policy and decision. 抗議者阻塞了市區交通，抗議市長的政策與決定。

The police **blocked off** the road after the traffic accident. 交通事故之後，警方將道路封鎖了。

Fire crews were still trying to get the fire under control several hours later. As of 9 p.m., the roads near the scene **were** still **blocked off** with fire trucks. 經過幾個小時之後，消防同仁仍在試著將火勢控制。至晚上 9 時為止，現場附近的道路仍然用消防車封鎖著。【美】(四面圍有街道的)街區。

James was discovered unresponsive in his room. His airway **was blocked** by food, which caused him to asphyxiate. 詹姆士被發現在他房間沒了反應，他的氣道被食物阻塞，造成他窒息。

n. 阻塞（物），障礙（物），【美】街區

As a result, several **blocks** are closed off. 結果，好幾個區域都被封閉。

應用 *airway block* 氣道阻塞（或 *airway obstruction*）

blockade	*vt.*	封鎖，道路阻塞
[blɑ`ked]		

Protesters **blockaded** the entrance to the city hall for three hours. 抗議者堵住市政廳的入口將近三小時。

n. 封鎖，道路阻塞

The protests and **blockades** have posed severe risks to public safety 抗議及阻塞道路已經對於共眾的安全造成嚴重的風險。

bloodstain	*n.*	血跡
[`blʌd,sten]		

Bloodstain pattern analysis (BPA) is one of several specialties in the field of forensic science. 血跡噴濺分析是刑事科學領域的其中一項專業。

body	*n.*	身體，屍體（參 corpse）
[`bɑdɪ]		

After the fire was extinguished, the victim's **body** was found inside the burned vehicle. 火勢撲滅後，被害者的屍體在燒毀的汽車內被找到。

應用 *body armor* 防彈衣

body camera (員警掛在胸前的) 隨身相機

body search 人身搜索

bodily [`bɑdɪlɪ]	*adj.*	*bodily harm* 身體上的傷害 *Bodily hurt* 身體上的傷害 *bodily injury* 身體上的傷害

bomb [bɑm]	*n.*	炸彈 On February 26, 1993, a bomb exploded in a parking garage of the World Trade Center (WTC) in New York City. 於 1993 年 2 月 26 日，一顆炸彈在紐約世貿大樓停車場爆炸。 The **bombing** occurred at 9:00 a.m. Six people were killed when the **bomb** exploded. 該爆炸發生於上午 9 時，炸彈爆炸時，造成有 6 人死亡。

bomber
[`bɑmɚ]   *n.*   炸彈客，使用炸彈的人
The **bombers** were were sentenced to life in prison. 該名炸彈客被判處無期徒刑。

應用   *car bomb* 汽車炸彈
         homicide bomber 殺人炸彈
         suicide bomber 自殺炸彈
         tear bomb 瓦斯彈

book [bʊk]	*vt.*	警方將……錄案登記以做指控之用(按：概念如同移送) After arrest, a criminal suspect is usually taken into police custody and **booked**. 逮捕之後，刑事罪犯通常會被警方拘禁並且錄案。

booking	*n.*	錄案 (按：概念如同移送，指犯罪嫌疑人被帶至警察局後登錄姓名、犯罪事實、拍照及按奈指紋等) Back in the police department, officers will register and enter charges against a person believed to have violated the law. The formal process is called **booking**. **Booking** creates an official arrest record. 回到警察局，員警對於認為已經違法之人，會做登錄並進行告訴，這個正式程序稱為錄案(booking)，錄案會形成正式的逮捕紀錄。

brandish [`brændɪʃ]	*vt.*	揮舞，揮動 The suspect **brandished** a knief at an employee and took money from a cash register. 嫌犯對雇員揮舞著刀子，並從收銀機拿走現金。

breach [britʃ]	*n.*	(對法律等的)破壞、違反，(對他人權利的)侵害 The lawyer told the court that it is clearly a **breach** of duty of care. 律師告訴法院那顯然違背了注意義務。 The suspect was arrested for **breach** of peace a few days ago outside of a club. 嫌犯因為幾天前在酒店外面的妨礙安寧而被逮捕。

break	*vt.*	破壞(約束)，違反
[brek]		The man was forced to quit his job after it was discovered that he had **broken** the law. 該男子被發現曾經違法之後，被迫離職。
	vt.	破(案)，偵破
		The Chief of Police declined to talk about any turning point that allowed investigators **to break** the case. 警察局長拒絕談論讓偵查人員得以破案的關鍵點。
		Police **broke up** the prostitution rign. Four suspects were arrested on suspicion of running brothels. 警方偵破應召集團，四名嫌犯因涉有經營應召站之嫌而被捕。

應用 *break into* 強行進入某處

The burglar **broke into** the victim's home. 竊賊侵入了被害人的家中。

| | *vi.* | 越(獄)，掙脫 |
| | | Three inmates **borke out of** prison last week and are still at large. 三名受刑人上星期越獄，而目前仍逍遙法外。 |

應用 *break out of jail / prison* 越獄
breaking and entering 非法侵入

| bribe | *vt.* | 向……行賄，收買 |
| [braɪb] | | The suspect attempted **to bribe** the detective **into** letting him go with offers of 1 million in cash. 嫌犯拿出 1 百萬現金，企圖行賄偵查員讓他離去。 |

應用 *to bribe one's way into* 用行賄手段達到……目的
to bribe sb. with sth. 用某物賄賂某人
to bribe sb. to do sth. 賄賂某人做某事

| | *n.* | 賄賂 |
| | | The officer was dismissed from office for taking **bribes** from the briber. 該官員因收受賄賂者的賄賂而被革職。 |

| bribery | *n.* | 賄賂 |
| [ˈbraɪbərɪ] | | |

---

bring	*vt.*	提起 (訴訟)
[brɪŋ]		The prosecutor **brought charges against** the defendant for several bad checks he had written. 檢察官對於被告提起了控訴，因為他開出多張空頭支票。
		The man **brought a lawsuit against** the officers because they arrested the wrong person. 該名男子對員警提起法律訴訟，因為員警逮捕錯人。
		The defendant argued that the prosecutor did not have jurisdiction **to bring the prosecution** because the alleged fraud

cases all happened abroad. 被告主張檢察官沒有管轄權可以起訴，因為這些詐欺案全都發生在國外。

He **was brought before the court** and was advised of his rights to counsel. But he waived the right and pleaded guilty. 他被逮捕到庭，並被告知有請求律師的權利，但他放棄了這項權利並且認罪。

The case **was brought before the court** two years age, the court found the defendant guilty of robbery early this year. 該案件在兩前被送進法院審理，法院在今年初判決被告強盜罪。

應用	*to bring a charge against sb.*	對(人)提起控告
	to bring a lawsuit	提起法律訴訟
	to bring prosecution	起訴
	to bring sb. to justice	使(人)歸案受審
	to bring sb. before the court	將(人)逮捕到庭

brothel [`brɔθəl]	*n.*	妓院

Police broke up the prostitution rign. Four suspects were arrested on suspicion of running **brothels**. 警方破獲應召集團，四名嫌犯因涉有經營應召站之嫌而被捕。

brutal [`brut!]	*adj.*	殘忍的，粗暴的，野蠻的

The **brutal** killing has shocked the whole country. 這起殘忍的殺入行為震驚了全國。

brutality [bru`tælətɪ]	*n.*	暴虐行為，蠻橫行為

Several Baltimore City police officers have been charged in a case of alleged police **brutality**. 好幾位巴爾的摩市警局的員警在一宗警察涉嫌暴力案件中被提告。

buckle [`bʌk!]	*vi. &* *vt.*	扣住，繫上

"**Buckle up**! It's the law". You may be pulled over if you **are** not properly **buckled up**. 「繫上安全帶，那是法律規定」。如果你沒繫好，你可能就會被攔下。

Even if the vehicle is equipped with air bags, always **buckle** your seat belt. Make it a habit that the vehicle does not go until everyone **is buckled up**. 即使車子配有安全氣囊，也要一直繫著安全帶。要養成每個人都繫安全帶才開車的習慣。

bug [bʌg]	*n.*	【俚】竊聽器

Police obtained a court permission to plant a bug in the suspect's office. Officers then attach a **bug** to the telephone line and record the conversation. 警方取得法院同意在嫌犯的辦公室安裝竊聽器，於是員警就在電話線上加裝竊聽器，並錄下對話。

	vt.	【俚】在⋯⋯安裝竊聽器
bullet	n.	子彈
[`bʊlɪt]		In the exhange of gunfire, officers fired more than a houdred **bullets** into the stronghold, and gun down the the suspects. 在槍戰中，員警對攻堅點發射超過 100 發子彈，並將嫌犯擊斃。

應用 *bullet wound* 槍傷
rubber bullet 塑膠子彈
bullet proof vest 防彈衣(或稱 *body armor*)

bully	vt.	霸凌，威嚇，脅迫，欺侮
[`bʊlɪ]		His life was miserable during his school years. He **was bullied** and subject to physical harm. 在學生時代他的生活真是悽慘，他受到霸凌並且受到身體上的傷害。
	n.	霸凌者，恃強欺弱者，惡霸
		Students might not report school **bullying** partly because they are afraid that the school authorities would tell the **bully** who told on him or her. 學生可能不會報告校園霸凌，有一部分是因為害怕校方會對惡霸者說出是誰告發的。

應用 *bully victim* 霸凌的被害人
cyberbullying 網路霸凌
school bullying 校園霸凌
workplace bullying 職場霸凌

bump	vt.	猛力撞擊⋯⋯，衝撞⋯⋯
[bʌmp]		He **bumped** his head in the accident and was sent to the hospital. 他在車禍中頭部猛力撞擊，並被送到醫院。
	n.	(因碰撞而引起的) 腫塊
		He got a large **bump** on his forehead. 他的前額腫了一大塊。

bumper-to-bumper	adj.	前後緊接而且行進緩慢的長車隊的
[`bʌmpɚtə`bʌmpɚ]		Traffic is **bumper-to-bumper** from the tunnel all the way out to the exit. Cars were lined up bumper-to-bumper along the whole length of the road. 交通從隧道到出口，一路上走走停停，整路車輛大排長龍。

burden	n.	重負，重擔，負擔
[`bɝdn]		**Burden of proof** includes both the **burden of production** and **burden of persuasion**. In general, prosecutors and the investigating officers **assume the burden of** proving the accused person guilty. 舉證負擔包括「提出之負擔(burden of production)」及「說服之負擔(burden of persuasion)」，通常，檢察官及偵查人員承擔被告有罪的舉證負擔。

burglar	n.	夜賊，破門盜竊者

[`bɝglɚ]		**Burglars** broke into his house last night. 竊賊在昨天夜裡闖入他家。
		Surveillance video revealed that the **burglar** broke in during the night. 錄影監視器顯示竊賊在夜間侵入。
		Police said the **burglar** has lengthy criminal histories for burglary charges. 警方說竊賊有很多侵入住宅竊盜的前科。
burglarize [`bɝglə,raɪz]	*vt.*	侵入竊盜/破門竊盜
		He **burglarized** three cars overnight. Also, seven restaurants **were** reportedly **burglarized** in the area. 他一夜之間侵入三輛車子行竊。該地區七家餐廳據報也被侵入而竊盜。
burglary [`bɝglərɪ]	*n.*	夜賊，破門竊盜，侵入竊盜
		Burglary means the breaking and entering of any building with the intent to commit larceny or felony. 竊盜(burglary)一詞指意圖犯竊盜罪而非法入侵 (breaking and entering) 建築物。
		【補充說明】在美國，theft、larceny 及 burglary 三個用語相似。各州可能使用 theft 用或 larceny 來描述偷竊
burn [bɝn]	*vi.*	燃燒，著火
		Firefighters estimated that the fire **had been burning** for more than 10 minutes before it was detected by the neighbor. 消防員估計這場火災被鄰居發現之前，已經燒了超過 10 分鐘。
	vt.	燃燒，著火
		Several houses **had been burnt to the ground** when the blaze was put out. 大火撲滅時，好幾間房子已經被燒毀。
		More than 50 firefighters were spraying nearby the buildings **to prevent the blaze from burning** other structures. 超過五十名消防員分散到建築物的附近，以防止火焰燒到其他建築物。
		Firefighters rushed to the scene of the car crash and rescued the driver from the **burning** car. 消防員警衝到車禍現場，並將駕駛從燃燒的車子中救出。
		After battling the blaze, a firefighter discovered a **burnt** dog among the debris. 火災撲滅之後，消防員在殘墟中找到一條被燒死的狗。
	n.	燒傷，灼傷，烙印，灼痛感
		Burns are classified as first, second or third degrees, depending on how deep and severe they penetrate the skin's surface. 燒傷分為一級、二級或三級，端看燒傷貫穿到皮膚表面有多深及多嚴重。
		His burn size is greater than 20% body surface area (BSA). 他的燒傷大於全身面積的 20%。

Jason suffered third and fourth degree burns over 70% of his body. 傑生全身百分之 70 受到三度及四度灼傷。

應用	*Burn Center* 燒燙傷中心
	burn injury 燒傷
	burn pattern analysis 燃燒型態分析
	burn pattern 燃燒型態
	burn rate 燃燒率
	electrical burn 觸電傷
	third-degree burn 三級燒傷

bury
['bɛrɪ]　*vt.*　Police said the victim's body **was buried in** the woods by the accused after the crime was committed. 警方說被告犯案後將被害人的屍體埋在樹林裡。

bust
[bʌst]　*vt.*　【口】逮捕，捕獲

City Police Department has **busted** the drug ringleaders for allegedly selling heroin. 市警局逮獲毒品集團的首腦涉嫌涉嫌販賣海洛因。

They **were busted** on drug possessions and sales charges.他們被依持有及販售之罪予以逮捕。

They **were busted** by the police in the raid. 他們被警方在掃蕩中逮捕。

n.　【口】逮捕，捕獲

Police said five people were arrested in the **drug bust**. 警方說，有五個人在毒品查緝中被逮捕。

應用	*drug bust* 毒品查緝
	prostitution bust 色情查緝
	illegal gambling bust 非法賭博查緝
	firemarms bust 槍枝查緝

camera
['kæmərə]　*n.*　照相機

應用	*body camera* (員警掛在胸前的)隨身相機
	red light camera 紅燈照相機
	speed camera detector 超速照相偵測器
	speed camera 超速照相機
	video surveillance camera 錄影監視器

cancel
['kæns!]　*vt.*　註銷

Under some circumstances, a driver license may be suspended, **cancelled** or revoked. Cancellation involves voluntarily giving up your driving privilege without penalty. Cancellation allows you to reapply for a license immediately. 有些情況下，駕照可能會被吊扣、註銷或吊銷。註銷涉及的是自願地放棄駕駛特權，沒

有處罰，註銷准許你立即重新申請駕照。

canine [`kenaɪn]	n.	警犬 (又稱 K-9)

---

caning [`kenɪŋ]	n.	鞭打，鞭刑 **Caning** is a form of punishment for convicted criminals, especially in Singapore and Malaysia. 鞭刑是針對有罪嫌犯的一種處罰形式，特別在新加坡及馬來西亞。

---

cannabis [`kænəbɪs]	n.	【植】印度大麻，大麻煙原料，大麻煙

---

capital punishment		死刑 **Capital punishment** is a legal process whereby a person is put to death by the law of the country as a punishment for a crime. In general, **capital punishment** is imposed for very serious offences such as murder. 死刑，是依國家法律將人處死，做為對於犯罪的懲罰的一個合法程序，通常，只有非常嚴重的犯罪諸如謀殺，才會獲判死刑。

---

captain [`kæptɪn]	n.	【警】隊長，【軍】上尉

---

captive [`kæptɪv]	adj.	被俘的，受監禁的，受控制的 They **were held captive** by masked gunmen. 他們被蒙面持槍歹徒劫持了。
	應用	*to hold (sb) captive* 囚禁或俘虜某人

---

capture [`kæptʃə]	vt.	紀錄，拍攝，留存 The murder **was captured** on the surveillance camera, and the perpetrator was identified from the images. "We have clear images on cameras. The footage **captures** the perpetrators of this crime," police said. 謀殺案被監視器拍到，行兇者已從影像被指認。警方說，「我們影帶上有清晰的影像，畫面拍到犯罪的行兇者。」
	vt.	捕獲，俘擄 The perpetrator **was captured** the following day. 行兇者在隔天被捕獲了。

---

caregiver [`kɛr͵gɪvə]	n.	照顧孩子(或老弱病殘者)的家人，受僱照顧孩子(或老弱病殘者)的人

---

caretaker [`kɛr͵tekə]	n.	照顧者，管理人

---

carpool [`kɑr͵pul]	n.	共乘，汽車合夥(車主協議輪流使用其自用車) You may use a **carpool lane** only if your vehicle carries the posted minimum number of people required for the **carpool**

lane. Typically, **carpool** in the United States is 2 or more person per vehicle. 只有當你的車子搭載高乘載專用道要求的最低公告人數時，你才可以使用共乘專用道，通常，美國的共乘是每車 2 人以上。

Carpool/High occupancy vehicle (HOV) lane is reserved for buses or vehicles with the minimum number of occupants specified on the signs. 共乘/高乘載專用道是保留給巴士，或載有標示規定的最低乘座人數的車輛。

cartridge	*n.*	彈殼
[`kɑrtrɪdʒ]		Spent **cartridge cases** not only help to identify the weapon used, they can also indicate where it was fired from. 用過的彈殼不僅可以幫助鑑定所使用的武器，也可以確認子彈是從何處發射。
casino	*n.*	賭場
[kə`sino]		【補充說明】gambling house 也是賭場。casino 通常附有住宿，飲食及其它娛樂，gambling house 通常只供賭博。如果是非法賭場，可先加 illegal 或 unlawful。
casualty	*n.*	(事故、災難等的)死者，傷者，受害人
[`kæʒʊəltɪ]		There were dozens of **casualties** in the train crash. 有數十人在那次火車事故中傷亡。
	應用	*heavy casualties* 重大傷亡
catastrophe	*vt.*	大災難，大敗，慘敗，翻天覆地的事件
[kə`tæstrəfɪ]		We were able to avoid a **catastrophe** because of the truck driver's assistance, police said. 警方說，由於卡車司機的協助，我們得以避免一場大災難。
catch	*vt.*	抓住，逮住，捕獲
[kætʃ]		The police decided to set up a controlled delivery of the marijuana **to catch** him. The suspect alleged that police illegally set trap **to catch** him. 警方決定安排大麻的控制下交付來抓他，嫌犯指控警方非法設陷阱抓他。
	vt.	趕上，及時趕到，沒錯過
		School Board said that it is dangerous that kids across the street **to catch** the bus. 學校委員會說，孩童直接穿過馬路去趕搭車是危險的。
	vt.	著(火)
		The building **caught fire** and burned down quickly. 建築物著火並很快地燒毀了。
	vt.	感染，染上(疾病)
		Detective Lee **has caught a cold**, and he needs to take

sick leave today. 李偵查員得了感冒，他今天必須請病假。

應用 *to catch a cold* 患了感冒

to catch a disease 染上疾病

to catch a fever 患了發燒

to catch fire 著火

---

causation   *n.*   因果關係

[kɔ`zeʃən]

In order to obtain a conviction, the prosecutor must prove **causation**. If an intervening factor breaks the **chain of causation** between the defendant's act and the result of the act, it would be difficult **to establish causation**. 為了取得定罪，檢察官必須證明因果關係，如果有介入的因素打斷被告的行為與結果之間的因果關係，因果關係就很難建立了。

---

cause   *vt.*   導致，引起

[kɔz]

An accident **has caused** traffic to back up on the highway. Eastbound traffic is backed up for miles. 車禍造成在高速公路上交通回堵，往東的交通回堵了好幾英里。

The super typhoon is expected **to cause** flash floods and mudslides. 這場超級颱風預期將造成豪雨成災及土石流。

    n.   原因，起因，理由，根據，動機

The **cause of the death** is unknown at this time and it could take seven to ten days to determine. 死亡原因目前仍不知道，可能要七天至十天才能確定。

The **cause of the fire** was under investigation. The **cause** has not been determined, but a **human cause** is suspected. 火災的原因還在調查中，原因還沒確定，但懷疑是人為因素。

原因，理由，根據

應用 *cause of death* 死亡原因 (或稱 *cause of the fatality*)

cause of fire 火災原因

probable cause 相當理由

reasonable cause 合理事由

without cause 無端地，沒有理由地

---

caution   *n.*   警告，小心，謹慎

[`kɔʃən]

Transportation authorities urge drivers to drive with caution and to slow down in work zones. 交通運輸當局呼籲駕駛人小心駕駛並且慢速通過施工區域。

應用 常見的 *caution* 標示文字如下：

Caution! Restricted area 警告！管制區

Caution! Work in progress 警告！工事進行中

Caution! Proceed with caution 警告！請小心前進
Caution! Area under construction 警告！本區施工中
Caution! Slippery surface 警告！地面濕滑

CCTV	*abbr.*	閉路監視器 closed circuit television (CCTV) **CCTV** images track the movement of offenders and witness to and from the scene. 閉路監視器影像可以追蹤犯罪者與證人往來於現場的動向。
	應用	*CCTV image* 閉路監視影像 *CCTV footage* 閉路監視影片
cell [sɛl]	*n.*	(監獄內一間一間的)牢房，囚房 The prisoner was locked in the **cell**. 受刑人被關在囚房內。
	應用	*holding cell* (治安機關的)留置室 (或稱 *luck up*) *cell tower* 細胞台 *cell tower id* 細胞台位址 *jail cell* 看守所囚房 *prison cell* 監獄囚房 *single cell housing* 獨居室，一人囚房 *out-of-cell time* (監獄的) 放風時間
certificate [sə`tɪfəkɪt]	*n.*	證明書，執照，(沒有學位的)結業證書
	應用	*Police Clearance Certificate* (或 *Police Certificate*) 無犯罪紀錄證明書。我國稱「警察刑事紀錄證明書 (Police Criminal Record Certificate)」，新加坡稱「稱良民證 (Certificate of Clearance)」
chain [tʃen]	*n.*	鏈，鏈條，一連串，一系列
	應用	*chain of causation* 因果關係歷程 *chain of command* 指揮體系 *chain of custody* 物證管制流程 *chain of possession* 物證管制流程
char [tʃɑr]	*n.*	燒焦物，炭
	vt.	把……燒成炭，把……燒焦 James was unresponsive when firefighters found him insides the **charred** apartment. 詹姆士被消防員在燒得焦黑的公寓內找到時，已經沒反應了。
charge [tʃɑrdʒ]	*vt.*	控告，指控[(+with)] The suspected drug dealer **is charged with** murder. 該名毒梟嫌疑犯被指控謀殺罪。
	n.	控告，指控 The prosecutor should not **bring charges against** the defendant or refuse **to dismiss** such **charges**, where admissible

evidence does not exist to support the charges. 如果不存在著有證據能力的證據可佐證指控，則檢察官不應該對被告提出告訴或拒絕撤掉告訴。

The owner agreed not **to press criminal charges against** them if they agreed to pay for the damages. 物主同意如果他們願意支付賠償的話，就不對他們提出刑事告訴。

At trial, the Judge must hear evidence presented by the prosecutor in order to decide whether enough evidence exist **to file charge against** a defendant. 審判時，法官必須聽取檢察官提出的證據，以決定是否有足夠的證據存在來對被告提出指控。

The suspect was arrested last week **on charge of** murder and confined in the jail. 嫌犯於上星期被捕，被指控殺人，並關在看守所。

Incident Commander **is in charge of** the incident. SWAT Commander **is in charge of** all tactics. 案件指揮官是負責案件；攻堅指揮官是負責所有戰術。

The mayor announced that the city police department **has taken charge of** the crowd control. 市長宣布說，市警局已經掌控群眾的管制了。

| charge [tʃɑrdʒ] | *vt.* | 指示，責令，賦予責任，委以責任 [(+ with)] |

Police **are charged with** the prevention and detection of crime and the enforcement of the law. 警察被賦予預防及發覺犯罪以及執法的責任。

Detectives **are charged with** the duty of investigating crimes. They are charged with the duty to prevent and detect crime, and granted full powers of arrest. 偵查人員被賦予偵查犯罪的任務，他們被賦予預防及偵查犯罪的任務，並被授與充分的逮捕權力。

| chase [tʃes] | *vi.* | 追逐，追趕，追捕 [(+ after)] |

Officers **chased after** the car at high speeds for more than 50 minutes. 員警以高速追捕該車將近 50 分鐘。

The suspect allegedly stole a car and **led police on chase** for more than 50 minutes. 嫌犯涉嫌偷了一輛車子並招致警方追逐超過 50 分鐘。

| | *n.* | 追逐，追趕，追捕 |

The suspect led authorities on a **high-speed chase** across Los Angeles. The **car chase** lasted for 50 minutes. 嫌犯引起當局以高速追逐了整個洛杉磯。整個汽車追逐持續了 50 分鐘。

checkpoint	n.	檢查站，關卡
[ˋtʃɛkˏpɔɪnt]	應用	*border checkpoint* 邊境檢查站
		DUI/DWI checkpoint 酒駕檢查站
		investigatory checkpoint 偵查檢查站
		random checkpoint 隨機(臨檢)檢查站
		security checkpoint 安檢站
		sobriety checkpoint 酒駕檢查站
chief constable	n.	【加拿大溫哥華；英國倫敦以外】警察局長
chief of police	n.	【美】警察局長
child	n.	兒童
[tʃaɪld]	應用	*child abduction for ransom* 兒童勒贖綁架
		child abuse 兒童虐待
		child custody 兒童監護
		child labor 童工
		child maltreatment 兒童不當對待
		child molestation 兒童性騷擾
		child neglect 兒童忽視
		child pornography 兒童色情圖片
		child prostitution 雛妓
		child support payment 子女撫養費
		child support 子女撫養
		children's court 少年法庭
		delinquent child 少年犯
CID	abbr.	刑事部門(刑事局、刑警大隊、偵查隊) *Criminal Investigation Department / Criminal Investigation Division*
citizen's arrest		公民扭捕 (公民發現罪犯可自行扭捕，送至執法機關) **Citizen's arrest** is an arrest of a private person by another private person on grounds that a public offense was committed in the arrester's presence, or the arrester has reasonable cause to believe that arrestee has committed a felony. 市民逮捕 (citizen's arrest)是指一個私人逮捕另一個私人，基於的是在逮捕人面前公然犯罪，或逮捕人有合理事由可信被逮捕人已犯下重罪。
citizenship	n.	公民(或市民)身分
[ˋsɪtəznˏʃɪp]		
civil	adj.	市民的，國民的，公民的
[ˋsɪvḷ]	應用	*civil disobedience* 公民不服從，不合作主義，(以拒絕遵守政府法令，拒絕納稅等方式進行的)非暴力反抗
		civil disorder 市民動亂

civil disturbance 內亂，內部騷動

	adj.	【律】民事的
	應用	*civil action* 民事告訴
		civil court 民事法庭
		civil damage 民事損害
		civil law 民法
		civil law country 大陸法系國家
		(*common law country* 普通法系國家)
		civil liability 民事責任
		civil right 民權(*removal of civil right* 剝奪公權)
		civil trial 民事審理

claim	*vt.*	聲稱，(依據權力)要求，主張
[klem]		The defendant **claimed that** he was coerced into illegal activity by police officers. 被告主張他是被員警誘使從事違法活動。
	vt.	(疾病，意外) 奪去(生命)
		The tragic fire at the warehouse **has claimed** four lives and injured ten people. 這場不幸的倉庫火災奪走了 4 人的生命並有 10 人受傷。
	n.	(對保險的) 索賠；(依據權力而提出的) 要求，主張
		Police said that the suspect staged the car accident made in order to **make false insurance claims**. 警方說，嫌犯假造這起車禍，為了申請不實的保險索賠。

clandestine	*adj.*	秘密的，暗中的，偷偷摸摸(做)的
[klæn`dɛstɪn]		Many illicit drugs are manufactured in **clandestine** drug labs. 許多非法毒品都是非法毒品工廠所製造的。
		When large amount of drugs is seized, usually the local police authorities will conduct citywide cleanup of **clandestine** drug labs. 當大量的毒品被查獲時，通常當地警察機關會進行全市的非法毒品工廠肅清。
	應用	*clandestine laboratory* 非法工廠 (或是簡稱 *clandestine lab*)
		clandestine drug laboratory 非法毒品工廠 (或是簡稱 *clandestine drug lab*)

clash	*n.*	衝突，糾紛 [(+with/between)]
[klæʃ]		About 50 alleged gang members were involved in the **clash**. The **clash** between the two rival street gangs left five people wounded. 大約五十名疑似幫派份子涉及這場衝突，這兩個敵對幫派的衝突造成五人受傷。

cleanup	*n.*	(對瀆職等行為的)肅清
[`klin,ʌp]		

clerk [klɝk]	*n.*	書記官(或稱 *Law clerk; court clerk; clerk to the court; clerk of the court; clerk of court*)
clue [klu]	*n.*	(解決疑案，問題等的) 線索，跡象，提示
		To urge people to tip off police about crime, police will set up an anonymous tip line for people **to give a clue**. 為了呼籲民眾向警方通報犯罪，警方會設置匿名報案專線，讓民眾提供線索。
		At the crime scene, examiners **look for clues** from hair, fiber, fabric, and dust. 在犯罪現場，鑑識人員從毛髮、纖維、織品及沙塵尋找線索。
cocaine [ko`ken]	*n.*	【藥】古柯鹼
code [kod]	*n.*	法典，法規
		Penal Code 刑法典 (或 *Criminal Code*)
		Civil Code 民法典
	n.	規則，規範，禮教習俗
		code of conduct 行為準則
		code of ethics 倫理準則
codify [`kɑdə,faɪ]	*vt.*	將……編成法典
		Common Law is generally **un-codified**. Civil Law, in contrast, is **codified**. 普通法通常是非法典化的，相對地，大陸法是法典化的。
coerce [ko`ɝs]	*vt.*	強制，迫使，脅迫
		The defendant claimed that he **was coerced into** illegal activity by police officers. 被告主張他是被員警脅迫從事違法活動的。
coercion [ko`ɝʃən]	*n.*	強制，強迫
cohabit [ko`hæbɪt]	*vi.*	(未婚者的) 同居
		She **cohabited** with the suspect as spouse for many years. They **cohabited** as husband and wife in a small apartment in the city. 她形同配偶與該嫌犯同居數年，他們形同夫妻同居在城市裡的一個小公寓。
cohabitant [ko`hæbɪtənt]	*n.*	同居人
		The law says that any crime that involves a **cohabitant** can be charged as domestic violence, as long as that crime has some sort of physical or emotional threat or violence. 法律指出，任何涉及同居人的犯罪，只要是該項犯罪有任何形式的身體或精神上的威脅或暴力，都可以用家暴來提告。
collapse [kə`læps]	*vi.*	倒塌，崩潰，瓦解
		Firefighters could not contain the fire and then by 4 o'clock they

decided to evacuate because they thought the building could **collapse**. 消防員無法遏制火勢，於是四點的時候他們決定撤離，因為他們認為建築物可能會倒塌。

vt. 使倒塌，使崩潰

Firefighters responded to the **collapsed** building and rescued people trapped in the **collapse** rubble. 消防員前往這處倒塌的建物，並且救出被困在坍塌瓦礫中的人。

n. 倒塌，崩潰

We establish the **collapse** zones. And keep people outside the **collapse** zones. 我們建立了坍塌區，並且將人們隔開在這些坍塌區之外。

At least 5 people died in the **collapse**, but the company denies any fault, saying the disaster was an act of God. 至少有五人在這次的倒塌中死亡，但是該公司否認有任何的錯，說這場災難是天災造成的。

應用	*bridge collapse* 橋樑倒塌
	building collapse 大樓倒塌
	collapse area 坍塌地區
	collapse rubble 坍塌瓦礫
	collapse site 坍塌地點
	structural collapse 建築物倒塌

| collide | *vt.* | 碰撞，相撞 |
| [kə`laɪd] | | The suspect's vehicle **collided with** several cars during the pursuit before it came to a stop. 嫌犯的車子在追逐中撞到好幾輛車之後，才停了下來。 |

| collision | *n.* | 碰撞，相撞 |
| [kə`lɪʒən] | | If you are involved in a **collision**, please stay at the scene. If anyone is hurt in the **collision**, call for an ambulance right away. 如果你發生碰撞，請停留在現場。如果任何人在碰撞中受傷，立即呼叫救護車。 |

combat	*vt.*	打擊，與……戰鬥，滅(火)
[`kɑmbæt]		Since gangsters may commit high profile crimes, each country's law enforcement authorities usually establish specialized unit **to combat**, disrupt and dismantle organized crime and gang violence. 由於幫派分子會從事重大犯罪，因此每一個國家的執法機關通常會設立專門的單位來打擊、分散及瓦解組織犯罪及幫派暴力。
		The blaze broke out this morning. More than 200 firefighters were working **to combat** the fire. 火災在今晨發生，有超過

200 名消防員在進行救火。

command	vt.	命令指揮，統率，控制
[kə`mænd]		The whole department **is commanded by** the Chief of Police. Each Division or police district **is commanded by** a director or commander. 整個警察局是由警察局長指揮，各科室或警察分局是由科長或分局長指揮。
	n.	命令，控制，控制(權)，指揮(權)
	應用	*chain of command* 指揮體系，指揮系統
		command and control center 指揮與控制中心
		command center 指揮中心
		command post 指揮所
		command staff 領導幹部
		command vehicle 指揮車
		mobile command vehicle 機動指揮車
		field command post 前進指揮所
		second in command 副手

commander	n.	指揮官，領導人，分局長或大隊長(台美大致相同)
[kə`mændɚ]	應用	*district commander* 分局長
		police commander 分局長
		incident commander 事件指揮官(IC)
		on-scene commander 現場指揮官

commission	n.	犯(罪)
[kə`mɪʃən]		The suspect was charged with the **commission** of murder. 嫌犯被指控犯下謀殺罪。
		High powered weapons were used **in the commission of** the crime. 高性能的武器被使用在這犯罪中。

commissioner	n.	【我國】警察局長
[kə`mɪʃənɚ]		【英/倫敦】警察局長
		【加、紐、澳】警政最高首長
		【新】警察總監
		【日、韓】Commissioner-General 警政最高首長

commit	vt.	犯(罪)
[kə`mɪt]		The suspect allegedly opened fire at her home, killing his girl friend. He then attempted **to commit** suicide. 嫌犯涉嫌對著她家開槍，殺了他的女友，他然後企圖自殺。
		The suspect claimed that he did not **commit** the murder. 嫌犯聲稱她並未犯該起謀殺。
		The motives **to commit** arson include vandalism, fraud, revenge, and pyromania. 犯縱火罪的動機包括為了破壞、詐

欺、報復及縱火狂。

| | *vt.* | 使承擔義務，把……交託給，把……付諸[(+to)] |

The Chicago Police Department, as part of and empowered by the community, **is committed to** protect the lives, property, and rights of all people. 芝加哥警察局作為社區的一部分，並在其賦予權力之下，承諾將保護所有人的生命、財產及權利。

應用 *to commit an offense* 犯罪
to commit a crime 犯罪
to commit a felony 犯重罪

---

common law 普通法

---

community
[kə`mjunətɪ] *n.* 社區，社會，公眾

As a law enforcement officer, my fundamental duty is to serve the **community**, and to safeguard lives and property. 身為執法人員，我的根本職責是服務社區，以及保障生命及財產。

應用 *community policing* 社區警政
community service 社區服務
police-community relations 警察與社區關係（或稱 *police-citizen relationship*）

---

comparison
[kəm`pærəsn] *n.* 比對，比較，對照

Many firearms examiners also perform tool mark **comparisons**. 許多槍枝鑑識人員同時也從事工具痕跡的比對。

應用 *voice comparison* 聲紋比對
fingerprint comparison 指紋比對
toolmark comparison 工具痕跡比對

---

compel
[kəm`pɛl] *vt.* 強迫，使……不得不

No person shall **be compelled** in any criminal case to be a witness against himself without due process of law. 未經正當法律程序，任何人均不得被強迫在任何刑事案件中，成為不利於己之證人。

Witnesses may not **be compelled** to testify. 證人不得被強迫作證。

---

compensate
[`kɑmpən,set] *vt.* 補償，賠償，酬報

The trial court ordered the accused to **compensate** the victim after the conviction. 地方法院命被告在有罪判決之後，對被害人進行補償。

The accused should **compensate** the victim **for** the damages caused by the criminal act. 被告對於犯罪行為所造成的損害，應補償被害人。

---

compensation *n.* 補償，賠償

[ˌkɑmpənˋseʃən]		The judge ordered the offender to pay money to the victims as **compensation** for their losses. 法官命令犯罪者支付金錢給受害人以補償他們的損失。
competence	*n.*	能力，資格，適格
[ˋkɑmpətəns]		**Competence** of a witness is determined before evidence is given; credibility of a witness is evaluated after evidence is given. 證人的適格是決定於證據提出之前；證人的可信度是評估於證據提出之後。
competent	*adj.*	【律】有法定資格的，適格的
[ˋkɑmpətənt]		At trial, it is important to determine whether someone **is competent** to be a witness or not considered to be a **competent witness**. 審判時，判斷某人是不是適格成為證人或不被認為是適格的證人，是很重要的。
complain	*vi.*	抱怨，【律】控訴，投訴 [(+to/about/of)]
[kəmˋplen]		The victim **complained to** the police many times **about** her cohabitant's behavior. 被害人多次向警方報案(申訴)關於同居人的行為。
		The victim **complained of** the verbal abuse by the defendant. 被害人報案受到被告言語辱罵。
	vt.	抱怨，【律】控訴，投訴 [(+that)]
		She **complained** to the police **that** her cohabitant had threated and beaten her many times. 她向警方報案(申訴)她的同居人多次威脅及毆打她。
complaint	*n.*	抱怨，抗議，【律】控告，控訴
[kəmˋplent]		At trial, the judge may decide to **dismiss the complaint** and discharge the defendant; or to admit the defendant to bail. 審判時，法官可以決定駁回訴狀並釋回被告，或准予被告交保。
		The plaintiff decided **to file a criminal complaint against** the defendant charging defendant with misappropriation. 原告決定對被告提起控訴，控告被告侵占。
		If you want to **make a complaint about** the way that your case has been handled by the police, you may write email to the Chief of Police or the Internal Affairs Office. 如果你要申訴員警對於你的案件的處理方式，你可以寫電子郵件給警察局長或是政風室。
	應用	*to resolve any complaint* 解決投訴(抱怨、抗議)
		noise complaint 噪音投訴
		officer complaint 申訴員警
		【補充說明】 在美國，indictment 及 information 都可以有起

訴書的意思，indictment 這種起訴書是控告犯罪的正式書面，是大陪審團認為有罪應起訴後做成的起訴書。如果被告在起訴階段認罪，並放棄以公開法庭的陪審團決定是否起訴的權利時，由檢察官直接起訴的起訴書稱為 information。

compliance [kəm`plaɪəns]	*n.*	順從，屈從

If an offender resists arrest, officers may use necessary force **to gain compliance**. 如果犯罪者抗拒逮捕，員警得使用必要的武力來取得服從。

comply [kəm`plaɪ]	*vi.*	(對要求、命令等)依從，順從，遵從[(+with)]

When offenders are released from prison on parole, parole officers will supervise them to ensure that they **comply with** the conditions of their parole. 當犯罪者被假釋出獄時，假釋官會監控他們，以確保他們遵守假釋條件。

conclude [kən`klud]	*vt.*	做出(最後)決定

The court **concluded that** on the evidence presented to it, the accused was proved to be the driver at the time of the fatal impact with the motor cyclist. 法院依據所提出的證據，認定被告證明就是在這場致命撞擊時撞到機車騎士的司機。

condemn [kən`dɛm]	*vt.*	責難，責備，譴責

The mayor **condemned** the violence and said all citizens need to work together to curb crimes. 市長譴責暴力，並且說全體市必須一起合作遏止犯罪。

conduct [kən`dʌkt]	*vt.*	進行

Police officer may **conduct** a warrantless search of the vehicle if there is probable cause for a search, and an exigent circumstance exists. 如果有搜索的相當理由以及有急迫情況存在時，員警可對車輛進行無令狀搜索。

應用
to conduct polygraph test 進行測謊
to conduct assessment 進行評估
to conduct autopsy 相驗
to conduct background check 進行背景清查
to conduct criminal prosecution 進行刑事起訴
to conduct drug sweep 進行毒品掃蕩
to conduct examination 進行詰問
to conduct gang business 從事幫派生意
to conduct gang sweep 進行幫派掃蕩
to conduct inspection 進行檢查
to conduct interception 進行攔截
to conduct interrogation 進行訊問

to conduct interview 進行訪談
to conduct investigation 進行偵查
to conduct lawful interception 進行通訊監察攔截
to conduct major crackdown 進行大取締
to conduct onself 表現鎮定沉著
to conduct police business 從事警察業務
to conduct prostitution (hooker) sweep 進行色情掃蕩
to conduct raid 進行突擊
to conduct scene reconstruction 進行現場重建
to conduct search 進行搜索
to conduct stop and frisk 進行攔檢及搜身
to conduct surveillance 進行偵監

confess [kənˋfɛs]	*vi.*	自白，坦白，承認，供認 [(+ to)] The murder suspect said that he had been forced **to confess to crime**. 殺人嫌犯說他被強迫而承認犯罪。The suspect **confessed to** beating her to death and dumping her body in a rivier. 嫌犯坦承將她毆打至死，並將屍體扔到河裡。 The arsonist **confessed to** starting several fires at six locations overnight. 消防局長說，縱火犯坦承一夜之間在六個地點放了好幾把火。
	vt.	自白，坦白，承認，供認 [(+ that)] He **confessed that** he had killed the victim. He also confessed that he was responsible for her death. 他坦承他殺了被害人，他也承認他應該為她的死亡負責。 The arsonist **confessed that** he set fires to six businesses. He **confessed that** he started the fires and killed 3 persons. 縱火犯坦承他對六個商家放火，他坦承放了火，而殺害了三人。
confession [kənˋfɛʃən]	*n.*	自白，坦白，承認，供認 A **confession** is inadmissible if it is extracted by any sort of coercion, threating, physical restraint or violence, or extended interrogation. 白自如果是用強制、威脅、強暴或疲勞訊問的方式取得時，無證據能力。
	應用	*to draw confession out of suspect* 從嫌犯取得自白 *to draw suspect to confess* 讓嫌犯進行自白 *to extract confession* 取得自白 *to make confession* 做出自白 *to obtain confession* 取得自白 *coerced confession* 被脅迫的自白 *false confession* 不實的自白

forced confession 被強迫的自白
voluntary confession 自願的自白
written confession 書面自白

confidential [ˌkɑnfəˈdɛnʃəl]	*adj.*	機密的

To use **confidential informants (CIs)** successfully, agencies must develop informant control procedures. In addition, officers should always take every possible measure to ensure that sources **are kept confidential**. 為了能夠成功地使用秘密線民，機關必須訂出線民管理程序，此外員警應要採取任何可能的措施，以確保消息來源被保密。

Information from a **confidential** source revealed that Mike was driving to Miami, and returning with large amounts of marijuana in his vehicle. 匿名消息來源顯示，麥克開車去了邁阿密，並且回來的時候車子內有大量的大麻。

confine [kənˈfaɪn]	*vt.*	禁閉，幽禁，使……臥床[(+to/in)]

Prisoners whose death sentences are confirmed **are confined in** single cells. 死刑確定的人犯通常被監禁在獨居的囚房。

vt. 限制，使局限，將火勢侷限……[(+to)]

During a fire, close all doors as you exit **to confine** the fire. Never use the elevator. 火災的時候，離開時將所有的門關閉，以阻絕火勢。不要使用電梯。

Firefighters began the interior attack and quickly **confined** the fire to the building of origin. 消防員開始內部滅火，並且很快地將火阻絕在原處。

confinement [kənˈfaɪnmənt]	*n.*	禁閉，幽禁

The suspect was arrested, taken into custody and charged with forcible **confinement**. 嫌犯被逮捕、拘禁，並被指控私行拘禁。

應用 *forcible confinement* 私行拘禁
solitary confinement 單獨監禁

confirm [kənˈfɝm]	*vt.*	證實，確定

Investigator should always **confirm** the source of information and **confirm** a suspect's alibi. 偵查人員都應該要確認資訊的來源，並確認嫌犯的不在場證明。

Police **have confirmed** the details of the incident but would not **confirm** the identities of the victims and the suspect. 警方確認了事件的細節，但不願意證實被害人與嫌犯的身分。

Fireman **confirmed** that the fire started on the third floor. 消防人員證實火災起源於三樓。

confiscate [`kɑnfɪs,ket]	vt.	沒收，將……充公，徵收 In order to control victims, traffickers will often **confiscate** their passports and legal documents. 為了控制被害人，販運分子經常會沒收他們的護照及法律文件。
conflict [`kɑnflɪkt]	n.	衝突 Police officers are regularly called upon to deal with **conflict** situations. Officers must be able to utilize **conflict management** and **conflict resolution** skills. 員警經常會被呼叫前往處理衝突情況，員警必須要能夠運用衝突管理與衝突解決的技能。
confront [kən`frʌnt]	vt.	對質[(+with)] In all criminal prosecutions, the accused shall enjoy the right **to be confronted with** the witnesses against him. At trial, the accused person has the right **to confront** the accuser. 在所有刑事起訴中，被告享有與不利於己的證人對質的權利。審判時，被告享有與控訴者對質的權利。 Show-up is the identification procedure in which a suspect **is confronted with** a witness or the victim of a crime. 當面指認是讓嫌犯面對證人或犯罪被害人的指認程序。
	vt.	迎面遇到，面臨，遭遇，對抗，使……面對，使……遭遇 The demonstrators **confronted** the police, getting close to their faces and shouting loudly during the protest. 示威者與警方對峙，在抗議的時候，貼近他們的臉並且大聲叫囂。 Riot police are trained and equipped **to confront** crowds and protesters. 鎮暴警察被訓練及賦予裝備來對抗群眾及示威者。
confrontation [ˌkɑnfrʌn`teʃən]	n.	對質，對峙，對抗 Show-up is a one-one-one **confrontation**. 當面指認是一對一的對質。 A suspect was injured during a **confrontation** at a convenient store. 有一名嫌犯在便利商店的對峙中受傷。
connect [kə`nɛkt]	vt.	連結 [(+ with/to)] According to Locard's exchange principle: Every scene cound **be connected to** a criminal, witness and victim, and every criminal, witness and victim could **be connected to** a crime scene. 依據「羅卡交換定律」：每一個現場都可以聯結到某個罪犯、證人及被害人；並且每一個罪犯、證人及被害人都可以聯結到某個現場。 Physical evidences allow the investigators **to connect** evidence

found at the crime scene **to** the suspect and victim. 物證，讓偵查人員能將犯罪現場找到的證據與被害人相連結。

connection [kə`nɛkʃən]	*n.*	關連

Police have arrested the suspect **in connection with** the robbery thanks to CCTV videos. Authorities say a second man has also been arrested in connection to the death of the robbery. 幸虧有 CCTV 影片，警方已逮捕到這名與強盜案有關連的嫌犯。當局說，與這起強盜致死有關連的第二名嫌犯也已被逮捕了。

As of this morning, the suspects **in connection to** this robbery **remain at large.** 直到今晨為止，與這起強盜案有關聯的嫌犯仍然在逃。

consent [kən`sɛnt]	*n.*	同意，贊成，答應

Police obtained his **consent** and conducted the search. 警方取得他的同意並進行了搜索。

應用　*consensual search* 同意搜索
consent search 同意搜索
express consent 明示同意
voluntary consent 自願同意

consignment [kən`saɪnmənt]	*n.*	委託，交付，託付物，託賣品，遞運的，委託貨物運送

Police intercepted an illicit **consignment** of heroin that weighed more than 10 kg. 警方攔截到重量超過 10 公斤的非法海洛因郵件。

consignor [kən`saɪnə]	*n.*	委託者，發貨人，貨主

Controlled delivery can prove that the **consignors**, transporters or receivers were knowingly in possession of the contraband. 控制下交付可以證明委託人、運送人或受領人是故意持有該違禁品。

conspiracy [kən`spɪrəsɪ]	*n.*	陰謀，謀叛，共謀

A person is guilty of **conspiracy** when he agrees with one or more persons to engage in criminal conduct. 任何人同意與其他一人或數人從事犯罪行為者，成立共謀罪。

conspirator [kən`spɪrətə]	*n.*	共謀者

Conspirators are two or more people who agree to commit a crime. A **conspirator** is a principal and shall be liable according to the provisions governing the attempted crimes. 共謀犯 (conspirator)是指兩個或以上之人同意做一項犯罪。共謀犯是正犯，並應依其企圖所犯之罪的規定負刑事責任。

conspire [kən`spaɪr]	*vi.*	同謀，密謀[(+with/against)][+to-v]

Investigation revealed that the defendants not only carried out brutal acts of violence in their turf, but also **conspired with** fellow gang members throughout the country to further the gang's criminal objectives. 調查發現，被告不只是在他們的地盤做出兇殘的暴力行為，也和全國各地的幫派份子共謀，以遂行其幫派的犯罪目的。

It is difficult to decide if the alien **conspires with** the citizen to enter into a marriage for the purpose of evading the immigration laws. 外國人是否為了逃避移民法，而與公民共謀締結婚姻，是很難判斷的。

	應用	*fraudulent marriage* 假結婚(或 *sham-marriage; fake marriage*)
constitute [ˈkɑnstəˌtjut]	*vt.*	構成，組成 Officers must understand that many police misconduct would **constitute** criminal offenses. 員警必須了解，許多的警察不當行為會構成刑事犯罪。
Constitution [ˌkɑnstəˈtjuʃən]	*n.*	憲法
constitutional [ˌkɑnstəˈtjuʃən!]	*adj.*	In many countries, it is the **Constitutional** Court that decides whether a law is **constitutional** or **unconstitutional**. 在許多國家，決定法律是合憲或違憲的是憲法法庭。 The death penalty has been declared **unconstitutional** in many countries. 死刑已經被許多國家宣告為違憲。
consult [kənˈsʌlt]	*vi.*	商議，磋商 [(+ with)] You have the right **to consult with** a lawyer and have that lawyer present during any questioning. 你有權利聘請律師，並在接受審訊時有律師在場。
consume [kənˈsjum]	*vt.*	飲，食 Officer shall not **consume** any intoxicating beverage while on duty. 員警執勤時，不得飲用酒精性飲料。
consumption [kənˈsʌmpʃən]	*n.* 應用	飲，食 *alcohol consumption* 酗酒 *drug consumption* 吸食毒品
contact [kənˈtækt]	*vt.*	接觸，交往，聯繫，聯絡[(+with)] If you have any information on the pictured subject, please **contact** our non-emergency telephone number to leave an anonymous tip. 如果您有相片上這個人的資訊，請打我們的非緊急電話號碼，留下匿名線索。
contact [ˈkɑntækt]	*n.*	接觸，交往，聯繫，聯絡 We need your **contact** information and we will have an officer **contact** you in person and take a report. 我們需要您的聯絡資

料，並且我們會有員警親自與你聯絡並製做報案。

Captain Raymond was designated as **point of contact** in the cross-border operation. 雷猛隊長被指定為這場跨境行動的聯絡窗口。

應用 *physical contact* 身體接觸
point of contact 聯絡人，聯絡對口，聯絡窗口
police-citizen contact 警民接觸
sexual contact 性接觸

contain	*vt.*	控制，遏制
[kən`ten]		

Police wore riot gear and formed a line to **contain** protesters. 警察穿著鎮暴裝備並組成一列以阻絕抗議者。

If necessary, police must deploy personnel to isolate and **contain** the people. 如果必要的話，警察必須佈署人員以隔絕及包圍民眾。

The fire broke out on the 5th floor of high-rise. Firefighters **contained** the fire around noon. 火災發生在高樓的第 5 樓，消防員大約在中午遏制火勢。

contaminate	*vt.*	弄髒，汙染，毒害
[kən`tæmə,net]		

Evidence is inadmissible if the sample **is contaminated**. 如果樣本被汙染時，證據就無證據能力。

His friend contracted AIDS after **being contaminated** during a transfusion. 他的朋友因為輸血時被傳染而染上愛滋病。

contempt	*n.*	【法律】(對法庭等的) 藐視 (+ of)
[kən`tɛmpt]		

Davis was in **contempt of court** for shouting at the judge. 戴維斯因為對法官咆哮而犯藐視法庭罪。

The court ruled that Davis was in **contempt of court** for disobeying the judge's order and sent him to jail. 法院判決戴維斯未遵守法官的命令而藐視法庭，並將他送去坐牢。

contend	*vt.*	堅決主張，聲稱 (+ that)
[kən`tɛnd]		

The defendant **contended that** the plaintiff was not in the cross walk at the time of the impact. He **contended that** he did not see the woman until after the accident. 被告聲稱原告在車禍撞擊當時並沒有在行人穿越道上，他聲稱直到車禍發生前都沒看到該名婦女。

contingency	*n.*	意外事故，偶然事件
[kən`tɪndʒənsɪ]	應用	*contingency plan* 應變計劃

contraband	*n.*	走私貨，違禁品
[`kɑntrə,bænd]		

contradict	*vt.*	否定(陳述等)，反駁，提出論據反對，與……矛盾/牴觸

[ˌkɑntrəˋdɪkt]		The defendant's contention **was contradicted by** the video evidence provided by the plaintiff. 被告的主張被原告提出的影像證據所駁斥。

---

control	*vt.*	控制，支配
[kənˋtrol]	*n.*	控制，支配
		During the riot, pepper spray was deployed. Police said they feared the crowd would **lost control of** the situation. Authorities urged parents to **take control of** their kids. 在暴動中，有使用了辣椒噴霧劑。警方說他們擔心群眾失去對情況的控制。當局呼籲家長要管好孩子。
		The fire has been brought **under control**. 火勢已受到控制。
		Fire crews immediately **gained control of** the blaze. 消防同仁立刻遏制了火勢。
		Fire crews were still trying **to get** the fire **under control**.消防同仁仍在試著將火勢控制。
		Firefighters spent three hours battling the blaze before they were finally able **to get it under control**. 消防員花了三小時滅火，才終於將火控制住
	應用	*to control crime* 控制犯罪
		to control traffic 控制交通

---

controlled	*adj.*	支配下的，被控制的
[kənˋtrold]	應用	*controlled delivery* 控制下交付
		controlled substance 管制物質，管制藥品

---

controversial	*adj.*	爭議的，可疑的
[ˌkɑntrəˋvɝʃəl]		Checkpoint has been a **controversial** issue. 臨檢站一直是個爭議的事項。

---

convict	*vt.*	證明……有罪，判……有罪，判決 [(+of)]
[kənˋvɪkt]		The judge **convicted him of** robbery. 法官判他搶劫罪成立。
		She **was convicted of** murder. 她被判謀殺罪成立。
convict	*n.*	被定罪之人
[ˋkɑnvɪkt]		A **convict** is a person found guilty of a crime and sentenced by a court to serve a sentence in prison. **Convicts** are often also known as prisoners or inmates. 「convict (定罪之人)」指一個被判有罪並且被法院判刑而在監獄服刑的人，「convict (定罪之人)」也稱為 prisoner 或 inmate。

---

conviction	*n.*	有罪判決
[kənˋvɪkʃən]		A **conviction** cannot be based solely on a confession. 有罪判決不能只依據自白。
		Defendant appeals from his **conviction** on firearms and

narcotics charges. 被告就槍枝與毒品的有罪判決提起上訴。

convince [kənˋvɪns]	*vt.*	使……確信，使……信服，說服 [(+ of)]
		The accused **convinced** the judge that he was innocent. 被告說服了法官他是無辜的。
		He **convinced** the judge **of** his innocence. 他說服了法官他的無辜。

| convinced
[kənˋvɪnst] | *adj.* | 確信的，令人相信的 |
| | | Based on the evidence, the judge **was convinced that** the suspect did not commit the crime intentionally. 根據證據，法官確信嫌犯並不是故意犯罪。 |

coordinate [koˋɔrdnet]	*vt.*	協調，調節，調和
		The Incident Commander must establish a field command post and staging area at or near the scene, from which he/she will control and **coordinate** police tactical operations. 事件指揮官必須在現場或其附近建立前進指揮所及集結地區，而在該等地區控制及協調警察的戰術行動。
	vi.	協調
	應用	*To coordinate with sb.* 與(人)協調 (而共同完成)
		New York Governo called on the FBI to investigate the incident, and also directed the State Police **to coordinate with** the FBI and NYPD on their investigation. 紐約州長請求聯邦調查局偵辦此一事件，同時也指示州警在偵查方面要與聯邦調查局及紐約市警局協調合作。

cordon [ˋkɔrdn]	*vt.*	包圍隔離(某地區)(常與 off 連用)
		Police **cordoned off** the area with yellow crime-scene tape. 警方用黃色刑案封鎖帶封鎖了該區域。
		Several streets around the building **were cordoned off** as firefighters battled the fire. 消防員在滅火時，靠近建築物的幾條街道都被封鎖了。
	應用	*cordon off* 封鎖 (或稱 *seal off, block off*)

coroner [ˋkɔrənə]	*n.*	法醫，驗屍官(或稱 medical examiner)
		The duties of the **coroner** are to investigate the causes of deaths, conduct autopsies, and help the prosecutions of homicide cases. 法醫的職責是調查死因、相驗及協助凶殺案件的起訴。
		【補充說明】 稱 medical examiner 的法醫不一定要是刑事病理學家，但他是受政府指派的醫生；而稱 coroner 的法醫通常不是醫生，但常是民選的。現在美國有的州使用 coroner 的制度；有的州使用 medical examiner 的制度。

corporal [`kɔrpərəl]	*n.* *adj.* 應用	(警)約為小隊長、(軍)下士 肉體的，身體的 *corporal punishment* 體罰
corpse [kɔrps]	*n.*	屍體【參閱 body】
correction [kə`rɛkʃən]	*n.*	矯正 The department of **corrections** is responsible for the custody of inmates and the supervision of offenders sentenced to probation or parole. 矯正部門是負責受刑人的拘禁，以及監控那些判處緩刑及假釋的人犯。
correctional [kə`rɛkʃən!]	*adj.* 應用	矯正的，修正的，改造的 *correctional facility* 矯正機關 *correctional institution* 矯正機關 *correctional officer* 矯正官員 （或稱 *corrections officer，correctional officer，detention officer，prison officer*，歷史上亦曾用過 *jailer，jail guard，prison guard*）
corroborate [kə`rɑbə,ret]	*vt.*	證實，確證 Police must **corroborate** the tip before acting on it. If police stop and search a defendant acting solely on an **uncorroborated** anonymous tip, the stop and search are not justified. 警察再依據線報行動之前，必須證實線報，如果警察只是依據未經證實的匿報就攔阻及搜索被告，則該項攔阻及搜索沒有正當化。 A conviction cannot be based solely on a confession. There must be other **corroborating evidences** to support the conviction. 有罪判決不能只依據自白，必須要有旁證來支持有罪判決。 確證的，可資佐證的 In other words, confession can be a piece of **corroborative**
corroborative [kə`rɑbə,retɪv]	*adj.*	**evidence** and not as the sole evidence.換言之，自白可以是一項補強證據，但不是唯一證據。
corruption [kə`rʌpʃən]	*n.*	貪瀆、貪污 Police **corruption** is a form of police misconduct in which officers abuse their power for personal gain. 警察貪污一種警察濫用權力以謀私人所得的不當行為。
cost [kɔst]	*vt.*	使……付出(時間，勞力，代價等)，損失，喪失 Fire may **cost human life** and the loss of money and property. 火災會造成人命損失及金錢與財產的損害。 Drug can **cost** you your life. 毒品是會要你命的。 Drink driving **costs** hundreds of live each year. This year, drink driving **has cost** 200 lives and around five seven thousand

injuries. 酒價每年都造成數百人死亡。今年，酒駕已經造成 200 人死亡以及大約五千人受傷。

counsel [`kaʊns!]	*n.*	律師，辯護人(或稱 *assigned counsel; court appointed attorney; court-apointed counsel, appointed counsel*) If you are arrested or detained by the police, you have the right **to retain counsel**. 如果你被警察逮捕或拘禁，你有權聘請律師。
count [kaʊnt]	*n.*	【律】(被控告的)罪狀，罪名，項(罪)，訴因 The drug dealer was charged with three criminal **counts**, including homicide, robbery, and drug abuse. The judge convicted him on all **counts**. 這名毒梟被指控三條刑事罪名，包括殺人、強盜及濫用毒品，法官對於他所有的罪都判決有罪成立。 Simpson is facing two **counts** of murder. In addition, he is also charged with three **counts** of possessing firearms. 辛普森面臨兩項謀殺罪，同時，他也被指控三項持有槍枝罪。
counter- [`kaʊntɚ]	應用	相反 *counter attack* 反擊 *counter measure* 反抗手段，反制措施 *counter terrorism* 反恐怖主義
counterpart [`kaʊntɚ,part]	*n.*	對口，對應的人 (或物) INTERPOL is a global organization, and shares criminal intelligence with foreign **counterpart** agencies. 國際刑警組織是一個全球性組織，並與外國的對口機關分享犯罪情報。 INTERPOL also enables police around the world to work directly with their **counterparts**, even between countries which do not have diplomatic relations. 國際刑警組織同時也讓全世界的警察能夠直接與對口機關直接合作，即使是沒有外交關係的國家之間。
counterfeit [`kaʊntɚ,fɪt]	*vt.*	偽造，仿造 It is a crime to **counterfeit** money. 偽造貨幣是犯罪行為。 Any person who forge, **counterfeit**, mutilate, or alter passport or travel document will be subject to criminal prosecution. 任何作假、偽造、撕掉或變造護照或旅行文件的人，會受到刑事起訴。
	n.	偽造，仿造品
	adj.	偽造的，假冒的
	應用	*counterfeit currency* 偽造貨幣 *counterfeit money* 偽幣，假鈔

		counterfeit passport 假護照
		counterfeit check 假支票
courier	*n.*	送遞急件的運送人
[ˋkʊrɪɚ]		Controlled delivery, if permitted by law, can also be operated through an undercover agent acting as a **courier**. 如果法律許可的話，控制下交付也可以透過以臥底幹員擔任運送人的方式操作。
	應用	*drug courier* 運送毒品的人
court [kort]	*n.*	法院
	應用	*appellate court* 上訴法院(或稱 *appeal court; court of appeals; court of appeal; appeals court*)
		Circuit Court【美】巡迴法院
		civil court 民事庭
		criminal court 刑事庭
		Constitutional Court 憲法法院
		court appointed counsel 指定辯護人(或稱 *assigned counsel*)
		family court 家事法庭 (或稱 *court of domestic relations* 或 *domestic court*)
		High Court 高等法院 (但在澳洲，*High Court of Australia* 為澳洲之最高法院)
		juvenile court 少年法庭 (或稱 *children's court*)
		Supreme Court 最高法院 (但紐約州 *Supreme Court of the State of New York* 為初審及上訴之法院)
		trial court 審理法院，地方法院 (或稱 *court of first instance; court of instance; instance court*)
courthouse	*n.*	法庭大廈
[ˋkort͵haʊs]		
courtroom	*n.*	法庭室，審判室
[ˋkort͵rʊm]		
cover up	*v.*	掩蓋，掩飾
		Usually, the alleged persons tend to give false alibi to the police to **cover up** their crimes, unless they are caught red-handed. 通常，涉嫌人傾向會給警方假的不在場證明，來掩蓋他們的犯罪，除非他們被當場逮到。
covert	*adj.*	隱蔽的，隱藏的，暗地的，秘密的
[ˋkʌvɚt]		Police said they need to add plainclothes police personnel to conduct **covert** surveillance. 警方說他們需要增加便衣警察人員來執行秘密偵監。
	應用	*covert action* 秘密行動

covert investigation 秘密調查

covert operation 秘密行動

covert military operaton 秘密軍事行動

covert surveillance 秘密偵監

CPR	*abbr.*	【醫】心肺復甦術 *cardiopulmonary resuscitation*

Cardiopulmonary resuscitation (CPR) is a lifesaving technique used in many emergencies, including heart attack or near drowning. 在很多緊急情況時，包括心臟病發或瀕臨溺斃時，心肺復甦術是被用來救命的技術。

After the EMT performed CPR, the man began to breathe again. 緊急救護技術員進行心肺復甦術之後，這個人就又開始呼吸了。

應用　*to conduct CPR* 進行心肺復甦術

to do CPR 進行心肺復甦術

to give CPR 進行心肺復甦術

to perform CPR 進行心肺復甦術

to start CPR 開始心肺復甦術

crackdown	*n.*	取締，制裁，對某事採取嚴厲措施
[`kræk,daʊn]		

Police **conducted** a major **crackdown** on violent gang-related crime. 警方針對與幫派有關的暴力犯罪進行了大取締。

Some **crackdowns** emphasize police visibility only, whereas others emphasize enforcement action. 有些取締強調的只是警察的能見度，其他則強調執法行動。

v. 取締，制裁，對某事採取嚴厲措施

City Police Department will conduct a week-long operation **to crack down on** speeding and aggressive drivers across the city. 市警局將會進行為期一周的行動，取締超速及咄咄逼人的駕駛人。

crash [kræʃ]	*vi.*	(發出猛烈聲音地)碰撞

Police have arrested a man suspected of **crashing into** three bicyclists in a hit-and-run incident. 警方逮捕到一人，疑似就是在肇事逃逸的車禍中撞到三個騎士的那個人。

Two trains **crashed** head-on. 兩輛火車迎面對撞。

n . 相撞(事故)

There were dozens of casualties in the train **crash**. Luckly, most passengers survived the **crash**. 有數十人在那次火車事故中傷亡。幸運地，大多數乘客都生還。

Two police officers rushed to the scene of the **car crash** and rescued the driver from the burning car. 兩名員警衝到車禍現

場，並將駕駛從燃燒的車子中救出。

應用		*staged car crash* 假車禍（或稱 *staged auto accident; fake accident*）
		chain-reaction crash 連環車禍(或稱 *multi-vehicle collision* 或是 *pile-up*)

credibility [ˌkrɛdəˋbɪlətɪ]	*n.*	可信度，可信性，確實性

Competence of a witness is determined before evidence is given; **credibility** of a witness is evaluated after evidence is given. 證人的適格是決定於證據提出之前；證人的可信度是評估於證據提出之後。

On cross-examination, a witness' **credibility** may be impeached by showing evidence of the witness' character and conduct. 在交互詰問時，證人的可信度可以透過提出證人的品格及行為的證據，予以彈劾。

At trial, any party, including the party that called the witness, may attack the witness's **credibility**. 審判時，任何一方，包括傳喚證人的一方，均可攻擊證人的可信度。

crime [kraɪm]	*n.*	罪，罪行，犯罪，犯罪活動
	應用	*to charge him with a crime* 控告他犯罪

to combat crime 打擊犯罪

to commit crime 犯罪

to confess to a crime 承認犯罪

to conseal crime 隱藏犯罪

to cover up crime 掩蓋犯罪

to crack down on crime 取締犯罪

to curb crime 遏止犯罪

to detect crime 察覺犯罪

to deter crime 制止犯罪

to escape crime scene 逃離犯罪現場

to fight crime 打擊犯罪

to investigate crime 調查犯罪

to punish crime 處罰犯罪

to reduce crime 降低犯罪

to report crime 犯罪報案

to seal off the crime scene 封鎖犯罪現場

to solve crime 解決犯罪

to stage a crime scene 假造犯罪現場

to take crime report 受理犯罪報案

to visit crime scene 親自到犯罪現場

crime analysis 犯罪分析

crime control 犯罪控制

crime lab 犯罪實驗室

crime mapping 犯罪繪圖

crime pattern 犯罪模式

crime prevention 犯罪預防

crime rate 犯罪率

crime report 犯罪報告

crime scene 犯罪現場

crime scene examination 犯罪現場鑑識

crime scene examiner 犯罪現場鑑識人員

crime scene investigation (CSI) 犯罪現場調查

crime scene reconstruction 犯罪現場重建

crime statistics 犯罪統計

crime trend 犯罪趨勢

crime watch 社區守望相助(或 *neighborhood crime watch*)

crime against humanity 違反人道罪

crime in progress 進行中的犯罪

computer crime 電腦犯罪

drug crime 毒品犯罪

evidence of a crime 犯罪證據

fear of crime 對犯罪的恐懼

fruit of a crime 犯罪所得之物

hate crime 仇恨罪（又稱 *biased crime*）

high crime area 高犯罪地區

high profile crime 重大犯罪

high-tech crime 高科技犯罪

international crime 國際犯罪

major crime 重大犯罪

Major Crimes Unit 重案組

organized crime 組織犯罪

primary crime scene 第一犯罪現場

secondary crime scene 第二犯罪現場

serial crime 連續犯罪

serious crime 重大犯罪

staged crime scene 故布疑陣的犯罪現場

street crime 街頭犯罪

transnational crime 跨國犯罪

unsolved crime 未破之犯罪

violent crime 暴力犯罪

war crime 戰爭罪

white collar crime 白領犯罪

crime-ridden [ˋkraɪm,rɪdn]	*adj.*	犯罪猖獗的 In the 1970s, New York was known as a **crime-ridden** city that was very dangerous especially after dark. 在 1970 年代，紐約是一個有名的犯罪猖獗的城市，特別是入夜之後非常危險。

criminal *n.* 罪犯

[ˋkrɪmən!]

Criminals frequently resort to violence if they perceive a victim is being uncooperative. 罪犯如果感覺被害人不配合時，經常就會訴諸暴力。

Criminals may stage a crime scene to misdirect investigators so as to get away with the crime. 罪犯可能會假造一個犯罪現場來誤導偵查人員，以逃避犯罪。

adj. 犯罪的，犯法的，刑事上的

應用

criminal action 刑事告訴

criminal activity 犯罪活動

criminal act 犯罪行為

criminal case 刑事案件

criminal charge 刑事控告

criminal code 刑法典(或 *penal code*)

criminal conduct 犯罪行為

criminal conspiracy 犯罪共謀

criminal court 刑事法院/刑事庭

criminal defendant 刑事被告

criminal enterprise 犯罪企業

criminal facilitation 刑事幫助罪

criminal history 犯罪紀錄

criminal immunity 刑事豁免

criminal informant 線民(CI)

criminal intelligence 犯罪情報

criminal intent 犯意

criminal interrogation 刑事偵訊

Criminal Investigation Department / Criminal Investigation Division 刑事部門(刑事局、刑警大隊、偵查隊)

criminal investigation 刑事調查

criminal jurisdiction 刑事管轄

criminal justice 刑事司法

criminal law 刑事法

criminal liability 刑事責任
criminal mischief 刑事毀損
criminal motivation 犯罪動機
criminal negligence 刑事過失
criminal network 犯罪網絡
criminal offense 刑事犯罪
criminal organization 犯罪組織
Criminal Procedure Code 刑事訴訟法
criminal proceedings 刑事訴訟
criminal profiling 罪犯剖繪
criminal prosecution 刑事起訴
criminal purpose 犯罪目的
criminal solicitation 刑事教唆
*criminal suspec*t 刑事犯罪嫌疑人
*criminal tria*l 刑事審理
criminal violation 刑事違反

Criminology [ˌkrɪməˈnɑlədʒɪ]	*n.*	犯罪學
crisis [ˈkraɪsɪs]	*n.* 應用	危機，緊急關頭 *crisis management* 危機管理 *crisis negotiation* 危機談判 *crisis situation* 危機情況
critical [ˈkrɪtɪk!]	*adj.*	緊要的，關鍵性的，危急的 Training is a **critical** part of firefighting. 訓練是消防重要的一部分。 A man was **critically** injured in the fire. He was rescued by firefighters and sent to the hospital in very **critical** condition. 男子在這火災中嚴重受傷，他被消防員救了出來，並且送到醫院，情況危急。
criticize [ˈkrɪtɪˌsaɪz]	*vt.*	批評，批判，苛求，非難[(+for)] If we **criticize** someone too much, his or her embarrassment may turn to anger. 如果我們對某人批評太多，他(她)的尷尬可能就會變成生氣。 Citizens have **criticized** police department **for** failing to take citizen complaints seriously. 民眾批評警察局不能認真看待民眾的抱怨。
cross [krɔs]	*adj.* 應用	交叉的，橫貫的 *cross examination*(一般通稱的)交互詰問、(在實際交互詰問中的)反詰問

		crossing gate 柵欄
		crossing 交叉，交叉點，十字路口，(穿過街道等的)橫道
		pedestrian crosswalk 行人穿越道
		railroad crossing 鐵路平交道
		school crossing guard 校園交通導護
	vt.	越過，渡過
		to cross the street 穿越馬路
cross-examination [ˋkrɔsɪɡˏzæməˋneʃən]	*n.*	(一般通稱的)交互詰問，(在實際交互詰問中)反詰問
cross-examine	*vt.*	交互詰問
		At trial, the defendant has the the right to confront and **cross-examine** adverse witnesses. 審判時，被告有權利與敵性證人對質及交互詰問。
crossfire [ˋkrɔsˏfaɪr]	*n.*	駁火
		An innocent pedestrian was injured in the **crossfire** between police and a suspect. The mastermind was killed by gunshot wounds he suffered in the **crossfire**. 一名無辜的路人在警匪的槍戰中受傷，首腦死於槍戰中所受的槍傷。
crossroad [ˋkrɔsˏrod]	*n.*	(與其他道路相交的)交叉路，十字路口，交叉點
crosswalk [ˋkrɔsˏwɔk]	*n.*	行人穿越道，斑馬線
crossway [ˋkrɔsˏwe]	*n.*	交叉路，岔道，十字路口
crowd [kraʊd]	*n.* 應用	人群，群眾 *crowd behavior* 群眾行為 *crowd control* 群眾控制 *crowd dispersal* 驅散群眾 *crowd leader* 群眾帶領者 *crowd management* 群眾管理 *crowd mood* 群眾情緒
cunning [ˋkʌnɪŋ]	*adj.*	狡猾的 The suspect is so **cunning** that no one knows his whereabouts. 嫌犯非常狡猾以至於沒人知道他的行蹤。
curb [kɝb]	*vt.*	控制，遏止 Law enforcement authorities use cutting edge technology **to curb** high-tech crimes and stay proactive in the high-profile cases. 執法機關使用尖端科技來遏止高科技犯罪，並且在重大矚目案件中，保持主動極積。

To curb gun violence, there is even a ban on the sale of imitation guns. 為了遏止槍枝暴力，甚至有販賣模型槍的禁令。

路邊，馬路邊緣

	n.	When you hear or see an emergency vehicle approach, you should immediately drive to the **curb** and stop. 當你聽到或看到緊急車輛靠近時，你必須立刻開到路邊並停下來。
custodian [kʌsˈtodɪən]	*n.*	監護人
custody [ˈkʌstədɪ]	*n.*	照管，保管，監護，拘留，監禁[(+in/into)]

The suspect used a vehicle to escape crime scene and avoid **being taken into custody** by officers. 嫌犯用車輛逃離犯罪現場及避免被執法人員拘禁。

The **chain of custody** is intended to trace the item of evidence from its discovery to court, prevent its loss or destruction. 物證管制流程是用來進行證據物件從發現直到法院這之間的追蹤、防止滅失或毀損。

Child custody is determined based on the best interests of the child. 兒童監護是依據兒童最佳利益而做決定的。

If the suspect **is in custody** when the police desire to conduct interrogation, police must inform the suspect of his or her constitution rights. 如果警方想偵訊時，嫌犯是在拘禁中，則警方必須將嫌犯的憲法權利告知他。

He **was taken into preventive custody**. 他被預防性羈押了。
He **was hold in preventive custody**. 他被預防性羈押了。

A peace officer or corrections officer may use reasonable force to prevent the escape of the arrested person from **custody**. 治安人員或矯正人員得使用武力以阻止被逮捕之人逃脫拘禁。

Any patrol officer who sees the crime of hit and run can pursue the suspect and **place him into custody**. 任何巡邏員警看到肇事逃逸，都可以追捕嫌犯並將其拘禁。

After arrest, a criminal suspect is usually taken into **police custody** and booked. 逮捕之後，刑事罪犯通常會被警方拘禁並且錄案。

應用
chain of custody 物證管制流程
child custody 兒童監護
joint custody 共同監護
joint legal custody 共同法定監護
joint physical custody 共同人身監護
legal custody 法律監護

physical custody 人身監護

police custody 警方的拘禁

protective custody 保護性留置

sole custody 單獨監護

to have the custody of (sb) 擁有對(人)的監護

to place him into custody 將他拘禁

to prevent the escape from custody of 防止從⋯⋯的拘禁中脫逃

to take a person into custody 拘禁某個人

cyber-attack		網路攻擊
cyberbullying		網路霸凌
		Cyberbullying can be very traumatic for a victim because, once posted online, the messages frequently cannot be removed. 網路霸凌對被害人而言會是非常創痛的，因為一旦張貼上網，訊息經常就無法移除。
damage [ˋdæmɪdʒ]	*n.*	損害，損失，賠償金
		The plaintiff seeks 10,000 in **damages** from the defendant. 原告要求被告賠償損失 1 萬元。
danger [ˋdendʒɚ]	*n.*	危險，威脅
		If you **are in danger**, call 1-1-0 immediately. 如果你身處危險中，請立即撥打 110。
		The driver is **in danger of** losing his life following a head-on car accident. 這名駕駛在一場迎面對撞的車禍後，正處於失去死命的危險中。
dead [dɛd]	*adj.*	死的
		This morning, officers spotted and confronted the murder suspect on 5th street. Suspect opened fire at the officers and **was** soon **shot dead** by the police. 今天上午，員警在第五街瞥見這名謀殺案嫌犯並與其對峙。嫌犯向員警開槍，而後來被警方開槍擊斃。
		The kidnapping suspect **was found dead** of a self-inflicted gunshot wound in his own room following a standoff that lasted about 15 hours. 在持續將近 15 小時的僵持之後，綁匪被發現因自己加工的槍傷而死在自己的房間。
		City Police Department is investigating the shooting that **left one fugitive dead** and two citizens wounded. 市警局正在調查這起造成一名逃犯死亡及兩位市民受傷的槍擊案。
		The car crash has **left three people dead**. The two people trapped inside the vehicle **were pronounced dead** at the

scene. One **was pronounced dead** at the hospital. The crash also left one passenger in a coma. 這起車禍造成了三人死亡，被困在車內的兩人被當場宣告死亡，一人到醫院被宣告死亡。這個車禍也讓一名乘客陷入昏迷。

The victim was stabbed and **left for dead**. 被害人遭刺，並被棄之而死。

adv. 完全地，全然地

You are **dead** wrong. I am **dead** right. 你完全錯了，我完全對了。I am dead tired. 我精疲力竭。

---

deadly
[`dɛdlɪ]

adj. 致命的，致死的

The suspect possessed a **deadly weapon** and attempted to escape. 嫌犯持有致命的武器，並企圖逃走。

An officer is justified in using **deadly force** when he believes that such force is necessary to prevent death or serious bodily injury to himself or such other person. 當員警相信使用致命武力是避免自己或他人死亡或重大身體傷害為有必要時，他就有使用此一致命武力的正當性。

The suspect poses a threat to the police officer, who was compelled to use **deadly force** to take his life in such a life-threatening situation. 嫌犯對員警作勢威脅，迫使員警在這樣的生命威脅情況之下，使用了致命武器結束他的生命。

Gang members often intimidate people who live and work within their turf, and are prepared for the **deadly encounters** with law enforcement officers and rival gangs. 幫派成員常恐嚇在他們地盤內生活及工作的人，並準備著與執法人員及敵對幫派做致命衝突。

---

death
[dɛθ]

n. 死，死亡

The offender **was sentenced to death** for a murder he committed in 2015. He **was put to death** for the homicide in 2023. 犯罪者因 2015 年犯下的謀殺而被判處死刑。在 2023 年，他因為這起殺人罪被處決了。

應用 *accidental death* 意外死亡

cause of death 死亡原因(或 *cause of the fatality*)

death certificate 死亡證書(或 *certification of death*)

death chamber 刑場(或 *execution chamber*)

death notification 死亡通知

death penalty 死刑(或稱 *capital punishment*)

death row inmate 死囚犯

death row 死囚區

death sentence 死刑判決
death toll 死亡人數
death warrant 死刑令
life and death 生死攸關的
natural death 自然死亡
traffic death 交通死亡
be punished by death 被處以死刑
to cause death 造成死亡
to put sb. to death 將(人)處決
to sentence sb. to death 將(判處死刑)

deceased [dɪˋsist]	*adj.* *n.*	已故的 死者

If **the deceased** dies from unnatural circumstances, coroner will need to further examine the remains of a deceased person prior to cremation. 如果死者死於非自然情況，法醫將必須在火化之前，進一步檢驗死者之遺體。

deception [dɪˋsɛpʃən]	*n.*	欺騙，欺詐

Although police are prohibited from using excessive physical force, they are able to use a variety of psychological ways to extract confessions from criminal suspects, including the use of **deception** during interrogation. 雖然長久以來，警方被禁止使用過度的身體武力，但他們是可以使用各種心理方式從嫌犯取得自白，包括偵訊時使用欺騙的方式。

decision [dɪˋsɪʒən]	*n.*	(法律上/法庭上的) 判決

The prosecutor decided to appeal the **decision** of the trial court. 檢察官決定對地方法院的判決進行上訴。

In the legal context, a **decision** is a judicial determination of parties' rights and obligation reached by a court based on facts and law. 就法律上來看，判決(decision)指的是法院依據事實及法律，對於各造權利及義務所做的司法決定(judicial determination)。

declarant [dɪˋklɛrənt]	*n.*	陳述者(判決書或證據法則常用)

Hearsay means a statement that the **declarant** does not make while testifying at the current trial or hearing. 傳聞，是指陳述者非在目前的審理或聽證的作證中所為的陳述。

defamation [ˌdɛfəˋmeʃən]	*n.*	誹謗

Defamation is a catch-all term for any statement that hurts someone's reputation. Written **defamation** is called libel, and spoken **defamation** is called slander. 誹謗(defamation)一詞是

指傷害他人名聲的言論的通稱，書面的誹謗用 libel 一詞，口頭的誹謗用 slander 一詞。

defend	vt.	防禦，保衛，保護，【律】為……辯護
[dɪ`fɛnd]		

A person may use physical force in defense of another person when and to the extent he or she reasonably believes such to be necessary **to defend** himself, herself or a third person. 任何人於其合理相信防衛自己或第三人所必要之時或限度內，得使用武力防衛他人。

Most people would look for someone with litigation experience when they file or **defend** lawsuits. 大多數人在提起或防禦訴訟時，會找有訴訟經驗的人。

defender	n.	防禦者，辯護人 (public defender 公設辯護人)
[dɪ`fɛndɚ]		

A defendant will be eligible for a **public defender** if he or she is in lack of the financial resources. 被告如果欠缺財力，就會有資格獲得公設辯護人。

A **public defender** can be refered to as an assigned counsel or a court appointed attorney. 公設辯護人也稱為 assigned counsel 或 court appointed attorney。

defendant	n.	被告
[dɪ`fɛndənt]		

The **defendant** is on trial for burglary. 被告因竊盜案受審。

The judge held that the **defendant** was innocent. 法官認定被告是無辜的。

At trial, the judge may decide to dismiss the complaint and discharge the **defendant**; or to admit the **defendant** to bail. 審判時，法官可以決定駁回訴狀並釋回被告，或准予被告交保。

In this case, the court, in its discretion, may sentence a **defendant** to a term of not less than twenty years. 這個案子，法院本於裁量得處被告 20 年以下的刑期。

The plaintiff decided to file a criminal complaint against the **defendant** charging **defendant** with misappropriation. 原告決定對被告提起刑事控訴，控告被告侵占。

All **defendants** are to be considered innocent until proven or adjudicated guilty in court. 所有的被告在被法院證明或判決有罪之前，應被認定為無辜。

defense	n.	抗辯
[dɪ`fɛns]		

Every day, law enforcement officers must draw their firearms for the **defense** of the public, fellow officers, and themselves. 每天，執法人員必須拔槍以保衛公眾、同僚及自己。

| | 應用 | *defense attorney* 辯護律師(或 *defense counsel, defense lawyer*) |

defraud	*vt.*	詐取，詐騙[(+of)]
[dɪˋfrɔd]		Officers arrested two men and charged them with **defrauding** the company of more than $1 million. 員警逮捕了兩人，並指控他們詐騙公司 100 萬元。
		The jewelry store owner staged a burglary with the intent of **defrauding** his insurance company. 珠寶店老闆意圖詐騙保險公司，假造有一個竊盜案。

| delinquency | *n.* | 違法行為，少年犯罪 |
| [dɪˋlɪŋkwənsɪ] | 應用 | *juvenile delinquency* 少年犯罪 |

delinquent	*n.*	青少年罪犯
[dɪˋlɪŋkwənt]	應用	*delinquent child* 犯罪兒童
		juvenile delinquent 少年犯

deliver	*vt.*	投遞，傳送，運送
[dɪˋlɪvɚ]		The suspect said he had used postol service to deliver the durg packages to the buyers. 嫌犯說他是利用郵政服務將毒品包裹送去給買主。
	vt.	生 (嬰兒)
		The EMTs loaded the pregnant woman into the ambulance, prepared her for delivery and headed for the hospital. Later, the baby was delivered in the ambulance. The EMTs delivered the baby in the ambulance. 緊急救護技術員將孕婦放進救護車，讓他準備生產並趕往醫院。後來，嬰兒在救護車上出生。緊急救護技術員在救護車上接生了嬰兒。

| delivery | *n.* | 交付，交貨 |
| [dɪˋlɪvərɪ] | 應用 | *controlled delivery* 控制下交付 |

demonstration	*n.*	示威
[͵dɛmənˋstreʃən]		Many people gathered at Central Station to demonstrate against government's new policies. After the **demonstration** officially ended, some demonstrators remained on the streets until late into the evening. 許多人聚集在中央車站示威反對政府的新政策。示威正式結束之後，許多的示威者仍然在街上，持續到深夜。
	應用	*demonstration leader* 示威帶領者
		mass demonstration 大規模示威

| demonstrator | *n.* | 示威者 |
| [ˋdɛmən͵stretɚ] | | |

| defy | *vt.* | 公然反抗，蔑視 |
| [dɪˋfaɪ] | | Armstrong **defied** the court's order, and was held in contempt of |

court. 阿姆斯壯違抗法院的命令，而被認定藐視法庭。

| denounce [dɪ`naʊns] | *vt.* | 指責，譴責，告發，指控 |

Activists **denounced** the police operation, in which many of them were handcuffed, not knowing what they had done wrong. 激進主義者譴責警方的行動，將許多他們的人上了手銬，而不知道他們有甚麼做錯了。

| deny [dɪ`naɪ] | *vt.* | 否定，否認 [(+ Ving)]， |

The suspect **denied having** any involvement in the robbery. He also **denied killing** the drug dealer. 嫌犯否認有任何涉入這起強盜案，他同時也否認殺死毒販。

The suspect **denied** that he had robbed the victim. 嫌犯否認他對被害人行搶。

Justice delayed is justice **denied**. 遲來的正義不是正義。

| deploy [dɪ`plɔɪ] | *vt.* | 展開，部署 |

Law enforcement agencies must effectively **deploy** resources, and come up with solutions to crime. 執法機關必須有效地佈署資源，並提出犯罪的解決策略。

If necessary, police must **deploy** personnel to isolate and contain the people. 如果必要的話，警察必須佈署人員，以隔絕及包圍群眾。

Riot police are organized, **deployed**, trained or equipped to confront crowds, protests or riots. 鎮暴警察被組織、佈署、訓練或配備來面對群眾、抗議或暴動。

Rescuers **deployed** air rescue cushion as a primary means of rescue or a safety backup. 救難人員鋪設救生氣墊做為一項主要的救援方法或安全備援。

| deport [dɪ`port] | *vt.* | 驅逐，遣返 |

In general, criminal aliens may become deportable aliens and will **be ordered deported**. 一般而言，犯罪外國人可能會成為可遣送的外國人，而會被命令驅逐。

| deportation [ˌdipor`teʃən] | *n.* | 遣送 |

US Congress enacted the term "removal" to refer to both **deportation** and exclusion. **Deportation** is for people already physically present inside the United States. 美國國會立法用遣返(removal)一字來指遣送(deportation)與拒入(exclusion)兩者，遣送(deportation)是針對人身已經在美國境內的人。

| depressant [dɪ`prɛsnt] | *n.* | 鎮定劑 |

deputy [ˋdɛpjətɪ]		副的 Deputy Commissioner 副局長
desert [dɪˋzɝt]	*vt.*	遺棄，拋棄，離棄 Some children are told to leave, abandoned, **deserted** and become thrownaway. 有些小孩被人叫他離開、被放棄、被捨棄，而成為被趕出家門的人。 A parent is guilty of abandonment of a child when he or she **deserts** a child in any place with intent to wholly abandon such child. 父或母基於徹底遺棄兒童之故意，而拋棄該兒童於任何地方者，犯遺棄兒童罪。
designate [ˋdɛzɪɡ͵net]	*vt.*	指定，指派 [(+ as)] Captain Raymond **was designated as** point of contact in the cross-border operation. 雷猛隊長被指定為這場跨境行動的聯絡窗口。 You will have to find a **designated** driver to avoid car accident if you are going to drink. 如果你打算喝酒，你將需要找一位指定駕駛(代駕)，以避免車禍。
destroy [dɪˋstrɔɪ]	*vt.*	毀壞，破壞，消滅 Simpson **destroyed** the evidence. Police said the evidence **was destroyed** to influence the court's final decision. 辛普森毀滅了證據，警方說證據被摧毀是要影響法院的最終判決。
destruction [dɪˋstrʌkʃən] n.	*n.*	破壞，毀滅，消滅 The chain of custody is intended to trace the item of evidence from its discovery to court, prevent its loss or **destruction**. 物證管制流程是用來進行證據物件從發現直到法院這之間的追蹤、防止滅失或毀損。 應用　*destruction of property* 毀損物品 *destruction of evidence* 毀損證據
detain [dɪˋten]	*vt.*	留置，拘留，扣留 The police officers can stop drivers at checkpoints and **detain** those suspected of driving under the influence (DUI). 員警可以在檢查站攔停駕駛人，並留置有酒駕可疑的人。 In Washington DC, parading without a permit is not an offense and shall not be used to **detain** anyone. 在華府，未經核准的遊行不是犯罪，而不得以之留置任何人。 The **detained person** may be discharged from custody if the executive authority of the requested State has not received the formal request for extradition within the specified period of time. 如果被請求國行政機關在所定的期間內，沒有收到正式的引

渡請求時，被留置之人可能就會從拘禁中被釋放。

detainee	n.	被拘留者
[dɪte`ni]		The judge set the bail at 1 million. However, the **detainee** could not gather enough funds to bail him out of jail. 法官訂出 1 百萬元保釋金額，然而，被拘禁人無法湊足資金將他保出來。

detect	vt.	發現，察覺，查出，看穿
[dɪ`tɛkt]		While on the streets, officers will observe crowds on the streets **to detect** problems or illegal activities. 在街上時，員警會觀察街上的群眾，以發現問題或不法活動。
		Police conducted an unannounced drug sweeps of the pubs and used canines **to detect** marijuana and other drugs. 警方局進行了無預警的酒吧毒品掃蕩，並且用警犬來偵測大麻與其他毒品。
		Fire Department was notified by a call within two to three minutes after the fire **was detected** at 11:30 p.m., but officials estimated the the fire had been burning for more than 10 minutes before it **was detected** by the neighbor. 消防局在火災 11:30 發現之後的 2 到 3 分鐘接到電話通報，但是官員估計這場火在被鄰居發現之前，已經燒了超過 10 分鐘。

detector	n.	探測器，檢驗器
[dɪ`tɛktɚ]	應用	*flame detector* 火焰偵測器
		gas detector 瓦斯偵測器
		hand-held metal detector 手持式金屬探測器
		life detector 生命探測器
		metal detector 金屬探測器
		smoke detector 煙霧偵測器

detective	n.	偵查員
[dɪ`tɛktɪv]		

detector	n.	探測器，檢驗器
[dɪ`tɛktɚ]	應用	*hand-held metal detector* 手持式金屬探測器
		lie detector 【口】測謊器
		life detector 生命探測器
		metal detector 金屬探測器
		radar detector 雷達偵測器
		smoke detector 煙霧偵測器
		speed camera detector 超速照相偵測器
		walk-through metal detector 金屬探測門

detention	n.	拘留，留置
[dɪ`tɛnʃən]		**Preventive detention** allows the judges to imprison anyone

89

who they have good reason to believe may commit a crime. 預防性拘禁讓法官有良好的理由相信某人將會犯罪時，將他監禁。

|應用| *detention center* 拘留所 (或 *detention home*)
immigration detention center 移民拘留所、移民收容所
juvenile detention center 少年教養院、感化院(或稱 *youth detention center, juvenile hall*)
preventive detention【律】預防性羈押、預防性拘禁

deter [dɪ`tɝ]	*vt.*	威懾住，使……斷念[(+from)]

A growing number of cities are using surveillance cameras **to deter** crime. 許多的城市現在都使用錄影監視器來嚇阻犯罪。

The exclusionary rule was designed primarily **to deter** police misconduct. 排除法則主要的設計是嚇阻警察的不當行為。

determine [dɪ`tɝmɪn]	*vt.*	確定

The cause of fire **has been determined**. Fire investigator **determined that** a flammable liquid had been used. That liquid **was determined to be** gasoline. 火災的原因已經確定，火災調查員確定有使用可燃性液體，該項液體確定是汽油。

The cause of fire **was determined to be** accidental but is still under investigation. 火災的原因已經確定是意外，但是仍在調查中。

deterrence [dɪ`tɝrəns]	*n.*	嚇阻

A major purpose of the exclusionary rule is the **deterrence** of police misconduct in obtaining evidence and unreasonable searches and seizures. 排除法則的主要的目之一，是嚇阻警察在取證時的不當行為及不合理的搜索與扣押。

detonate [`dɛtə,net]	*vt.*	使……爆炸，使……觸發

At 9:00 a.m., the suicide bomber **detonated** a bomb aboard a train travelling between K Street station and M Street station. 上午九點，自殺炸彈客搭火車在 K 街站與 M 街站之間引爆了一顆炸彈。

detour [`ditʊr]	*vi.*	繞路(而行)，迂迴(而行)

The driver ignored a "**Detour Ahead. Road Closed to Thru Traffic**" sign and caused the car accident. 駕駛忽視了「前方請繞路，直行線道封閉」的標誌，而造成了車禍。

	n.	繞路(而行)，迂迴(而行)

Other drivers were forced **to take a detour** because of the car accident. 由於這場車禍，其他駕駛被迫繞路。

detrimental [dɛtrəˋmɛnt!]	*adj.*	有害的，不利的 Domestic violence in a household **is detrimental to** the child. 家戶中的家庭暴力，對兒童是有害的。 The improper use of controlled substances has a **detrimental** effect on the health of the people. 不當使用管制物質對於人的健康有不利的影響。
develop [dɪˋvɛləp]	*vt.*	開發，使……成長，使……發達 Drug investigation relies heavily on information from outside sources in order to **develop** a case. It is extremely important to **develop** investigative leads. 毒品偵查相當仰賴外界資訊來讓案件開展，發展偵查線索是極為重要的。 Detectives have to **develop** new ways of drawing confessions out of suspects, e.g. psychological techniques. 偵查員必須發展新的方法從嫌犯獲取自白，例如心理技巧。
die [daɪ]	*vi.*	[(+of)] 因……而死亡(因疾病, 寒冷, 飢餓, 悲傷等) Simpson **died of** heart failure. His mother **died of** lung cancer. 辛普森因心臟衰竭而死，他的媽媽死於肺癌。 [(+ from)] 因……而死亡 (因受傷或其他外界因素) Simpson **died from** drug overdoses. 辛普森死於吸毒過量。
dignity [ˋdɪgnətɪ]	*n.*	尊嚴，莊嚴 In conducting a search of a prisoner's body, correctional authorities should strive to preserve the privacy and **dignity** of the prisoner. 進行受刑人身體搜查時，矯正機關應致力保持受刑人的隱私及尊嚴。
dilemma [dəˋlɛmə]	*n.*	困境，進退兩難 The majority of police pursuits involve a stop for a traffic violation. The **dilemma** faced by officers is whether or not to continue a chase. 大多數的警察追逐涉及交通違規的攔檢，員警所面臨的兩難困境是要不要繼續追逐。
disarm [dɪsˋɑrm]	*vt.*	繳……的械，解除……的武裝 The suspect pointed a handgun at the officer. The officer **disarmed** the suspect and arrested the suspect for attempted murder and unlawful carrying of a weapon. 嫌犯將手槍指著員警，員警卸除了嫌犯的武器並將他以殺人未遂及非法攜帶武器予以逮捕。
disaster [dɪˋzæstə]	*n.*	災害，災難，不幸 The activation of the Emergency Operation Center (EOC) is based on the levels of threats and seriousness of the **disaster**. 「緊急應變中心(EOC)」 的開設依據的是災害的威脅等級與災害的

嚴重性。

	應用	*disaster area* 災區
		disaster loss 災損
		disaster management 災難管理
		man-made disaster 人為災害
		natural disaster 天然災害

disastrous [dɪz`æstrəs]	*adj.*	災害的，災難性的，悲慘的 Any breakdown in communications during a crime in progress could have **disastrous** results. 在犯罪還在進行的時候，任何通訊方面的故障，都可能產生災難的結果。
discharge [dɪs`tʃɑrdʒ]	*vt.*	允許……離開，釋放，【律】撤銷(法院命令)，使……免除，使……卸脫 At trial, the judge may decide to dismiss the complaint and **discharge** the defendant; or to admit the defendant to bail. 審判時，法官可以決定駁回訴狀並釋回被告，或准予被告交保。 The detained person will be **discharged** from custody if the requested State does not receive the formal request for extradition. 如果被請求國沒有收到正式的引渡請求時，被留置之人就會從拘禁中被釋放。
	vt.	射出，開(砲) Firearms examiners may test a weapon to discover whether it can **be discharged**. 槍枝鑑定人員會測試武器，瞭解該槍是否還能擊發。
discipline [`dɪsəplɪn]	*n.*	紀律 Law enforcement officers may use reasonable force to maintain order and **discipline**. 執法人員得使用合理武力以維持秩序與紀律。
	vt.	訓練，使……有紀律，懲戒 Some abusive parents may use physical force to **discipline** their children. 有些施虐的父母會用身體的武力去訓誡子女。
disclose [dɪs`kloz]	*vt.*	揭露，揭發，透露，公開 At trial, prosecutors have the duty to **disclose** evidence to defendants. 審判時，檢察官有義務揭示證據給被告。
discover [dɪs`kʌvɚ]	*vt.*	查明，發現，找到 The Chief of Police said that the medical examiner would perform autopsies to **discover** the cause of death. 警察局長說，法醫將會進行驗屍，以查明死亡原因。 The Chief of Police also said that firearms examiners would test a weapon **to discover** whether it can be discharged. 警察局長還

說，槍枝鑑定人員將會測試武器，以查明該槍是否還能擊發。

discretion	*n.*	裁量(權)，斟酌(或行動)的自由

[dɪ`skrɛʃən]

The admissibility of evidence shall be determined by the court. In other words, the question of admissibility of evidence is left to the **discretion** of the trial court. 證據能力應由法院認定，換言之，證據能力的問題，是留給審理法院裁量。

In this case, the court, **in its discretion**, may sentence a defendant to a term of not less than twenty years. 這個案子，法院本於裁量得處被告 20 年以下的刑期。

Society and the media frequently criticized police inaction **as abuse of discretion**. They complained about the abuse of **police discretion**. 社會與媒體經常批評警察的不做為是濫用裁量，他們抱怨警察裁量的濫用。

Officers may **exercise discretion** in deciding whether and how to intervene in an incident. 員警得行使裁量權，決定在事件中是否介入及如何介入。

應用　*at sb's discretion* 由……自行處理/斟酌處理

at the discretion of 由……自行處理/斟酌處理

administrative discretion 行政裁量

judicial discretion 司法裁量

police discretion 警察裁量

prosecutorial discretion 起訴裁量

discriminate	*vt.*	有差別地對待；歧視 [(+against)]

[dɪ`skrɪmə,net]

Chief of Police said the police department did not **discriminate against** the officer with long hair. 警察局長說，警局對於留長髮的員警沒有差別對待。

discrimination	*n.*	不公平待遇，歧視

[dɪ,skrɪmə`neʃən]

Police must apply laws without prejudice or **discrimination**. 警察適用法律必須沒有偏見或歧視。

應用　*age discrimination* 年齡歧視

gender discrimination 性別歧視

race/racial discrimination 種族歧視

sexual discrimination 性別歧視

workplace discrimination 職場歧視

disguise	*vt.*	假裝，掩飾

[dɪs`gaɪz]

Two men **disguised as** law enforcement officers, forced their way into the victim's home and demanded to know where they kept the money. 兩名男子喬裝執法人員，強行進入被害人的家中，並要求知道他們把錢藏在何處。

The suspect **disguised himself as** the staff and committed the theft. 嫌犯喬裝自己為員工並行竊。

disk cutter		(消防)圓盤切割器
dismantle	*vt.*	拆除，解散，瓦解
[dɪs`mænt!]		Since gangsters may commit major crimes, each country's law enforcement authorities usually establish specialized unit to combat, disrupt and **dismantle** organized crime and gang violence. 由於幫派分子會從事重大犯罪，因此每一個國家的執法機關通常會設立專門的單位，來打擊、分散及瓦解組織犯罪及幫派暴力。
dismember	*vt.*	肢解，分割
[dɪs`mɛmbɚ]		The murderer confessed that he had forced other accomplices to help **dismembering** the body of the deceased. 殺人犯承認他強迫其他共犯幫助肢解死者的屍體。
dismiss	*vt.*	【律】駁回(起訴)，不受理，(未經開庭審理而) 終結訴訟
[dɪs`mɪs]		At trial, the judge decided to **dismiss the complaint** and discharge the defendant. 審判時，法官決定駁回訴狀並釋回被告。
disorder	*n.*	脫序，不符合司法程序的行為
[dɪs`ɔrdɚ]		Pyromania is a **mental disorder** behavior. 縱火狂是一項精神障礙的行為。
		In the US, people commit the crime of **disorderly conduct** while intoxicated in a public place, engaging in conduct that is likely to offend, scare, or annoy others. 在美國，當在公共場所成醉態，並從事有可能侵犯、驚嚇，攪擾他人的行為時，為觸犯妨害安寧(罪)。
	應用	*disorderly conduct* 妨害安寧(罪)
dispatch	*vt.*	派遣
[dɪ`spætʃ]		If officers are available, **dispatch** the call. It is important that calls **be dispatched** quickly. 如果員警有空，就派遣電話事項。快速進行電話派遣，是重要的。
		Patrol officers **are** often **dispatched to** deal with domestic disputes. 巡邏員警常被指派去處理家庭糾紛。
		Firefighters **were dispatched** to the scene at 6:00 p.m. It is not known what ignited the fire. 消防員在下午 6 點被派出去，還不知道是什麼引燃火災的。
dispatcher	*n.*	派遣官，派遣員
		While performing the duties, **radio dispatcher** must determine the priority based on current staffing, activity, location of

officers, citizen information, and location of the incident. 在執行勤務時，無線電派遣官必須依據目前的人力、事項、員警的位置、市民的資訊及事件的位置，確定優先順序。

Police, fire, and ambulance **dispatchers** are also called public safety telecommunicators. **Dispatchers** answer emergency and nonemergency calls, and must be available around the clock. 警察、消防及救護的派遣員(dispatcher)也稱為「公共安全通訊連絡員(public safety telecommunicator)」。派遣員(dispatcher)接聽緊急與非緊急電話，並且必須全天都在。

dispersal order		驅散命令

disperse *vt.* 驅散，解散，疏散
[dɪ`spɝs]

In a violent civil disturbance, the primary objective of the Incident Commander is to **disperse** threatening crowds in order to eliminate the immediate risks of continued escalation and further violence. 在暴力的騷動中，事件指揮官的主要目標是驅散有威脅性的群眾，以消除持續升高及進一步暴力的立即風險。

displace *vt.* （從原來的地方）移開，迫使（人）離開
[dɪs`ples]

As of last night, 55 people **were displaced by** the fire. 20 of the **displaced** residents slept at the shelter. The majority of residents stayed with relatives and friends. 到昨天晚上為止，55 人因為火災而被迫離開，20 位被迫離開的居民睡在收容(庇護)處，大部分的居民是跟親戚及朋友暫住。

display *n.* The driver was ticketed for failure **to display** the number plate.
[dɪ`sple] 該駕駛因為未懸掛車牌而被開單。

dispute *n.* 爭論，爭執，爭端
[dɪ`spjut]

Patrol officers are often dispatched to deal with **domestic disputes**. 巡邏員警常被指派去處理家庭糾紛。

In general, most **legal disputes** are settled in the trial court. 通常，大部分法律爭議是在一審解決了。

應用 *disputed waters* 爭議水域(海巡)

disrupt *vt.* 使……分裂，使……瓦解
[dɪs`rʌpt]

Since gangsters may commit major crimes, each country's law enforcement authorities usually establish specialized unit to combat, **disrupt** and dismantle organized crime and gang violence. 由於幫派分子會從事重大犯罪，因此每一個國家的執法機關通常會設立專門的單位，來打擊、分散及瓦解組織犯罪及幫派暴力。

disruption *n.* 分裂，崩潰，瓦解

[dɪs`rʌpʃən]		If there is any **disruption** during the reading of the verdicts, the bailiffs will have the obligation to remove any persons disrupting these proceedings. 如果宣讀判決的時候有任何擾亂，法警會有義務排除任何擾亂程序的人。
distress [dɪ`strɛs]	*n.*	愁苦，悲傷，憂傷，苦惱，不幸 Officers **were in distress** because of death of the hostage. 員警因為人質的死亡而感到悲傷。
distressed [dɪ`strɛst]	*adj.*	愁苦的，悲傷的，憂傷的 Officers **were distressed by** the death of the hostage during the operation. 因為人質在行動中死亡，使得員警感到悲傷。
distribute [dɪ`strɪbjʊt]	*vt.*	散佈，分布，分配 Street gangs pose the greatest threat to many communities because they **distribute** large quantities of illicit drugs throughout the country. 街頭幫派對很多社區形成了最大威脅，因為他們散布大量非法毒品遍及全國。
Distribution [ˌdɪstrə`bjuʃən]	*n.*	散布，分發，分配 The illegal importation, manufacture, **distribution**, possession and improper use of controlled substances have a substantial and detrimental effect on the health and general welfare of the people. 非法進口、製造、散布、持有，及不當使用管制物質，對於人的健康及全般福祉具有實質及有害的影響。
disturb [dɪs`tɝb]	*vt.*	妨礙，打擾，干擾，使……心神不寧 The nearby residents complained that their lives **were disturbed by** the noise coming from the religious festivals. Other residents said the street performances **disturbed** their lives. 附近的住戶抱怨，他們的生活受到宮廟活動的噪音所干擾，其他住戶說街頭表演干擾了他們的生活。
disturbance [dɪs`tɝbəns]	*n.*	騷擾，混亂，引起騷動的事物 (指擾亂他人安寧、引起他人憤怒焦慮不安的行為) If a peaceful assembly escalates to a **civil disturbance**, the official in charge shall make an evaluation as to the additional manpower required to manage the situation. 如果和平的集會升高成為騷動，負責的官員應針對控制情況所需的額外人力進行評估。 應用 *civil disturbance* 內亂，內部騷動
divorce [də`vors]	*n.*	離婚 應用 *action for divorce* 離婚訴訟 *divorce agreement* 離婚協議 *divorce decree* 離婚判決

do (sb) justice do justice to		公平地對待(某人) He believes that the jury will **do him justice**. 他相信陪審團會公平地對待他。 People expect the court to fairly try the case and **do justice to** the victim. 人們期待法院公平審理案件，給被害人一個公道。
do time		服刑 The warden said that last year the drug dealer **did time** at this prison for selling marijuana. He **did time** at this prison before being paroled this January. 典獄長說，去年這名毒販曾因販賣大麻在這所監獄服刑，他在今年一月被假釋之前，是在這個監獄服刑。 Al Capone **did time** for tax evasion on Alcatraz for four and half years. He is one of the most famous prisoners that you will learn about on a trip to Alcatraz. 卡彭因為逃稅案在「惡魔島(Alcatraz)」服刑四年半，他將是你的「惡魔島(Alcatraz)」之旅會認識的最有名囚犯。
DOB	*abbr.*	出生日 date of birth
document [`dɑkjəmənt]	*vt.*	紀錄 A photography unit is an essential part of any crime lab because photography is widely used **to document** evidence. 影像組是任何犯罪實驗室不可或缺的一部分，因為相片被廣為用來記錄證據。
	n. 應用	文件，文書 *questioned document examiner* 文書鑑定人員 *documentary evidence* 書證，書面證據，文書證據 *identity document* 身分文件 *travel document* 旅行文件 *document fraud* 證件詐騙 *undocumented immigrant* 無證件的(無身分的)移民
domestic [də`mɛstɪk]	*adj.* 應用	家庭的，家事的 *domestic abuse* 家庭虐待、家庭暴力 *domestic call* 家事報案 *domestic conflict* 家庭衝突 *domestic court* 家事法庭 (或稱 *family court*) *domestic dispute* 家庭糾紛 *domestic violence* 家暴 (也稱 *domestic abuse* 或 *family violence*) *domestic disturbance* 家庭問題
	adj. 應用	國內的 *domestic law* 國內法

domestic legal system 國內司法系統

domicile	*n.*	【法律上的】住所
[ˋdɑməsḷ]		The police went to visit his domicile when he was reported missing.警方據報他失蹤時，前往了他的住所訪查。
		【補充說明】domicile 指有久住之意思，為民法上所稱的「住所」；dwelling 為民法上所稱的「居所」。另 dwelling 與 residence 都指住處、住宅、寓所，dwelling 為較正式之用詞。
domiciled	*adj.*	定居的
[ˋdɑməsaɪld]		The police checked with the immigration authorities, and discovered that the suspect **is domiciled in** foreign country. 警方向移民機關連繫，發現嫌犯居住在外國。
door to door	*adv.*	一戶一戶地，逐戶
[ˋdortəˏdor]		Firefighters are going **door to door** to check on neighbors. 消防人員正逐戶檢查鄰居。
doubt	*vt.*	懷疑，不相信 [+whether/if][+that]
[daʊt]		Because he has an alibi, there is no reason to **doubt** him. 由於他有不在場證明，因此沒有理由懷疑他。
		The FBI **doubted that** the attack was made by hackers abroad. 聯邦調查局懷疑這起攻擊是國外的駭客所為。
	n.	懷疑，不相信
		If you think there is a real possibility that he is not guilty, you must give him **the benefit of the doubt** and find him not guilty. 如果你認為確實有可能他是無辜的話，你必須將疑點利益歸於他並判他無罪。
		Criminal courts must prove an accused guilty **beyond a reasonable doubt**. 刑事法庭對於被告有罪必須證明至無合理可疑。
		Officers **cast doubt on** the defendant's confenssion. 員警對於被告的自白產生懷疑。
doubtful	*adj.*	可疑的，令人生疑的
[ˋdaʊtfəl]		It **is doubtful that** the offense was completed by the accused alone. 犯罪由被告單獨一人完成，這點令人懷疑。
		Police **are doubtful of** the statement of the accused. 警方對於被告的陳述是懷疑的。
draw	*vt.*	(法律上) 推斷出，作出，形成
[drɔ]		You are not permitted to **draw** any inference against the defendant because he did not testify. 你不得因為被告沒有作證，而對他做不利的推論。
	vt.	拔出，掏出

The responding officer immediately **drew** his firearms and shot the suspect multiple times. 前往處理的員警立即掏出武器,並數度對嫌犯射擊。

| | *vt.* | 吸引,招來,招致 |

The gunshots **drew the attention of** police. 槍擊聲引起了警方的注意。

Officers said the suspect was firing a handgun into a crowd of people, and the gunshots **drew their attention** to the suspect. 警方說嫌犯對著群眾開槍,槍擊聲讓警方注意到嫌犯。

| drill [drɪl] | *n.* | 操練,訓練,演習 |

Fire drill is a practical method of practicing the evacuation of a building for a fire or emergency. 消防演習是一個練習在火災或緊急情況時撤離建築物的實際方法。

| dropout
[ˋdrɑpˏaʊt] | *n.*
應用 | 退出(學校等),中輟生
to drop out of school 輟學
to drop out of gang 脫離幫派 |

| drown
[draʊn] | *vt.* | 把⋯⋯淹死,溺斃 |

Police said the boat capsized in the river and three of the occupants were **drowned**. The **drowning** accident occurred at approximately 10:00 a.m. 警方說該船在河中翻覆,三名乘客溺斃,這起溺斃的事件發生在大約上午 10 時。

| | *vi.* | 溺斃 |

Fire Chief said that most passengers **had drowned** when their vessel overturned. It was also reported that many of them on board **had drowned** because they were trapped on the boat's lower level. 消防局長說,大部分乘客在船隻翻覆時溺斃了,同時據報其中許多人溺斃,是因為被困在船隻的下層。

| | 應用 | *near drowning* 瀕臨溺斃的 |

| drug
[drʌg] | *n.* | 藥品,毒品 |

Officer found that he **takes durgs**. Urine test showed that he **was on drugs**. But he said he **used drugs** once in a while. Officers then told him "**don't do drugs**." 員警發現他吸毒,尿液測試顯示他有染上毒品。但是他說他是偶爾吸毒。於是員警告訴他「不要吸毒。」

| | 應用 | *club drug* 夜店毒品
controlled drug 管制類毒品
drug abuse 毒品濫用
drug addict 吸毒成癮者
drug addiction 毒品成癮 |

drug chemist 毒品化學專家

drug dealer 毒品販子

drug mule 毒驢 (代為攜帶毒品闖關的人)

drug paddler 毒品販子

drug raid 毒品掃蕩

drug rehabilitation 毒品戒治

drug residue 毒品殘留

drug screening 毒品篩檢

drug sniffing dog 緝毒犬 (又稱 *drug dog* 或 *sniffing dog*)

drug test 毒品檢測

drug smuggling 毒品走私

drug trafficking 毒品走私

drug treatment 毒品勒戒

drug trend 毒品趨勢

illicit drug 非法毒品

應用	常見毒品：

Cocaine [ko`ken] 古柯鹼

Ecstasy [`ɛkstəsɪ] 合成迷幻藥(俗稱 MDMA 快樂丸)

GHB 也稱為液態快樂丸(liquid ecstasy)

hallucinogen[hə`lusnə,dʒɛn]迷幻劑

Heroin [`hɛro,ɪn]海洛因

Ketamine K 他命

Marijuana [,mɑrɪ`hwɑnə]大麻，大麻煙，大麻毒品

Methamphetamine [,mɛθæm`fɛtəmin]甲基苯丙胺，脫氧麻黃鹼

morphine [`mɔrfin]嗎啡

DUI	*abbr.*	酒駕 driving under the influence (也稱為 driving while intoxicated (DWI); drunken driving; drunk driving; drink driving; operating under the influence; drinking and driving)
		The police officers can stop drivers at checkpoints and detain those suspected of **driving under the influence (DUI)**. So be resonaible. Let designated driver takes you and your car home. 員警可以在檢查站攔阻駕駛人，並留置可疑的酒駕者。所以，要負責任，讓指定駕駛連人帶車帶你回家。
duress [`djʊrɪs]	*n.*	強迫，脅迫
duty [`djutɪ]	*n.*	責任，義務，職責，職務
		An officer was assaulted **in the line of duty**, and sustained

injuries. 有一位員警在執勤中受到攻擊並且受傷。

應用	*in the line of duty* 在執行任務時
	in the performance of duty 在執行任務時
	duty officer 值勤員
	off duty 退勤
	on duty 執勤
	reflective duty vest 反光背心 (或稱 *reflective safety vest*)
	to report for duty 到勤 (同 *to report to work*)

dwelling [`dwɛlɪŋ]	*n.*	住處，住宅，寓所

NY State Penal Law 140.30: A person is guilty of burglary when he knowingly enters or remains unlawfully in a **dwelling** with intent to cimmit a crime. 紐約州刑法 140.30 條：任何人意圖犯罪，而故意進入或非法停留在某一住居所，犯竊盜罪。

【補充說明】domicile 指有久住之意思，為民法上的「住所」；dwelling 為民法上的「居所」。dwelling 與 residence 都指住處、住宅、寓所，dwelling 為較正式之用詞

DWI	*abbr.*	酒駕，全稱為 driving while intoxicated，也稱 driving under the influence (DUI)

A police officer can arrest the person without a warrant in case of **driving while intoxicated (DWI)** if such violation is coupled with an accident or collision. 在酒駕的案件，如果該項違規有伴隨發生車禍或擦撞時，員警可以無令狀逮捕該人。

eavesdrop [`ivz,drɑp]	*vt.*	竊聽，偷聽

Eavesdropping and wiretapping are similar, but they're not identical. Basically, the difference is that wiretapping is the act of intercepting and listening in on phone conversations by using a machine to tap into the phone line. **Eavesdropping**, on the other hand, is the act of listening in on conversations (including those that don't take place over the phone) with the aid of an electronic device that is not a wiretap of a phone line. 竊聽與監聽相似，但不相同。基本上，區別在於，監聽是藉由機器接上電話線，而攔截與聽取電話中的對話；竊聽是藉由電話線路監聽以外的電子設備的輔助去聽取對話(包括非電話中所進行的對話)。

effect [ɪ`fɛkt]	*vt.*	實現，達到(目的)，做成

An officer is justified in the use of any force which he reasonably believes to be necessary to **effect** the arrest, for example, to prevent the escape. 員警合理認為，武力的使用是完成逮捕所必要時——例如避免脫逃——員警使用武力是有正當性的。

		效果，作用，影響，(法律的)效力
	n.	The illegal importation, manufacture, distribution, possession and improper use of controlled substances have a substantial and detrimental **effect** on the health and general welfare of the people. 非法進口、製造、散布、持有及不當使用管制物質，對於人們的健康及全般福祉具有實質及有害的影響。

---

egress
[`igrɛs]　　　*n.*　　外出，出路

Put the fire out if you can, but if that is not possible, protect the **means of egress**, so that people can escape and rescuers can enter. 如果可以的話，你就滅火，但是如果不可能的話，要保護好「出路(means of egress)」，以便人們可以逃離，並且救援者可以進入。

Means of egress is the way out of a building during an emergency. It may be by door, window, hallway, or exterior fire escape. 「出路(means of egress)」是指緊急時離開建築物的路線，那可以是由門、窗、廊道或是外部的防火梯。

---

electrocution
[ɪ,lɛktrə`kjuʃən]　　　*n.*　　電刑處死

Execution by **electrocution** is a form of execution in the U.S. usually performed by using an electric chair. 以電刑執行是美國的一種執行方式，通常是使用電椅執行。

---

electronic
[ɪlɛk`trɑnɪk]　　　*adj.*　　電子的，電子操縱的

應用

electronic monitoring 電子監控 (或 *electronically monitored supervision*)

*electronic monitoring bracele*t 電子監控手環

electronic surveillance 電子監察

---

eligible
[`ɛlɪdʒəb!]　　　*adj.*　　法律上合格的

If the immigration officer determines that you **are eligible for** admission under its immigration law, he or she will stamp your passport and let you in. 如果移民官依據移民法，認定你有入境資格的話，他會在護照上蓋章，並讓你入境。

---

eliminate
[ɪ`lɪmə,net]　　　*vt.*　　排除，消除，消滅，(比賽中)淘汰[(+from)]，【口】殺(人)

DNA evidence **eliminated** him as a suspect. DNA 證據將他排除為涉嫌人。

---

elude
[ɪ`lud]　　　*vt.*　　(巧妙地) 逃避，躲避

The fugitive **eluded** the police for five days before being captured. Police said that he had **eluded** capture for five days. 通緝犯躲避警方 5 天後被捕，警方說他逃避逮捕五 5 天。

---

embassy
[`ɛmbəsɪ]　　　*n.*　　大使館

embezzlement [ɪm`bɛz!mənt]	*n.*	侵占，挪用，侵吞，盜用公款(或 misappropriation) **Embezzlement** involves taking property that you already possess, but do not own. Misappropriation is **embezzlement** of money only. 侵占(用 embezzlement 一詞)是指取走已經持有但非擁有的財產，侵占(用 misappropriation 一詞)是僅指金錢的侵占。
emblem [`ɛmbləm]	*n.*	徽章
emergency [ɪ`mɝdʒənsɪ]	*n.* 應用	緊急事件 *emergency aid* 緊急救援 *emergency alarm* 緊急警報 *Emergency Call Box* 緊急電話箱 *emergency evacuation* 緊急撤離 *emergency exit* 緊急出口 *emergency management* 應急管理 *Emergency Medical Services (EMS)* 緊急醫療服務 *Emergency Medical Technician (EMT)* 緊急救護技術員 *Emergency Operations Center (EOC)* 緊急應變中心 *emergency power system* 緊急電源系統 *emergency rescue and evacuation* 緊急救援及撤離 *emergency toll-free number* 緊急免付費電話 *emergency vehicle* 應急車輛 *fire emergency number* 火災緊急電話 (110) *police emergency number* 報警緊急電 (119)
employ [ɪm`plɔɪ]	*vt.*	使用，利用 Riot police may **be employed** to disperse or control crowds. However, they should never **employ** unnecessary force or violence. 鎮暴警察得用來驅散或控制群眾，然而，絕對不可以使用不必要的武力或暴力。
empower [ɪm`pauɚ]	*vt.*	授權，准許，賦予權力 In general, police **are empowered to** do almost anything if they believe on reasonable grounds that it is necessary. 基本上，如果有合理事由認為必要的話，警察被授權做的幾乎是全部。 In the protest, District Commander **was empowered to** decide how many plain clothes officer to assign. He **was empowered to** assign officers as he saw fit – in uniform or in plain clothes. 在這抗議中，分局長被授權決定要指派多少便衣警察，他被授權依其認為適合而指派員警，包括制服警察與便衣警察。
EMT	*abbr.*	緊急救護技術員 *emergency medical technician*

An **Emergency Medical Technician (EMT)** provides basic life support (BLS) in a pre-hospital setting to individuals during medical emergencies. Basic Life Support may include CPR, oxygen administration, bleeding control, spinal immobilization, etc. 緊急救護技術員提供到院前基本救命術給醫療緊急中的人，基本救命術包括：心肺復甦術、給予氧氣、控制出血、脊椎固定等等。

enact [ɪnˋækt]	*vt.*	制定（法律） The new traffic law **was enacted** to protect the safety of pedstrians. 為保護行人的安全，新的交通法已經制定。 It **was enacted** to protect pedestrians and other road users from injuries caused by reckless drivers. 其制定是為了保護行人及其他用路人免於受到不注意的駕駛人所造成的傷害。
encounter [ɪnˋkaʊntɚ]	*vt.*	遭遇(敵人)，遇到(困難，危險等)，意外地遇到 Police received a call about a robbery in progress. While at the scene, the responding officers **encountered** the armed suspect who opened fires at them. "We **encountered** the suspect outside the shop and returned fire," officers said. 警方接到一通電話是關於一件進行中的強盜竊案。在現場時，回應的員警遭遇攜械嫌犯朝員警開槍。員警說，「我們在店門口外面遭遇嫌犯，並且開槍還擊」。
	n.	偶然相遇，遭遇 Officers must understand that negative public attitudes toward the police stem from negative police **encounters**. 員警必須知道，公眾對警察的負面態度，源自於負面的警察接觸。 Gangsters often intimidate people who live and work within their turf, and are prepared for the deadly **encounters** with law enforcement officers and rival gangs. 幫派分子常恐嚇在他們地盤內生活及工作的人，並準備著與執法人員及敵對幫派做致命的衝突。
endanger [ɪnˋdendʒɚ]	*vt.*	危及，危害到……，使遭到危險 The arsoner started the fire using gasoline. Police said his action **endangered** the residents of the apartment building. 縱火犯使用汽油引燃火災，警方說他的行為使公寓的住戶陷入危險。
enforce [ɪnˋfors]	*vt.*	實施，執行 As a law enforcement officer, I will **enforce** the law courteously and appropriately without fear or favor. 身為執法人員，我會禮貌而適當地執法，沒有畏懼或偏袒。
enforcement	*n.*	執行

[ɪn`fɔrsmənt]	應用	*enforcement of foreign penalties* 外國刑罰之執行 *law enforcement authorities / agency* 執法機關 *law enforcement officer* 執法人員 *selective enforcement* 選擇性執法 *traffic enforcement* 交通執法
engage [ɪn`gedʒ]	*vi.*	從事，參與 [(+ in)] The accused was arrested because officers reasonably believed that the accused **engaged in** the crime of robbery. 被告遭到逮捕，因為員警合理相信被告幹下這起強盜罪。
engulf [ɪn`gʌlf]	*vt.*	吞沒，捲入 I woke up and found the neighbor's building **was fully engulfed in** flames. 我醒來並發現鄰居的建築物被吞噬了。 The blaze broke out in the basement of a seven-story apartment and soon **engulfed** the entire structure. 大火從一棟七層樓公寓的地下室發生，並且很快地將整個建物吞噬。
enjoy [ɪn`dʒɔɪ]	*vt.*	享受，享有 In all criminal prosecutions, the accused shall **enjoy** the right to have the assistance of counsel for his defense. The accused also **enjoy** the right to be confronted with the witnesses against him. 在所有刑事起訴中，被告享有由律師協助辯護權利。被告也享有與不利於己的證人對質的權利。 The Permanent Court of International Justice (PCIJ) held that the flag State does not **enjoy** exclusive territorial jurisdiction in the high seas in respect of a collision with a vessel carrying the flag of another State 常設國際法院認定，船旗國在公海上，對於與懸掛另一國旗幟的船隻的碰撞，並不享有專屬的屬地管轄。
entrap [ɪn`træp]	*vt.*	使……投羅網，欺騙，使……陷入 Officers must understand that the defendant may claim that he or she **was entrapped into** committing the crime by a law enforcement officer. 員警必須了解，被告會主張他是被執法人員誘陷而犯罪的。
entrapment [ɪn`træpmənt]	*n.*	誘陷，誘捕，圈套 **Entrapment** can be explained as the conduct to induce the suspect to commit an offense. 誘陷可以被解釋為引誘嫌犯從事犯罪的行為。
EOC	*abbr.*	緊急應變中心 *Emergency Operation Center* The activation of the **Emergency Operation Center (EOC)** is based on the levels of threats and seriousness of the disaster. Level 1 Activation is full activation; Level 2 Activation is partial

activation; Level 3 Activation is limited activation. 「緊急應變中心(EOC)」的開設是依據威脅的等級與災害的嚴重性，一級開設是完全開設，二級開設是部分開設，三級開設是有限開設。

EOD robot	*abbr.*	防爆機器人 Explosive Ordnance Disposal robot
equal [`ikwəl]	*adj.*	平等的 All **are equal** before the law and are entitled without any discrimination to **equal** protection of the law. (Article 7 of the Universal Declaration of Human Rights, UDHR) 法律之前人人平等，並享有法律之平等保護，不受任何歧視。(世界人權宣言第 7 條)
err [ɝ]	*vi.*	犯錯誤，出差錯 (常見在判決書上使用) The defendant appeals and arguing that the court **erred** in denying his request. 被告提起上訴並主張法院拒絕其請求核有違誤。 The court **erred** in admitting improper evidence, and excluding proper evidence. 法院接受不當的證據並排除了適當的證據，核有違誤。
error [`ɛrə]	*n.*	錯誤，失誤，差錯 If court finds an **error** which will affect the result, the higher court will reverse the lower court's **error** in whole or in part. 如果法院發現有會影響結果的錯誤，上級法院將會對下級法的錯誤為全部或局部撤銷。
escalate [`ɛskə,let]	*vi.*	逐步上升(增強或擴大) If a peaceful assembly **escalates** to a civil disturbance, the official in charge shall determine if a recall of off-duty personnel may be necessary. 如果平和的集會升高成為騷動，負責的官員應決定是否有召回退勤人員的必要。 The fire **escalated** very quickly. I've never seen a fire travel that fast, a neighbor said. 火勢很快升高，我從未看過火勢蔓延得如此快地，一位鄰居說。
escape [ə`skep]	*n.*	脫逃 In the course of making an arrest, officers may use necessary physical force to prevent the **escape** from custody of an offender. 進行逮捕之際，員警得使用必要的身體武力，以防止人犯逃脫拘禁。
	vt.	脫逃，逃脫 A handcuffed man attacked an officer guarding him and **escaped** police custody in Manhattan Tuesday night, according to the NYPD. 根據紐約市警局，星期四晚上在曼哈頓，一名被上手

銬的男子攻擊戒護他的員警，並逃脫逃警方的拘禁。

The master decided to drop anchor in the bay **to escape** the storm. 船長決定拋錨將船停泊在港灣中，以躲避暴風雨。

| | *vi.* | 逃跑，逃脫[(+from)] |

The attempted-murder suspect who **escaped from** the police in handcuffs last month was captured on Monday, the police said. 警方說，這名上個月戴著手銬從警方脫逃的殺人未遂嫌犯，在星期一被抓到的。

應用　*escape ladder* 逃生梯

escape rope 逃生索

escape route 逃生路線

escape training 逃生訓練

fire escape 防火梯

---

escaped
[ə`skept]
adj. 脫逃了的，逃跑了的

Police said the **escaped prisoner** is still at large. 警方說逃逸人犯仍然在逃。

應用　*escaped person* 逃逸者

escaped prisoner 逃逸人犯

escaped suspect 逃逸嫌犯

---

escort
[`ɛskɔrt]
n. 戒護

vt. **Escort** duty is dangerous. When you **escort** the inmate to court, you should park in the designated parking for institutional vehicle when arriving at the courthouse, and then **escort** the inmate to the proper courtroom. 戒護任務是危險的，當你戒護受刑人到法院，你抵達法庭大廈時，應將車子停在提供給機關車輛的指定停車處，然後戒護受刑人前往法庭。

The house was raided. Three suspects were arrested for dealing drugs, and **were scorted** to the police department. 該房子被查抄，三位嫌犯因交易毒品被捕，並被戒護至警察局。

應用　*medical escort* 戒護就醫 (*medical parole* 保外就醫)

---

establish
[ə`stæblɪʃ]
vt. Officers may conduct an immediate search of a vehicle when they **have established** probable cause to believe that evidence of a crime is present in the vehicle. 當員警確認有相當理由可信汽車內出現有犯罪的證據時，得對該汽車立即進行搜索。

Firefighters **established** collapse zones, and keep people outside the collapse zones. 消防員建立了坍塌區，並且將人們隔開在這些坍塌區之外。

ETA
abbr. 預估抵達時間 estimated time of arrival (或 ETOA)

---

ethical
adj. 道德的，合乎道德的

[ˋɛθɪk!]		Although entrapment is not a crime, it is sometimes considered **unethical**. 雖然誘陷不是犯罪，但有時被認為是不道德的。
EUROPOL	*abbr.*	歐盟警察組織 European Police Office
evacuate	*vt.*	撤空，撤離，從……撤退
[ɪˋvækjʊˏet]		Fire drill is a practical method of practicing the evacuation of a building for a fire or emergency. When the fire alarm or smoke detector sounds, the building **is evacuated** as though a real incident had occurred. 消防演習是一個練習在火災或緊急情況時撤離建築物的實際方法，當火災警報或煙霧偵測器響起時，建築物進行撤離，就一如真實事件發生一樣。
		Police **have evacuated** the riverside area. More than 10 thuosand people **have been evacuated from** the city's coastal area. 警方已經將河岸地區撤離，有超過一萬人已經被從城市的海岸地區撤離。
		Firefighters **evacuated** the building. 消防人員撤空了建築物。
	vi.	撤出
		Firefighters could not contain the fire and decided to evacuate because they thought the building could collapse. 消防員無法遏制火勢而決定撤離，因為他們認為建築物可能會倒塌。
evacuation	*n.*	撤空，撤離，撤退，疏散
[ɪˏvækjʊˋeʃən]		An **evacuation** was ordered for the community near the river, Fire Chief said. 消防局長說，已經對於靠近河流的社區下令撤離了。
	應用	*emergency evacuation* 緊急撤離
		evacuation center/shelter 疏散撤離收容中心/所
		evacuation order 撤離命令
		evacuation plan 撤離計畫
		evacuation route 撤離路線
		evacuation training 撤離訓練
		fire evacuation 火災疏散撤離
		forced evacuation 強制疏散撤離
		massive evacuation 大規模疏散撤離
		medical evacuation 醫療後送
evacuee	*n.*	被疏散者
[ɪˏvækjʊˋi]		City government has opened two community centers and five elementary schools for **evacuees.** 市政府已經開啟了兩個社區中心及五所學校給被疏散者。
evade	*vt.*	到躲避，逃避，迴避
[ɪˋved]		Police said that the sex offender used his dead brother's identity

to evade arrest. 警方說 性侵犯使用了死掉的哥哥的身分躲避逮捕。

Police claimed that the man climbed onto the rooftop of his house **to evade the arrest** and accidentally fell off from there. 警方指稱，該名男子為了躲避逮捕爬到房子的屋頂上，然後意外從那裡跌了下來。

evaluate [ɪ`væljʊˌet]	*vt.*	對……評價，為……鑑定

Competence of a witness is determined before evidence is given; credibility of a witness **is evaluated** after evidence is given. 證人的適格是決定於證據提出之前；證人的可信度是評估於證據提出之後。

evaluation [ɪˌvæljʊ`eʃən]	*n.*	估算，評估

If a peaceful assembly escalates to a civil disturbance, the official in charge shall **make an evaluation** as to the additional manpower required to manage the situation. 如果平和的集會升高成為騷動，負責的官員應針對控制情況所需的額外人力進行評估。

evidence [`ɛvədəns]	*n.*	證據

The forensic analyst and examiner will run tests on the **evidence** brought to the lab. 刑事分析人員與鑑識人員會將帶回實驗室的證據進行檢驗。

The court concluded that on the **evidence** presented to it, Mr. Dean was proved to be the driver at the time of the fatal impact with the motor cyclist. 法院認定，依據呈送該院的證據，Dean(林克穎)被證明就是當時撞到機車騎士的司機。

應用

to collect evidence 蒐集證據

to document evidence 記錄證據

to examine evidence 鑑驗證據

to exclude evidence 排除證據

to gather evidence 蒐集證據

to introduce evidence 引入證據

to obtain evidence 取得證據

to present evidence 呈遞證據

to preserve evidence 保存證據

to produce evidence 提出證據

to seize evidence 查扣證據

to suppress evidence (法庭中)不採為證據

to weight evidence 衡量證據

to give evidence 提供證據

admissibility of evidence 證據能力

admissible evidence 有證據能力的證據 (*inadmissible evidence* 無證據能力的證據)

circumstance evidence 情況證據

clear evidence 明確(切確)的證據

computer evidence 電腦證據

concerte evidence 具體證據

corroborating evidence 旁證、佐證、補強證據

corroborative evidence 旁證、佐證、補強證據

credible evidence 可靠 (可信)的證據

digital evidence 數位證據

direct evidence 直接證據

documentary evidence 文書證據

electronic evidence 電子證據

evidence processing room 證物處理室

evidence room 證物室

evidence security bag 物證袋

evidence storage room 證物儲藏室

evidence tape 物證膠帶

false evidence 不實證據

hard evidence 有力證據、鐵證

hearsay evidence 傳聞證據

impression evidence 印痕證據

indirect evidence 間接證據

insufficient evidence 證據不足

irrevelent evidence 無關聯性的證據

oral evidence 口頭證據

physical evidence 物證

preponderance of evidence 優勢的證據

probative evidence 有證明力的證據

property room 證物室

relevancy of evidence 證據關聯性

relevant evidence 關聯性證據

Rule of Evidence 證據規則

scientific evidence 科學證據

solid evidence 確鑿的證據

strong evidence 有力的證據

substantial evidence 實質證據

testimonial evidence 供述證據

took-mark evidence 工具痕跡證據
trace evidence 微物證據
video evidence 影像證據
vital evidence 關鍵證據
wiretap evidence 監聽證據

examination	n.	(刑事的)鑑定，鑑識
[ɪg͵zæmə`neʃən]	應用	*arson examination* 縱火鑑定

audio examinations/voice comparison 聲音鑑定/聲紋比對
chemical examination 化學鑑定
computer examination 電腦鑑定
controlled substance examination 管制物質鑑定
drug residue examination 毒品殘留鑑定
explosive examination 爆裂物鑑定
explosive residue examination 爆裂物殘留鑑定
firearm examination 武器鑑定
glass examination 玻璃鑑定
hair and fiber examination 毛髮與纖維鑑定
image analysis examination 影像分析鑑定
latent print examination 指紋鑑定
polygraph examination 測謊鑑定
questioned document examination 文書鑑定
shoe print and tire thread examination 鞋印及胎痕鑑定
soil examination 土壤鑑定
toolmark examination 工具痕跡鑑定
toxicology examination 毒物鑑定
video examination 影像鑑定

examination	n.	(法庭或證據法的)詰問
[ɪg͵zæmə`neʃən]		

The **examination** of all witnesses during a trial should be conducted fairly and objectively. 審判中對所有證人的詰問，應公平而客觀地進行。

The purpose of **cross-examination** is to discredit a witness. 交互詰問的目的是要打擊證人的信用。

應用 *to conduct examination* 進行詰問
direct examination 主詰問
cross examination 反詰問
redirect examination 覆主詰問
recross examination 覆反詰問

examine	vt.	詰問
[ɪg`zæmɪn]		At trial, the court may **examine** a witness regardless of who calls

		the witness. 審判時，法院得詰問證人，不管證人是誰傳喚的。
	vt.	檢驗，詳細檢查
		If the death of a person is suspicious or unexpected, medical examiner will be required **to examine** the body before the body is to be removed. 如果某人的死亡是可疑或無預期的，法醫就會需要在屍體被移動之前，去檢驗屍體。
	vt.	鑑定，鑑識
		Firearm examiners will **examine** the bullet using a comparison microscope to match the bullet to the gun it was fired from. 槍枝鑑識人員會使用比對比對顯微鏡鑑定子彈，將子彈與發射的槍枝比對吻合。
examiner [ɪgˋzæmɪnɚ]	*n.* 應用	鑑識人員、鑑定人員 *crime-scene examiner* 犯罪現場鑑識人員 *fingerprint examiner* 指紋鑑定人員 *firearms examiner* 槍枝鑑識人員 *forensic examiner* 刑事鑑識人員 *medical examiner* 法醫(*coroner*) *polygraph examiner* 測謊人員 *questioned document examiner* 文書鑑定人員
exchange [ɪksˋtʃendʒ]	*vt.*	交(戰)，交(火) The suspect **exchanged** gunfire **with** police and barricaded himself in a home. 嫌犯與警方槍戰，並且把自己封閉在家裡。
	n.	交戰，交火 Officers surrounded the house and there was an **exchange** of gunfire. Authorities said an armed man was critically wounded during an **exchange** of gunfire with police. 員警將房子包圍並發生槍戰，當局說，有一位持槍的男子在與警方槍戰過程中嚴重受傷。
exclude [ɪkˋsklud]	*vt.*	把……排除在外，不包括[(+from)] The exclusionary rule is used to **exclude** or suppress evidence obtained in violation of an accused person's constitutional rights. 排除法則，是用來排除或駁回違反被告憲法權利之下所取得的證據。 The court may **exclude** evidence obtained in violation of an accused person's constitutional rights. 法院得排除違反被告憲法權利之下所取得的證據。
exclusion [ɪkˋskluʒən]	*n.*	排斥，排除在外，(美國移民法)拒絕入境 US Congress enacted the term removal to refer to both **exclusion** and deportation. **Exclusion** is designed to prevent the

alien from staying in the country when he has not been admitted on a visa at the port of entry. 美國國會立法用遣返(removal)一字來指拒絕入境(exclusion)與遣送(deportation)兩者，拒絕入境(exclusion)的設計是為了讓外國人在入境港埠還沒准予依簽證入境時，就防止其在國內留下。

execute	*vt.*	實行，執行，將……處死
[`ɛksɪ,kjut]		

Police **executed** a search warrant at the suspect's house, where they found four loaded firearms. Earlier this week, police had obtained the search warrant based on information from an informant. 警方在他家執行搜索票，在那裡警方發現四把裝填彈藥了的武器，這星期稍早，警方依據線民的資訊即已取得了搜索票。

The murderer **wes executed** last week. 殺人犯在上周已經伏法了。

execution	*n.*	實行，執行，處決
[,ɛksɪ`kjuʃən]		

Shooting, lethal injection, and electrocution are common methods of **execution**. 槍決、注射、電刑是常見的執行方式。

應用 *execution chamber* 刑場 (或 *death chamber*)

exercise	*vt.*	(權力，權利等的)行使，運用
[`ɛksə,saɪz]	應用	*to exercise due care* 行使注意義務

to exercise jurisdiction over 對……行使管轄權
to exercise official power 行使公權力
to exercise one's right not to testify 行使不作證的權利
to exercise good judgment 運用良好了判斷
to exercise control over 行使對……的控制
to exercise reasonable diligence 盡合理注意
to exercise due diligence 盡注意義務

exhale	*vi.*	呼氣，吐氣，吹氣
[ɛks`hel]		

Police asked the driver **to exhale** into the mouthpiece. The driver then breathed into the mouthpiece. The driver blew into the mouthpiece for three 5 seconds. 警方要求駕駛人對著吹嘴呼氣，於是駕駛人對著吹嘴吹氣，駕駛人吹入吹嘴有 5 秒鐘。

exhibit	*n.*	【律】證據物件，物證物件
[ɪg`zɪbɪt]		

Prosecuter: Mr. Jones, I hand you a paper here marked **exhibit 1**, and I ask you to state what this is.

檢察官：瓊斯先生，我這裡手上拿給你的一張紙，標示著 [物證 1 (exhibit 1)]，我請你說明這是甚麼。

Mr. Jones: It is a letter fom my ex-girlfriend.

瓊斯先生：那是我前女友給我的一封信。

【補充說明 exhibit】
證據物件(exhibit)是證據，通常是文件，被標示了標記以便法院及另一造知道目前所討論的證據是哪一件。證據物件通常會用字母標記例如 Exhibit A、Exhibit B 或 Exhibit C；或用數字標記例如 Exhibit 1、Exhibit 2 或 Exhibit 3。 (An exhibit, often a document, is evidence that is marked so that the court and the other side can know what piece of evidence you are discussing. Exhibits are usually marked with letters (Exhibit A, Exhibit B, Exhibit C, etc) or numbers (exhibit 1, Exhibit 2, Exhibit 3, etc)

exigent [ˈɛksədʒənt]	n.	緊急的，危急的，急需的 **Exigent search** is a warrantless search carried out under **exigent** circumstances, but police cannot create **exigent** reasons for the emergency by their own actions. 急迫搜索是一種在急迫情況下所執行的無票搜索，警察不可以用自己的行為，來為緊急情況製造急迫原因。
expel [ɪkˈspɛl]	vt.	驅逐，趕走 The defendant's family **was expelled from** the courtroom for interrupting the judge and mocking the plaintiffs. 被告的家人因為打斷法官講話以及嘲笑原告，被逐出了法庭。
	vt.	開除 The student **was expelled from** school for smoking marijuana. 該名學生因為吸大麻而被學校開除。
expert [ˈɛkspɚt]	n. 應用	專家 *expert witness* 專家證人 *expert testimony* 專家證詞
expire [ɪkˈspaɪr]	vi.	屆期，(期限)終止 If your passport **has expired** but the US visa in it is still valid, you just have to renew your passport and travel with both old and new passport. The visa does not **expire** with the passport. 如果你的護照到期了，但是護照內的美國簽證還有效的話，你就只需要換新照護，並帶著新舊兩本護照旅行。簽證不回隨著護照而過期。
	vi.	呼氣，吐氣，斷氣 Although EMS was called, the victim **expired** at the scene. 雖然有呼叫急救醫療服務，但是被害人在現場就已經斷氣了。
explode [ɪkˈsplod]	vt.	燃放 Many cities enact rules that it shall be unlawful for any person to **explode** any dangerous fireworks or **explode** any rocket, firecracker, Roman candle, sparkler, or other explosive substance,

except with permission by a public agency. 許多城市制訂規定，任何人燃放任何危險爆竹煙火，或燃放沖天炮、鞭炮、焰火筒、仙女棒，或其他爆裂物質者，是違法的，除非是有公務機關許可。

exploitation	*n.*	剝削
[ˌɛksplɔɪˈteʃən]		

Any person may choose to be smuggled into another country, but when a person is forced into a situation of **exploitation** and their freedom is taken away, he or she is then a victim of human trafficking. 任何人都可以選擇被偷渡到另一個國家，但是當某個人被迫變成一個被奪走自由的剝削狀態時，這個人就成為人口販運的被害人。

financial exploitation 財產上的剝削

應用 *sex (sexual) exploitation* 性剝削

explosion	*n.*	爆炸
[ɪkˈsploʒən]		

The victims were shopping when the **explosion** occurred. It wasn't clear what caused the **explosion**. 爆炸發生時，被害人正在逛街。造成爆炸的原因目前尚不清楚。

explosive	*n.*	爆裂物，炸藥
[ɪkˈsplosɪv]	*adj.*	爆炸(性)的，爆發性的

應用 *explosive substance* 爆裂物質

explosive examination 爆裂物鑑定

explosive residue examination 爆裂物殘留鑑定

expose	*vt.*	使……暴露於，使……接觸到[(+to)]
[ɪkˈspoz]		

Many women **are** constantly **exposed to** marital violence, but such violence is often treated as a family matter. 許多婦女經常暴露於婚姻暴力，但這樣的暴力卻常被當成家務事處理。

Experts said if a building **is exposed to** heavy fire for 20 minutes or more, it may be too dangerous to enter. 專家說，如果一間建築物已經暴露在大火 20 分鐘或更長的話，要進去就可能會太危險。

Several first responders **were exposed to** the poisonous fumes. They were taken to the hospital to be examined. Fortunately, they were not injured. 好幾位初期應變者暴露在有毒煙氣中，他們被送到醫院檢查，幸運地，他們沒有受傷。

extend	*vt.*	延長，延伸
[ɪkˈstɛnd]		

You may apply **to extend** your stay if you were lawfully admitted into our country. If your job **is extended**, you must apply **to extend** your work permit. 如果你是合法入境本國，你可以申請延長停留，如果你的工作延長了，你必須申請延長你的工

		作許可。
extension	*n.*	延長，延期
[ɪk`stɛnʃən]		If you commit any crime during your stay in the country, this will make you ineligible for re-entry or **extension**. 如果你在這國家停留的期間內從事任何犯罪的話，這會讓你不合於重入境或延期。
extinguish	*vt.*	撲滅(火)
[ɪk`stɪŋgwɪʃ]		In the event of a fire, do not attempt **to extinguish** the fire unless you activate the fire alarm to notify building occupants of the emergency. 萬一火災時，不要試想著要去滅火，除非你開啟了火災警鈴通報大樓住戶該緊急事件。
		The blaze **was** quickly **extinguished**. 這場火很快地就被撲滅了。
		Fire crews **extinguished** the blaze, but the car was destroyed. 消防同仁撲滅了火災，但車子已經被毀了。
extinguisher	*n.*	滅火器
[ɪk`stɪŋgwɪʃɚ]		Do not attempt to fight a large or spreading fire with a **fire extinguisher**. Make sure you have activated the fire alarm before you use an **extinguisher**. 不要想用滅火器去撲滅大火或是蔓延的火災，要確保你在使用滅火器之前，已經先啟動火災警鈴。
	應用	*carbon dioxide fire extinguisher* 二氧化碳滅火器
		dry chemical fire extinguisher 乾式化學滅火器
		dry powder fire extinguisher 乾粉滅火器
		hand held fire extinguisher 手持式滅火器
		portable fire extinguisher 攜帶式滅火器
		water and foam fire extinguisher 泡沫水滅火器
extort	*vt.*	敲詐，勒索
[ɪk`stɔrt]		The victim said she **was extorted by** a man who claimed to have indecent photos of her. 被害人說她被一名聲稱有她不雅照片的男子所勒索。
extortion	*n.*	敲詐，勒索
[ɪk`stɔrʃən]		Simpson was arrested on charges of robbery, **extortion** and using his position as a police officer to commit criminal acts. 辛普森被逮捕，被指控強盜、勒索及使用警察職務從事犯罪行為。
extract	*vt.*	(供詞的)取，用力取出，使勁拔出，抽出
[ɪk`strækt]		A confession is inadmissible if it **is extracted by** any sort of coercion, threatening, physical restraint or violence, or extended

interrogation. 白自如果是取自於強制、威脅、強暴或疲勞訊問的方式，是無證據能力的。

Patients that are tagged red or "immediate" are **to be extracted** first, followed by those tagged yellow or "delayed". 被標示紅色或「立即(immediate)」的傷患要優先被撤出來，之後是標示黃色或「暫緩(delayed)」的。

extricate [`ɛkstrɪ,ket]	*vt.*	使擺脫，解救 Firefighter **extricated** two victims trapped inside the voids. 消防員解救出兩名受困在空隙內的遇難者。
extraditable [`ɛkstrə,daɪtəb!]	*adj.*	可引渡的 In the extradition proceedings, court must determine whether the fugitive **is extraditable**. If the court finds the fugitive **to be extraditable**, he would be surrendered to the requesting government. 在引渡程序中，法院必須決定逃犯是否可引渡，如果法院認定逃犯為可引渡的話，他就會被遞解給請求國政府。
extradite [`ɛkstrə,daɪt]	*vt.*	引渡(逃犯)

US-UK Extradition Treaty

ARTICLE 1 Obligation to Extradite

The Parties agree to extradite to each other, pursuant to the provisions of this Treaty, persons sought by the authorities in the Requesting State for trial or punishment for extraditable offenses.

美國與英國引渡條約
第 1 條　引渡義務
締約各方同意，依照本條約之條文，對於請求國基於審判或處罰可引渡之犯罪而請求之人，予以引渡他方。

While common law countries will **extradite** their own nationals, it should be noted that many countries, primarily civil law countries, prohibit the extradition of their own nationals. 儘管普通法系國家會引渡本國國民，應注意的是，很多國家—主要是大陸法系國家—禁止引渡本國國民。

extraditable [`ɛkstrə,daɪtəb!]	*adj.*	可引渡的 Money laundering is an **extraditable** offence. 洗錢是一項可引渡之罪。
extradition [,ɛkstrə`dɪʃən]	*n.*	引渡 The day after the suspect's arrest, prosecutor said he planned to

seek his extradition to face trial in the court, but **extradition proceedings** can take years to complete. 嫌犯被捕次日，檢察官說，他打算請求引渡該人以面對法院的審判，但引渡程序會耗時數年完成。

A country may wish **to obtain the extradition of** a fugitive whose whereabouts is located abroad. 當逃犯的下落在國外被查到時，國家可能希望取得逃犯的引渡。

Many countries will **grant extradition** only when there is a treaty or convention for **extradition** with the foreign government. 許多國家通常只在與外國政府訂有引渡條約或公約時，才會給予引渡。

extremist [ɪkˋstrimɪst]	n.	極端主義者，過激分子
eyewitness [ˋaɪˏwɪtnɪs]	n.	目擊證人
fair [fɛr]	adj.	The right to a **fair trial** is a basic human right. 公平審判的權利是一項基本人權。 At appeal, the defendant argued that the district court was not **fair and just**. 上訴時，被告主張地方法院不公平公正。
faithful [ˋfeθfəl]	adj.	忠實的，忠誠的，忠貞的 [(+to)] As law enforcement officers, we **are faithful to** the law. We **are faithful to** our mission and to our organization. 身為執法人員，我們對法律忠誠，我們對我們的使命及組織忠誠。
fake [fek]	adj. 應用	假的，冒充的 *fake accident* 假車禍（或 *staged auto accident; staged car crash*） *fake address* 假地址 *fake diamond* 假鑽石 *fake identity* 假身分 *fake marriage* 假結婚(或 *marriage fraud; fraudulent marriage; sham-marriage*) *fake name* 假名 *fake note* 假鈔，偽鈔
false [fɔls]	adj. 應用	不正確的，不真實的，假的 *false accusation* 誣告 *false alarm* 假警報 *false alibi* 假的不在場證明(*give false alibi*) *false answer* 虛假的回應 *false arrest* 不法逮捕，非法拘留（又稱 *wrongful arrest*）

false certificate 虛假的證件

false confession 不實的自白

false imprisonment 錯誤的監禁

false memory 錯誤的記憶

false police complaint 不實的報案(*to file false police complaint* 做不實的報案)

false report 謊報(*to make false report* 做謊報)

false statement 不實的陳述(*to make false statement* 做不實的陳述)

false testimony 不實的證詞

fault [fɔlt]	*n.*	(法律上因為過失的) 責任，過錯，瑕疵
		The plaintiff claims the defendant **was at fault** in that he was negligent. The court found the plaintiff 25 % **at fault** and defendant 75 % **at fault**. 原告主張被告因為有過失而有責任。法院判決原告有百分之 25 的責任，而被告有百分之 75 的責任。
fasten [`fæsn]	*vt.*	扣緊，繫緊
		The driver and all passengers in the vehicle must **fasten** a seat belt. 保持您的安全帶繫好，車內的駕駛人及所有乘客都必須繫上安全帶。
	應用	*to buckle up* 繫安全帶 *to buckle your seat belt* 繫安全帶 *to keep seat belt fastened* 繫安全帶 *to fasten seat belt* 繫安全帶 *to wear seat belt* 繫安全帶
fatal [`fet!]	*adj.*	致命的，生死攸關的，無可挽回的，毀滅性的
		City police department was called to a hit-and-run crash which resulted in a fatality. Officers are still searching for the **fatal** hit-and-run suspect. 市警局被呼叫前往一件導致死傷的肇事逃逸車禍，員警仍在尋找該起致命肇事逃逸的嫌犯。
fatality [fə`tælətɪ]	*n.*	(因意外事故的)死亡，死者，死亡事故，災禍
		Officers must understand that high-speed pursuits may end in a crash and result in a **fatality**. 員警必須了解，高速追逐可能會以撞車結束並造成死亡。
felon [`fɛlən]	*n.*	重罪犯
		An aider is someone who, knowing that a **felon** has finished committing a crime helps the **felon** avoid arrest or trial. 幫助犯是指一個知悉重罪罪犯已經完成犯罪，而幫助該重罪罪犯逃避逮捕或審判的人。

felony [ˋfɛlənɪ]	*n.*	重罪 In the United States, criminal law divides crimes into two main categories: **felony** and misdemeanor. 在美國，刑法將犯罪分為兩大類：重罪與輕罪。

---

fictitious [fɪkˋtɪʃəs]	*adj.*	假的，假裝的，虛構的，非真實的 Accounts must not be opened or operated in **fictitious** names. 帳戶的開立或操作，不可以用假名。
	應用	*fictitious account* 假帳戶 *fictitious name* 假名 *fictitious story* 虛構的故事 *fictitious website* 虛構的網站

---

field sobriety test		現場清醒測試

---

fight [faɪt]	*vt.*	打（仗），與……作戰，與……鬥爭 A total of 50 firefighters **fought** the blaze, which was brought under control shortly after midnight. 總計有五十名消防員在滅火，而這場火在子夜過後不久被控制住。
	vi.	戰，鬥，打鬥 The witness testified that the defendant and the victim **were fighting** when the fatal shots were fired. 證人作證表示，致命的槍擊發射時，被告與被害人正在打鬥。 The man was caught on a surveillance camera as he **fought with** the cashier. Suddenly he set fire to a store and then set the car outside ablaze with a lighter. 這名男子跟店員打鬥的時後正被監視器拍到。突然間，他就對店家放火，然後點火燒了汽車。
	n.	打鬥 During the **fight**, someone pulled out a gun and fired shots. 打鬥的過程中，有人掏出一把槍並開了好幾槍。

---

file [faɪl]	*vt.* 應用	提出(申請等)，提起(訴訟等)　(或 lodge) *to file a petition for asylum* 提出庇護請求 *to file a request with immigration officer* 向移民官員提出請求 *to file action against* 對……提出訴訟 *to file appeal* 提起上訴 *to file charge* 提起告訴 *to file criminal charge* 提起刑事告訴 *to file complaint* 報案 *to file lawsuit* 提起法律訴訟 *to file motion* 提出聲請 *to file petition* 提起請願

---

find	*vt.*	(經司法調查後的)裁決，認定，判定；(陪審團的)裁決，認定，

[faɪnd]		判定

Ladies and gentlemen of the jury, have you reached a verdict? Yes we have, your honor. We **find** the defendant guilty. 「陪審團先生及女士，你們已經做成判決了嗎？是的，庭上。我們認定被告有罪。」

The jury **found** him guilty of murder. This Court **finds that** the evidence presented at trial was sufficient for the trial judge to determine beyond a reasonable doubt that defendant is guilty of murder. 陪審團認定他謀殺罪成立。本院認定，審判所提的證據足以讓審理法官決定被告成立殺人罪，無合理可疑之處。

vi. 裁決，判決

Defendant's dogs killed plaintiff's cat. The trial court found for the plaintiffs. The trial court **found that** defendant was negligent. 被告的狗弄死了原告的狗，審理法院做出有利原告的判決，審理法院認定被告有過失。

應用 *to find for* (人)【律】做出對（人）有利的裁決

In a civil case, the verdict is usually "We the jury **find for** the plaintiff" or "We the jury **find for** the defendant." 在在民事案件中，裁決通常是：「本陪審團認定有利原告」，或「本陪審團認定有利被告」。

finding [ˈfaɪndɪŋ]	*n.*	【律】(正式法律調查後的) 裁決，判決

The appellate court decided that the trial court's **finding** was supported by the facts and evidence. 上訴法院認為地方法院的裁判有事實與證據作為支撐。

fine [faɪn]	*n.*	(刑事的)罰金，(行政的)罰鍰

A judge may convert the imprisonment into a **fine**. But if the **fine** is not paid, it may be converted into imprisonment. 法官得將徒刑易科為罰金，但如果罰金未繳納時，得易科為監禁。

In New York, the driver and front-seat passenger would **be fined** up to $50 if they're not wearing a seat belt. 在紐約，駕駛人與前座乘客如果沒有繫安全帶，會被罰 50 美金以上。

fingerprint [ˈfɪŋɡɚˌprɪnt]	*n.*	指紋
	應用	*to collect fingerprint* 採集指紋

to take fingerprint 採集指紋

to enhance fingerprint 讓指紋顯相

fingerprint comparison 指紋比對

fingerprint examiner 指紋鑑定人員

latent fingerprint 指紋

fire	*vi.*	開火，射擊[(+at)]

[faɪr]

The two burglars allegedly broke into a home, shot a man, and then **fired at** officers during a chase. 這兩名竊賊涉嫌侵入一戶住家，開槍擊中一名男子，然後在追逐中對著員警開槍。

n. 砲火，火力

The officer **returned fire** and arrested the shooter. 員警開槍還擊，並逮捕了開槍者。

n. 火，火災

Firefighter said at least two arsonists **set** the vehicle **on fire** using a flammable liquid. The **fire** spreaded quickly. 消防員說，至少兩名縱火犯使用可燃液體點火燒車，火勢蔓延迅速。

He said his building **was on fire** when firefighters started knocking on everyone's apartment doors. 他說他的房子起火了的當時，消防員開始對公寓逐戶敲門。

應用 *apartment fire* 公寓火災

arson fire 縱火

fire alarm system 火災警報系統

fire alarm 火災警報

fire attack 滅火

fire blanket 防火毯

fire cause investigation 火災原因調查

fire death 火災死亡

fire department 消防局、消防部門

fire detection system 火災偵測系統

fire door 防火門

fire drill 消防演習

fire engine 消防車

fire exit 火災逃生出口

fire extinguisher 滅火器

fire hose 消防水帶

fire hydrant system 消防栓系統

fire hydrant 消防栓

fire investigation 火災調查

fire origin 起火點、火源

fire prevention 火災預防

fire scene reconstruction 火場重建

fire scene 火災現場

fire truck 消防車

fire wall 防火牆

high-rise fire 高樓大火

home fire 家庭火災

residential fire 住宅火災

structure fire (或 *structural fire*) 建物火災

to attack fire 滅火

to catch fire 著火

to extinguish fire 滅火

to fire several shots at 朝……開了數槍

to open fire at 對……開槍射擊

to put out fire 滅火

to return fire 開槍還擊

to set fire to 對……放火

to start a fire 放火

firearms [`faɪr,ɑrmz]	*n.*	武器，槍砲(尤指手槍) Every day, law enforcement officers must draw their **firearms** for the defense of the public, fellow officers, and themselves. 每天，執法人員必須拔槍以保衛公眾、同僚及自己。 Defendant appeals from his conviction on **firearms charges**. 被告對於他的槍枝案件的有罪判決提起上訴。 Many **firearms examiners** also perform tool mark **comparisons**. 許多槍枝鑑識人員同時也從事工具痕跡的比對。
	應用	*firearms smuggling ring* 槍械走私集團 *firearms trafficking* 槍械走私 *firearms training* 武器訓練 *homemade firearms* 改造槍枝、土製槍枝
fireboat [`faɪr,bot]	*n.*	救火船，消防船
firecracker [`faɪr,krækə]	*n.*	鞭炮
fireground [faɪr graʊnd]]	*n.*	火場 Fire department said that large structures are required by law to contain standpipe systems to eliminate the loss of time between their arrival at the **fireground** and initiation of fire attack. 消防局說，大型建築物依法應有給水立管系統，以便消除「抵達火場之後到開始滅火」之間損失的時間。
firefighter [`faɪr,faɪtə]	*n.* 應用	消防員 *career firefighter* 專職消防員 *volunteer firefighter* 義消
fireman	*n.*	消防隊員，救火隊員

[ˋfaɪrmən]

fireworks	n.	爆竹煙火
[ˋfaɪrˏwɝks]		

flame	n.	火焰，火舌
[flem]		

There was a lot of smoke, a lot of **flames**. Residents attempted to put out the flames. Minutes later, the house was fully engulfed in **flames**. 有很大的煙，很大的火，住戶試圖滅火。幾分鐘之後，這個房子就全部被吞噬在火焰中了。

The major risks of firefighting are created by the **flames**, heat, smoke and toxic gases produced by fire. 消防員的主要風險是產生自火焰、熱氣、煙霧及有害氣體。

Suddenly I heard an explosion and I looked outside and saw the building **in flames**. 突然，我聽到一聲爆炸，我往外看，並看到建築物陷入了火焰中。

flammable	adj.	易燃的，可燃的，速燃的
[ˋflæməb!]		

Firefighter said at least two arsonists set the vehicle on fire using a **flammable** liquid. The fire spreaded quickly. 消防員說，至少兩名縱火犯用可燃液體點火燒車，火勢迅速蔓延。

flashover	n.	閃燃【電】閃絡
[ˋflæʃˏovɚ]		

Fire scene reconstruction is based upon burn pattern analysis, burn rates, **flashover**, ventilation, etc. 火場重建依據的是燃燒型態分析、燃燒率、閃燃、排煙等等。

flee	vi.	逃，逃走
[fli]		

The suspect inflicted injury upon the officer and then began to **flee**. 嫌犯對員警施加傷害，然後開始逃逸。

He robbed the bank and **fled with** the cash. He **fled with** the accomplice on a motorbike. 他搶了銀行然後帶著現金逃走，他與共犯乘摩托車逃走。

	vt.	逃避，逃離

He decided to **flee** the police. So he **fled the scene**. He **fled** the prusuing officers for a few hundred meters and was found by authorities a couple of blocks away. 他決定逃避警方，所以他逃離了現場，他逃離追逐員警有數百公尺，然後在幾個轉角之遠被找到。

The District Commander has confirmed that the **fleeing suspect** was connected to the bank robbery occurred last week. 分局長證實逃逸的嫌犯與上星期發生的銀行搶案有關。

footprint	n.	腳印
[ˋfʊtˏprɪnt]		

footwear impression	*n.*	鞋印
force	*vt.*	強迫，迫使，勉強作出
[fors]		Officers encountered the armed suspect and **were forced to** return fire to protect their own lives. 員警迎面遭遇攜械嫌犯，並被迫開槍還擊保護自身的性命。
	n.	力，力量，武力
		A police officer or a peace officer may use **physical force** in the course of making an arrest or preventing the escape from custody of an offender. 員警或治安人員於進行逮捕或防止人犯逃脫拘禁之際，得使用身體武力。

應用 *deadly force* 致命的武力
excessive force 過度的武力
excessive use of force 過度的武力使用
forced labor 強迫勞力
nondeadly force 非致命的武力
reasonable force 合理的武力
tactical force 攻堅武力，攻堅部隊
task force 專案組
Joint Task Force 聯合專案組
Special Task Force 特勤組、特勤部隊

forcible	*adj.*	強迫的，強制的
[`forsəb!]		We tried to open the front door, it was locked. We had to make **forcible** entry into the residence, officer said. 員警說，「我們試著打開前門，門是鎖著的，我們必須強行進入這間住宅」。

應用 *forcible entry* 強行進入(*to make a forcible entry*)
forcible rape 強制性交
forcible confinement 私行拘禁

forensic	*adj.*	法醫的
[fə`rɛnsɪk]	應用	*foreisic scientist* 刑事鑑識科學專家

forensic analyst 刑事分析人員
forensic anthropology 法醫人類學
forensic chemistry 鑑識化學
forensic entomology 刑事昆蟲學
forensic evidence 刑事鑑識證據
forensic examination 刑事鑑定
forensic examiner 刑事鑑識人員
forensic expert 刑事鑑識專家
forensic lab 刑事實驗室
forensic photography 刑事攝影學

forensic science laboratory 刑事實驗室
Forensic Science 刑事科學（或稱 *Forensics*）
forensic serology 刑事血清學

foreperson [ˋforpɚsn]	*n.* 應用	(陪審團的)首席 *deputy foreperson*(陪審團的)副首席

forfeit [ˋfɔr,fɪt] *vt.* (因犯罪、失職、違約等)喪失(權利、名譽、生命等)

The judge may decide to admit the defendant to bail, but if a condition of the bond is breached, the court will declare the bail **forfeited**. 法官得決定准予被告交保，但如果違背交保條件的話，法院會宣告沒收保釋金。

forfeiture [ˋfɔrfɪtʃɚ] *n.* (財產等的)沒收，(權利、名譽等的)喪失

Criminal forfeiture operates as punishment for a crime. As US former President George Bush said, "**Asset forfeiture** laws allow the government to take the ill-gotten gains and use them to put more cops on the streets." 刑事沒收是用來當作犯罪的處罰，一如美國前總統喬治布希說的，「資產沒收的法律讓政府拿走不義之財，並用以增加更多的警察在街上」。

forge [fɔrdʒ] *vt.* 偽造，編造

She **forged** a suicide note to make the murder look like a suicide. 他偽造了一張自殺字條，讓這起謀殺看起來像是自殺。

forgery [ˋfɔrdʒərɪ] *n.* 偽造文書

Passport **forgery** is a serious offense. People may use **forged** passport to gain entry into another country. A passport **forger** may steal a passport, then erase and reprint information. **Forger** may also obtain a valid passport by using a fraudulent name. Furthermore, a **forger** could steal a valid passport and assume that person's identity. 護照偽造是嚴重的犯罪，人們可能會使用偽造護照來進入另一個國家，護照偽造者會偷取護照，然後擦掉資訊並重印，偽造者也可能用假名來取得合法有效的護照，此外偽造者也會偷取合法有效的護照，並僭用該人的身分。

forgive [fəˋgɪv] *vt.* 原諒，寬恕[(+for)]

The plaintiff said he **forgave** the defendant for his mistake. 原告表示他原諒了被告的錯誤。

forgiveness [fəˋgɪvnɪs] *n.* 原諒，寬恕

Forgiveness of the victim and the victim's family is one of the basic considerations in imposing a sentence on the perpetrator of a crime. 被害人及其家人的寬恕，是對犯罪行為者所犯之罪在科以刑罰時的一項基本考慮事項。

foster	*vt.*	促進
[`fɔstɚ]		Hosting liaison meetings can **foster** cooperation between prosecutors and the police. 聯繫會議的舉行可以強化檢警的合作。
	adj.	養育的，收養的
	應用	*foster care* 寄養照顧
		foster child 領養的小孩
		foster family 寄養家庭
		foster home 寄養家庭
		foster father/mother 養父/養母

frame	*n.*	架構，骨架，結構
[frem]	*vt.*	【俚】陷害 (指因虛假或捏造的證據而變成有罪)
		The convicted person claimed that he **was framed by** the police. He said he **was framed for** the murder that he did not commit. 被判刑之人聲稱她被警察陷害，他說他因為一件不是他所犯的殺人罪而被陷害。

fraud	*n.*	欺騙，詐騙
[frɔd]		In recent years, **frauds** are on the rise. 近年來，詐欺不斷增加。
	應用	*bank fraud* 銀行詐欺(騙)
		computer fraud 電腦詐欺(騙)
		credit card fraud 信用卡詐欺(騙)
		document fraud 證件詐欺(騙)
		health care fraud 健保詐欺(騙)
		insurance fraud 保險詐欺(騙)
		internet auction fraud 網拍詐欺(騙)
		internet fraud 網路詐欺(騙)
		investment fraud 投資詐欺(騙)
		marriage fraud 婚姻詐騙(騙)
		online auction fraud 線上拍賣詐欺(騙)
		staged auto accident fraud 假車禍案件詐欺(騙)

fraudulent	*adj.*	欺詐的，欺騙的，騙得的，騙取的
[`frɔdʒələnt]		Marriage fraud is also known as **fraudulent** marriage, sham-marriage or fake marriage. 婚姻詐騙又稱假結婚 (fraudulent marriage、sham-marriage 或 fake marriage)。

free	*adj.*	自由的
[fri]		The police **set** the man **free** when they decided that there was not enough evidence to charge him with a crime. 當警方認定沒有足夠的證據指控該人犯罪時，便將該人釋放了。
		The man who confessed to the murder may **go free** because

		authorities say there simply isn't enough evidence to win the prosecution. 坦承謀殺的那個人很可能就這樣沒事了，因為當局說，根本沒有足夠的證據可贏得起訴。
	adv.	自由地 The suspect walked **free** on bail. 嫌犯交保後就行動自由了。
	vt.	使…自由，解放 They were held hostage for 20 hours before **being freed by** SWAT team. 他們被挾持了 20 小時，才被 SWAT(特種武器與戰術部隊)解救自由。
freedom [`fridəm]	*n.* 應用	自由，自由權，獨立自主 *freedom of assembly* 集會自由 *freedom of expression* 表現自由 *freedom of religion* 宗教自由 *freedom of speech* 言論自由
freeway [`frɪ,we]	*n.*	【美】高速公路
freeze [friz]	*vi.*	(警察用語) 站住不動 **Freeze!** You are under arrest. 不要動，你被捕了。
frisk [frɪsk]	*n.*	【口】(用手或探測器)搜身 Unless a police officer has probable cause to make an arrest or a reasonable suspicion to conduct a **stop and frisk**, a person is generally not required to answer an officer's questions or allow an officer to conduct a search. 除非員警有相當理由進行逮捕，或有合理懷疑進行攔阻及搜身(stop and frisk) ，否則一般而言，任何人並不需要回答員警的問題，或讓員警進行搜索。
fugitive [`fjudʒətɪv]	*n.* 應用	逃亡者，逃犯，亡命者 He is a **gugitive** from justice. 他是一名司法通緝犯。 *fugitive from justice* 逃犯 *wanted fugitive* 通緝犯 *to arrest fugitive* 逮捕逃犯 *to locate fugitive* 找到逃犯 *to pursue fugitive* 追緝逃犯 *to apprehend fugitive* 逮捕逃犯 *to capture fugitive* 逮捕逃犯
gain [gen]	*vt.*	取得控制 The suspect retreated to his car as backup officers arrived. The officers on scene **gained control of** the situation and arrested the man later that day. 支援警力抵達後，嫌犯撤回到他的車子，當天後來，現場的員警控制狀況並將該男子逮捕。

The fire broke out on the 20th floor of high-rise. Firefighters contained the fire around noon. Fire crews immediately **gained control of** the blaze. 消防同仁立刻遏制了火勢。火災發生在高樓的第 20 層，消防員大約在中午控制住火勢。

On arrival, police **gained entry to** the building and discovered around 200 cannabis plants in one bedroom. 警方到場後，找到建築物入口的入口並在其中一間房間找到 200 株大麻。

Police said the offender broke the front window and **gained access to** the building. 警方說犯罪者打破前方的玻璃並進到大樓內。

---

gamble [ˋgæmbl]	*vi.*	賭博

They took a vacation to Las Veges, stayed at the hotel and **gambled** in the casino every night. 他們去拉斯維加斯度假，待在飯店並且每天晚上都在賭場賭博。

Police raided the house, and 10 people were arrested on **gambling** charges. 警方突擊掃蕩該屋，而有 10 人被捕並以賭博罪指控。

【補充說明】casino 賭場 gambling house/den/hell 賭場，賭窟，按 casino 通常附有住宿，飲食及其它娛樂，gambling house 通常只供賭博。如果是非法賭場，可先加 illegal 或 unlawful。

---

gang [gæŋ]	*n.*	幫派

應用	
gang violence 幫派暴力	
street gang 街頭幫派	
rival gang 敵對幫派	

---

gangster [ˋgæŋstɚ]	*n.*	幫派分子

---

gas [gæs]	n.	氣體，瓦斯 【美】【口】汽油

Firefighters were called to the apartment near K street around 4 p.m. for a reported odor of **natural gas.** 消防員在下午四點被請求前往 K 街，據報有瓦斯氣味。

應用

deadly gas 致命的氣體

gas cylinder 瓦斯鋼瓶

gas detector 瓦斯偵測器

gas emission 氣體外洩

gas leaking 氣體外洩

gas mask 防毒面具

gas water heater 瓦斯熱水器

natural gas explosion 天然氣爆炸

natural gas 天然氣

noxious gas 有毒氣體

gathering [`gæðərɪŋ]	*n.* 應用	集會，聚集 *spontaneous gathering* 自發性的聚集
gear [gɪr]	*n.* 應用	（尤指特種用途的）衣服 *fire gear* 消防服裝

get

[gɛt]

vi. 變成，成為，被……[+v-ed]

Criminal stages a crime scene to misdirect investigators so as to **get away with** the crime. 罪犯會假造一個犯罪現場來誤導偵查人員，以逃避犯罪。(get away with 受到(較輕的懲罰)，【口】不因某事受懲罰)

Somebody **got shot**! **Get down**! Get down! Everybody get down! 有人中彈了，趴下，趴下，大家趴下。

If you **get** a traffic ticket, you can challenge the law enforcement officer who has given you the ticket and **get** it dismissed. 如果你拿到罰單，你可以挑戰開單的執法人員，而讓罰單被撤銷。

The murder suspect **got** 20 years in prison after guilty plea for murder. 謀殺案嫌犯認罪之後，獲判 20 年徒刑。

getaway

[`gɛtə,we]

n. 逃走

Police released video that shows the possible **getaway** car used by the suspect. Later, the black **getaway** vehicle used by the suspects involved in the campus shootout has been found, police said. 警方公布了影帶，顯示了嫌犯可能使用的逃逸車輛。之後，警方說，涉及該起校園槍擊案的嫌犯所使用的黑色逃逸車輛已經找到。

go

[go]

vi. 便成，處於……的狀態

go free 脫離束縛，自由

The man who confessed to the murder may **go free** because authorities say there simply isn't enough evidence to win the prosecution. 坦承謀殺的那個人很可能就這樣沒事了，因為當局說，根本沒有足夠的證據可贏得起訴。

go missing 失蹤

Police have pubicly identified the prime suspect in the case of the student who **went missing** three years ago on his way to school and have asked the public for help with their investigation. 警方公開指出三年前在上學途中失蹤學生一案中的的主要嫌犯，並請大眾協助他們調查。

go undetected 沒被發現

In the UK, it is estimated that 65% of all fraudulent insurance claims **go undetected**. 在英國，估計有百分之六十五的詐欺

保險請領沒有被發現。

go unpunished 沒受處罰

The victim was shot in the chest and died. His family says all they want is justice and that this crime should not **go unpunished**. 被害人胸部中彈而死，他的家人說他們所要的是正義，並且這個犯罪不可以就這樣沒受到處罰。*go unreported* 沒有報案

For some reasons, many sexual harassment cases **go unreported**. 因為一些原因，很多騷擾案件沒有被報案。

go unsolved 沒有結案/破案

In the US, the clearance rate for arsons is low. Statistics show that many arson cases often **go unsolved**. 在美國，縱火的破案率是低的，統計顯示，許多縱火案件常常沒有破案。

應用 *go free* 脫離束縛，自由

go missing 失蹤

go undetected 沒被發現

go unpunished 沒受處罰

go unreported 沒有報案

go unsolved 沒有破案/結案

---

go-between	*n.*	中間人，掮客 (同義字 middleman)

The defendant acted as a **go-between** in the drug deal. He acted as a **go-between** for the drug suppliers and drug addicts 被告在毒品交易中擔任中間人。他在毒品供應者與吸毒者之間擔任中間人。.

---

grant	*vt.*	授予(權利等)，同意，准予，給予
[grænt]		

Some visas can **be granted** on arrival. A visa **granted** at a port of entry is called visa on arrival. 有些簽證可以在抵達時核發，在入境港埠核發的簽證稱為落地簽證。

The court finally **granted** the divorce. 法院最後核准離婚。

The judge may **grant** an order authorizing or approving the interception of electronic communications. 法官得核准命令，授權或同意攔截電子通訊。

應用 *to grant extradition* 准予引渡

to grant parole 准予交保

to grant privileges or favors 給予特權或好處

to grant visa 准予簽證

to grant visitation 准予訪視

---

gratuity	*n.*	餽贈
[grəˋtjuətɪ]		

---

graze	*vt.*	擦傷，抓破

[grez]		He fell of my bike and **grazed** my left hand. 他從自行車跌倒，左手受到擦傷。
		He suffered a **graze** on the left hand. 他左手受到擦傷。
	n.	擦過，掠過
gridlock [`grɪd,lɑk]	n.	交通癱瘓，極端嚴重的全面交通壅塞(無車能動)
grievance [`grivəns]	n.	不滿，不平，抱怨，牢騷 [(+against)]
		Officers shall not use their police powers to resolve personal **grievances**. 員警不得使用警察權來解決個人的不滿。
ground [graʊnd]	n.	根據，理由
		The court will issue an emergency protective order where a law enforcement officer asserts **reasonable grounds** to believe that a person or a child is in immediate danger of domestic violence by a family or household member. 當執法人員提出合理事由，相信有人或有孩童處在家人或家戶成員家暴的立即危險時，法院會核發緊急保護令。
groundless [`graʊndlɪs]	adj.	無根據的，無理由的，無基礎的
		The defendant argued that the prosecution was **groundless** and without any probable cause. He said it was a **groundless** charge. 被告主張起訴毫無根據而且沒有相當理由，他說那是毫無根據的指控。
guard [gɑrd]	n.	守衛，警戒，衛兵
		Chief of Police said that more than 200 riot police were **on guard** to prevent further violence. 警察局長說，有超過 200 名鎮暴警察在警戒中，以防止進一步的暴力。
	應用	*coast guard* 海巡 (U.S. Coast Guard 美國海岸防衛隊)
		corporate guard 公司衛警
		executive guard 私人安全警衛(指高階主管聘請)
		residental guard 住宅衛警
		security guard 安全警衛
guardian [`gɑrdɪən]	n.	【律】監護人
		legal guardian 法定監護
guilt [gɪlt]	n.	有罪，犯罪
		Confession is a criminal suspect's oral or written **acknowledgement of guilt**. A false confession is an **admission of guilt**. 自白，是犯罪嫌疑人的口頭或書面的有罪承認。不實的自白是有罪的自認。
		Silence cannot be used **to establish guilt**. Silence is not probative of **guilt**. Otherwise, it is the **presumption of guilt**.

沉默不能被用來認定有罪，沉默不能做為有罪的證明，否則就是有罪推定。

guilty [ˋgɪltɪ]	*adj.*	有罪的，犯……罪的[(+of)]

Ladies and gentlemen of the jury, have you reached a verdict? 「陪審團先生及女士，你們已經做成判決了嗎？Yes we have, your honor. 是的，庭上。 What is your verdict? 你們的判決為何？ We **find the defendant guilty**. 我們認定被告有罪。」

Criminal courts must **prove an accused guilty** beyond a reasonable doubt. 刑事法庭對於被告有罪必須證明至無合理可疑。

應用　*is found guilty* 被認定有罪
is guilty of 有……罪
guilty plea 有罪的認諾
guilty verdict 有罪的判決
to find the defendant guilty 認定被告有罪

gun [gʌn]	*n.*	槍

應用　*gun law* 槍枝法律
gun locker 槍櫃(或稱 *gun safe*)
gun powder residue 火藥殘留
gun vault 槍械室
gun violence 槍枝暴力
toy gun 玩具槍
stun gun 電擊槍 【補充說明】Taser 為美國泰瑟公司，專門生產電擊槍，因而 taser 一字也因其名而被意譯為電擊槍
imitation gun 模型槍
radar speed gun 雷達測速槍(*radar gun or speed gun*)
riot gun 鎮暴槍

vt. 　向……開槍

A suspected drug dealer **was gunned down** in an encounter with the police over the weekend. 周末的時候，一名可疑的毒販在一場與警方的對峙中，被開槍擊斃。

gunfire [ˋgʌn͵faɪr]	*n.*	砲火，用槍砲作戰

The suspects and police also exchanged **gunfire** during the pursuit. One suspect was critically injured and transported to the hospital where he was pronounced deceased. 在追逐中，嫌犯與警方槍戰，一名嫌犯嚴重受傷並且被送到醫院，而在醫院被宣告死亡。

gunman [ˋgʌn͵mæn]	*n.*	持槍者，持槍歹徒，職業殺手

gunpoint	n.	槍口
[ˋgʌn͵pɔɪnt]		The victim was carjacked **at gunpoint** by two males. He told police that he was robbed **at gunpoint**. 被害人在兩名男子用槍口抵著的情況下被劫車，他告訴警方說，他被用槍口抵著而被洗劫。

gunshot	n.	開槍，射擊
[ˋgʌn͵ʃɑt]		An innocent pedestrian was injured in the crossfire between police and a suspect. The mastermind was killed by **gunshot wounds** he suffered in the crossfire. 一名無辜的路人在警匪的槍戰中受傷，首腦死於槍戰中所受的槍傷。
	應用	*gunshot residue* 火藥殘餘

habitual	adj.	慣常的，習以為常的
[həˋbɪtʃʊəl]		A **habitual offender** is also known as a repeat offender. It refers to a person who has been previously convicted of one or more crimes in the past and is currently facing new charges. 關於 habitual offender (慣犯，再犯)也稱為 repeat offender，指過去曾被判處一個或數個有罪確定而仍面臨新指控的人。
		Although many **habitual offenders** tend to commit the same type of crime over and over again, a person does not necessarily have to commit the same crime in order to be called a repeat offender or **habitual offender**. 雖然許多慣犯常會一再地犯同類的犯罪，但其實稱「慣犯/再犯(repeat offender 或 habitual offender)」不一定是要犯同類的犯罪。
		The man was described by the the police as a **habitual housebreaker**. 該名男子被警方形容為侵入住宅慣犯。
	應用	*habitual criminal* 慣犯
		habitual drunkard 酗酒慣犯
		habitual gambler 賭博慣犯
		habitual housebreaker 侵入住宅慣犯
		habitual offender 慣犯

hack	vt.	駭，(駭客)入侵
[hæk]		Cyber Crime Unit said the victim's Facebook account **was hacked**. His bank account **was** also **hacked**. 網路犯罪小組說，被害人的臉書被駭客入侵，他的銀行帳號也被入侵。
	vi.	駭，(駭客)入侵 [(+into)]
		Police said the suspect allegedly **hacked into** the computer systems of the company and downloaded customers' information. 警方說，嫌犯涉嫌駭入公司的電腦系統並下載了客戶資料。

The St. Louis Cardinals are being investigated by the FBI for allegedly **hacking into** networks of the Houston Astros and trying to steal information about the players, The New York Times reported Tuesday. 美國紐約時報星期二報導,聖路易紅雀隊(Cardinals)正受到美國聯邦調查局調查涉嫌駭入休士頓太空人隊(Houston Astros)網路,意圖竊取球員資料一事。

hacker [`hækə]	n.	駭客

---

hallucination [hə,lusn`eʃən]	n.	幻覺,妄想,【醫】幻想症

---

hallucinogen [hə`lusnə,dʒɛn]	n.	迷幻劑

---

handcuff [`hænd,kʌf]　　*n.*　　手銬

Officers should not use **handcuffs** as a form of punishment or retaliation. 員警不應使用手銬做為一種處罰或報復的形式。
給……戴上手銬

vt.　　Police **handcuffed** the man's left arm to the wall during the interrogation. 警方在偵訊時,將該男子的左手銬在牆上。

---

handicapped [`hændɪ,kæpt]　　*adj.*　　有生理缺陷的,殘障的

A non-moving violation is usually related to parking violations, such as parking in a **handicapped zone** without a permit. 靜態違規通常與停車違規有關,例如無許可證而停在殘障車位。

---

handwriting [`hænd,raɪtɪŋ]	n.	筆跡

---

hang [hæŋ]　　*vt.*　　絞死,吊死 (過去式/過去分詞 hanged/hanged)

The man was **hanged** for murder. 該男子因謀殺罪被處絞刑。

Medical examiner determined that the inmate **had hanged himself** with a bedsheet. 法醫認定該名受刑人用床單上吊自盡。

vi.　　逗留,徘徊 (過去式/過去分詞 hung/hung)

應用　　*to hang out with sb.* (與某人) 出去玩、消磨時間、到外面晃晃、廝混

Many at-risk youths tend to **hang out with** gang members. 許多高風險青少年容易跟幫派分子廝混。

At risk youths spend more time **hanging out with** friends than their families. 高風險青少年跟朋友在一起的時間比跟家人的時間還長。

---

harass [`hærəs]　　*vt.*　　騷擾

She alleged that she had been sexually harassed by her

		supervisor. 她聲稱她被她的上司性騷擾。
harassment [ˋhærəsmənt]	*n.*	騷擾
		Many women's advocacy groups said that based on their studies, most cases of **sexual harassment** in the workplace still go unreported. 許多婦女倡議團體表示，依據他們的研究，許多職場的性騷擾案件仍然沒有報案。
hazard [ˋhæzɚd]	*n.*	危險，危害物，危險之源
		It is important that responding officers can identify **hazards** to reduce risk. 處理人員能夠確認危害以便降低風險，是重要的。
	應用	*fire hazards* 火災災害
		human-caused hazards 人為造成的災害
		natural hazard 天然災害
		unexpected hazards 無法預期的災害
hazardous [ˋhæzɚdəs]	*adj.*	有危險的，冒險的
		To ensure the safety of all building occupants, we must call the fire department and report **hazardous** conditions in the event of a fire. 為確保建築物的所有居住者的安全，萬一火災時，我們必須打電話給消防局並通報危害情況。
	應用	*hazardous material* 有害物質(HAZMAT)
head-on	*adv. & adj.*	迎面地，直接地，面對面地
		Two trains crashed **head-on**. 兩輛火車迎面對撞。
		In a serious **head-on** collision or a multi-vehicle collision, the possibility to survive the crash is difficult. 在重大的對撞或連環車禍中，從這種車禍生還的可能性不易。
hearsay [ˋhɪr,se]	*n.*	(證據規則的)傳聞
		In general, **hearsay** is not admissible. 通常，傳聞沒有證據能力。
high [haɪ]	*adj.*	高的
	應用	*high occupancy vehicle (HOV)* 高乘載
		high rise 摩天大樓
		high-rise fire 高樓火災
		high seas 公海
		high speed police pursuit 高速警察追逐
		high speed police chase 高速警察追逐
		high speed pursuit 高速警察追逐
		high-crime area 高犯罪地區 (或稱 *hot spot* 熱區)
		high-power 強有力的(同 high-powered)
		high-power(ed) weapon 高性能武器

high-profile 受到矚目的

high risk 高風險

high tech 高科技 *(或稱 cutting edged technology)*

high profile case 重大矚目案件

hijack	*n.*	劫持，攔路搶劫
[`haɪˌdʒæk]		A man has been arrested for allegedly **hijacking** a car, after police received a tip-off. 警方接獲報案之後，將一名涉嫌劫車的男子予以逮捕。

hit	*vt.*	襲擊，使遭受
[hɪt]		The victim **was hit** from behind with an unknown object by a man. 被害人被從後面用不詳的東西襲擊。
		His car **was hit** from behind by a truck. 他的車被一輛卡車從後方撞上。
		Authorities say a magnitude 5.0 earthquake **has hit** the San Francisco Bay Area this morning. 當局說，一場震級為 5 級的地震在今天早上襲擊舊金山灣區。
		Two men have died and one man has been rescued after their small fishing boat **hit** rocks and capsized in rough seas off Botany Bay on Sunday afternoon. 星期日下午，一艘小船在 Botany 灣外洶湧的海面撞到岩石而翻覆之後，其上的兩名男子死亡，一人被救起。
	vi.	襲擊
		Authorities said many people were in the building when the fire **hit**. 當局說，火災襲擊時，有很多人在建築物裡。
		Before the storm **hit**, Mayor issued a warning to the citizens urging them to keep off the roads through the duration of the storm. 暴風雨來襲之前，市長發出警告給市民，呼籲他們在暴風雨期間不要上街。

hit and run	*n. &*	肇事逃逸／肇事逃逸的
[hɪt]	*adj.*	Police are seeking help from the public with any information about a fatal **hit-and-run** accident that occurred Friday. 警方正在尋求大眾協助提供任何關於星期五發生的致命肇事逃逸車禍意外的資料。

hobo	*n.*	遊民
[`hobo]		

hold	*vt.*	握著，抓住，拘留，扣留
[hold]		Prisons are designed to **hold** individuals convicted of crimes. 監獄是設計來關押有罪確定之人。
		During the standoff, the armed suspect **held** the student

hostage at gunpoint inside the conference room. He was held hostage for 20 hours before being freed by SWAT team. 在僵持之際，這名武裝嫌犯用槍挾持了學生做為人質在會議室裡，他們被挾持了 20 小時，才被 SWAT(特種武器與戰術部隊)解救自由。

The suspect pretended to be a police officer and **held** the victim **captive** for several days. 嫌犯佯裝是員警，並將被害人囚禁了數日。

Minister expressed that the government also seeks to protect public safety and **hold** offenders **accountable for** their actions. 部長表示，政府也致力於保護公眾的安全並讓犯罪者為自己的行為負責任。

	vt.	(法律上)認定，認為，持有(見解)

The district court **held** that the evidence presented at trial was sufficient to support the conviction. However, the court of appeals **held** that the evidence should not be admitted and discharged the defendant. 地方法院認定，審判所提的證據足以支持有罪判決，然而上訴法院認為，該證據不應該被採用，然後並釋放了被告。

The judge **held** that the defendant was innocent. 法官認定被告是無辜的。

應用	
	to hold (sb) accountable for 讓(人)為……負責
	to hold (sb) hostage 將……挾持做為人質
	to hold (sb.) captive 囚禁或俘虜(某人)

---

holding cell		(警察局內的)留置室，拘留所 (或稱 lockup)

---

holdup	*n.*	持槍攔劫
[`hold,ʌp]		Police have charged two men involved in a convenience store **holdup** last week. 警方已經將涉及上星期便利商店搶劫的兩人提出控訴。

---

homade	*adj.*	自製的，家裡做的
[`hom`med]	應用	*homemade firearms* 自製/改造槍械
		homemade toy gun 自製/改造玩具槍
		homemade weapon 自製/改造武器
		homemade bomb 自製炸彈
		homemade explosives 自製爆裂物
		homemade grenade 自製手榴彈

---

homicide	*n.*	殺人
[`hɑmə,saɪd]		**Homicide** is the killing of one person by another. Murder and manslaughter are two different types of **homicide**. 殺人是一人

殺死另一人，murder(謀殺)與 manslaughter(包括殺人與致死兩個意義)是殺人的兩種不同的態樣。

hospital	*n.*	醫院
[ˋhɑspɪt!]		The motorcycle rider **is in hospital** after being hit by a car at a busy crossroads. 機車騎士在繁忙的十字路口被一輛汽車撞到後，目前在住院中。
hospitalize		
[ˋhɑspɪt!͵aɪz]	*vt.*	使……住院治療
		John **has been hospitalized** for a serious respiratory infection. 約翰因為嚴重的呼吸道感染而住在醫院。

hostage	*n.*	人質
[ˋhɑstɪdʒ]		In domestic violence, perpetrators may **take** a spouse, partner, or children **hostage**. 在家暴案件中，犯罪者有可能會將配偶、伴侶或小孩當作人質。
		During the standoff, the armed suspect **held** three students **hostage** at gunpoint inside the conference room. They were **held hostage** for 20 hours before being freed by SWAT team. 在僵持之際，這名武裝嫌犯以槍挾持了三名學生在會議室裡，他們被挾持了 20 小時，才被 SWAT(特種武器與戰術部隊)解救自由。

應用
- *be held hostage* 被拘禁/挾持當做人質
- *to hold (sb) hostage* 將(人)挾持當做人質
- *to take (sb) hostage* 將(人)挾持當做人質
- *hostage negotiation* 人質談判
- *hostage negotiator* 人質談判官
- *hostage-taker* 人質挾持者

hot spot		熱區，又稱 high-crime area (高犯罪地區)

housebreaker	*n.*	侵入家宅者，入屋盜賊
[ˋhaʊs͵brekɚ]		The man was described by the the police as a habitual **housebreaker**. 該名男子被警方形容為慣性侵入住宅者。
housebreaking	*n.*	(為偷盜等目的) 侵入住宅
[ˋhaʊs͵brekɪŋ]		He pleaded guilty to the **housebreaking** and larceny.他對於侵入住宅竊盜認罪。
		He was arrested for suspected **housebreaking** and theft. 他因為有侵入住宅行竊的嫌疑而被逮捕。
		He we found guilty on three counts of **housebreaking** with intent to steal. 他因為三項侵入住宅意圖行竊罪名被判有罪。

household	*n.*	家庭，戶
[ˋhaʊs͵hold]		*single-parent household* 單親家庭
	adj.	家的，家庭的

應用		*Household Registration Office* 戶政事務所
		household member 家戶成員
		household safety 家戶安全

---

householder
[`haʊs,holdɚ]

n. 住戶，居住者

The **householder** immediately called the police after returinning home to find an intruder in his home. 住戶回家發現有一位入侵者在他家裡之後，立即打了電話給警方。

HOV

abbr. 高乘載 *high occupancy vehicle*

High occupancy vehicle (HOV) lane is reserved for buses or vehicles with the minimum number of occupants specified on the signs. 高乘載專用道是保留給巴士，或載有標示規定的最低乘座人數的車輛。

---

human
[`hjumən]

n. 人，人類

adj. 人的，人類的

Fire may cost **human** life and the loss of money and property. 火災會造成生命損失及金錢與財產的損害。

應用
human right 人權
human trafficking 人口販運

IC

abbr. 事件指揮官 Incident Commander

ICS

abbr. 事故現場指揮體系 Incident Command System

The Incident Command System (ICS) was developed to eliminate the mass confusion during the emergency. There are five major functional areas: management, operation, planning, logistics and finance. 「事故現場指揮體系(ICS)」是發展來消除重大緊急事件中的重大混亂。一共有五個主要功能面向：管理(management)、行動(operation)、計畫(planning)、後勤(logistics)及財務(finance)。

---

identification
[aɪ,dɛntəfə`keʃən]

n. 識別，鑑定

Mistaken **identifications** may lead to the arrest of innocent persons. 錯誤的指認會導致無辜者被逮捕。

Lineup is the police **identification** procedure to determine whether the suspect is the perpetrator of the crime. 排列指認是警方確認嫌犯是不是犯罪的行兇者的確認程序。

應用
Identification Card 身分證件(或 *ID card*)
Picture ID 有相片的證件(或 *photo ID*)
Engine Identification Number (EIN) 引擎號碼
Vehicle Identification Number (VIN) 車身號碼

---

identify
[aɪ`dɛntə,faɪ]

vt. 確認，識別，鑑定，驗明[(+as)]，視……(與……)為同一事物[(+with)]

Cartridge cases not only help to **identify** the weapon used, they can also indicate where it was fired from. 彈殼不僅可以幫助確認所使用的武器，也可以確認子彈是從何處發射。

Search warrant must **identify** the person or property to be searched or seized. 搜索票必須指明應搜索或扣押之人或物。

Field officers can better **identify** and understand the problems in the beat. 轄區員警比較能確認及了解轄區內的問題。

Officers will arrange line-ups to **identify** the suspect as part of their follow-up investigation and surveillance. 員警會安排指認，以指出嫌犯，做為後續調查與偵監的一部分。

When the recipient took possession of the drugs, officers then **identified themselves**, seized the contraband, and arrested the currier and recipient. 當受領人持有該毒品之後，員警即表明身分、查扣違禁物並逮捕運送人及受領人。

identity [aɪ`dɛntətɪ]	*n.*	身分

The FBI and law enforcement officials are seeking the public's assistance in locating the person believed to be connected to the abduction of Paul Smith. The suspect is described as a white male, approximately 5'10" tall, 180 pounds, with short hair and eyeglasses. If you have any information as to the **identity** or whereabouts of the suspect, who is featured in the surveillance video above, please contact authorities. 聯邦調查局及執法人員正尋求大眾的協助找尋這位據相信與 Paul Smith 綁架案有關的人，嫌犯的特徵為白人男子、身高約 5 呎 10 吋、180 磅、蓄留短髮、戴眼鏡。如果你有任何關於上述監視影帶中的嫌犯的身分及下落的資訊，請與當局聯絡。

ignitable [ɪg`naɪtəbl]	*adj.*	易發火的，可燃性的

According to firefighters, someone threw an **ignitable** liquid at the house and set it on fire, but firefighters have declined to comment on what is in the **ignitable** liquid. 根據消防員表示，有人將可燃液體丟向房子點燃火災，但消防員不願評論這可燃液體是什麼。

ignite [ɪg`naɪt]	*vt.*	點燃，使……燃燒

Sparks from the wires can **ignite** fires. 電線產生的火花會引燃火災。

The arsonist **ignited** the fire, ran outside and fled from the scene. 縱火犯引燃火災，跑了出去並逃離現場。

Firefighters were dispatched to the fire scene at 6:00 p.m. It is not known what **ignited** the fire. 消防員在下午六時被派出去

了，還不知道什麼引燃火災的。

The fire chief confirmed the homeowner is a fireworks distributor and that the blaze **ignited** some of the explosives. 消防局長證實屋主是鞭炮盤商，並且火災引燃了一些爆炸。

Igniter	*n.*	點火器，點火者
[ɪgˋnaɪtɚ]		The scene should be searched for **igniters**. The most common igniter is a cigarette-lighter. 在現場應該要尋找點火物，最常見的點火物是香菸打火機。

ignition	*n.*	著火，燃燒
[ɪgˋnɪʃən]		The **ignition** of the forest was caused by lightning. 這場森林起火是由雷電引起的。
	應用	*autoignition* 自燃
		spontaneous ignition 自燃

illegal	*adj.*	不合法的，非法的，違反規則的
[ɪˋlig!]		To protect their interests and benefits, gang members will acquire high-powered weapons and equipment through **illegal** purchases via middle-men. 為了保護利益及好處，幫派成員會透過中間人的不法購買，取得高性能武器及裝備。

ill-gotten gains	*n.*	不法所得，不義之財
		As traditional responses such as imprisonment and fines are said to be ineffective, many countries have amended criminal code and procedural laws to facilitate seizure and forfeiture of **ill-gotten gains**. 由於傳統的回應像監禁及罰金據說沒有效果，因此，許多國家修訂了刑法及程序法，以便利不法所得的扣押與沒收。

illicit	*adj.*	非法的，不法的，違禁的，不正當的
[ɪˋlɪsɪt]		Police intercepted an **illicit** consignment of heroin that weighed more than 10 kg. That was the largest seizure of heroin ever made in the country. 警方攔截到一件非法海洛因運送，秤重超過 10 公斤，這是國內有史以來最大的海洛因查扣案。
	應用	*illicit drug* 非法毒品

immediate	*adj.*	立即的，即刻的，直接的
[ɪˋmidɪt]		Protective search is a search of a detained suspect and the area within the suspect's **immediate control**. 「保護性搜索」是對於被拘禁之人及其立即可控制之區域的搜索。
	應用	*child's immediate welfare* 兒童的直接福祉
		immediate action 立即的行動
		immediate danger 立即的危險
		immediate death 立即的死亡

immediate family 近親(例如父、母、繼父母、寄養父母、兄弟姊妹、配偶及子女)

immediate precursor 先驅物質，原料

immediate risk 立即的風險

immediate supervisor 直接上級

immigrant	*n.*	移民
[`ɪməgrənt]	*adj.*	移民的
	應用	*immigrant visa* 移民簽證
		illegal immigrant 非法移民

immigration	*n.*	【美】(總稱)(外來的)移民
[ˌɪmə`greʃən]	應用	*Immigration* (在機場)證照查驗
		immigration officer 查驗員

imminent	*adj.*	(危險等)逼近的，即將發生的
[`ɪmənənt]	應用	*imminent danger* 急迫的危險

immunity	*n.*	免除，豁免，豁免權
[ɪ`mjunətɪ]		Officials said that diplomat does not enjoy **immunity** from criminal prosecution on charges of visa fraud. 官員說，外交官對於簽證詐欺的指控，不享有刑事起訴的豁免。

impair	*vt.*	削弱，減少，損害，損傷
[ɪm`pɛr]		No one shall report to work as law enforcement officer when his judgment **has been impaired by** alcohol. 任何員警如果其判斷力已因酒精而受到減損時，不得到勤擔任執法人員。

impartial	*adj.*	不偏不倚的，公正的，無偏見的
[ɪm`parʃəl]		Every person accused of crime is entitled to a fair and **impartial** trial. 每一個被指控犯罪的人都享有公平而不偏袒的審判。

impeach	*vt.*	【律】彈劾，控告，檢舉[(+for/of/with)]
[ɪm`pitʃ]		On cross-examination, a witness' credibility may **be impeached by** showing evidence of the witness' character and conduct. 在交互詰問時，證人的可信度可以透過提出證人的品格及行為的證據，予以彈劾。

importation	*n.*	進口，輸入
[ˌɪmpor`teʃən]		The illegal **importation**, manufacture, distribution, possession and improper use of controlled substances have a substantial and detrimental effect on the health and general welfare of the people. 非法進口、製造、散布、持有，及不當使用管制物質，對於人的健康及全般福祉具有實質及有害的影響。

impose	*vt.*	科(刑)，判處(刑)，加(負擔)，徵(稅), 將……強加於 [(+on/upon)]
[ɪm`poz]		The prosecutor recommended life imprisonment, but the trial

judge imposed a 15-year prison sentence on the defendant. 檢察官求處無期徒刑，但審理法官判被告 15 年有期徒刑。

應用	*to impose a fine* 科以罰金
	to impose death penalty 判處死刑
	to impose life sentence 判處無期徒刑
	to impose probation 科以緩刑

impound	*vt.*	扣押，沒收
[ɪmˋpaʊnd]		The suspect was charged with reckless driving. Police also **impounded** his car. 嫌犯被指控莽撞駕駛，警方也扣押了他的車子。

imprison	*vt.*	監禁，關押
[ɪmˋprɪzn]		The murder suspect **was imprisoned** for nearly two years but maintained his innocence. He was granted a new trial. Later, he was acquitted for lack of evidence. 謀殺案兇嫌被關了將近 2 年，但堅稱他無辜，他獲准了新的審理，後來因為缺乏證據而無罪釋放。

imprisonment	*n.*	監禁，關押
[ɪmˋprɪznmənt]		If a prisoner receives **life imprisonment**, he may be held in captivity until he dies. But in reality, a life sentence does not always mean **imprisonment** for life. 如果受刑人獲得無期徒刑，他可能會被囚禁直到死亡，但事實上，無期徒刑並非都是意味著監禁一生。
應用		*life imprisonment* 無期徒刑 (或稱 *life in prison; life sentence; life incarceration*)
		unlawful imprisonment 非法拘禁
		wrongful imprisonment 非法監禁(*false imprisonment*)

inaction	*n.*	無所做為，沒有做為 (刑法的「不作為」是 omission)
[ɪnˋækʃən]		The society and the media frequently criticize police **inaction** as abuse of discretion. 社會與媒體經常將警方的無所作為批評為濫用裁量。

inadmissible	*adj.*	無證據能力的
[ˌɪnədˋmɪsəbl̩]		Evidence derived from an illegal search, arrest, or interrogation is **inadmissible** because the evidence was tainted by the illegality. 非法搜索、逮捕或訊問所取得的證據，無證據能力，因為，證據已經被不法所污染了。
		A confession is **inadmissible** if it is extracted by any sort of coercion, threatening, physical restraint or violence, or extended interrogation. 白自如果是用強制、威脅、強暴或疲勞訊問的方式取得時，則為無證據能力。

Evidence is **inadmissible** if the sample is contaminated. 如果樣本被汙染時，證據就無證據能力。

adj. 不合於入境的

Any alien who is wanted by the Interpol or foreign judicial authorities is **inadmissible** and shall be taken into custody for deportation. 任何受國際刑警組織或外國司法機關通緝的外國人，不得許可入境，並應予拘禁，以便遣送。

incarcerate	*vt.*	監禁

[ɪnˋkɑrsə‚ret]

Many people believed that the murder suspect's actions and his continued threat to public safety would keep him **incarcerated** for life. 很多人相信，該名殺人犯的行為以及他對於公眾安全的持續性威脅，會讓他一輩子都被關著。

incarceration	*n.*	監禁

[ɪn‚kɑrsəˋreʃən]

Probation should not be confused with parole. Probation replaces **incarceration**. Parole, on the other hand, follows **incarceration**. 緩刑不要與假釋混淆，緩刑取代監禁，假釋則是接在監禁之後。

應用 *incarceration rate* 監禁率

life incarceration 無期徒刑 (或稱 *life in prison; life sentence; life imprisonment*)

Incendiary	*adj.*	放火的

[ɪnˋsɛndɪ‚ɛrɪ]

Witness told fire investigators an **incendiary** device may have caused the fire. The arsonist used a car as an **incendiary** device to set buildings on fire. 證人告訴火災調查員說，可能是一個放火裝置造成這場火災，縱火犯使用一輛汽車做為放火裝置，引起建築物發生火災。

inchoate	*adj.*	剛開始的，未完的

[ɪnˋkoɪt]

Not every crime will be completed. Uncompleted crimes are referred to as **inchoate** crimes. 並不是所有犯罪都會完成，未完成的犯罪被稱為未遂之罪。

incident	*n.*	事件

[ˋɪnsədnt]

Finally, police arrived and took control of the **incident**. 終於，警察抵達了並掌控了這個事件。

Fire investigators believed the **incident** could have been a natural gas explosion. 火災調查員相信，這個事件可能是一件天然氣爆炸。

應用 *incident commander at scene* 案件的現場指揮官

incident report 案件報告

search incident to arrest 附帶搜索

| incite | vt. | 煽動，激勵，激起 [(+to)] |
| [ɪn`saɪt] | | Authorities believed that the riot **was** mostly **incited by** demonstrators. 當局相信，這場暴動大部分是被示威者煽動所激起的。 |

Incriminate	vt.	使(某人)看似有罪，控告，歸咎於
[ɪn`krɪmə,net]		Constitution protects people from being compelled to **incriminate** oneself. 憲法保障人民不被強迫自證有罪。
		Police have searched his apartment and found **incriminating evidence**. 警方搜索了他的公寓並找到足以入罪的證據。

| incriminating | adj. | 顯示有罪的，入人於罪的 |
| [ɪn`krɪmɪneɪtɪŋ] | | **Incriminating statements** can be very harmful evidence. Therefore, the suspect decided to retain a lawyer before officers ask him questions that could make him **incriminate** himself. 陷人入罪的陳述會是非常有傷害性的證據。因此，該嫌犯決定在員警問他一些會讓他入罪的問題之前，先聘請律師。 |

應用
Incriminating document 入人於罪的文件
Incriminating evidence 入人於罪的證據
Incriminating photo / picture 入人於罪的相片
Incriminating statement 入人於罪的陳述
Incriminating texting message 入人於罪的簡訊
Incriminating video 入人於罪的影片

| incrimination | n. | 顯示有罪 |
| [ɪn,krɪmə`neʃən] | | The right against **self-incrimination** forbids the government from compelling any person to give evidence that would likely **incriminate** him in a criminal case. 「不自證己罪權」禁止政府強迫任何人提出可能會讓自己在刑事案件中成為有罪的任何證據。 |

| Indict | vt. | (尤其指陪審團)對……起訴 |
| [ɪn`daɪt] | | The jury **indicted** the suspect on 3 felony counts. He **was indicted** on three counts of murder. He **was indicted** for the murder of his assiciates. He **was indicted** on the murder charges. 陪審團起訴嫌犯三項重罪。他被起訴三項謀殺罪。他因殺害同夥被起訴。他被以殺人罪起訴。 |

| indictment | n. | (經陪審團而提起的)起訴書 |
| [ɪn`daɪtmənt] | | In the U.S., **indictment** and information are two charging instruments. **Indictment** is the formal written accusation of a crime, made by a grand jury and presented to a court for prosecution against the accused person. 在美國，indictment 及 information 是兩種控告文書，indictment 這種起訴書是控 |

告犯罪的正式書面，由大陪審團做成，並向法院對被告提起告訴。(參看 information 一字)

induce	*vt.*	引誘
[ɪn`djus]		Entrapment can be explained as the conduct to **induce** the suspect to commit an offense. 誘陷可以被解釋為引誘嫌犯從事某項犯罪。

infect	*vt.*	傳染，侵染，感染
[ɪn`fɛkt]		Hepatitis B is dangerous, but most people who **are infected with** hepatitis B are unaware of their infection. B 型肝炎是嚴重的，但是大部分患有 B 型肝炎的人並不知道他們感染。

infiltrate	*vt.*	透入，滲透
[ɪn`fɪltret]		The young police officer volunteers to go undercover to **infiltrate** the crime ring. 這名年輕的員警自願臥底滲透這個犯罪組織。

inflict	*vt.*	給予(打擊)，使……遭受(損傷等)，加以(處罰或判刑)[(+on)]
[ɪn`flɪkt]		It is forbidden by law to **inflict** corporal punishment upon the school students. Under no circumstances shall a teacher **inflict** corporal punishment on any student. 法律禁止對學校的學生施加體罰，老師在任何情況下都不得對任何學生施予體罰。
		The suspect **inflicted** injury **upon** the officer and then began to flee. 嫌犯對員警施加傷害，然後開始逃逸。

informant	*n.*	線民，消息(或情報)提供者，告密者
[ɪn`fɔrmənt]	應用	*confidential informant (CI)* 秘密線民
		criminal informant 線民
		informer 線民
		cooperating individual 線民

information	*n.*	(由檢察官提起的)起訴書 (或稱 bill of information)
[ˌɪnfə`meʃən]		In the U.S., indictment and **information** are two charging instruments. **Information** is a formal criminal charge made by a prosecutor without a grand-jury indictment. 在美國，indictment 及 information 是兩種控告文書，information 這種起訴書是檢察官不經大陪審團起訴而提出的正式刑事控告。(參看 indictment 一字)

infringe	*vi.*	侵犯，侵害[(+on/upon)]
[ɪn`frɪndʒ]		Activists called on people across the nation to come together this weekend and claimed that government cannot **infringe upon** the rights of the people to assemble. 激進分子號召全國人民在這個周末聚集一起，並且聲稱政府不可以侵犯人民集會的權利。

	vt.	侵犯，侵害

The Second Amendment to the U.S. Constitution provides that the right of the people to keep and bear arms shall not **be infringed**. 美國憲法第 2 修正案規定，人民擁有及攜帶武器的權利不得受到侵犯。

---

inhale	*vt.*	吸入，吸食
[ɪn`hel]		

The drug addicts admitted he **inhaled** cocaine powder everyday. 吸毒者承認他每天吸食粉末古柯鹼。

---

inhalation	*n.*	吸入
[,ɪnhə`leʃən]		

The victim suffered **smoke inhalation** and carbon-monoxide poisoning, and died several days later at the hospital. 遇難者受到吸入濃煙及一氧化碳中毒，而數日後在醫院死亡。

Authorities said the victim was taken to the hospital for **smoke inhalation**. The man is in stable condition. 當局說，遇難者因吸入濃煙被送到醫院，這個人的狀況穩定。

---

inhuman	*adj.*	不人道的，無人性的
[ɪn`hjumən]		

---

initiate	*vt.*	開始，創始，開始實施
[ɪ`nɪʃɪt]		

In order to **initiate** a traffic stop, police must have reasonable suspicion to believe that a crime is or has been committed. 為了進行交通攔檢，警方必須有合理懷疑相信犯罪正在發生或以經發生。

The FBI **initiated** the investigation based on information provided by the informant. 聯邦調查局依據線民提供的資料發動了調查。

Police **initiated** an internal investigation to determine who is leaking information about the murder case to the press. 警方展開內部調查，以了解是誰洩漏這起謀殺案的資訊給媒體的。

應用　*to initiate the arrest* 展開逮捕
to Initiate CPR 開始進行心肺復甦術
to initiate investigation 展開調查
to initiate the pursuit 展開追逐
to initiate the evacuation 展開撤退

---

inject	*vt.*	注射(藥液等)[(+into)]，為(某人)注射[(某人)+with)]
[ɪn`dʒɛkt]		

Cocaine is highly addictive and it can **be injected**, snorted as a powder. 古柯鹼具有高度的成癮性，它可以用注射、以粉末用鼻子吸食。

---

injure	*vt.*	傷害
[`ɪndʒɚ]		

Officers often feel stressed if fellow officer **are injured** or killed in the line of duty. 如果同僚員警在值勤中受傷或死亡，員警常會感到挫折。

injury	*n.*	傷害
[ˈɪndʒərɪ]		The suspect inflicted **injuries** upon the officer and then began to flee. 嫌犯對員警施加傷害，然後開始逃逸。

inmate	*n.*	(監獄的)被收容者，囚犯，同坐牢的人
[ˈɪnmet]		When you escort the **inmate** to court, courthouses will have a lock up area where you can secure the inmate while they are waiting for court appearance. 當你戒護受刑人到法院時，法庭大廈會有一個拘留區，在受刑人等待出庭時，讓你可以將受刑人保全在那裡。
		Several **inmates** broke out of jail last week and are still at large. Authorities still wondered how they broke jail. 好幾名囚犯在上星期越獄而出，並且仍然逍遙法外，當局還不知道他們是如何越獄的。
	應用	*death row inmate* 死囚犯

innocence	*adj.*	無罪，清白，無知，幼稚
[ˈɪnəsns]		**The presumption of innocence** is a legal principle that every person accused of any crime is considered innocent until proven guilty. 無罪推定是一項法律原則，意即任何被控告任何犯罪，在還沒證明有罪之前，都被認定為是清白的。

innocent	*adj.*	無罪的，清白的；天真的，幼稚的
[ˈɪnəsnt]		Criminal laws require that every one charged with a criminal offence shall be presumed **innocent** until proved guilty according to law, known as the presumption of innocence. 刑法要求，每一個被指控刑事犯罪之人，在依法被證明有罪之前，應推定為無罪，稱為無罪推定。
		They person brought a false accusation against the **innocent** man. 他們對這名無辜者提起了誣告之訴。
		The judge held that the defendant was **innocent**. 法官認定被告是無辜的。

inquire	*vi.*	查問，詢問，調查 [(+about/into)]
[ɪnˈkwaɪr]		Police **are inquiring about** the cause of the murder. 警方在調查這起謀殺案的起因。
		They **are inquiring into** this matter. 他們正在調查這件案件。
		Police **are inquiring into** his connection with the gang. 警方正在調查他與幫派的關聯。
		查問，詢問，調查 [(+子句)]
		Officers **are inquiring** why she was attacked. 員警正在查問他

	vt.	她為何被攻擊。
inquiry [ɪnˋkwaɪrɪ]	*vt.*	詢問，打聽[(+about/into]，調查[(+into)] Many people saw the gang fight but declined to cooperate with police **inquiries**. 有許多人看到幫派鬥毆，但對於警方的詢問則婉拒合作。
	n.	詢問，打聽 Police **inquiries** are ongoing, and police urge any witnesses or anyone with information to come forward. 警方的調查仍在持續，並且警方呼籲任何證人或任何有資訊的人能出面。
insignia [ɪnˋsɪgnɪə]	*n.*	階級章
inspect [ɪnˋspɛk]	*vt.*	檢查，檢驗 Police set up roadblocks or checkpoints to stop and **inspect** drivers and vehicles passing along a road. 警察設置路障或檢查站以攔檢過路的駕駛人及車輛。 檢查，審查 Authorities say the fire equipment must **be inspected** and maintained periodically. 當局說，消防設備必須定期檢查及維護。
inspection [ɪnˋspɛkʃən]	*n.*	檢查，檢驗，審視 Fire Department said they would initiate a new program **to perform** home fire safety **inspection** and install free smoke detectors for low income households. 消防局說他們開啟一個新計畫，為低收入戶進行家戶防火安全檢查及裝置免費煙霧偵測器。
	應用	*airport inspection* 機場檢查 *annual fire safety inspection* 年度防火安全檢查 *baggage inspection* 行李檢查 *fire extinguisher inspection* 滅火器檢查 *fire Safety inspection* 防火安全檢查 *motor vehicle inspection* 行車檢查 *periodic inspection and test* 定期檢測 *random inspection* 隨機檢測 *vehicle safety inspection* 車輛安全檢查
install [ɪnˋstɔl]	*vt.*	安裝，設置 According to the law, smoke alarms are compulsory and must **be installed** in every new building, on or near the ceiling of every storey to wake sleeping occupants. 根據法律，煙霧警報器是強制的，並且在每棟新的建築物天花板上或靠近的地方，都

必須安裝，以便喚醒睡著的居住者。

If you are renting an apartment, it is the landlord's responsibility to ensure smoke alarms **are installed** and kept in working condition. 如果你租公寓，屋主有責任確保有安裝煙霧警報器，並且堪用。

instrument of crime		供為犯罪之工具

Any material determined to be contraband or **instrument of crime** are subject to seizure by law enforcement officers. 任何被認定為違禁物或犯罪工具的物品，都應受執法人員扣押。

integrity [ɪnˋtɛɡrətɪ]	*n.*	正直，廉正，誠實

intelligence [ɪnˋtɛlədʒəns]	*n.*	情報，消息

Intelligence officer admitted that they used cutting edge technologies to take videos and photos to spy on suspicious citizens. 情報人員承認他們用先進的科技錄影及拍照，來監視可疑的市民。

Intelligence indicates that the world's most powerful drug syndicate continues to operate in this area. 情報顯示，全球最有勢力的毒品犯罪集團仍然繼續在這個地區運作。

intend [ɪnˋtɛnd]	*vt.*	意圖要，想要，計畫

Suspect admitted in the interrogation that he **intended to** kill the victim. 嫌犯在偵訊中承認他是意圖要殺害被害人。

Alarms **are intended to** alert building occupants that a fire or other life-threatening situation exists. 警報器是用來警示建築物居住者有火災或其他有生命威脅情況存在。

An immigrant visa is issued to a foreign national who **intends to** live and work permanently in this country. 移民簽證是核發給有意在本國永久居住及工作的外國國民。

intent [ɪnˋtɛnt]	*n.*	犯意，意圖(或稱 *mens rea*; guilty mind)

The basic elements of a crime consist of **intent**, conduct, and causation. **Intent** is also known as *mens rea* or guilty mind. 犯罪的基本要素包含犯意、行為及因果關係，犯意也稱為 *mens rea* 或 guilty mind。

	應用	*criminal intent* 刑事犯意

intention [ɪnˋtɛnʃən]	*n.*	意圖，意向，目的

The accused admitted his **intention** was to kill the ringleader. 被告承認他的意圖是要殺了這幫派老大。

intentional [ɪnˋtɛnʃənl]	*adj.*	有意的，故意的

The defendant contended the shooting was an accident. The

court, however, contended that the killing was **intentional**. 被告堅稱槍擊純屬意外，然而法院認定這個殺害行為是故意的。The defendant shot and killed the victim **intentionally**.被告是故意開槍殺害被害人。

【補充說明】

按刑法的故意與過失，在英文為：

1. 故意(intentionally)：真心要造成結果(類似於明知並有意使其發生)，與 purposely 相同。

2. 故意(knowingly)：知悉其行為之本質或情狀(類似於其發生不違背本意)。

3. 過失(recklessly)：知悉此等結果將發生或有此等情狀存在的風險，並真心不注意該實質而難辭其咎的風險(類似於預見其發生而自信其不發生)。

4.過失(negligently)：未能察覺此等結果即將發生，或有此等情狀存在的實質與難辭其咎的風險(類似於雖非故意，但應注意、能注意而不注意)，詳《實用執法英文》一書第 3 課

interact [ˌɪntəˈrækt]	*vi.*	互動 The society expects officers to **interact with** citizen with respect. 社會期待警察與民眾互動要有尊重。
intercept [ˌɪntəˈsɛpt]	*vt.*	攔截，截住，截擊 When contraband **is intercepted**, controlled delivery is useful to identify the recipients. 當違禁物被攔截時，控制下交付對於確認收件人，是有用的。 The CID has been authorized **to intercept** the communications of the drug ring. 刑警大隊業已獲得授權攔截毒品集團的通訊。
interception [ˌɪntəˈsɛpʃən]	*n.* 應用	攔截，竊聽 *lawful interception* 合法攔截(或稱 *telephone tapping, wire-tapping or wiretapping*) *real time interception* 即時攔截 *voice telephone interception* 語音電話攔截
interchange [ˌɪntəˈtʃendʒ]	*n.*	交流道
intercourse [ˈɪntəˌkors]	*n.*	性交 The rapist was arrested for sexual **intercourse** by force against the will of the victim. 強姦犯因為以強制力違反被害人的意願性交而被逮捕。
interest [ˈɪntərɪst]	*n.*	利益，利害 Child custody is determined based on **the best interests of the**

child. 兒童監護是依據兒童最佳利益而做決定的。

| 應用 | *interested party* 有利害關係的一方 |

interested party 有利害關係的一方
party in interest 有利害關係的一方
in the public interest 基於公眾利益

---

interfere　*vi.*　介入，干涉，干預，妨礙，衝突，抵觸 [(+with)]
[ˌɪntəˈfɪr]

It shall be unlawful **to interfere with** fire department operations such as obstructing or restricting the mobility of or blocking the path of travel of a fire department emergency vehicle. 妨礙消防局的行動是違法的，例如阻礙或限制消防局緊急車輛的機動性或阻塞其行進路線。

---

internal　*adj.*　內的，內部的
[ɪnˈtɜn!]

應用　*Internal Affairs Office* 政風室
Internal investigation 內部調查
Internal administrative investigation 內部行政調查

---

international crime　國際犯罪

應用　國際犯罪包括以下之罪：
aggression 侵略
crime against humanity 違反人道
genocide 種族滅絕
piracy 海盜
slavery 奴隸
terrorism 恐怖主義
torture 酷刑
war crime 戰爭

INTERPOL　*abbr.*　國際刑警組織 International Criminal Police Organization

---

interrogate　*vt.*　訊問，偵訊
[ɪnˈtɛrəˌget]

Interrogation is different from interview. Investigators will **interrogate** suspect, and interview victim or witness. 訊問與訪談不同，偵查人員訊問(interrogate)嫌犯；並訪談(interview)被害人或證人。

---

interrogation　*n.*　訊問，偵訊
[ɪnˌtɛrəˈgeʃən]

If the suspect is in custody when the police desire to conduct **interrogation**, police must inform the suspect of his or her constitution rights. 如果警方想偵訊時，嫌犯是在拘禁中，則警方必須將嫌犯的憲法權利告知他。

應用　*interrogation room* 偵訊室
extended interrogation 疲勞訊問
to conduct interrogation 進行偵訊

---

interrogator　*n.*　偵訊者

[ɪn`tɛrə,getə]

intersection	*n.*	十字路口

[,ɪntəˋsɛkʃən]

iIntervene	*vi.*	干涉，干預，調停[(+in/between)]

[,ɪntəˋvin]

Traditionally, in many countries, police officers have been reluctant **to intervene in** family quarrels. 傳統上在許多國家，員警向來不願介入家庭口角。

Intervention	*n.*	介入，調停，斡旋

[,ɪntəˋvɛnʃən]

Patrol officers responded to the domestic violence and determined that the situation required police **intervention**. 巡邏員警前往處理家暴，並判斷該狀況需要警方的介入。

應用　*Crisis Intervention Team (CIT)* 危機處理小組

crisis intervention 危機處理

drug abuse intervention 毒品濫用防治

hostage crisis intervention 人質危機處理

suicide intervention 自殺防阻

interview	*n.*	訪談，詢問

[ˋɪntə,vju]

While **interviews** are conducted for the purpose of gathering information from a victim or witness, interrogation is designed to match information to a particular suspect. 訪談進行的目的是為了從被害人或證人蒐集資訊；偵訊的用意，則是把資訊與某個特定嫌犯做吻合比對。

	vt.	訪談，詢問

Interview is different from interrogation. Investigators will interrogate suspect, and **interview** victim or witness. 訪談與訊問不同，偵查人員訊問(interrogate)嫌犯；並訪談(interview)被害人或證人。

"You were arrested this morning at about 9 a.m. for an assault. I **am interviewing** you to establish your involvement in the incident. Do you understand why you **are being interviewed**?" 「你在今早 9 時因為一起攻擊事件被捕，我現在對你進行訪談以便確定你在這起事件中的涉入情況，你知道你為何在被訪談嗎？」

Interviewer	*n.*	訪談人，談話人

[ˋɪntəvjuə]

A good investigator must also be a good **interviewer**. **Interviewer** should start the interview with an explanation of the case. 一位好的偵查員必須也同時是一位好的訪談員。訪談員進行訪談必須從案件的解釋開始。

interviewee	*n.*	被訪談人，被談話人

[ˌɪntə·vjuˋi]		Interviewers must be able to demonstrate to the **interviewee** that they are listening and understanding. 訪談員必須能夠向受訪者證明他們有傾聽也能諒解。
intimidate [ɪnˋtɪməˌdet]	*vt.*	威嚇，脅迫 Gang members often **intimidate** people who live and work within their turf. 幫派份子經常恐嚇在他們地盤內生活及工作的人。
intimidation [ɪntɪməˋdeʃən]	*n.*	恐嚇 Gang members frequently use violence or **intimidation** to further their criminal objectives. 幫派分子經常使用暴力或恐嚇來助長其犯罪目標。
intoxicated [ɪnˋtɑksəˌketɪd]	*adj.*	喝醉了的 A police officer can arrest the person without a warrant in case of **driving while intoxicated** if such violation is coupled with an accident or collision. 在酒駕的案件中，如果該項違規伴隨發生車禍或擦撞時，員警可以無令狀逮捕該人。
intoxicating [ɪnˋtɑksəˌketɪŋ]	*adj.*	使人醉的，使人興奮的 The defendant consumed **intoxicating** liquor. He was affected by the use of **intoxicating beverage** at the time of the accident. 被告喝了酒精飲料，車禍的當下，他受到酒精飲料所影響。
introduce [ˌɪntrəˋdjus]	*vt.*	引進 At trial, the prosecutor **introduced** evidence to show that it was the defendant's gun which killed the victim at close range. The killing was caught on video by a bystander. 審判時，檢察官引進了證據顯示，就是被告的這把槍在近距離殺死了被害人。殺害剛好被路人錄影拍到。
	應用	*to introduce evidence* 引進證據 (或稱 *to present evidence* 提出證據)
intrude [ɪnˋtrud]	*vi.*	侵入，闖入，侵擾，打擾 The suspect **intruded into** the residence of his ex-girlfriend and assault her. 嫌犯闖入前女友的住處並攻擊她。
intruder [ɪnˋtrudə·]	*n.*	侵入者，闖入者，干擾者 According to the police, the victim was assaulted by **intruder** at his residence in New York. 根據警方表示，被害人在他紐約的住所遭到入侵者的攻擊。
intrusion [ɪnˋtruʒən]	*n.*	侵入，闖入，【律】非法侵入他人土地 Illegal wiretapping constitutes an **intrusion** of privacy. 非法的監聽構成隱私的侵犯。
intrusive	*adj.*	有侵入性的

[ɪnˋtrusɪv]		Police couldn't arrest him because their **intrusive** surveillance still could not find any evidence of any crime. 警方無法逮捕他，因為他們的侵入性偵查仍無法找到任何犯罪的任何證據。
invade [ɪnˋved]	*vt.*	侵入，侵犯
		The homeowner told the police his home **was invaded by** three masked robbers. The robbers **invaded** his home and stole over 10,000 in cash and jewellery, along with several other items. 屋主告訴警方他家被三位蒙面強盜侵入，強盜侵入他家並且偷走超過 1 萬元現金及珠寶以及其它一些物品。
invader [ɪnˋvedə]	*n.*	入侵者
invasion [ɪnˋveʒən]	*n.*	入侵，侵略，侵害，侵犯

Home invasion is the most serious burglary charge because it involves an act of violence. 入室竊盜是最嚴重的竊盜，因為那涉及暴力行為。

In the US, A residential burglary becomes a **home invasion** when the offender knew that someone was likely to be at the residence and: (1) possessed a weapon; (2) committed violence against an occupant; (3) fired or threatened to fire a gun; or (4) sexually assaulted or abused an occupant. 在美國，「住宅竊盜 (residential burglary)」如果犯罪者知道該住宅內可能有人並且有以下四種情況時，會變成「入宅竊盜(home invasion)」：(1) 持有武器、(2)對住居者從事暴力、(3)開槍或威脅開槍，或(4) 性侵或性虐待住居者。

應用	*invasion of privacy* 侵犯隱私
	home invasion 入室竊盜

investigate [ɪnˋvɛstəˏgetə]	*vt.*	調查，偵查

Police **are investigating** the deaths of the man who was found with a gunshot wound to the head in Central Park. 警方正在調查該名在中央公園被發現而頭部有槍傷的男子的死亡案件。

Police believe that Johnson is the prime suspect and continue **to investigate** him for years. 警方相信強生是主要嫌疑人，並且多年來持續在調查他。

investigator [ɪnˋvɛstəˏgetə]	*n.*	調查員，偵查員
investigation [ɪnˏvɛstəˋgeʃən]	*n.*	調查，偵查

Chief of Police said that the FBI would **open an investigation** on the police shooting of an unarmed teen. The FBI has announced their plans **to launch an investigation** on the case.

警察局長說，聯邦調查局會對這起「警方槍擊沒有攜帶武器的青少年」事件開啟調查。聯邦調查局宣布他們計畫展開本案的調查。

The suspect was **under investigation** for murder. 該嫌犯因謀殺案在被調查中。

It took **firefighters** only about 10 minutes to knock down the blaze. One resident was treated for smoke inhalation. The cause of the fire **is under investigation**, authorities said. 這場火勢只花了消防員十分鐘的時間就撲滅了，一位居民因吸入濃煙接受治療，火災原因還在調查中，當局說。

應用　*to open investigation* 開啟調(偵)查
　　　to launch investigation 發動調(偵)查
　　　to start investigation 開始調(偵)查
　　　to initiate investigation 展開調(偵)查
　　　to conduct investigation 進行調(偵)查
　　　to commence investigation 開始調(偵)查
　　　is/am/are under investigation 受到調查、被調查中
　　　follow-up investigation 後續調(偵)查

| investigative | *adj.* | 調查的，偵查的 |
| [ɪnˋvɛstəˌgetɪv] | | |

應用　*investigative assistance* 偵查協助
　　　investigative lead 偵查線索
　　　investigative procedure 偵查程序
　　　investigative tool 偵查工具
　　　investigative process 偵查過程
　　　investigative technique 偵查技巧
　　　investigative technology 偵查科技

| investigator | *n.* | 偵查人員 |
| [ɪnˋvɛstəˌgetɚ] | | |

Criminals may stage a crime scene to misdirect **investigators** so as to get away with the crime. 罪犯可能會假造一個犯罪現場來誤導偵查人員，以逃避犯罪。

In general, it is the responsibilities for the crime scene **investigators** to go to crime scenes, collect evidence, and process the scene. 一般來說，犯罪現場調查人員的責任是前往犯罪現場、蒐集證據並做現場採證。

應用　*private investigator* 私家偵探　(或稱 *private eye*)

| involve | *vt.* | 使……捲入，連累，牽涉[(+in/with)] |
| [ɪnˋvɑlv] | | |

Police have charged two men **involved in** a convenience store holdup last week. 警方已經對上星期涉及便利商店搶劫的兩人提出控訴。

應用		*officer-involved shooting* (用槍時機中的)警察開槍事件

Police confirm that the suspect involved in the **officer-involved shooting** has been taken into custody and is being transported to a local hospital. 警方證實，涉及警察開槍事件的嫌犯已經被警方拘禁，且正在被送到當地的一家醫院。

involvement [ɪn`vɑlvmənt]	*n.*	參與，牽連，牽涉，涉入

The detained suspect has confessed to his **involvement in** the robbery, but denied any **involvement with** the drug dealer's murder. 被拘禁的嫌犯坦承他涉入強盜案，但否認有任何涉及毒販的謀殺案。

irrelevant [ɪ`rɛləvənt]	*adj.*	無關的，無關聯性的

Rules of Evidence provide that relevant evidence is **admissible**; irrelevant evidence is not **admissible**. Hearsay is not **admissible**. 證據法則規定，有關聯性的證據有證據能力；無關聯性的證據無證據能力。傳聞，沒有證據能力。

isolate [`aɪsḷ͵et]	*vt.*	使……孤立，把……隔離

If necessary, police must deploy personnel to **isolate** and contain the people. 如果必要的話，警察必須佈署人員以隔絕及包圍群眾。

issue [`ɪʃjʊ]	*vt.*	核發

When Incident Commander determines there is a need to take police action, commander at scene will need to **issue** warnings to the crowd to disperse. 當案件指揮官認定有必要採取警察行動時，現場指揮官就必須向群眾發出解散的警告。

If police investigation establishes probable cause to believe that an offense has been committed and that the defendant committed it, the judge must **issue** an arrest warrant to an officer to execute it. 如果警方的調查確認有相當理由足認犯罪已完成，而且是被告所為時，法官必須核發逮捕令給員警執行之。

item [`aɪtəm]	*n.*	(證據的)物件，項目，品項

The chain of custody is intended to trace the **item** of evidence from its discovery to court. 「物證管制流程」是用來對證據物件進行追蹤，從發現直到法院。

jail [dʒel]	*n.*	看守所，監獄，拘留所

Inventory search is a complete search of an arrestee's body before that person **is booked into jail**. 清查搜身是被逮捕人在被錄案進入看守所之前，所做的完整搜索。

Several inmates **broke out of jail** last week and are still at large.

Authorities still wondered how they **broke jail**. 好幾名囚犯在上星期越獄而出，並且仍然逍遙法外，當局還不知道他們是如何越獄的。

監禁，拘留

	vt.	The murder suspect was only 18 years old when he **was jailed**. 這殺人兇嫌被關的時候只有 18 歲。
jailor [`dʒelə]	*n.*	監獄管理員，看守監獄的人 (或 jailer)
jaywalk [`dʒe,wɔk]	*vi.*	不守交通規則橫行穿越馬路 Although pedestraians have the right-of-way in crosswalks, **jaywalking** can be ticketed. 雖然行人在十字路口有路權，但不守交通規則橫行穿越馬路會被開罰。
jeopardize [`dʒɛpə,aɪz]	*vt.*	使瀕於危險境地，冒……的危險，危及…… While performing the duties of radio dispatcher, never **jeopardize** the safety of citizens or officers by delaying a dispatch. 在執行無線電派遣官的任務時，切勿因為延誤派遣，而危害到市民或員警的安全。
jeopardy [`dʒɛpədɪ]	*n.*	危險，風險，危難 If a crime is in progress and someone's safety **is in jeopardy**, please call 1-1-0 immediately. 如果一項犯罪尚在進行的狀態，而某個人的安全處在危險之中，請立即撥打 110。 If you do not determine that weapons are involved or fail to relay the getaway car's description or direction, arriving officers may **be put into jeopardy**. 如果你沒能確認有槍枝牽涉，或沒能傳達逃走車輛的描述或方向的話，抵達的員警很可能會被置於險境中。
judge [dʒʌdʒ]	*n.*	法官(大法官稱為 Justice)
judgment [`dʒʌdʒmənt]	*n.*	審判，裁判，判決 Accordingly, we vacate the Fourth Circuit's **judgment**, and remand the case for resentencing consistent with the jury's verdict. 據此，我們廢棄第四巡迴法院的判決，並將案件發回重為與陪審團裁判一致的判決。 The trial court properly denied Mr. Bean's **motion for judgment of acquittal**. 事實審法院已適當地否決 Bean 的無罪判決聲請。
	n.	判斷 Good **judgment** comes from experience; experience comes from bad **judgment**. (Rita Mae Brown) 好的判斷來自於經驗；

		經驗來自於不好的判斷(美國作家 Rita Mae Brown)。
judicial [dʒu`dɪʃəl]	*adj.* 應用	司法的，審判的，法院判定的 *judicial authorities* 司法機關 *judicial decision* 司法判決 *judicial discretion* 司法裁量 *judicial officer* 司法官 *judicial proceedings* 司法訴訟 *judicial process* 司法過程 *judicial review* 司法審查
jump [dʒʌmp]	*vt.* *n.* 應用	跳過，越過 The suspect subsequently **jumped bail** and fled the country. 嫌犯後來棄保並逃離國家。 跳過，越過 *suicide jump* 跳樓自殺 *suicide jumper* 跳樓自殺者
junction [`dʒʌŋkʃən]	*n.*	(公路、鐵軌等的)聯接點，匯合處，交叉口 The traffic accident occurred at the **junction** of two highways. 這件交通事故發生在兩條公路的會合處。
jurisdiction [‚dʒʊrɪs`dɪkʃən]	*n.* 應用	管轄權，司法權，審判權，裁判權，權限，管轄範圍 The trial court is a court of original **jurisdiction** where the evidence is first received and considered. Appellate court is a court with **jurisdiction** to review decisions of lower courts. 初審法院是接受及認定證據的原始管轄法院，上訴法院是一個具有管轄權得審查下級法院裁判的法院。 *to exercise jurisdiction over* 對……行使管轄權 *criminal jurisdiction* 刑事管轄 *territorial jurisdiction* 屬地管轄 *extraterritorial criminal jurisdiction* 領域外刑事管轄權
juror [`dʒʊrə]	*n.*	陪審員
jury [`dʒʊrɪ]	*n.*	陪審團 *grand jury* 大陪審團 *petty/petit jury* 小陪審團
just [dʒʌst]	*adj.*	正義的，正直的，公平的 At appeal, the defendant argued that the district was not **fair and just**. 上訴時，被告主張地方法院沒有公平公正。
justice [`dʒʌstɪs]	*n.*	正義，公平，司法，審判 **Justice** delayed is **justice** denied. 遲來的正義不是正義。 **Justice** will prevail. 正義會獲得伸張。

He believes that the jury will **do him justice**. 他相信陪審團會公平地對待他。

People expect the court to fairly try the case and **do justice to** the victim. 人們期待法院公平審理案件，對被害人公正。

Police continue to search for the suspect in the building, hoping to be able to track him down and **bring him to justice**. 警方持續在建築物內搜索嫌犯，希望能追蹤到他並將他歸案受審。

The job of an investigator is not just to seek convictions but **to seek justice**. 偵查人員的工作不只是在追求有罪判決，更是追求正義。

The suspect was brought home **to face the justice** he evaded for more than 20 years. He was arrested in Mexico back in April and was extradited back to California **to face justice**. 嫌犯被帶回國面對他逃避超過 20 年的司法。他四月時在墨西哥被捕，並且被引渡回加州面對司法。

n.	大法官（通常開頭為大寫 Justice）

Sandra Day O'Connor was the first female **Justice** appointed to the US Supreme Court. 珊卓拉·戴·歐康納是美國最高法院第一位女性被任命的大法官。

應用	*associate justice* (美國的)大法官
	chief Justice 首席大法官
	criminal justice system 刑事司法體系
	miscarriage of justice 審判不公，誤判
	to deny sb. justice 對(某人)不公平

---

justifiable	*adj.*	可證明為正當的，有道理的
[ˋdʒʌstə‚faɪəb!]		

The use of force **is justifiable** when the person believes that such force is immediately necessary to prevent someone from committing suicide, inflicting serious bodily injury upon himself, or committing a crime. 當一個人相信，武力的使用是「防止某人自殺、防止對他自己加諸嚴重的身體傷害，或防止犯罪」所立即必要時，該武力的使用有正當性。

---

justify	*vt.*	證明……是正當的，為……辯護，是……的正當理由
[ˋdʒʌstə‚faɪ]		

Police must have probable cause **to justify** the arrest. Prosecutors must have probable cause **to justify** the prosecution. 警方必須有相當理由，讓逮捕具有正當性，檢察官必須有相當理由，讓起訴具有正當性。

Officer **is justified** in using deadly force only when the officer believes that such force is necessary to prevent death or serious bodily injury to himself or another. 員警使用致命武力，僅在

其相信武力的使用是為防止自己或他人死亡或嚴重之身體傷害所必要時，該武力的使用有正當性。

juvenile	*adj.*	少年的
[`dʒuvən!]	應用	*juvenile court* 少年法院/庭(或稱 *children's court*)

juvenile crime 青少年犯罪

Juvenile delinquency 青少年犯罪

juvenile delinquent 青少年犯

juvenile offender 青少年犯

juvenile reformatory 少年感化院(現多稱為 *juvenile correctional facilities* 或訓練學校 *training school*，也有使用 *juvenile detention center; youth detention center* 及 *juvenile hall*)

kidnap	*vt.*	誘拐，綁架，劫持
[`kɪdnæp]		

The alleged kidnappers called the victim's family and said that his daughter **was kidnapped**. 涉嫌的綁匪打電話給被害者的家人，並且說他的女兒被綁架了。

Police and FBI agents have launched a desperate search in Arizona for a six-year-old girl who disappeared from her home on Friday. They fear that the little girl might **have been kidnapped**. 對於星期五從家中失蹤的這個 6 歲女孩，警方與聯邦調查局已在亞歷桑納展開拼命搜尋，他們擔心這個小女孩可能已經被綁架了。

Kidnapping is the taking away of a person against his or her will by force or threat. Abduction is the taking away of a person by persuasion or by fraud. 「擄人(kidnapping)」是以武力或威脅違反他人意願而將人帶走，「誘拐/綁架(abduction)」是以說服或詐欺的方式將人帶走。

kidnapper	*n.*	The **kidnapper** abducted the victim and demanded a total of
[`kɪdnæpɚ]		one million in ransom. 綁匪綁架了被害人並要求 100 萬贖金。

knowingly	*adv.*	故意(或稱 with knowledge)
[`noɪŋlɪ]		

Application will be denied if the applicant **knowingly** makes false statement. 申請人如果故意做不實陳述的話，該申請將會被拒絕。

In general, statements given by a witness are presumed to be truthful. Those who are caught **knowingly** misleading a court will face serious criminal charges of perjury. 通常，證人的供訴是被推定所言屬實，被逮到故意誤導法院的人，會面臨嚴重的偽證罪刑事告訴。

laboratory	*n.*	實驗室，化學工廠，藥廠
[`læbrə,torɪ]	應用	*clandestine lab* 非法(毒品)工廠

crime lab 犯罪實驗室

laboratory accreditation 實驗室認證

larceny [ˋlɑrsnɪ]	*n.*	竊盜 【補充說明】theft、larceny 及 burglary 是相似的用語。在美國，各州可能使用 theft 用或 larceny 來描述偷竊) 應用 *aggravated larceny* 加重竊盜
large [lɑrdʒ]		be at large 逍遙法外，在逃中，(指罪犯、動物等)自由的 After the shootout, one suspect turned himself in to police, but the second suspect remained **at large**. 槍戰之後，有一名嫌犯向警方自首，但第二位嫌犯仍然在逃。
launch [lɔntʃ]	*vt.*	發動，開展，發出 The FBI has announced their plans to **launch** an investigation on the case. 聯邦調查局宣布他們計畫對本案發動調查。 Police and FBI agents **have launched** a desperate search in Arizona for a six-year-old girl who disappeared from her home on Friday. They fear that the little girl might have been kidnapped. 對於星期五從家中失蹤的這個 6 歲女孩，警方與聯邦調查局已在亞歷桑納展開拼命搜尋，他們擔心這個小女孩可能已經被綁架了。
law enforcement agency		執法機關 (或 law enforcement authorities)
law enforcement officer		執法人員
law-abiding [ˋlɔ,baɪdɪŋ]	*adj.*	守法的 Most people are **law-abiding** citizens who never have any problems with the law. 大部分的人都是從未有法律麻煩的守法市民。
lawful [ˋlɔfəl]	*adj.*	合法的，法律上正當的 應用 *lawful arrest* 合法的逮捕 (*to make a lawful arrest* 進行合法逮捕) *lawful excuse* 合法的理由、法律上的理由 *lawful interception* 合法攔截 (即：電話監聽 *telephone tapping*、*wire tapping* 或 *wiretapping*) *lawful order* 合法的命令
lawsuit [ˋlɔ,sut]	*n.*	訴訟(尤指非刑事案件) Most people would look for someone with litigation experience when they file or defend **lawsuits**. 大多數人在提起或防禦訴訟時，會找有訴訟經驗的人。
lawyer [ˋlɔ,sut]	*n.*	律師 (或稱 *attorney; attorney-at-law; counsel; solicitor*)

lead [lid]	vi.	導致......後果，帶到某處
		Mistaken identifications may **lead to** the arrest of innocent persons. 錯誤的指認會導致無辜者被逮捕。
		The information provided by the informant **has led to** the apprehension of the criminal suspect. 線民提供的資訊導致了嫌犯的逮捕。
	n.	線索，提示
		Police say hundred of officers are investigating **leads** related to the convicted murderer who escaped from the prison over the weekend. 警方說，數百位員警正在調查周末時從監獄脫逃的殺人定讞人犯的相關線索。

leading ['lidɪŋ]	adj.	帶領的
	應用	*leading question* 誘導性詰問

leave [liv]	vt.	使處於某種狀態，留下
		The apartment building fire **left** four people dead. 公寓火災造成四人死亡。
		City Police Department is investigating the shooting that **left one fugitive dead** and two citizens wounded. 市警局正在調查這起造成一名逃犯死亡及兩位市民受傷的槍擊案。
		The car crash has **left three people dead** and 5 others **injured**. The two people trapped inside the vehicle **were pronounced dead** at the scene. One **was pronounced dead** at the hospital. 這起車禍造成了三人死亡及五人受傷，被困在車內的兩人被當場宣告死亡，一人到醫院被宣告死亡。
		The victim was stabbed and **was left for dead**. 被害人遭刺，並被棄之而死。
		Always keep in mind that it is illegal to **leave** a child **unattended** in a motor vehicle. 要隨時記得，將小孩單獨留在汽車裡，是違法的。
		Sometimes, the undercover agent would **leave** a car **unattended** in a high crime area, with the door unlocked, and then round up the suspect while he is committing the car theft. 有時候，臥底幹員會把車子留在高犯罪地區，讓車門沒上鎖，然後等嫌犯進行竊車時圍捕他。
	n.	休假，休假期
		He takes sick **leave** today. He will **be on** sick **leave** for five days. 他今天請病假，他會掛病假五天。
		Police department has placed one of its officers **on** dministrative **leave**. He was put on paid administrative **leave**, pending the

outcome of an internal investigation. 警察局已經給予其中一位員警行政假(停職)，他被放行政假(停職)，等待政風調查的結果。

應用	*administrative leave* 行政假
	annual Leave 年休假
	marriage leave 婚假
	offical leave 公假
	personal leave 事假
	sick leave 病假
	two weeks' leave 休假兩周

legal [`lig!]	*adj.*	法律上的，合法的，正當的
	應用	*joint legal custody* 共同法律監護
		legal action 法律追訴
		legal advice 法律意見
		legal age 法定年齡
		legal aid 法律扶助
		Legal Attache (Legat)(聯邦調查局派駐國外的)法務官
		legal dispute 法律爭議
		legal document 法律文件
		legal guardian 法定監護人
		legal issue 法律問題
		legal limit 法律限度
		legal officer 法律官員
		legal process 法律程序
		legal right 法律權利
		legal scholar 法學家
		legal standard 法律標準
		legal system 司法系統
		legal term 法律術語
		mutual legal assistance 司法互助
		Mutual Legal Assistance Agreement 司法互助協定
		to take legal action against 對……採取法律行動

leg-cuff	*n.*	腳鐐 (或稱 *shackle; foot-cuff; leg iron*)
legislation [,lɛdʒɪs`leʃən]	*n.*	立法
legislator [`lɛdʒɪs,letə]	*n.*	立法者
lethal [`liθəl]	*adj.*	致命的，危險的，毀滅性的 Riot police often use **non-lethal** force or **less-lethal** weapons,

such as Tasers, rubber bullets, pepper spray, and tear gas against demonstrators. 鎮暴警察常使用非致命武力或低致命武器來對抗示威者，例如電擊槍、塑膠子彈、胡椒噴霧，及催淚瓦斯。

liability [ˌlaɪəˈbɪlətɪ]	*n.* 應用	責任，義務 *civil liability* 民事責任 *criminal liability* 刑事責任 *legal liability* 法律責任 *political liability* 政治責任 【補充說明】按 liability 及 responsibility 的中文翻譯都是「責任，義務」，但略有差別在於 liability 指的比較是法律方面；responsibility 指的比較是道德倫理方面。(By definition, liability is a legal issue, and responsibility is a moral and ethical issue)
liable [ˈlaɪəbl̩]	*adj.* 應用	負有法律責任的，有義務的[(+for)][+to-v] In general, helping people or choosing not to help is a moral dilemma and not a crime. Therefore, people should not **be held** criminally **liable for** not helping people in need. 一般而言，幫助人或選擇不幫助人是道德困境而不是犯罪，因此，人們不會因為不幫助有需要的人而負刑事責任。 *hold (sb) liable for* 讓(人)為……負起責任
liaison [ˌlɪeˈzɑn]	*n.* 應用	【軍】聯絡，聯繫 *police liaison officer* 警察聯絡官
libel [ˈlaɪbl̩]	*n.*	【律】(利用文字、圖畫等的)誹謗(罪)，誹謗的文字(或圖畫等) Defamation is a catch-all term for any statement that hurts someone's reputation. Written defamation is called **libel**, and spoken defamation is called slander. 誹謗(defamation)一詞是指「傷害他人名聲的言論」的通稱，書面的誹謗用 libel 一詞，口頭的誹謗用 slander 一詞。
lie [laɪ]	*n.* *vi.* 應用	謊言 Officer said, "it is not an offence to **tell a lie**, but If you **tell a lie**, this may be used in evidence." 員警說，說謊不是犯罪，但如果你說謊，這可以被用來作為證據。 撒謊 The suspect **lied** to police **about** his name and date of birth. He **lied about** his age. 嫌犯向警方謊報他的姓名及出生年月日。他謊報年齡。 *to lie in wait (+for)* (為謀殺他人而)事先埋伏 The suspect **was lying in wait** in the garage. He **was lying in wait for** the victim to exit the gum before opening the fire. 嫌

犯在停車場事先埋伏，他在開槍之前，事先埋伏在健身房出口等待被害人出來。

life	*n.*	(個人的)性命，一生，無期徒刑
[laɪf]		

Fire may **cost human life** and the loss of money and property. 火災會造成人命損失及金錢與財產的損害。

If a prisoner receives **life imprisonment**, he may be held in captivity until he dies. But in reality, a **life sentence** does not always mean imprisonment **for life**. 如果受刑人獲得無期徒刑時，他可能會被囚禁直到死亡，但事實上，無期徒刑並非都是意味著終生監禁。

Many people believed that the murder suspect's actions and his continued threat to public safety would keep him incarcerated **for life**. 很多人相信，殺人犯的行為以及他對於公眾安全的持續性威脅，會讓他終生都被關著。

life-threatening	*adj.*	（疾病等）威脅生命的，致命的
[ˈlaɪfθrɛtənɪŋ]		

The suspect posed a threat to the police officer, who was compelled to use deadly force **to take his life** in such a **life-threatening** situation. 嫌犯對員警作勢威脅，迫使員警在這樣的生命威脅情況之下，使用了致命武器結束他的生命。

EMTs said that he was able to determine the presence of a **life-threatening** hemorrhage at the scene. 緊急救護技術員說，他在現場時判斷，有生命危險的出血。

應用 *inflatable life raft* 充氣橡皮製救生艇
life detector 生命探測器
life imprisonment 無期徒刑 (或稱 *life in prison; life sentence; life incarceration*)
life threatening 有生命威脅受的
lifeboat 救生艇，救生船(又稱 *survival craft*)
lifebuoy 救生圈，救生帶
lifejacket 救生衣
lifeline 救生索
liferaft 橡皮製救生艇
life-saving 救命(用)的
take one's life 結束某人的生命
to put one's life at risk 將某人的生命置於險境

life-and-death	*adj.*	生死攸關的，重大的
[ˈlaɪfənˈdɛθ]		

Everyday, firefighters make many **life-and-death** decisions when they are on duty. 消防員每天在出勤時，都在做生死攸關的決定。

lineup ['laɪn,ʌp]	n.	(證人指認嫌犯讓數人排成的) 排列指認

Lineup is the police identification procedure. In the **lineup process**, the victim or witness will be brought into the **lineup room**. In addition to **physical lineup**, investigators may decide to use **photo lineup**. 排列指認是警方的確認程序，在排列指認的程序中，被害人或證人會被帶到指認室。除了人身指認之外，偵查人員得決定使用相片指認。

load [lod]	vt.	裝，裝載[(+with)]

The suspect **loaded** a semi-automatic handgun magazine and then opened fire. 嫌犯裝填半自動手槍的彈夾，然後開火。

loaded ['lodɪd]	adj.	(槍等)裝彈藥的

Police executed a search warrant at the suspect's house, where they found four **loaded** firearms. 警方在他家執行搜索票，在那裡警方發現四把裝填彈藥了的武器。

loan-shark ['lon,ʃark]	n.	放高利貸者
	vi.	以放高利貸為業

locate [lo`ket]	vt.	確定……的地點，探出，找出

Authorities said that police searched the area, but they were unable to **locate** the suspects. 當局說，警方搜索了這個地區，但他們無法找到嫌犯。

A country may wish to obtain the extradition of a fugitive whose whereabouts **is located** abroad. 逃犯的下落在國外被查到時，國家可能希望取得逃犯的引渡。

Thermal imager helps firefighter to find their way in the dark building and **to locate** fire victims. 熱影像儀幫助消防員在黑暗的建築物中找到路及找到火災遇難者。

Firefighters said high heat and heavy smoke conditions hampered the search. A victim **was located** in the second floor'sbedroom and was brought out. Firefighters removed several victims from the structure. 消防員說，高熱及濃煙狀況阻礙了搜尋。有一位遇難者在二樓的臥室被找到並被帶出來。消防員從建築物帶出了幾個遇難者。

lock [lak]	vt.	(人的) 關押 (通常多加 up)

The offender **was locked up** for the murder of Justin. He **was locked up** for eight years. 這名罪犯因為謀殺賈斯汀被關，他被關了八年。

	vt.	鎖住

The suspect purposely **locked** the victim in the basement. The door **was locked from** the outside. 嫌犯故意將被害人鎖在地

下室，門從外面被上鎖。

| | vi. | 鎖住 |

The door **locked**. 門鎖住了。

| lockdown | n. | 禁閉室 |
| [`lɑk,ʌp] | | |

Solitary confinement is referred to in the U.S. as **lockdown**. Correctional officials should not use a **lockdown** to substitute for disciplinary sanctions. 單獨監禁在美國稱為禁閉，矯正官員不可以用禁閉取代訓誡懲罰。

| lockup | n. | (臨時)拘留所 |
| [`lɑk,ʌp] | | |

A police lockup is neither a jail nor a prison. **Police lockups** should be monitored to ensure that their human rights are respected. 警方的留置室不是看守所也不是監獄，警方的留置室應該要予以監控，以確保他們的人權有被顧及。

| lodge | vt. | 提出(申訴，抗議等)[(+with)]、[(+against)] |
| [lɑdʒ] | | |

The man decided to **lodge** a complaint against the company. 該人決定對這家公司提出控告。

| look into | v. | 調查 |

Police **are looking into** the death of the gang member. 警方正在調查這個幫派分子的死因。

Investigators **are looking into** whether stowaways are tucked inside a shipping container. 偵查員正在調查偷渡客是否有被塞進船隻的貨櫃內。

| lookout | n. | 守望，警戒，監視 |
| [`lʊk`aʊt] | | |

If a traffic signal light is green and a police officer signals you to stop, you should obey the traffic officer and **be on the lookout for** red light runners. 如果交通號誌燈為綠燈，而員警示意你停車，你必須遵從交通警察，並小心闖紅燈的人。

| loot | vt. | 搶劫，洗劫，強奪 |
| [lut] | | |

Rioters turned violent and **looted** several stores during the protest. 聚眾鬧事者變得暴力，並且在抗議時洗劫了幾家商店。

| lost and found | | 失物招領處 |
| [,lɑstənd`faʊnd] | | |

| lure | vt. | 引誘，誘惑 |
| [lʊr] | | |

Investigators should always confirm the source of information and be careful not to **be lured into** a trap. 偵查人員都得要確認資訊的來源，並小心不被引入陷阱。

| Mafia | n. | (義大利)黑手黨，(m-)祕密犯罪集團 |
| [`mɑfɪ,ɑ] | | |

magazine [ˌmægəˈzin]	*n.*	(槍上的) 彈閘，彈盒，彈盤子彈夾

The suspect loaded a semi-automatic handgun magazine and then opened fire. 嫌犯裝填半自動手槍的彈夾，然後開火。

maintain [menˈten]	*vt.*	維持，保持，堅持，主張，斷言

Law enforcement officers may use reasonable force to **maintain** order and discipline. 執法人員得使用合理武力以維持秩序與紀律。

It is important that dispatchers **maintain** control of all telephone conversations and **maintain** radio contact with the field officers. 派遣官對所有電話的對話維持掌控，並與轄區員警保持無線電聯絡，是重要的。

major [ˈmedʒɚ]	*adj.*	主要的，重要的

The **Major Crimes Unit** investigates all serious crimes such as homicides, kidnappings, robberies, etc. Personnel with the Unit are responsible for **major** criminal investigations. 重案組偵查所有嚴重的犯罪例如殺人、綁架、強盜等。該組人員負責重大犯罪的調查。

應用

major case 重大案件

Major Case Unit 重案組

major causes of death 主要死因

major crime 重大犯罪

Major Crimes Unit 重案組 (或 *Major Crime Unit*)

major explosion 重大爆炸

major fire 重大火災

major responsibility 首要責任

major suspect (prime suspect) 主嫌犯、重大嫌犯

make [mek]	*vt.*	做

應用

to make a case against 對⋯⋯立案

to make a forcible entry 強制進入⋯⋯

to make a formal accusation against 對⋯⋯嫌犯做正式的控告

to make a judgment 做出判決

to make a left turn 右轉

to make a right turn on red 紅燈時左轉

to make a U-turn 迴轉

to make a confession 做出自白

to make a motion 提出聲請

to make a plan 做策畫

to make a report to 向⋯⋯報告/報案

to make a roll call 點名

to make a ruling / order 做成裁決/裁定

to make an appeal 提出上訴

to make an arrest 進行逮捕

to make an effort 努力

to make an evaluation 進行評估

to make any public statement 發表公開言論

to make application to the judge 向法官提出申請

to make child support payment 支付子女撫養費

to make court appearance 出庭

to make false insurance claim 不實申請保險索賠

to make false report 謊報

to make false statement 做不實陳述

to make voice comparison 做聲紋比對

to make warrantless arrest 進行無令狀逮捕

maltreatment [mæl`tritmənt]	*n.*	虐待，粗暴對待，不當對待 In general, there are four major types of **maltreatment**, including physical abuse, sexual abuse, neglect, and emotional abuse. 大致而言，不當對待有四種，包括身體虐待、性虐待、忽視及精神虐待。
mandatory [`mændə,torɪ]	*adj.*	義務的，強制的 Law enforcement officers believe that it is necessary for repeat sex offenders to undergo **mandatory** therapy. 執法人員相信，讓性侵害慣犯接受強制治療是必要的。
manhunt [`mæn,hʌnt]	*n.*	搜索，追捕 According to a press release from the police, a **manhunt** was initiated to capture the suspect, following the issuing of an arrest warrant on the charge of murder. 依據警方的新聞發布，在指控殺人的逮捕令發布之後，即展開一場追捕以抓拿嫌犯。
manslaughter [`mæn,slɔtɚ]	*n.*	【律】一般殺人罪，過失致死 Murder and **manslaughter** are two different types of homicide. Murder is the killing of human being with malice aforethought, and is subdivided by degrees. **Manslaughter** is the unlawful killing of a human being without malice aforethought. 謀殺(murder)與殺人(manslaughter 包括殺人與致死兩個意義)是 homicide 的兩種不同的態樣，Manslaughter 這個字的殺人是沒有惡意預謀的非法殺人。
manufacture [,mænjə`fæktʃɚ]	*n.*	(大量)製造，加工 The illegal importation, **manufacture**, distribution, possession and improper use of controlled substances have a substantial and

		detrimental effect on the health and general welfare of the people. 非法進口、製造、散布、持有，及不當使用管制物質，對於人的健康及全般福祉具有實質及有害的影響。
	vt.	製造
		The FBI confirmed that the drugs **were manufactured** in Mexico. 聯邦調查局證實這些毒品是墨西哥製的。
		Many illicit drugs **are manufactured** in clandestine drug labs. 許多非法毒品都是非法毒品工廠所製造的。
march [mɑrtʃ]	*n.*	遊行抗議，遊行示威 Protesters pledged not to cross the picket line during the **march**. 示威者保證在遊行的時候，不會跨越過警戒線。
marijuana [ˌmɑrɪˈhwɑnə]	*n.*	【植】大麻，大麻煙，大麻毒品，(又稱 hashish)
marked police vehicle		制式警車 (unmarked police vehicle 一般警車)
mask [mæsk]	*n.*	口罩，防護面具 應用 *gas mask* 防毒面具 *face mask* 口罩
masked [mæskt]	*adj.*	戴假面具的，戴防護面具的，偽裝的，隱蔽的 They were held captive by **masked** gunmen. 他們被蒙面槍手劫持了。 應用 *masked gunman* 蒙面槍手 *masked robber* 蒙面搶匪 *masked suspect* 蒙面嫌犯
mastermind [ˈmæstə-maɪnd]	*n.*	幕後主使者 One of the suspects that robbed the store was arrested. Under questioning, he revealed the names of two other members of the gang but said he did not know the identity of the **mastermind** behind the holdup. 行搶商店的嫌犯之一被捕了，問訊中，他透露其他兩名幫派分子的姓名，但是說他不知道搶案幕後主使者的身分。
MCI	*abbr*	大量傷患事件 **Mass Casualty Incident** (另有稱：Mass Fatality Incident 或 Multiple Casualty Incident) **MCI** includes initial triage, patient extraction, medical treatment and transportation of patients. Types of **MCI** incidents include, but not limited to: multiple vehicle collision, building collapse, mass transit accidents, HAZMAT incidents, chemical exposure, etc. 「大量傷患事件(MCI) 」包括初步檢傷分類(initial triage)、傷患挑出(patient extraction)、醫治(medical treatment)以及傷患運送(transportation of patients)。「大量傷患事件(MCI) 」的

型態包括，但不限於：連環車禍、建築物倒塌、大眾運輸意外、有害物質、化學爆炸等等。

mediate [ˈmidɪˌet]	vt.	調停解決 Traditionally, the police response to a domestic call has been to try to **mediate** the situation or to simply get the batterer out the house for the night. 傳統上，警察對於家事電話的回應一向是試著調解狀況，或只是在當天晚上把實施暴力的一方帶離開而已。
mediator [ˈmidɪˌetɚ]	n.	調停者
medical examiner [ˈmɛdɪk!] [ɪgˈzæmɪnɚ]		法醫(又稱 coroner) The duties of the **medical examiner** are to investigate the causes of deaths, conduct autopsies, and help the prosecutions of homicide cases. 法醫的職責是調查死因、相驗及協助凶殺案件的起訴。 Fire investigators haven't completely ruled out the possibility that the male was the arisonist, and the **medical examiner** said further study was being done to determine how they died. 消防員還沒完全排除這個男子就是縱火犯，並且法醫說，正在做進一步的研究，已確定他們是如何死的。 【補充說明】稱 medical examiner 的法醫不一定要是刑事病理學家，但他是受政府指派的醫生；而稱 coroner 的法醫通常不是醫生，但常是民選的。現在美國有的州使用 coroner 的制度；有的州使用 medical examiner 的制度。
mental [ˈmɛnt!]	adj.	精神的，心理的 A witness is ordinarily presumed to have the **mental** capacity to testify. 證人通常推定有作證的精神能力。
	應用	*mental illness* 精神疾病 *mental health* 精神健康 *mental condition* 精神情況 *mental disorder* 精神障礙
merge [mɝdʒ]	vi.	(車道的)匯合，匯入 As you **merge into** the highway, you have to maintain a nice distance from the cars behind you and in front of you. 當你匯入高速公路時，你必須與前後車維持良好的距離。
Methamphetamine [ˌmɛθæmˈfɛtəmin]	n.	【藥】甲基苯丙胺，甲基安非它命 (比安非他命更強的興奮劑)
middleman [ˈmɪd!ˌmæn]	n.	中間人，掮客 (同義字 go-between) Most traffickers shipped their drugs to Miami, and then sold

them to **middlemen** with connections around the country. 大部分私梟將毒品運到邁阿密，然後賣給與國內各地有管道的中間人。

The defendant acted as a **middleman** in the drug deal. He acted as a **middleman** for the drug suppliers and drug addicts 被告在這個毒品交易中擔任中間人。他在毒品供應者與吸毒者之間擔任中間人。

Miranda warnings		米蘭達警語(源於美國聯邦最高法院 Miranda v. Arizona, 384 U.S. 436, 1966 一案)

You have the right to remain silent. If you do say anything, what you say can be used against you in a court of law. You have the right to consult with a lawyer and have that lawyer present during any questioning. If you cannot afford a lawyer, one will be appointed for you if you so desire. If you choose to talk to the police officer, you have the right to stop the interview at any time. 你有權保持緘默；如果你說任何話，則你所說的任何話可以在法庭中被用來做為對你不利的證供；你有權利聘請律師，並在接受審訊時有律師在場；如果你請不起律師，而如果你想的話，法院會替你指派；如果你選擇與員警談，你有權在任何時間停止訪談。

misapprivation [ˌmɪsəˌprɪpɪˈeʃən]	n.	侵占

Misapprivation is embezzlement of money only. Embezzlement involves taking property that you already possess, but do not own. 侵占用 misappropriation 一詞是僅指金錢的侵占，侵占用 embezzlement 一詞是指取走已經持有但非擁有的財產。

miscarriage of justice		【律】審判不公，誤判

misconduct [mɪsˈkandʌkt]	n.	不當行為，對(異性)行為不端

From citizen's perspective, the excessive use of physical force and excessive abuse of police power are often seen as police brutality, not just police **misconduct**. 從市民的角度，過度使用身體武力及過度的濫用警察權，常被視為是警察暴力，而不只是警察行為不當而已。

Police corruption is a form of police **misconduct** in which officers abuse their power for personal gain. 警察貪汙是一種警察濫用權力以謀私人所得的不當行為。

misdemeanor [ˌmɪsdɪˈminə]	n.	【律】輕罪

In the United States, criminal law divides crimes into two main categories: felony and **misdemeanor**. 在美國，刑法將犯罪分

為兩大類：重罪與輕罪。

misdirect [,mɪsdə`rɛkt]	*vt.*	誤導 Criminal will stage a crime scene to **misdirect** investigators so as to get away with the crime. 罪犯會假造一個犯罪現場來誤導偵查人員，以逃避犯罪。
miserable [`mɪzərəb!]	*adj.*	悽慘的，悲哀的 His life was **miserable** during his school years. He was bullied and was subject to physical harm. 在學生時代他的生活真是悽慘，他被霸凌並且受到身體上的傷害。
misfortune [mɪs`fɔrtʃən]	*n.*	(非因自己的原因而發生的) 不幸，厄運，災難 **Misfortune** never come single [singly]. 真是禍不單行。
misjudge [mɪs`dʒʌdʒ]	*vt.*	對……判斷錯誤 The truck driver **misjudged** the time and distance needed to pass safely and subsequently collided with another truck. 卡車司機對於要安全通過所需的時間與距離判斷錯誤，結果與另一輛卡車擦撞。
	vt.	對……判斷不公，錯判 No matter in whichever country, **misjudged** criminal cases are inevitable. 不管任何國家，有錯判的刑事案件是不可避免的。 A judge will be punished only when he intentionally **misjudges** a case. If the judge accidentally **misjudges** a case because of his carelessness, then he will not be punished at all. 法官只有當他故意將案件錯判時才會被處罰，如果法官偶然地因為疏忽而錯判案件，那他完全不會被處罰。
	應用	*misjudged case* 錯判的案件 *misjudged criminal case* 錯判的刑事案件
mislead [mɪs`lid]	*vt.*	誤導 The jury **was misled by** the false evidence. 陪審團被不實證據誤導。 The police **were misled by** an informant that there were illicit drugs at Jackson's residence. 警方被線民誤導傑克森的住處有非法毒品。
misleading [mɪs`lidɪŋ]	*adj.*	誤導的 The trial court found the suspect's statements to be **misleading**. 審理法院認定嫌犯的陳述是誤導的。 In general, statements given by a witness are presumed to be truthful. Those who are caught knowingly **misleading** a court will face serious criminal charges of perjury. 通常，證人的供述是被推定所言屬實，被逮到故意誤導法院的人，會面臨嚴重

的偽證罪刑事告訴。

mitigate [ˋmɪtə͵get]	vt.	使緩和，減輕 Authorities said they will come up with strategies **to mitigate** the impact of natural hazards. "We will do our best to prepare the communities **to mitigate** the impact of natural disasters. We will provide funding **to mitigate** future disaster damage, the Mayor said. 當局說他們會提出策略來減輕自然災害的衝擊。「我們會盡力讓我們的社區準備好，去減輕自然災害的衝擊。我們會提供資金援助，來減輕未來的災損」，市長說。
mitigation [͵mɪtəˋgeʃən]	n.	緩和，減輕，(災防的)減災 One of our priorities is to reinforce our role in disaster mitigation and prevention, the Mayor said. 我們的優先是項之一就是強化我們在災害的減災與預防方面的角色，市長說。
mob [mɑb]	n.	暴徒，暴民，烏合之眾 **Mobs** were spreading throughout the city and began throwing stones through windows. 暴徒竄到城市各地，並開始用石頭砸窗戶。
mobster [ˋmɑbstɚ]	n.	暴徒(或流氓)集團的一分子，匪徒
mock [mɑk]	vt.	對……嘲弄，對……嘲笑 The defendant **mocked** the victim **as** a clown, and caused the victim to suffer servere emotional distress before the suicide. 被告嘲笑被害人是小丑，造成被害人在自殺前受到嚴重的情緒困擾。
	vi.	嘲弄，嘲笑 [(+at)] They **mocked at** him. They **mocked at** his idea. 他們嘲笑他，他們嘲笑他的構想。
modus operandi [ˋmodəs ͵ɑpəˋrændɪ]	n.	(犯罪的)手法 (或縮寫為 m.o.) The suspect gave us a detailed account of his **modus operandi**. 嫌犯給我們詳盡說明了他的犯罪手法。
molest [məˋlɛst]	vt.	猥褻，調戲，性騷擾 Sociologists and social workers indicated that many adults **were molested** as children. 社會學家與社工指出，許多大人在兒童時有被猥褻。
molestation [͵moləsˋteʃən]	n.	猥褻，調戲，性騷擾 The suspect was arrested on **child molestation** charges for allegedly abusing a 14-year-old student. 嫌犯因涉嫌性虐待一名 14 歲的學生，而被以兒童性騷擾罪逮捕。
money laundering		洗錢

In some countries, casinos have become a haven for **money laundering**. They allow criminals to use their bank accounts for money laundering purposes. 許多國家，賭場已成為洗錢的天堂，它們讓罪犯以洗錢的目的使用銀行帳戶。

monitor [ˋmɑnətɚ]	*vt.*	監控，監聽，監測，監視

Police lockups should **be monitored** to ensure that their human rights are respected. 警方的留置室應該要予以監控，以確保他們的人權有被顧及。

Electronic monitoring (or electronically monitored supervision) is considered a highly economical alternative to the cost of imprisoning offenders. Sex offenders are often required to wear an **electronic monitoring bracelet**. 相對於監禁人犯的費用來說，電子監控被認為是一項相當經濟的替代方式，性侵害罪犯經常被要求戴上電子監控手環。

Because transshipments often take place in remote locations, it is difficult to **monitor** transshipment at sea. 因為轉載經常發生在遙遠的地方，要監控海上轉載是困難的。

監測，監視，監控

The EMT testified he has properly assessed and treated the patient. He said he had assessed vital signs, administered oxygen and continued **to monitor** the patient's vital signs during the transport. 緊急救護技術員作證說，他有適當地對患者評估及治療。他說他有評估生命跡象、給予氧氣，並且在運送之際，有持續監控患者的生命跡象。

	n.	監測器，監視器，監控器
	應用	*vital sign monitor* 生命跡象監視器
		patient monitor 病患監視器

moral [ˋmɔrəl]	*adj.*	道德(上)的，品性端正的，精神上的，心理上的，道義上的

morale [məˋræl]	*n.*	士氣，道德，品行

motion [ˋmoʃən]	*n.*	【律】(訴訟人提出的)聲請，請求，申請
	應用	*to grant one's motion* 准予某人的聲請
		to deny one's motion 駁回某人的聲請
		motion for default judgment 聲請缺席判決
		motion for judgment of acquittal 聲請無罪判決
		motion for new trial 聲請重新審理
		motion for protective order 聲請保護令
		motion for summary judgment 聲請簡易判決

motion to alter or amend the judgment 聲請變更或修改判決
motion to dismiss for lack of jurisdiction 以欠缺管轄為由聲請駁回
motion to dismiss for lack of standing 以欠缺訴訟資格聲請駁回
motion to dismiss 聲請駁回(原告)起訴
motion to enforce 聲請執行
motion to remand 聲請發回
motion to suppress 聲請排除非法證據
motion to transfer venue 聲請移轉管轄地

motivate [`motə,vet]	*vt.*	促動 The preliminary investigation indicates that the assault **was motivated by** a dispute over parking. 初步調查指出，該項攻擊是起因於停車糾紛。
motivation [,motə`veʃən]	*n.*	動機 Both pyromania and arson involve setting fires. The major difference between the two is the **motivation**. Arsonists usually have criminal **motivations**, while pyromaniacs do not. Pyromania does not have any obvious motive. 縱火狂(pyromania)與縱火(arson)都涉及放火，兩者主要的不同在於動機，縱火犯通常有犯罪動機，但縱火狂不是，縱火狂沒有任何明顯的動機。
motive [`motɪv]	*n.*	動機，主旨，目的[(+of/for)] Revenge is the most common **motive** for a serial arsonist. 報復，是連續縱火犯最常見的動機。
mourn [morn]	*vt.*	為……哀痛，為……哀悼 The day after the shooting, more than 200 people gathered at the scene **to mourn** the victim. 槍擊案的隔天，超過 2 百人聚集在現場哀悼被害人。
	vi.	哀痛，哀悼[（+for/over）] They **mourned for** the death of the victim. 他們為被害人的死亡哀悼。
movement [`muvmənt]	*n.*	動向 CCTV images can track the **movement** of offenders and witness to and from the scene. 閉路影像可以追蹤犯罪者與證人往來於現場的動向。
moving violation		動態違規 應用 *non-moving violation* 靜態違規
mugshot [`mʌgʃat]	*n.*	(嫌犯檔案)臉部照片 If the accused is arrested, he or she must cooperate with the

booking process, and must allow officers to take his or her **mugshot**. 如果被告被逮捕，他必須配合錄案(移送)程序，並且必須讓員警拍攝他的臉部照片。

murder	*vt.*	殺人(基於惡意的預謀而殺死人)
[ˋmɝdɚ]		Detectives investigating the death of victim have revealed that they cannot rule out the possibility she **was murdered**. 偵辦這起被害人死亡的偵查員透露，他們不能排除她是被謀殺的可能。
	n.	謀殺，殺人(基於惡意的預謀而殺死人)

The man was arrested on suspicion of **murder**. 該男子因涉有謀殺之嫌而被捕。

The suspect claimed that he did not commit the **murder**. 嫌犯聲稱他沒犯下這起謀殺案。

The suspect went on trial on **murder charges** last week. Prosecutors said DNA on the cartridge connects him to the crime. 嫌犯在上星期就謀殺案的指控出庭，檢察官說，彈殼上的 DNA 連結了他與這件犯罪。

The **murder suspect** was confined to a prison's psychiatric ward. She was convicted of **murder**. 謀殺案嫌犯被關在監獄中的精神病囚室，她被判謀殺罪成立。

The **murderer** wes executed last week. 殺人犯在上周已經伏法了。

In the **murder for hire** conspiracy (or plot, scheme), both the hired killer and the mastermind who hired him were found guilty of murder. 在這起雇傭殺人的共謀案件中，被雇用的殺手與雇用的幕後藏鏡人雙雙被認定謀殺罪成立。

應用　*murder for hire* 雇傭的殺人

murderer	*n.*	殺人犯，兇手
[ˋmɝdərɚ]		
mutual legal assistance		司法互助，Mutual Legal Assistance Agreement 司法互助協定
nab	*vt.*	抓住，逮捕 (現行犯)
[næb]		The suspect **was nabbed by** the police at his home and charged with murder and weapon possession. Police did not release his name because he is a juvenile. 嫌犯在家中被警方抓到，並被指控殺人及持有槍枝。由於他是未成年，因此警方並未公布其姓名。
narcotic	*n.*	麻醉劑，致幻毒品
[nɑrˋkɑtɪk]	*adj.*	麻醉的，有麻醉作用的，與毒品有關的

A successful drug investigation depends on how well **narcotics** investigators can locate and identify leads. Drug canines or drug dogs are extremely useful to **narcotics** investigations. 一個成功的毒品偵查，端看毒品偵查員能多麼順利地找到及確認線報，緝毒犬對於毒品偵查是相當有用的。

naturalization [`nætʃərələˋzeʃən]	*n.*	(外國人的)歸化

neglect [nɪgˋlɛkt]	*n.* 應用	忽視，忽略 *child neglect* 兒童忽視 *developmental neglect* 成長忽視 *educational neglect* 教育忽視 *emotional neglect* 情緒忽視 *health care neglect* 健康照顧忽視 *neglect of household safety and sanitation* 家戶安全及衛生的忽視 *neglected child* 被忽視的孩童 *nutritional neglect* 營養忽視 *physical neglect* 身體忽視

negligence [ˋnɛglɪdʒəns]	*n.* 應用	過失 *criminal negligence* 刑事過失 (*with negligence* 為 *negligently* 同義詞)

negligently [ˋnɛglɪdʒəntlɪ]	*adv.*	過失地 (或稱 with negligence) A person is not guilty of an offense unless he acted purposely, knowingly, recklessly or **negligently**. **Negligently** has equivalent term such as with negligence. 任何人之行為非基於故意(purposely 或 knowingly)或過失(recklessly 或 negligently)者，不成立犯罪。negligently 有同義詞為 with negligence.

negotiate [nɪˋgoʃɪ,et]	*vi.*	談判，協商，洽談[(+with/for)] During the standoff, police attempted **to negotiate with** the hostage taker. At last, officers successfully **negotiated with** the suspect. 在僵局對峙之時，警方試圖與人質劫持者談判，最後員警成功地與歹徒談判。
negotiator [nɪˋgoʃɪ,etɚ]	*n.*	談判人員，交涉者 The hostage taker did not cooperate with **negotiators** in the begining. 人質劫持者一開始並未與談判人員合作。
negotiation [nɪ,goʃɪˋeʃən]	*n.* 應用	談判，協商 The n**egotiation** lasted for 6 hours. 這場談判持續了 6 小時。 *hostage negotiation* 人質談判 *crisis negotiation* 危機談判

neighborhood watch		守望相助 (或稱 *crime watch; neighborhood crime watch*)

nervious [ˋnɝvəs]	*adj.*	緊張不安的[(+about)] The suspect **appeared nervous** during the interview. 嫌犯在訪談時顯得緊張不安。 "I can see you **are nervous**. If you're innocent, you have nothing to **be nervous about**." 「我可以看得出來你緊張，如果你是無辜的，你沒甚麼好緊張的。」
next-of-kin	*n.*	直系親屬 The police notified the **next of kin** of the woman who was killed in the car accident. 警方通知了車禍中喪生婦人的親屬。
nickname [ˋnɪk,nem]	*n.*	綽號 Police are seeking a suspect whose **nickname** is "CoCo". 警方正在尋找一名綽號「CoCo」的嫌犯。
	vt.	給……起綽號 He **was nicknamed** "CoCo" by other inmates when he was in prison. 他在監獄的時候被其他受刑人取綽號「CoCo」。
notice [ˋnotɪs]	*vt.*	注意，注意到 Police **noticed** a suspicious vehicle parked in front of the store. Officers **noticed** a suspected drug transaction at the scene. 警方注意到一輛停放在商店前的可疑車輛，員警注意到現場有一個可疑的毒品交易。
	n.	公告，通知，(國際刑警組織發布的)通報 【補充說明】 國際刑警通報(Interpol Notice)包括：(1)紅色通報(Red Notice)請求逮捕通緝者；(2)藍色通報(Blue Notice)蒐集的身分、下落或與犯罪活動；(3)綠色通報(Green Notice)通報週知某人從事刑事犯罪，而有可能在其他國家重施這些犯罪」的警示或犯罪情報；(4)黃色通報(Yellow Notice)請求協尋失蹤人；(5)黑色通報(Black Notice)尋求無名屍體的資訊；(6)橘色通報(Orange Notice)警示警察及其他國際組織關於偽裝之武器、郵包炸彈或其他危險物質的潛在威脅；(7)紫色通報(Purple Notice)提供罪犯使用的犯罪手法、程序、物品、裝置及躲藏地點的資訊。
notify [ˋnotə,faɪ]	*vt.*	通知，告知[(+of)][+that] You **are** hereby **notified that** a hearing will be held at the date, time, and location indicated above. 謹此向您通知，聽證將於上述日期、時間及地點舉行。 You will **be notified of** the date and location of the hearing based upon the contact information that you provide. 依據您提供的連絡資訊，您將會被通知聽證的日期及地點。
notorious	*adj.*	惡名昭彰的，聲名狼藉的[(+for)]

[no`torɪəs]		There are some **notorious** and dangerous criminal street gangs in this area. 有一些惡名昭彰而危險的街頭犯罪幫派在這一帶。
obedience [ə`bidjəns]	*n.*	服從，順從[(+to)]
obey [ə`be]	*vt.*	服從，聽從 You should **obey** the traffic signals and be on the lookout for red light runners. 你必須遵從交通號誌，並小心闖紅燈的人。
obligate [`ɑblə,get]	*vt.*	使……負有法律義務 When there is probable cause to make an arrest, officers **are obligated to** identify themselves, advise the person that he or she is under arrest, and explain why. 當有相當理由進行逮捕時，員警有義務表明身分，告知該人已被逮捕並解釋原因。
obligation [,ɑblə`geʃən]	*n.*	(道義上或法律上的)義務，責任 If there is any disruption during the reading of the verdicts, the bailiffs will have the **obligation** to remove any persons disrupting these proceedings. 如果宣讀判決的時候有任何擾亂，法警會有義務驅離任何擾亂程序的人。
obscene [əb`sin]	*adj.*	猥褻的，淫穢的 She filed a complaint at the police station and accused her neighbor of making **obscene** gesture. 她向派出所報案，控告她的鄰居比了猥褻的手勢。
observantion [,ɑbzɚ`veʃən]	*n.*	觀察，注意，監視 Prosecutor asked the investigator about his **observation** of the suspected drug transaction in the parking lot. Investigator testified that he saw the transaction. 檢察官問偵查員有關他對於在停車場疑似毒品交易的觀察狀況，偵查員作證說他有看到這個交易。
observe [əb`zɝv]	*vt.*	觀察，觀測，監視，看到，注意到[+(that)] While on the streets, police officers will **observe** people to detect problems or illegal activity. 在街上時，員警會觀察人群以發現問題或不法活動。 Officers shall adhere to this agency's use-of-force policy and shall **observe** the civil rights of the citizens. 員警應恪遵機關的武力使用政策，並應注意到市民的公民權利。
obstruct [əb`strʌkt]	*vt.*	阻塞，堵塞，妨礙，阻擾，阻止 No person shall **obstruct** the operations of the fire department. 任何人均不得阻礙消防局的行動任務。
obstruction	*n.*	阻塞，堵塞，妨礙，阻擾，阻止

[əb`strʌkʃən]

During the protest, several activists were arrested on charges of riot, resisting arrest and **obstruction** of government administration. 在抗議中，幾個激進人士被逮捕，被指控暴動、拒捕及妨礙政府行政。

應用 *obstruction of justice* 妨害司法公正罪 (此為普通法規定的犯罪，指妨礙司法人員在法庭上履行職務，或者妨害出庭人員以影響審判的行為。)

| obtain | *vt.* | 得到，獲得 |
| [əb`ten] | | |

應用
to obtain a driver license 取得駕駛執照
to obtain arrest warrant 取得逮捕令狀
to obtain confession 取得自白
to obtain credible information/ intelligence 取得可靠的資訊/情報
to obtain evidence 取得證據
to obtain formal approval 取得正式的核准
to obtain money, drug, and goods 取得金錢、毒品及物資
to obtain order of protection 取得保護令
to obtain statement 取得陳述
to obtain the assistance of foreign countries 取得外國的協助
to obtain the defendant's consent 取得被告的同意
to obtain the extradition of a fugitive 取得人犯的引渡
to obtain visa 取得簽證
to obtain consent 取得同意

| occupant | *n.* | (房子的)居住者，(車子的)乘客 |
| [`ɑkjəpənt] | | |

Smoke alarm can only alert the **occupants** to a fire in the house. It cannot contain or extinguish a fire. 煙霧警報器只能向住戶警示房子內有火災，它無法將火隔絕或撲滅。

Carpool/High occupancy vehicle (HOV) lane is reserved for buses or vehicles with the minimum number of **occupants** specified on the signs. 共乘/高乘載專用道是保留給巴士，或載有標示規定的最低乘座人數的車輛。

| offender | *n.* | 違法者 |
| [ə`fɛndə] | | |

應用
adult offender 成年犯
career offender 常業犯
first offender 初犯
habitual offender 慣犯
juvenile offender 少年犯
known offender 熟識的犯人
offender profiling 罪犯剖繪 (或稱 *psychological profiling* 心理

剖繪、*criminal profiling*)
repeat offender 累犯
serial offender 連續犯
sex offender 性侵犯
suspected offender 嫌疑犯

offense	*n.*	罪過，犯法(行為)，過錯
[əˋfɛns]		

All reports of crimes in progress shall receive first priority without regard to the nature of the **offense**. 所有進行中的犯罪的報案，應收到第一優先，不管其犯罪性質為何。

Entrapment can be explained as the conduct to induce the suspect to commit an **offense**. 誘陷可以被解釋為引誘嫌犯從事犯罪的行為。

According to the Penal Code, a person is not guilty of an **offense** unless he acted purposely, knowingly, recklessly or negligently. 依據刑法，人之行為非基於故意(purposely 或 knowingly)或過失(recklessly 或 negligently)者，不成立犯罪。

應用　*aggravated offense* 加重之罪
capital offense 死罪 (死刑為 *capital punishment*)
criminal offense 刑事犯罪
drug offense 毒品犯罪
extraditable offense 可引渡之犯罪
offense report 犯罪報告
prior offense 先前的犯罪
serious offense 嚴重的犯罪
sexual offense 性侵害罪

omission	*n.*	不作為
[oˋmɪʃən]		

The basic elements of a crime consist of intent, conduct, and causation. Conduct means an act or **omission**. 犯罪的基本要素包含犯意、行為及因果關係。行為指作為或不作為。

on	*prep.*	
[ɑn]	應用	*is/am/are admitted on a visa* 獲准依簽證入境

is/am/are arrested on suspicion of……疑涉有……之嫌而被逮捕
is/am/are on appeal 在上訴中
is/am/are on bail 在交保中
is/am/are on duty 在執勤中
is/am/are on fire 著火了*(The house is on fire.)*
is/am/are on patrol 在巡邏
is/am/are on probation for 因……在緩刑中

is/am/are on the lookout for red light runner 小心闖紅燈的人

is/am/are on the loose 在逃亡中， 逍遙法外

is/am/are on the run 在逃亡中

is/am/are on the track of……正在追蹤……

is/am/are on tow(車子的)被拖吊

is/am/are on trial 受審

is/am/are onvicted on all counts 所有各項的罪都被判有罪成立

is/am/are released on bail 被交保釋放

on the evidence presented 依據所提的證據

on the spot 當場

on-scene commander 現場指揮官

to come out on your own terms 自願投降出來

to crack down on crime 取締犯罪

to go on strike against……抗議反對……

to make a right turn on red 紅燈時左轉

to set the vehicle on fire 放火燒車

visa on arrival 落地簽證

open [`opən]	*vt.*	開，打開

13 people are dead and at least 8 others were injured after a gunman **opened fire at** the Washington Navy Yard on Monday, officials said. 在持槍歹徒星期一對華府海軍園區開槍後，已有 13 死及至少 8 人受傷，官員說。

Police Chief says that the FBI will **open an investigation** on the shootout. 警察局長說，聯邦調查局對於槍戰將會開啟調查。

Police **reopened** the case and decided to reconstruct the crime scene. 警方決定重啟案件並決定重建犯罪現場。

operate [`apə,ret]	*vt.*	運作，經營；(機器，車輛的) 開，開動，操作

Controlled delivery, if permitted by law, can also **be operated** through an undercover agent acting as a courier. 控制下交付如果受法律許可的話，也可以透過以臥底幹員擔任交通的方式操作。

A person who **operates** a motor vehicle while in an intoxicated condition is called driving while intoxicated. 在酒醉情況下駕駛機動車輛的人，稱為醉態駕駛(DWI)。

	vi.	運作，營業，營運

Interpol's General Secretariat **operates** 24 hours a day, 365 days a year. 國際刑警組織的祕書處每天 24 小時、一年 365 天運作

Gang members often **operate** as pimps, luring or forcing at-risk

		young females into prostitution，幫派分子常充當皮條客，引誘或迫使弱勢年輕女性從事賣淫。
operation [͵ɑpəˋreʃən]	*n.*	行動，操作，營運 Police launched a **joint operation** to crack down on drug offenses in this district. 警方發動一場聯合行動，取締本區毒品犯罪。

應用
emergency operation 急救行動
joint operation 聯合行動
rescue operation 救援行動
salvage operation 救援行動
surveillance operation 偵監行動
undercover operation 臥底行動
Emergency Operation Center (EOC) 緊急應變中心

opinion [əˋpɪnjən]	*n.*	意見，見解，主張

應用
concurring opinion 協同意見
dissenting opinion 不同意見
opinion testimony 意見證詞
plurality opinion 多數意見

opium [ˋopjəm]	*n.*	鴉片

order [ˋɔrdɚ]	*n.*	秩序，治安，規律

Generally speaking, the bailiff shall **preserve order** in the court. He must **keep order** in the court. 通常而言，法警應維持法院的秩序，他必須保持法院的秩序。

The defendant shouted in the courtroom. In order to maintain **order** in the courtroom, the judge banged his gavel and yelled: **"Order, Order in the Court"**. 被告在法庭叫囂，為了維持法庭秩序，法官敲擊法槌並喊道：「保持秩序，保持法庭秩序！」

vt. 命令，指揮[+(that)]

The court **ordered that** the defendant should receive psychological treatment. 法院命令被告應接受心理治療。

n. 令，命令

應用
protection order 保護令(或 *protective order*)
restraining order 保護令，禁制令

【補充說明】
按 protection order, protective order, 與 restraining order 中文都是「保護令」，通常會被互換使用(People use the terms **protection order, protective order** and **restraining order** interchangeably.)

通常而言，protective order 這種保護令特別是與家暴有關，protective order 的核發特別是針對暴力、跟蹤或性虐待的被害人。(Generally speaking, **protective orders** are typically associated with family violence. **Protective orders** are typically issued when you've been a victim of violence, stalking, or sexual abuse.)

另一方面，restraining order 這種保護令通常與刑事案件無關，而是多與民事案件有關。(On the other hand, **restraining orders** are generally not associated with criminal cases, and are almost always linked to civil case proceedings.)

origin	*n.*	起源
[ˋɔrədʒɪn]		

The **point of origin** Is the specific location at which a fire was ignited. 起火點是火被引燃的那個特定的地點。

應用　*to find fire's origin* 尋找起火源
to locate the fire's origin 找到起火源
to identify the fire's origin 確定起火源
probable origin 可能的起火源
the point of origin 起火點、起始點
place of origin 籍貫、先人所來自的地方 (本身的出生地是 *place of birth* 簡稱 POB)

outage	*n.*	（水、電等的）中斷供應
[ˋaʊtɪdʒ]		

The storm caused trees to topple onto home in downtown, sparked **power outages** across the city. 暴風雨造成在市區有樹木壓倒住家，並引發整個城市停電。

outnumber	*vt.*	在數量上超過，有優勢(人的)數量
[aʊtˋnʌmbɚ]		

Protesters took to the street but they **were** later surrounded and **outnumbered** by the police. 抗議者占據街頭，但後來被警方包圍，而警方有優勢人數。

As a police officer, it is a tough situation when you **are** surrounded and **outnumbered**, and you could not take out your weapeon to defend yourself because you are surrounded by unarmed citizens. 身為警察，當你被包圍而沒有無優勢人數，而你又因為是被沒有武裝的市民包圍而不能拿出武器自衛時，那真是一個艱困的情況。

out-of-court testimony	法庭外的證詞
out-of-home care	家外安置

overdose	*n.*	藥劑過量，服過量的藥，吸食過量
[ˋovɚˏdos]		

Police have arrested a suspected drug dealer in connection with the **overdose** death of a drug user. 警方逮捕到一名與這起吸

毒者吸毒過量致死有關的可疑毒販。

Simpson died from drug **overdoses**. 辛普森死於吸毒過量。

overhaul [ˌovəˈhɔl]	vt. & n.	全面檢查，拆開檢修，大修，【消防】殘火處理 Overhauling is a late stage in fire-suppression process during which the burned area is carefully examined for remaining sources of heat that may re-ignite the fire. 殘火處理 (overhauling 原意為全面檢查)是滅火過程中的後面階段，這個階段中，燒毀的區域會被仔細檢查，尋找剩餘可能會再燃起火災的熱源。 **Fire overhaul** includes searching for possible sources of re-ignition, and investigating the origin of the fire. 殘火處理 (overhaul 原意為全面檢查) 包括「尋找可能會再燃起火災的源頭」以及「調查起火點」。 Firefighter conducted **overhaul operations** at a fire scene. 消防員在火場進行了殘火處理 (overhaul 原意為全面檢查)。
overload [ˈovəˌlod]	vt.	超載，超負荷 使超載，使負荷過多[(+with)] Firefighters said an **overloaded** extension cord caused the fire. The fire was sparked by **overloaded** extension cord. 消防員說，一條延長線超過負荷造成火災，這場火災是延長線超過負荷引起的。
overpower [ˌovəˈpaʊə]	vt.	擊敗，制伏 In general, corrections officers carry no weapons because prisoners might **overpower** them and use the seized weapon. 通常，矯正人員並不攜帶武器，這是因為受刑人有可能壓制矯正人員，並使用這些擄獲的武器。
overrule [ˌovəˈrul]	vt.	否決(或駁回)……的意見 District ourt **overruled** his objection. 地方法院駁回了他的異議。
overstay [ˈovəˈste]	vi. & vt.	逾期居留停留 Do not **overstay** your visa. If you **overstay** your visa, the visa can be voided and cancelled. If the visa holder **overstays** his lawful status, he becomes deportable under the immigration law. 不要逾期停留，如果你逾期停留，簽證會無效及取消，如果簽證持有人居留超過其合法狀態，則在移民法之下，他就變成可以遣送。
overtake [ˌovəˈtek]	vt.	超車 Many traffic accidents are caused by reckless **overtaking**. To safely **overtake** another vehicle, you need to be extremely careful. 很多交通事故是因為輕率超車而造成的，若要安全超

越它車，你必須相當小心。

overtime	*n.*	加班
[ˌovɚˈtaɪm]		Police department must pay officers **overtime pay** when they work more than an average of 40 hours a week. 當員警工作超過平均每星期 40 小時的時候，警察局必須支付超勤費給員警。
	adv.	加班
		Officers must be paid **overtime** when they work more than the limit. 員警工作超過限度時，應該要有超勤費。

overturn	*vt.*	推翻
[ˌovɚˈtɝn]		The court of appeal **overturned** the conviction based on new evidence. 上訴法院依據新證據推翻了判決。
	vi.	翻覆，傾覆
		Police said that most passengers had drowned when their vessel **overturned**. 警方說，大部分乘客在船隻翻覆時溺斃了。

pedestrian	*n.*	行人
[pəˈdɛstrɪən]		**Pedestrians** have the right of way in all crosswalks. Drivers must yield the right of way to **pedestrians**. 行人在人行穿越道擁有路權，駕駛人必須禮讓路權給行人。
		Pedestrians must use the sidewalk instead of walking in the road. 行人必須使用人行道而不是走在路中。

parade	*n.*	遊行
[pəˈred]		It is unlawful for any person to hold, manage, conduct or participate in any **parade** or any other similar display on any public street, park, sidewalk or any other public grounds in the city, unless there has first been obtained from the city police department a permit to do so. 除非已先取得警察局許可，否則任何人在城市內的任何公共道路、公園、人行道或任何公共場地舉辦、管理、進行或參與任何遊行或相類似的展演者，是不合法的。

parking	*n.*	停車，停車處
[ˈpɑrkɪŋ]	應用	*angle parking* 斜角停車
		double parking 併排停車
		free parking 免費停車場
		parallel parking 順向停車
		parking fine 停車罰款
		parking garage 停車庫
		parking light 停車信號燈
		parking lot 停車場

parking meter 停車收費表
parking permit 停車證
parking space 停車位
parking ticket 違規停車罰單
parking violation 停車違規
valet parking 代客泊車

parole	*vt.*	假釋
[pə`rol]		Sometimes, a prisoner may **be paroled** after certain years of imprisonment. 有時候，囚犯在監禁若干年之後，可以被假釋。
	n.	假釋
		Once the prisoner is released **on parole**, the parolee will be returned to prison if he or she fails to abide by the condition of **parole**. 一旦受刑人被假釋時，該假釋人如果未能遵守假釋條件，就會被送回監獄。
	應用	*medical parole* 保外就醫
		parole officer 假釋官
		parole revocation 假釋的撤銷
		parolee 被假釋之人

parolee	*n.*	被假釋者，假釋犯人
[pə,ro`li]		Once the prisoner is released on parole, the **parolee** will be returned to prison if he or she fails to abide by the condition of parole. 一旦受刑人被假釋時，被假釋人如果未能遵守假釋條件，就會被送回監獄。

partnership	*n.*	合夥(或合作)關係
[`partnɚ,ʃɪp]		We will provide quality police service **in partnership with** other members of the community. 我們會與社區成員合為夥伴關係，提供有品質的警察服務。
	應用	*in partnership with……* 與……結為夥伴合作

party	*n.*	(法律或訴訟上的) 一造，一方
[`partɪ]	應用	*adverse party* 對造

passenger		乘客，旅客
[`pæsndʒɚ]		The driver and all **passengers** in the vehicle must fasten a seat belt. 駕駛人及車內的所有乘客都必須繫上安全帶。

pat	*vt.*	拍(搜); (pat-down *n.* 拍搜)
[pæt]		Officers are allowed to **pat** the person's outer clothing If they reasonably suspect the person to be armed. **Pat-down** is not an arrest. It is conducted for the officers' safety. Therefore, the Miranda warnings need not be given. 如果員警合理懷疑某個人攜帶武器，即被容許拍搜此人的外部衣服。拍搜並不是搜

索，其進行是為了員警的安全，所以不需要告知 Miranda 警語。(參看 Miranda Warnings)

| patrol | *vt.* | 巡邏 |
| [pə`trol] | | |

Police **patrolled** the shopping mall and urged shoppers to take precaution against theft. 警方巡邏了賣場，並且呼籲逛街的人慎防遭竊。

The chief of police decided to put more officers on the street to **patrol** high crime areas. 警察局長決定增加街上的警力來巡邏高犯罪區域。

n. 巡邏

In fact, **patrol officers** are often the first ones summoned to the crime scenes. 事實上，巡邏員警經常是最早被呼叫前往犯罪現場的人。

When officers are **on patrol** and they see something that looks suspicious, they will take appropriate action immediately. 當員警進行巡邏，並且看到有東西可疑時，他們會立刻採取適當的作為。

應用　*air patrol* 空中巡邏
automobile patrol 汽車巡邏
bicycle patrol 自行車巡邏
border patrol 邊境巡邏
directed patrol 定點巡邏
foot patrol 徒步巡邏
motorcycle patrol 機車巡邏
mounted patrol 騎警巡邏
patrol officer 巡邏員警
preventive patrol 預防性巡邏
routine patrol 例行巡邏 (或稱 *random patrol* 隨機巡邏)
water patrol 水上巡邏

pavement marking　路面標誌
應用　*broken white line* 白虛線
broken yellow line 黃虛線
double solid white line 雙白實線
double yellow lines (one solid, one broken) 雙黃線(一實線一虛線)
solid white line 白實線
solid yellow line 黃實線

| pedestrian | *n.* | 步行者，行人 |
| [pə`dɛstrɪən] | | |

If you are about to turn left at an intersection, you must yield the right-of-way to other **pedestrians** and vehicles until it is safe to turn. 如果你正要在十字路口左轉，你必須禮讓路權給其他行人及車輛，直到可以安全轉向。

	應用	*pedestrian accident* 人、車相撞的車禍 (或 *car-pedestrian accident)*
		pedestrian crosswalk 行人穿越道

---

peeping Tom	*n.*	偷窺癖者

There was a report of a **peeping Tom** near our apartment building. 有報案在我們公寓大樓附近有偷窺癖者。

---

penal	*n.*	刑事的，刑法上的
[`pin!]	應用	*Penal Law* 刑法 (或稱 *Penal Code, Criminal Code)*

---

penalty	*n.*	處罰，刑罰
[`pεn!tɪ]		

If the offender voluntarily surrenders himself to the authorities, the presiding judge may consider a reduction of the **penalty**. 如果犯罪者自願向機關自首的話，主審法官可考慮減刑。

	應用	*death penalty* 死刑(或 *capital punishment)*

---

pend	*vi.*	等候判定或決定
[pεnd]		

Police said the suspect had a murder charge **pending** against him. 警方說嫌犯有一件謀殺指控案件還在等待判決。

There were five criminal cases **pending** against him. 他有 5 件刑案正在等待判決。

pending	*adj.*	懸而未決的，未定的，待定的
[`pεndɪŋ]		

警方說 The case is **pending** before the court of appeal. The case is **pending** on appeal. 本案在上訴法院等待判決中，本案正在上訴等候中。

---

penetrate	*vt.*	穿過，刺入，(情報或執法人員的)滲透/滲透入
[`pεnə,tret]		

Police said officers successfully **penetrate** the smuggling enterprise. 警方說，員警成功滲透入走私集團。

The smuggling ring **was penetrated by** undercover police. 走私集團被臥底警察滲透。

Undercover officer **penetrated** the smuggling network. 臥底警察滲透進入走私網絡。

---

perform	*vt.*	履行，執行，完成，做
[pə`fɔrm]		

A medical examiner **performed** the autopsy to discover the cause of death. 有一位法醫進行了驗屍，要找出死亡原因。

Many firearms examiners also **perform** tool mark comparisons. 許多槍枝鑑識人員同時也從事工具痕跡的比對。

While **performing** the duties, Radio dispatcher must determine the priority based on current staffing, activity, location of officers, citizen information, and location of the incident. 在執行勤務時，無線電派遣官必須依據目前的人力、事項、員警的位置、市民的資訊及事件的位置，確定優先順序。

After the EMT **performed** CPR, the man began to breathe again. 緊急救護技術員進行心肺復甦術之後，這個人就又開始呼吸了。

The patient was found unconscious. EMTs arrived at the scene and **performed** chess compression on him, since he had stopped breathing. 患者被發現失去意識，緊急救護技術員抵達了現場並對她進行胸部按壓，因為她的呼吸停止了。

performance [pɚ`fɔrməns]	*n.*	履行，實行，完成[(+of)]

The Police have a serious concern for safety **in the performance of** police duties. 警察執行職務時，對於安全非常重視。

In the performance of their duties, officers may have to use force to effect a detention or arrest, to overcome resistance, or to protect themselves or others from serious injury. 在執行職務時，員警可能必須使用武力以完成留置或逮捕、壓制抗拒，或保護自己或他人免於重大的傷害。

peril [`pɛrəl]	*n.*	(嚴重的) 危險

The gunman was shot and his life **is in peril**. 槍手被擊中而生命垂危。

perish [`pɛrɪʃ]	*vi.*	消滅，死去

Police said a fatal car accident occurred this morning, and all four occupants **perished** on the spot. They **perished** at the scene. 警方說今晨有一死亡車禍發生，全部四位乘客當場死亡，他們在現場就死亡了。

perjury [`pɝdʒərɪ]	*n.*	偽證

Those who are caught knowingly misleading a court will face serious criminal charges of **perjury**. 凡是被發現故意誤導法院的人，會面臨嚴重的偽證刑事告訴。

I hereby declare that the above made statements are true to the best of my knowledge and belief, and that I understand it is made for use as evidence in court and is subject to penalty for **perjury**. 本人謹此聲明，就本人所知及認知，以上所做的陳述都是真實無誤。我也了解它將在法院作為證據之用，並且會受到偽證罪的處罰。

permission [pɚ`mɪʃən]	*n.*	允許，許可，同意 [+to-v]

Following the arrest and formal charge of a suspect, sensitive information relating to investigation shall not be released without the express **permission** of the Police Department. 在逮捕及正式控訴嫌犯之後，有關偵查的機密資料若沒有警察局的明示同意，不得公布。

permit [pɚ`mɪt]	*vt.*	允許，許可，准許

An officer **is permitted** to use the amount of force necessary only to overcome the resistance or aggression that is presented by the subject. 員警容許使用武力的多寡，僅得在制伏對象表現出來的抗拒或侵犯所必要的程度內，使用之。

permit [`pɝmɪt]	*n.* 應用	許可證，執照

entry permit 入境許可證
re-entry permit 重入境許可
parade without a permit 未經核准的遊行
parking permit 停車證
work permit 工作證

perpetrate [`pɝpə,tret]	*vt.*	做(壞事)，犯(罪)

Many sexual abuse cases **are perpetrated by** offenders known to the victims. 許多性侵害案件是被害者所認識的犯罪者所為。

Gun violence is an issue regularly debated in the United States because a large number of homicides **were perpetrated** using a firearm. 槍枝暴力在美國是每隔一陣子就會被討論的議題，因為許多凶殺案都是用槍枝來犯案的。

perpetrator [,pɝpə`tretɚ]	*n.*	行兇者

In domestic violence, **perpetrators** may take a spouse, partner, or children hostage. 在家暴案件中，加害人有可能會將配偶、伴侶或小孩當作人質。

Lineup is the police identification procedure to determine whether the suspect is the **perpetrator** of the crime. 排列指認是警方確認嫌犯是不是犯罪的行兇者的確認程序。

persecute [`pɝsɪ,kjut]	*vi.*	迫害，殘害

Refugees claimed they can't go back to their home country because they will **be persecuted**. 難民主張他們不能回母國，因為他們會遭到迫害。

persecution [,pɝsɪ`kjuʃən]	*n.*	迫害

Undocumented or illegal immigrants come from different cultures for different purposes, e.g. to seek protection from political or religious **persecution**. 無證件或非法之移民來自不同文化，為了不同目的，例如為尋求保護免於政治或宗教迫害。

petition [pə`tɪʃən]	*n.*	請願，請願書[(+for/against)]，(向法院遞交的)申請書[(+for)] **The right to petition** gives citizens the right to appeal to the government to change its policies. 請願權讓民眾有權利訴請政府改變政策。 Historically, when the individual **files a petition** for asylum, the final determination is usually made by the Head of State. 在歷史上，當個人提起庇護的請求時，最終的決定通常是由國家元首做成。
physical [`fɪzɪk!]	*adj.* 應用	身體的，物質的 *physical custody* 人身監護 *physical evidence* 物證 *physical force* 身體的武力 *physical harm* 身體的傷害 *physical injury* 身體的傷害 *physical restraint or violence* 身體上的強制或暴力
picket line		示威(罷工)者的糾察線，警戒線 Protesters pledged not to cross the **picket line** during the march. 示威者保證在遊行時不會越過警戒線。
pickpocket [`pɪk,pɑkɪt]	*n.*	扒手 The witness saw a **pickpocket** pinch a wallet from an old man. 證人看到扒手偷走老人的皮夾。
piece [pis]	*vt.*	拼湊，將……拼湊一起 [(+together)] Detectives **pieced together** the evidence. Then they located and arrested the suspects. 偵查員拼湊了證據，然後他們找到嫌犯並逮捕。
pike pole		消防勾
pileup [`paɪl,ʌp]	*n.*	連環車禍 (也稱 multivehicle collision 或 chain-reaction crash)
pimp [pɪmp]	*n.*	(男)妓院老板，拉皮條者
pinch [pɪntʃ]	*vt.*	【俚】偷取，擅自拿取 The witness saw a pickpocket **pinch** a wallet from an old man. 證人看到扒手偷走老人的皮夾。
	vt.	【俚】逮捕，拘留[H][(+for)] He **was pinched** for selling drugs. 他因為販賣毒品被捕。
piracy [`paɪrəsɪ]	*n.*	海盜行為
pistol [`pɪst!]	*n.*	手槍 (或稱 hand gun)

place	*vt.*	放置，安置，將……寄託於
[ples]		The driver **was placed into custody** for driving while intoxicated. 駕駛人因為酒駕而被拘禁。
		Officers ordered the suspected driver to turn off the car, turn on the internal light, and **place his hands on** the wheel. 員警命令該名可疑的駕駛人將車輛熄火、打開車內燈光，並將雙手放在方向盤上。
		He was accussed of international drug trafficking, and **was placed on** Interpol's red notice. 他被指控國際毒品走私，並被放上國際刑警組織的紅色通報。
		He **was placed in** the holding cell waiting for transfer to the Prosecutor's Office. 他被置於留置室等待送到地檢署。
	應用	*to take place* 發生
		The car accident **took place** at around 10 a.m. in the westbound lane of Highway No 3. 這起車禍大約上午 10 時左右發生在 3 號高速公路西向。

plainclothes	*n.*	便衣(警察)
		In general, **plainclothes officers** are known to most of the uniformed officers in their districts. If you are in **plainclothes**, remember that it's your responsibility to identify yourself as quickly and clearly as possible. 通常，便衣警察都是轄區內制服警察所認識的人，如果你擔任便衣，要記得，快速而明確地出示身分，是你的責任。

plaintiff	*n.*	原告
['plentɪf]		The **plaintiff** decided to file a criminal complaint against the defendant charging defendant with misappropriation. 原告決定對被告提起控訴，控告被告侵占。

plea	*n.*	【律】抗辯，答辯
[pli]		He **entered a plea of** not guilty to the charges filed against him. 他對於不利於他的指控抗辯無罪。
		The murder suspect got 20 years in prison after **guilty plea** for murder. 謀殺案嫌犯認罪之後，獲判 20 年徒刑。
	應用	*guilty plea* 認諾有罪
		plea bargain 【律】(以被告承認犯有輕罪而獲從輕處罰的)認罪協商

plead	*vt.*	【律】為(案件)辯護，作為答辯提出，承認
[plid]		A defendant may **plead** guilty or not guilty. 被告可認罪或不認罪。
		Offender might also decide to turn himself in and **plead** guilty.

犯罪者也可能會決定自首及認罪。

plot	*n.*	陰謀，秘密策畫
[plɑt]		

The suspect has been arrested after detectives uncovered the alleged **plot** to shoot the drug dealer. 嫌犯在幹員發現這個槍殺毒販的密謀之後，以經將逮捕了。

While checking the inmate's cell, prison officers found the notes and several pieces of metal, and uncovered the escape **plot**. 監獄人員在檢查受刑人囚房之時，發現了字條以及幾片金屬片，而揭發了這起脫逃陰謀。

Airport authorities uncovered a **plot** to blow up an airplane. Suspect was arrested after the port authorities uncovered the bomb plot. 機場當局發現了這起炸掉飛機的陰謀。在機場當局揭發炸彈策畫之後，嫌犯已被逮捕。

應用　*bomb plot* 爆炸策畫

criminal plot 犯罪策畫

escape plot 脫逃策畫

fraud plot 詐欺策畫

murder plot 謀殺策畫

shooting plot 開槍殺人計畫

terrorist plot 恐怖策畫

	vt.	密謀，秘密策劃

The suspect was sentenced to 5 years imprisonment on charges that he **plotted** to kill the witness who testified against him in the trial. 嫌犯被判處 5 年徒刑，相關的指控是他策劃殺害在審判中對他做不利作證的證人。

PMI	*abbr.*	死後間隔時間，死亡時間(postmortem interval，屍體發現時距離死亡發生時刻的間隔時間)
POB	*abbr.*	出生地 place of birth
poison	*n.*	毒，毒藥，毒物，
[`pɔɪzn]	*vt.*	下毒，服毒，中毒

Under the evidence in this case, the jury could believe that the victim **was poisoned** by the defendant on three separate occasions. 在本案的證據之下，陪審團相信被害人是受到被告在三次分別的場合下毒。

James was admitted to the hospital for **food poisoning**. 詹姆士因為食物中毒住進了醫院。

	adj.	有毒的，有害的
poisonous		
[`pɔɪznəs]		

"Fruit of the **poisonous** tree" is a legal doctrine used to explain that evidence obtained illegally is generally inadmissible in court.

		毒樹果是法律學說，用來解釋非法取得的證據在法庭上無證據能力。
police [pə`lis]	*n.* 應用	警察 *armored police vehicle* 警用裝甲車 *marked police vehicle* 制式警車 *unmarked police vehicle* 一般警車 *police academy*【美】警察學校 *police authorities* 警察機關 *police beat* 警勤區 *police brutality* 警察暴力 *police cadet* 警校生 *police call* 報警電話 *police chase* 警車追逐 *police department* 警察局 *police duty* 警察勤務，警察任務 *police force* 警力 *police investigation* 警察的偵查 *police liaison officer* 警察聯絡官 *police misconduct* 警察的不當行為 *police officer* 警員，員警 *police power* 警察權 *police precinct* 警察分區，(美國)警察分局 *police pursuit* 警車追逐，警察追捕 *police radio* 警用無線電 *police radio dispatcher* 警察無線電派遣員 *police service* 警察服務 *police tactical operation* 警察的戰術行動 *police tape* 現場封鎖帶（或稱 *barricade tape; barrier tape; crime scene safety tape*) *police-citizen contact* 警民接觸 *police-public interaction* 警察與公眾的互動 *riot police* 鎮暴警察
polygraph [`palɪ,græf]	*n.*	測謊器 **Polygraph examiner** conducts **polygraph investigations** of suspects, witnesses, and victims of criminal activity. To conduct the actual **polygraph examination**, the examiner will attach the equipment to the examinee. The opinion of the examiner is based solely on the **polygraph charts**. 測謊人員對犯罪活動的嫌犯、證人及被害人進行測謊調查，為了進行測謊，測謊

鑑定人員會將設備貼在受測者，測謊鑑定人員的意見所依據的，惟有測謊圖表。

應用 *polygraph examination* 測謊鑑定

polygraph examiner 測謊鑑定人員

to conduct polygraph test 進行測謊

---

pornography
[pɔr`nɑgrəfɪ]
　　　　n.　色情書刊，色情圖片，色情電影

---

posess
[pə`zɛs]
　　　　vt.　擁有，持有

The suspect admitted that he illegally **possessed** firearms after officers found 5 pistols and 50 rounds of bullet in his residence. 嫌犯在員警從他住處查獲 5 把手槍及 50 發子彈後，承認他非法持有武器。

---

possession
[pə`zɛʃən]
　　　　n.　擁有，持有

The illegal importation, manufacture, distribution, **possession** and improper use of controlled substances have a substantial and detrimental effect on the health and general welfare of the people. 非法進口、製造、散布、持有，及不當使用管制物質，對於人的健康及全般福祉具有實質及有害的影響。

Controlled delivery can prove that the consignors, transporters or receivers **were** knowingly **in possession of** the contraband. 控制下交付可以證明委託人、運送人或受領人是故意持有該違禁品。

---

positive
[`pɑzətɪv]
　　　　adj.　確定的，確實的，有把握的

Officers were **positive** that the person they had arrested was the man who sold the heroin to the undercover agent. 員警很肯定他們所逮捕的人就是賣海洛因給臥底幹員的男子。

　　　　adj.　【醫】陽性的 (*negative* 陰性的)

The blood tests **positive**.　驗血結果呈陽性。

The arrestee will be detained If his drug test **is positive** for cocaine. 被逮捕之人如果毒品檢測呈現古柯鹼陽性反應，將會被拘禁。

Official said that all inmates were tested for drug and the many tested **positive** for marijuana. 官員說，全部的獸行人都要被進行毒品檢測，而有許多受刑人經檢驗結果為大麻陽性反應。

---

prank
[præŋk]
　　　　n.　胡鬧，惡作劇

Officer received a call for assistance, and responded to the scene only to find that it was a **prank call.** 員警接到請求協助的電話並趕往處理，卻發現那只是一通惡作劇的電話。

---

precaution
　　　　n.　預防，警惕，謹慎，預防措施

[prɪˋkɔʃən]		Police patrolled the shopping mall and urged shoppers to take **precaution** against theft. 警方巡邏了賣場，並且呼籲逛街的人慎防遭竊。
precedent [ˋprɛsədənt]	n.	判決先例，判例 Common Law is generally un-codified. It is largely based on **precedent**. 普通法通常是非法典化的，其大部分是依據判決先例。
precinct [ˋprisɪŋkt]	n.	【美】(警察) 管轄區，分局 New York City is divided into 77 **police precincts**. 紐約市分為 77 個警察分局。 【補充說明】 (美國有些警局所稱的) 警察分局，例如紐約市警局(NYPD)以數字編排分局，第五分局稱為(*The 5th Precinct*)。 另外有些警察局的分局用 District 一字。例如華府市警(MPD)也是以數字編排分局，從 First District 到 Seventh District。
precursor [priˋkɜsɚ]	n. 應用	先驅，前導 *drug precursor* 毒品原料 *immediate precursor* 先驅物質、原料
prejudice [ˋprɛdʒədɪs]	n.	偏見，歧視 In the performance of my duty, I will never act officiously or permit personal feelings, **prejudices**, political beliefs, aspirations, animosities or friendships to influence my decisions. 在執行職務時，我不會恣意行事，或容許個人的情感、偏見、政治理念、期盼、憎惡或友誼影響我的決定。
preliminary [prɪˋlɪmə͵nɛrɪ]	adj. 應用	初步的，預備的 In major crime investigations, one of the priorities of the crime scene investigation (CSI) unit is to seal off the crime scene and conduct a **preliminary** examination. 在重大犯罪的偵查中，犯罪現場調查小組有一項優先事項，就是封鎖現場並進行初步的鑑識。 *preliminary investigation* 初步偵查 *preliminary examination* 初步鑑識
preparedness [prɪˋpɛrɪdnɪs]	n.	準備、戰備(的狀態) ，(消防的) 整備
press [prɛs]	vt. n.	控告 She agreed not to **press** criminal charges against him if he agreed to pay for the damages. 如果他同意負擔損壞費用，她同意不對他提出刑事告訴。 報刊，新聞輿論

應用		*press room* 記者室
		press conference 記者會
		press release 新聞發布

presume	*vt.*	推定，假定，假設，推測
[prɪˋzum]		Criminal laws require that every one charged with a criminal offence shall **be presumed** innocent until proved guilty according to law, known as the presumption of innocence. 刑事法要求，每一個被指控刑事犯罪之人，在依法被證明有罪之前，應推定為無罪，稱為無罪推定。
		Generally, a witness **is presumed** to have the mental capacity to testify. 證人通常推定有作證的心智能力。

presumption	*n.*	【律】推定
[prɪˋzʌmpʃən]	應用	*presumption of innocence* 無罪推定
		presumption of guilt 有罪推定
		presumption of death 推定死亡

prevent	*vt.*	防止，預防，阻止，制止，妨礙[(+from)]
[prɪˋvɛnt]		Emergency protective order is an important tool **to prevent** the occurrence or recurrence of domestic violence. 緊急保護令對於避免家暴的發生或再發生，是一項重要的工具。
		A peace officer or corrections officer may use reasonable force **to prevent** the escape of the arrested person from custody. 治安人員或矯正人員得使用合理的武力以阻止被逮捕之人逃脫拘禁。
		Over 50 firefighters were spraying nearby the buildings **to prevent** the blaze **from** burning other structures. 超過五十名消防員分散在這建築物的附近，以防止火勢燒到其他建築物。

prevention	*n.*	預防，防止，阻止
[prɪˋvɛnʃən]		Immersion suit can assist in prevention of hypothermia. 突然泡在冷水中的反應包括冷休克(0 至 2 分鐘)、功能殘疾(2 至 15 分鐘)，及失溫(15 至 30 分鐘)，保溫救生衣可以幫助預防失溫。
	應用	*crime prevention* 犯罪預防
		drug prevention 毒品預防
		fire prevention 火災預防
		disaster prevention 災害預防
		suicide prevention 自殺預防

preventive	*adj.*	預防的
[prɪˋvɛntɪv]		**Preventive patrol** is also known as routine patrol or random patrol. 預防性巡邏也稱為例行巡邏或隨機巡邏。

He was taken into **preventive custody**. 他被預防性羈押了。

He was hold in **preventive custody**. 他被預防性羈押了。

---

principal	*n.*	正犯
[`prɪnsəp!]		Parties to crimes include conspirators, **principals**, aider and abettor. A **principal** is a person who commits the offence himself or through another. If more than one person commit the offence jointly, each shall be liable as a **principal**. Both **principals** and secondary participants are defined as accomplices. 犯罪的參與者包括共謀者(conspirator)、正犯(principal)、幫助犯(aider)及教唆犯(abettor)。正犯(principal)是親自或藉由他人而犯罪的人，如果超過一人以上共同從事犯罪時，每個人都承擔正犯之責，正犯與從犯兩者被定義為共犯(accomplice)。

---

prior	*adj.*	先前的，在先的，在前的
[`praɪɚ]	應用	*prior identification* 先前的指認
		prior inconsistent statement 先前不一致的陳述
		prior offense 先前的犯罪
		prior statement 先前的陳述
		prior testimony 先前的證言

---

prison	*n.*	監獄
[`prɪzn]		It seems unlikely that the **prison escape** took place without some form of inside help. A manhunt has been launched. 此一越獄若無內部的幫助，似乎不太可能發生，一場搜捕已經展開。
		The murder suspect got 20 years in **prison** after guilty plea for murder. 謀殺案嫌犯認罪之後，獲判 20 年徒刑。
		The person is convicted of robbery and sentenced to six years in **prison**, he will be put behind bars to serve the **prison sentence**. 這個人被判強盜罪確定並判刑 6 年監禁，他將就會放被到牢裡服刑。
		Wrongful incarceration means that you are incorrectly arrested, prosecuted, and found guilty and ordered to serve a **prison term**. 非法的監禁是指你被不當地逮捕、起訴並且被判有罪，並且被命令服刑。
	應用	*prison escape* 越獄(又稱 *prison break*)
		【補充說明】 美國的聯邦監獄的用語有：*United States Penitentiaries*，*Federal Correctional Institution*，*Federal Prison Camp*，*Federal Correctional Complex*

---

prisoner	*n.*	受刑人，犯人，囚犯 (或稱 inmate)
[`prɪznɚ]		

privacy [`praɪvəsɪ]	*n.* 應用	隱私，私事，私生活 *invasion of privacy* 侵犯隱私(權) *right of privacy* 隱私權
private [`praɪvɪt]	*adj.* 應用	個人的，私人的 *private communication* 私人通信 *private eye* 私家偵探 *private investigator* 私家偵探 *private interests* 私人利益 *private person* 私人 *private prosecution* 自訴 *private prosecutor* 自訴人 *private residence* 私人住宅
probable cause		相當理由 Officers must have **probable cause** to make an arrest or a reasonable suspicion to conduct a stop and frisk. 員警必須要有相當理由，以進行逮捕，或有合理懷疑，以進行攔阻及搜身。 Police must have **probable cause** to justify the arrest. Prosecutors must have **probable cause** to justify the prosecution. 警察必須有相當理由，逮捕才有正當性，檢察官必須有相當理由，起訴才有正當性。 If police investigation establishes **probable cause** to believe that an offense has been committed and that the defendant committed it, the judge must issue an arrest warrant to an officer to execute it. 如果警方的調查確認有相當理由足認犯罪已完成，而且是被告所為時，法官必須核發逮捕令給員警執行之。
probation [pro`beʃən]	*n.* 應用	【律】緩刑 The man **was on probation for** robbing a small store last year. 這個人正在為去年搶奪商店的案件受緩刑中。 *probation officer* 緩刑監督官，緩刑觀護人 *to revoke one's probation* 撤銷某人的緩刑（或 probation revocation)
probationer [prə`beʃənə]	*n.* 應用	緩刑之人犯 *probation officer* 緩刑監督官，緩刑觀護員
probative [`probətɪv]	*adj.* 應用	供作證明或證據的 Admissibility, relevance and **probative value** are three important issues for evidence to be considered. 證據能力、關聯性及證明價值，是證據被考慮的三個重要事項。 *probative value*(證據的)證明價值，證明力
probe	*vt.*	探查，徹底調查

[prob]		The Internal Affairs Office **is probing** the suicide of a suspect who hung himself with his own belt in a police holding cell. 政風室正在調查這起嫌犯在警察留置室用自己的皮帶上吊的自殺案件。
	vi.	探查，徹底調查 [(+into)]
		They are probing into the cause of the incident. 他們正在調查這起事件的原因。
	n.	探查，徹底調查
		The sexual abuse allegation did not surface until the authorities' recent **probe**. 這起疑似性侵害的指控，直到當局最近的調查，才浮出檯面。

proceed [prə`sid]	*vi.*	繼續進行，繼續做(講)下去[(+to /with)]；開始，著手 [(+to)]
		If you have the right-of-way and others yield it to you, **proceed** immediately. 如果你有路權而其他人禮讓路權給你時，應立即前進。
		The examination of a witness generally **proceeds** along the following lines: direct examination, cross-examination, redirect examination, and recross-examination. 證人的詰問通常循著以下的順序：主詰問、反詰問、覆主詰問及覆反詰問。
		起訴 [(+against)]
	vi.	District Prosecutors Office said that prosecutors have enough evidence **to proceed against** the man charged with beating his wife to death. 地檢署說，檢察官有足夠的證據將該名毆打妻子致死的男子起訴。

proceedings [prə`sidɪŋz]	*n.*	訴訟、法律程序
		Prosecutor is the legal officer who represents the government **in criminal proceedings**. 檢察官是刑事訴訟中代表政府的法律官員。
		In **the criminal proceedings**, the prosecutor will make a formal accusation against the suspect. 在刑事訴訟中，檢察官會對嫌犯做正式的控告。
		Bailiff is responsible for maintaining order during **court proceedings**. If there is any disruption during the reading of the verdicts, the bailiffs will have the obligation to remove any persons disrupting these **proceedings**. 法警負責在開庭程序中維持秩序。如果宣讀(陪審團的)判決的時候有任何擾亂，法警會有義務排除任何擾亂訴訟程序的人。
	應用	*civil proceedings* 民事訴訟程序 *court proceedings* 法院程序

criminal proceedings 刑事訴訟程序

deportation proceedings 遣送(訴訟)程序

divorce proceedings 離婚訴訟程序

extradition proceedings 引渡(訴訟)程序

judicial proceedings 司法程序

【補充說明】proceedings 所指的訴訟程序，以刑事訴訟 (criminal proceeding)來說，指的是嚴格意義上從訴訟開始到判決確定的整個聽審、開庭審理的正式程序；如果加上前端的偵查、後續處罰時，廣範意義的訴訟程序，可以用 criminal procedure 表示。

process	*vt.*	過程，進程；處理，辦理
[`prasɛs]		There are several steps that need to be taken in order to **process** a crime scene. Some of the steps include: securing the scene, a detailed search, documenting the crime scene, collecting and preserving evidence, etc. 為了要作現場處理，有些步驟需要採取，包括：保全現場、詳細的搜索、現場紀錄、證據的採集與保存等等。
	n.	【律】訴訟程序 vita
		Plaintiff's claimed that defendants deprived him of his property without **due process of law**. 原告主張被告未經正當法律程序剝奪了他的財產。
	應用	*due process of law* 正當法律程序
		legal process 法律程序
		to process the wound 處理傷口(*to dress the wound*)

proclaim	*vt.*	宣告，公布，聲明
[prə`klem]		As early as in 1829, Sir Robert Peel **proclaimed** that "the police are the public and the public are the police" 早在 1829 年，羅伯皮爾爵士宣稱「警察即是民眾，民眾即是警察。」
		Police **proclaimed** the demonstration to be an unlawful assembly. 警方宣稱該項示威是非法集會。

produce	*vt.*	生產，出產，製造，創作
[prə`djus]		In general, the prosecutor and police are required to **produce** sufficient evidence for the judge to determine whether there is probable cause. At trial, public prosecutor is expected to **produce** evidence in his possession in support of the prosecution. 通常，檢察官及警察必須提出充分的證據向法官證明有無相當理由。審判時，檢察官被期待提出其持有的證據，來支持起訴。

profile	*n.*	輪廓，外形，外觀，【美】傳略，人物簡介，概況

[`profaɪl]	應用	*high-profile* 受到矚目的
		high profile case 重大矚目案件
		psychological profiling 心理剖繪（或稱 *offender profiling; criminal profiling; profiling*）

progress	*n.*	進行，進步，前進，進展
[prə`grɛs]		If a crime **is in progress** and someone's safety is in jeopardy, please call 1-1-0 immediately. 如果一項犯罪尚在進行的狀態，而某個人的安全處在危險之中，請立即撥打 110。
		All reports of **crimes in progress** shall receive first priority without regard to the nature of the offense. 所有進行中的犯罪的報案，應收到第一優先，不管其犯罪性質為何。
		If CPR **is in progress**, continue until the AED is turned on. 如果 CPR 在進行中，那就一直持續到 AED 開啟。
		in progress 進行中
	應用	*crime in progress* 進行中的犯罪

prohibit	*vt.*	禁止 [(+from)]
[prə`hɪbɪt]		Once police initiate the pursuit, roadblock and excessive force **are prohibited**. 一旦警察展開追逐，路障及過度的武力是禁止的。

pronounce	*vt.*	(法官的)宣判，(醫生的)宣告
[prə`naʊns]		The trial judge **pronounced** a sentence of death on the murderer. The appallete judge **pronounced** the defendant guilty but imposed life sentence. 地院法官宣判兇手死刑；高院法官宣判該名被告有罪，但判處無期徒刑。
		One gunman was shot by the sniper and **was pronounced dead** at George Washington University Hospital. 一名持槍歹徒被狙擊手擊中，並在喬治華盛頓大學醫院被宣告死亡。

proof	*n.*	檢驗，證明
[pruf]	應用	*burden of proof* 舉證責任
	adj.	不能穿透的，能抵擋的
	應用	*bullet proof vest* 防彈衣(或稱 *body armor*)
		fireproof [`faɪr`pruf] 防火的，耐火的

property room		證物室

proportion	*n.*	比例，比率
[prə`porʃən]		The use of force should be **in proportion to** the degree of threat. Punishment should always be **in proportion to** the crime. 武力的使用應與威脅的程度成比例，處罰應與犯罪成比例。

prosecute	*vt.*	起訴

[ˌprɑsɪˋkjut]

The defendant **was prosecuted** by the District Prosecutor's Office (District Attorney's Office). He **was prosecuted** for murder. He **was prosecuted** under Article 271 of the Penal Code. 被告被地檢署起訴，他被以謀殺起訴，他被以刑法第271 條起訴。

---

prosecution   *n.*   起訴

[ˌprɑsɪˋkjuʃən]

Any person who commits a crime will be subject to criminal **prosecution**. 任何犯罪的人都將會受到刑事起訴。

Illegally-seized evidence cannot be used as evidence against defendants in a criminal **prosecution**. 非法扣押的證據，不得用在刑事起訴中做為不利被告的證據。

In all criminal **prosecutions**, the accused shall enjoy the right to be confronted with the witnesses against him. 在所有刑事起訴中，被告享有與不利於己的證人對質的權利。

The **prosecution** proved that the accused killed the deceased. 檢方證明是被告殺了被害人。

---

prosecutor   *n.*   檢察官，公訴人 (或稱 public prosecutor; 【美】attorney)

[ˋprɑsɪˌkjutɚ]

prosecuting attorney 起訴檢察官

應用   *private prosecutor* 自訴人

---

prostitute   *n.*   娼妓

[ˋprɑstəˌtjut]

Sex-for-money and sex-for-drug are two major reasons for being **prostitutes**. 為錢賣淫或為毒賣淫是從娼的兩大原因。

Undercover officer might act as a drug dealer or even trafficker and participate in the crime. Such operations are frequently used to catch **prostitutes** on city streets. 臥底幹員可能會扮演毒品交易者或甚至走私者的角色並參與犯罪，這種行動常被用來抓街上的娼妓。

---

prostitution   *n.*   賣淫

[ˌprɑstəˋtjuʃən]

Prostitution is a major source of income for many gangs and organized crime groups. Gang members often operate as pimps, luring or forcing at-risk young females into **prostitution** and controlling them through violence and psychological abuse. 對許多幫派及組織犯罪團體而言，賣淫是一項主要收入，幫派分子常充當皮條客，引誘或迫使弱勢年輕女性從事賣淫，並以暴力及心理虐待的方式控制她們。

---

protect   *vt.*   保護 [(+against/from)]

[prəˋtɛkt]

The mission of the prison is to **protect** society by confining offenders in the controlled environments of prisons to assist offenders in becoming law-abiding citizens. 監獄的任務在於保

		護社會，藉由將犯罪人監禁在監獄，來協助犯罪者成為守法的公民。
protection order		保護令(也稱 protective order; order for protection)
		The traditional response of the criminal justice system to domestic violence has been to issue **protection order** or restraining orders. **Order for Protection** is the court order that enables the couple to live apart but remain married. 刑事司法體系對於家暴的傳統回應，一直以來都是核發保護令或限制令。保護令是一種讓雙方分開居住但仍然維持結婚狀態的法院命令。
	應用	*restraining order* 限制令
protective [prə`tɛktɪv]	*adj.* 應用	保護的，防護的，(對人)關切保護的 *emergency protective order* 緊急保護令 *full protective clothing* 全套防護衣 *protective clothing* 防護衣 *protective custody* 保護性管束 *protective hood* 防護頭套(罩) *protective order* 保護令 *temporary protective order* 暫時保護令
protest [prə`tɛst]	*vt.*	抗議，反對[(+about/against/at)] Protesters blocked downtown traffic to **protest** mayor's policy and decision. 抗議者堵住交通，抗議市長的政策與決定。
	n.	抗議，反對 [`protɛst] Riot police are organized, deployed, trained or equipped to confront crowds, **protests** or riots. 鎮暴警察被組織、佈署、訓練或配備來面對群眾、抗議或暴動的警察人員。
protester [pro`tɛstɚ]	*n.*	抗議者，反對者，拒絕者 **Protesters** blocked downtown traffic to protest mayor's policy and decision. 抗議者堵住市中心的交通，以抗議市長的政策與決定。 Police wore riot gear and formed a line to contain **protesters**. 警察穿著鎮暴裝備並形成一列，以阻絕抗議者。
prove [pruv]	*vt.*	證明，證實 [+(that)] The prosecution **proved that** the accused killed the deceased. 檢方證明是被告殺了被害人。 Criminal courts must **prove** an accused guilty beyond a reasonable doubt. 刑事法庭對於被告有罪必須證明至無合理可疑。 Johsnon **was proved** to be the driver at the time of the fatal

impact with the motor cyclist. 強生被證明就是當時撞到機車騎士的駕駛人。

	vi.	證明是……

When the DNA test **proved positive**, he confessed to raping the victim. 當 DNA 檢測證明是陽性/符合時,他承認性侵了被害人。

provide [prə`vaɪd]	*vt.*	規定 [+(that)]、[(+for)] (或稱 stipulate, set forth)

Criminal Law **provides** that a person is guilty of theft if he unlawfully takes movable property of another with purpose to deprive him thereof. 刑法規定,任何人基於剝奪之目的,而不法拿取他人動產者,成立竊盜罪(theft)。

Article 3 of the United States Constitution **provides** that the trial of all crimes shall be by Jury. 美國憲法第 3 條規定,犯罪的審判應由陪審團為之。

provision [prə`vɪʒən]	*n.*	(法規的)條文,條款
provocation [ˌprɑvə`keʃən]	*n.*	挑釁,挑撥,激怒
provoke [prə`vok]	*vt.*	對……挑釁,煽動, 激怒,激起

The remarks of the defense lawyer **provoked** much discussion. 辯護律師的言論引發了許多議論。

The defense lawyer claimed that the killing **was provoked by** the deceased. He said the violence **was provoked by** victim's own actions. 被告的律師主張這個殺害事件是死者挑釁所引起的,他說暴力是由於被害人自己的作為所挑起的。

prowler [`praʊlə]	*n.*	徘徊者,小偷
psychological [ˌsaɪkə`lɑdʒɪkl̩]	*adj.*	心理的,精神的

psychological abuse 心理虐待

psychological profiling 心理剖繪 (或稱罪犯剖繪 *offender profiling*、*criminal profiling*)

psychological treatment 心理治療

pull [pʊl]	*vt.*	拉,拔出

pull over 把……開到路邊,攔下

A police officer can **pull you over** for any traffic violation. You may **be pulled over** if you are not properly buckled up. 員警可以因為交通違規而將你攔下,如果你沒繫好安全帶,你會被攔下。

	vi. &	*pull up* 使……停下來 *vi. Vt.*

	vt.	Officer turned on his flashing lights and pulled up behind the suspicious vehicle. 員警打開他的閃燈，然後在這輛可疑的車子後面停了下來。
	vt.	*pull (out)* 拔出，掏出
		The driver was pulled over for speeding. Officers **pulled out** his service weapon when he noticed the gun in the hand of the driver. 該駕駛人因未超速被員警攔下，員警於發現駕駛人手上有槍時，即掏出勤務用槍。
punch [pʌntʃ]	*vt.*	用拳猛擊 [(+in/on)]
		The suspect **punched** the victim in the face several times and removed the victim's wallet. 嫌犯對著被害人的臉揮拳好幾次，然後拿走被害人的皮夾。
	n.	拳，擊 [(+in/on)]
		Simpson **gave her a punch** in the face and broke her nose. 辛普森揮了一拳在她臉上，而打斷了她的鼻梁。
punish [`pʌnɪʃ]	*vt.*	罰，懲罰，處罰
		The suspect may **be punished by** death penalty or imprisonment for life if he is found guilty of murder, police said. 警方說，如果嫌犯獲判謀殺罪成立，他可能會被處以死刑或無期徒刑。
punishable [`pʌnɪʃəb!]	*adj.*	可罰的
		The crime of murder **was punishable** by more than 10 years' imprisonment or death. 謀殺罪可處 10 年以上徒刑或死刑。
punishment [`pʌnɪʃmənt]	*n.*	處罰，懲罰，刑罰
		The principle of legality means no crime without law, no **punishment** without law. 罪刑法定原則的意義是「無法律即無犯罪；無法律即不處罰」。
	應用	*capital punishment* 死刑
		corporal punishment 體罰
purposely [`pɝpəslɪ]	*adv.*	故意（或稱 with purpose; intentionally; with intent）
		Any person who **purposely** violates the provisions of this chapter is guilty of a class A felony. 任何人故意違反本章的條文者，犯 A 級重罪。
pursue [pɚ`su]	*vt.*	追趕，追蹤，追捕
		A patrol officer who sees the crime of hit and run can **pursue** the suspect and place him into custody. 看到肇事逃逸的巡邏員警，可以追捕嫌犯並將其拘禁。
	vi.	追求，追趕[(+after)]
	應用	*to pursue after a fugitive* 追捕一名逃犯

pursuit	*n.*	追蹤
[pə`sut]		During the **pursuit**, one suspect was critically injured and transported to the hospital where he was pronounced deceased. Another suspect took (drove/transported) himself to the hospital and was later arrested at the hospital. 在追逐中，一名嫌犯嚴重受傷並且被送到醫院，而在醫院被宣告死亡。另一名嫌犯自行(開車/運送)就醫，並且後來在醫院被捕。
	應用	*hot pursuit* 緊急追捕(也稱 fresh pursuit)

put	*vt.*	放，置，使……處於(某種狀態)
[pʊt]	應用	*is/am/are put into jeopardy* 置於險境中
		to put out fire 將火熄滅
		to put people in prison 把人關在監獄
		to put the person on hold 讓該人在電話線上等待
		to put……at danger 置……於危險中
		to put……at the risk 置……於風險中
		to put……behind bars 讓……被關、讓……去監獄服刑
		to put……to death 將……處死

pyromania	*n.*	縱火狂
[ˌpaɪrə`menɪə]		**Pyromania** is a mental disorder behavior. While both **pyromania** and arson involve setting fires, the major difference between the two is the motivation. Arsonists usually have criminal motivations, while **pyromaniacs** do not. **Pyromania** does not have any obvious motive. 縱火狂是一項精神障礙的行為。雖說縱火狂(pyromania)與縱火(arson)都涉及放火，兩者主要的不同在於動機，縱火犯通常有犯罪動機，但縱火狂不是，縱火狂沒有任何明顯的動機。

pyromaniac	*n.*	縱火狂(人)
[ˌpaɪrə`menɪˌæk]	*adj.*	放火狂的

question	*vt.*	問話，對……問話，詢問，訊問，審問[(+about)]，懷疑，對……表示疑問
[`kwɛstʃən]		At 10:00 a.m., the suspect arrived at police headquarters and two detectives started **to question** the suspect. 嫌犯上午 10 時抵達警察總局，兩位偵查人員開始對嫌犯問話。
		He **was questioned** for three hours by two detectives in the interrogation room. 他被兩位偵查人員在偵訊室裡問了三個小時。
	n.	問話，問題，疑問，爭端，難題
		You have the right to consult with a lawyer and have that lawyer present during any **questioning**. 有權利聘請律師，並在接受

問話時，有律師在場。

The **incident in question** happened last Sunday. 所談的這個事件發生在上星期日。

He insisted that he was not responsible for the disappearance of the **object in question**. 他堅持他對於所談物品的消失不用負責任。

	應用	*In question* 正在談論的(問題等)，【例如：*the case in question* 所談案件、the incident in question 所談事件、*the person in question* 所談之人】
		leading question 誘導性詰問
		legal question 法律問題
		questioned document examination 文書鑑定
		questioned document examiner 文書鑑定人員
radar detector		雷達偵測器
radar speed gun		雷達測速槍 (或 radar gun; speed gun)
radio	*n.*	無線電
[ˋredɪˏo]	應用	*patrol car radio* 巡邏車無線電
		police radio 警察無線電
		portable radio 隨身無線電(*portable transceiver* 手持無線電)
		radio channel 無線電頻道
		radio dispatcher 無線電派遣員
rage	*n.*	（風浪，火勢等）狂暴，肆虐
[redʒ]	*vi.*	猖獗，肆虐，激烈進行
		The fire raged through the building, causing serious damage before it was extinguished. 大火熊熊燃燒這棟建築物，造成嚴重損害之後才被撲滅。
		The storm was raging outside and two hours later the power went off. 外面正暴風雨肆虐，兩小時後停電了。
raging	*adj.*	肆虐的
[ˈreɪdʒɪŋ]		The historical church was destroyed in the raging fire. 這棟歷史教堂被熊熊燃燒的大火給摧毀了。
		A raging fire swept over several houses in downtown, and luckly no victim was trapped. 一場熊熊燃燒的大火橫掃過市區的幾間房子，幸運地，沒有人受困。
raid	*vt.*	(警察等)對……突然查抄(或搜捕)
[red]		Police **raided** the house, and 10 people were arrested on gambling charges. 警方突擊掃蕩該屋，而有 10 人被捕並以賭博罪指控。
		The house **was raided**. Three suspects were arrested for dealing

drugs, and were scorted to the police department. 房子被查抄，三位嫌犯因交易毒品被捕，並被戒護前往警察局。

| | *n.* | (警察等的)突然查抄，搜捕 |

At least 5 suspects were rounded up in **raids** involving the FBI and the Los Angeles Police Department. 在聯邦調查局與洛杉磯警局的突擊中，至少有 5 名嫌犯被捕。

應用 *drug raid* 毒品掃蕩
to conduct drug raid 進行毒品掃蕩

| rally | *n.* | 集會 |
| [`rælɪ] | | |

Many education associations held an anti-violence **rally** in response to the increased incidents of school bullying. 許多教育團體舉行了反暴力集會，以回應漸增的校園霸凌事件。

| ramp | *n.* | 斜面，斜坡，坡道 |
| [ræmp] | | |

Traffic backed up significantly on highway near the St. Francis **off ramp**. The St. Francis northbound **off-ramp** will require a full closure for 5 days. 高速公路靠近「聖法蘭西斯」閘道出口的交通嚴重回堵了，「聖法蘭西斯」北向出口將會需要完全封閉 5 天。

應用 *on-ramp* (高速公路等的)駛進匝道，匝道入口
off-ramp (高速公路等的)駛出匝道，匝道出口

| rampage | *n.* | 暴跳，橫衝直撞 |
| [`ræm,pedʒ] | | |

Hours after the **rampage** began, police were strill trying to track down several suspicious persons to determine whether those individuals had any involvement. 動亂之後數小時，警局仍在試著對幾個可疑的人進行追蹤，以判斷他們是否有任何涉入。

| random | *n.* | 任意行動，隨機過程 (現只用於 at random) |
| [`rændəm] | | |

The gunman opened fire **at random** on the street. He killed two innocent pedestrians **at random**. 槍手在街上隨機開槍，他隨機殺害了兩名無辜的路人。

| | *adj.* | 隨機的，無規則的，任意的，胡亂的 |

Police set up traffic checkpoint **on a random basis** to apprehend drunk drivers, and check for drugs and illegal weapons. The stops are conducted **on a random basis**. 警方採隨機的方式設置交通攔檢點逮捕酒駕者，並檢查毒品及非法武器，這些攔檢都是以隨機的方式進行。

應用 *random attack* 隨機攻擊
random crime 隨機犯罪
random killer 隨機殺人犯
random killing 隨機殺人

		random patrol 隨機巡邏
		random stop 隨機攔阻
rank and file	*n.*	普通成員
	adj.	一般成員的
		Supervisors must ensure that the **rank and file** officers comply with established policy, standard, and rules. 督導人員必須確保全體員警有遵守既定的政策、標準及規範。
ransom	*n.*	贖金
[`rænsəm]		The police are investigating the alleged kidnapping for **ransom** of a little girl who has been missing since April 1. The victim's parents were sent a **ransom note**. They were told to follow directions. 警方正在調查這起 4 月 1 日以來失蹤的女孩擄人勒贖案。被害人的父母收到了勒贖字條，他們被要求照著指示去做。
rape [rep]	*n.&vt.*	強姦
	應用	*date rape* 約會強暴
		forcible rape 強制性交
		marital rape 婚姻強暴
		spousal rape 配偶強姦
		statutory rape 準強制性交
rapid entry device		破門器
rate	*n.*	比例，比率
[ret]	應用	*clearance rate* 破案率
		apprehension rate 逮捕率
		burn rate 燃燒率
		detention rate 收容率
		crime rate 犯罪率
		reporting rate 報案率
		recidivism rate 再犯率
		reoffending rate 再犯罪率
razor wire barrier		蛇籠鐵絲網
reach	*vt.*	抵達，到達，達成
[ritʃ]		Ladies and gentlemen of the jury, have you **reached** a verdict? 陪審團先生及女士，你們已經做成判決了嗎？Yes, we have. Your honor. 是的，庭上。
		Defnese lawyer claimed that he does not agree with the conclusion **reached by** the court of appeal. 被告辯護律師表示他不同意高等法院達成的結論。
		When officers **reached** the location, they discovered a male

victim suffering from a gunshot wound. However, the suspect was gone by the time officers **reached** the scene. 當員警抵達該地點時，他們發現一名男性被害人受到槍傷，然而，嫌犯在員警抵達該現場時已經跑了。

| | *vt.* | 與……取得聯繫 |

The man was killed in a fatal hit-and-run. Police are still trying **to reach** the victim's family. Officers are asking anyone with information to contact police. 男子在一場肇事逃逸車禍中死亡，警方正試圖與被害人家屬取得聯絡，員警請任何有相關資訊的人與警方聯絡。

| real-time
[`ril,taɪm] | *adj.*
應用 | 即時的
real-time interception 即時攔截 |

| reasonable
[`riznəb!] | *adj.*
應用 | 合理的，正當的，適當的
reasonable doubt 合理懷疑(或稱 *rational doubt*)
reasonable suspicion 合理懷疑 |

| recede
[rɪ`sid] | *vi.* | 退，後退 |

Although the the floodwaters **had receded**, the street was full of mud. 雖然洪水已經遠去，街道上還是充滿泥濘。

| receive
[rɪ`siv] | *vt.* | 收到，接到，受到，遭受 |

When prisons **receive** new inmates, correctional officers will firstly conduct body cavity search. 當監獄收容新的囚犯時，矯正人員首先會進行身體搜查。

The defendant **received** life imprisonment for killing the victim. His lawyer claimed that the defendant didn't **receive** fair trial. 被告因殺害被害人獲判無期徒刑，他的律師主張被告並沒有受到公平審判。

Inmates have the right **to receive** medical treatment when they are sick or injured. 受刑人在他們生病或受傷時，有接受醫療的權利。

Usually, sex offenders are required **to receive** psychological treatment. 通常性侵犯會被要求接受心理治療。

Last year, about 500 poilice officers **received** training at the police academy. 去年大約有 500 名員警在警察學校受訓。

接待

| | *vt.* | He **received** his guests warmly. 他熱情接待他的客人。 |

| recidivist
[rɪ`sɪdəvɪst] | *n.* | 再犯之人，累犯之人 |

A repeat shoplifter is a **recidivist**. 一個重複冒充顧客進行偷竊的人，就是一個累犯。

【補充說明】repeat offender 也是再犯、累犯之意思。

recipient [rɪˋsɪpɪənt]	*n.*	收件人，受領者 Controlled delivery is useful in identifing the **recipients**. When the **recipient** takes possession of the drugs, officers then identify themselves, seize the contraband, and arrest the currier and **recipient**. 控制下交付對於確認收件人是有用的，當受領人握有該毒品之後，員警即表明身分、查扣違禁物並逮捕運送人及受領人。
reciprocity [ˌrɛsəˋprɑsətɪ]	*n.*	互惠 Extradition is usually based on **reciprocity**. 引渡通常是基於互惠。
recklessly [ˋrɛklɪslɪ]	*adv.*	過失（或稱 with recklessness）
reconstruct [ˌrikənˋstrʌkt]	*vt.*	重建，再建，改組，（按原樣）修復 Police reopened the case and decided **to reconstruct the crime scene**. 警方決定重啟案件並決定重建犯罪現場。 【補充說明】 按 reconstruct 與 restore 的意思與中文翻譯很接近，就犯罪現場而言，如果是現場已經摧毀的重建，應使用 to reconstruct the crime scene；對於現場不是摧毀，或僅局部毀損的修補或移動回原來樣貌的話，可使用 to restore the crime scene。
reconstruction [ˌrikənˋstrʌkʃən]	*n.* 應用	重建，(按原樣)修復 *crime scene reconstruction* 犯罪現場重建 *facial reconstruction* 臉部重建 *fire scene reconstruction* 火場重建 *traffic accident reconstruction* 交通事故重建
record [rɪˋkɔrd]	*vt.*	記載，記錄，進行錄音(或錄影) In many countries, law enforcement agencies are required **to record** interrogations of people accused of servious crime. 在許多國家，執法機關被要求對於被指控重大犯罪之人的偵訊要錄影錄音。
record [ˋrɛkəd]	*n.* 應用	記錄，記載，成績，前科記錄 *arrest record* 逮捕紀錄 *court record* 法院紀錄 *criminal record* 刑案(前科)紀錄 *fingerprint record* 指紋紀錄 *immigration record* 移民紀錄 *Police record* 警察紀錄（指警察保管的犯罪、前科、報案、逮捕、移送及各項註記等記錄） *public record* 公開資訊

telephone record 電話紀錄
telephone tall record 電話通聯紀錄
toll record 通聯紀錄

recover [rɪ`kʌvɚ]	*vt.*	重新找到，起出 Police recovered the weapons in his home. Police said two weapons **were recovered** at the scene, and the victim's body **was recovered** from below the bridge. 警方在他家起出武器，警方說有兩把武器在現場被起出，並且被害者的屍體在橋下被找到。 Fire department reported that divers **recovered** the body of a drowning victim from the river this evening. 消防局報告說，潛水員在今晚找到了在河流溺斃的遇難者 Fire Department Dive Team **recovered** his body about 50 meters from shore. 消防局潛水隊員在離岸五十公尺的地方找到大體。
	vi.	(身體的) 復原，康復 He was shot in his chest. The gunfire struck him in his chest, and luckly he **recovered** from the injury. 他胸部中彈，砲火擊中他的胸部，幸運地，他從傷勢中康復。
recruit [rɪ`krut]	*vt.*	徵募(新兵)，吸收(新成員) The street gang was accused of running a prostitution ring that **recruited** high school girls for paid sex. 這個街頭幫派被指控經營招募高中女生性交易的色情集團。
	n.	新兵，新手，新成員 A **police recruit** or police cadet must complete the **recruit training** while in the police academy. 新進警察學生(police recruit 或 police cadet)必須在警察學校時，完成新進人員訓練。
red-handed [`rɛd`hændɪd]	*adv.*	在犯罪現場，當場 Usually, the alleged persons tend to give false alibi to the police to cover up their crimes, unless they are caught **red-handed**. 通常，涉嫌人傾向會給警方假的不在場證明，來掩蓋他們的犯罪，除非他們被當場逮到。
refer [rɪ`fɚ]	*vt.*	將……提交，交付[(+to)] Usually, criminal cases **are referred** to the CID. 刑事案件通常被移給刑警隊。 When the police have solved a crime and **refer** the investigation report and evidence **to** the prosecutor, the prosecutor will make a formal accusation against the suspect. 當警察解決一件犯罪，

並移送調查報告及證據給檢察官時，檢察官會對嫌犯做正式的控告。

referral [rɪ`fɝəl]	n.	推薦，介紹，（經介紹）轉診病人

---

reflective duty vest — 反光背心 (或稱 reflective safety vest)

---

refuge
[`rɛfjudʒ]　　n.　躲避，避難，庇護[(+from)]

They smelled smoke, so they managed to rush down the fire escape and took refuge in friend's home nearby. 他們聞到煙霧，所以他們設法衝下防火梯，並在附近的朋友家避難。

Residents lost their homes to the fire and have taken refuge at a Red Cross shelter. 居民們的房子付之一炬，並一直在紅十字會的避難所避難。

應用　*to take refuge in the cellar* 在地下室避難
　　　　area of refuge 避難地區

---

refugee
[,rɛfjʊ`dʒi]　　n.　難民，流亡者
應用　*political refugee* 政治難民

---

registrant
[`rɛdʒɪstrənt]　　n.　登記者
應用　*registrant of the vehicle* 車輛登記人

---

regret
[rɪ`grɛt]　　vt.　痛惜，哀悼，懊悔，因……而遺憾 [+v-ing][+that]

He **regretted killing** the man. He said he **regretted doing** so. 他後悔把男子殺了，他說他後悔這麼做。

He **regretted himself for** pulling the trigger and killed him. He **regretted himself that** he was so stupid. 他後悔扣板機殺了他，他後悔他自己如此愚蠢。

He **regretted that** the victim was pronounced dead on arrival at the hospital. 他感到傷痛遺憾被害人被宣告到院前已經死亡。

　　　　n.　痛惜，哀悼，懊悔，遺憾

The battered woman said she had no **regret** for killing her husband. 受暴婦女說她不後悔將她丈夫殺了。

The defendant expressed his **regret** and apologized for his misconduct. 被告表達他的後悔並為他的不當行為道歉。

---

regulate
[`rɛgjə,let]　　vt.　管理，控制，管控，為……制訂規章

Legislator said it is important to enact a new law **to regulate** traffic and parking. 立法者說，制定新法來管控交通與停車是重要的。

---

regulation
[,rɛgjə`leʃən]　　n.　規章，規則，規定，條例

---

rehabilitation
[,rihə,bɪlə`teʃən]　　n.　（病殘人的）康復，更新，（罪犯的）改過遷善
應用　*social rehabilitation* 社會康復

drug rehabilitation 毒品戒治

drug rehabilitation center 毒品勒戒所

release [rɪ`lis]	*vt.*	釋放，解放[(+from)]，

Once the prisoner **is released** on parole, the parolee will be returned to prison if he or she fails to abide by the condition of parole. 一旦受刑人被假釋時，該假釋人如果未能遵守假釋條件，就會被送回監獄。

| | *vt.* | 發表、發布 |

Police **released** a surveillance video of the suspect who set fire to a shopping center last week. Police also **released** a sketch of the suspect.警方公布了上星期在賣場縱火嫌犯的監視影帶。警方也公布了嫌犯的畫像。

Authorities have captured the man who abducted the little girl. The man's name **has not been released**. 當局抓到了綁架小女孩的人，該人的名子還沒公開。

Police have **released** video that shows the possible getaway car used by the suspect. 警方公布了影帶，顯示嫌犯可能使用的逃逸車輛。

Fire Chief said he admitted to setting the three fires after being arrested. Later, he **was released** on bail. 消防局長說，他在被捕之後承認了三件縱火，後來，他被交保釋放。

Three firegithers got sick at the scene and were all treated and then **released** from the hospital. 三名消防員在現場覺得想嘔吐，並且被治療，之後被醫院准予出院。

The other seven occupants were evaluated, treated and **released**. 其他 7 名住戶被撤離、治療並准予出院了。

| | *vt.* | 施放 |

The man **released** chemical gases in his apartment Thursday, killing himself. 該名男子在公寓內施放化學毒氣，導致自己死亡。

| | *n.* | 發行，發表，(發布的) 新聞稿 |

Police will hold a **press release** to release more details about the homicide. 警方會舉行記者會公布更多有關這起兇殺案的細節。

relevance [`rɛləvəns]	*n.*	(證據的)關聯性

Admissibility, **relevance** and probative value are three important issues for evidence to be considered. 證據能力、關聯性及證明價值，是證據被考慮的三個重要事項。

relevant	*adj.*	有關的，有關聯的

[ˋrɛləvənt]		Rules of Evidence provide that relevant evidence is **admissible**; irrelevant evidence is not **admissible**. 證據法則規定，有關聯性的證據有證據能力；無關聯性的證據無證據能力。 Hearsay is not **admissible**. 傳聞，沒有證據能力。
reliable [rɪˋlaɪəb!]	adj.	可信賴的，可靠的 Researches indicate that eyewitness testimony is not a **reliable** form of evidence and may cause more miscarriages of justice. 研究指出，目擊證人的證詞不是一種可靠的證據，並可能造成司法誤判。
relief [rɪˋlif]	n.	(痛苦，負擔等的) 緩和，減輕，解除 It is a great **relief** to know that everyone is safe and unharmed, police said. 警方說，得知大家都平安沒有受傷，真是鬆了一大口氣。
relieve [rɪˋliv]	vi.	緩和，減輕，解除 The mother **felt relieved that** her son was safe. 母親覺得鬆了口氣，因為她兒子平安。 He **felt relieved that** the case against him is over. 她覺得鬆了口氣，因為他被提告的案件已經結案。 The defendant pleaded guilty to the charge and told detectives he **felt relieved** to have been caught. 被告對於指控事項認罪，並且告訴偵查員說他在被捕後覺得鬆了口氣。
remand [rɪˋmænd]	vt.	(案件)發回重審，(人)還押候審 The court of appeals vacated in full the lower court's judgment and **remanded** the case to a new trial. 上訴法院撤銷了下級法院的判決，並將案件發回重新審理。 The judge ordered that the suspect **be remanded** in jail custody for another 3 months. 法官命令嫌犯還押看守所三個月。 【請參看 affirm, uphold, vacate】
removal [rɪˋmuv!]	n.	【美】遣返 【補充說明】 美國國會立法用遣返(removal)一字來指遣送(deportation)與拒絕入境(exclusion)。遣送(deportation) 是對人身已經在美國境內的人，拒絕入境(exclusion)的設計是為了在外國人在入境港埠還沒准予依簽證入境時，就防止其在國內留下。US Congress enacted the term "**removal**" to refer to both deportation and exclusion. Deportation is for people already physically present inside the United States. Exclusion is designed to prevent the alien from staying in the country when he has not been admitted on a visa at the port of entry.

remove	*vt.*	脫掉，除去，去掉，消除[(+from)]
[rɪˋmuv]		

After battling the blaze, firefighters soon **removed** protective clothing in order to prevent heat exhaustion. 火撲滅之後，消防員快速地脫去防護衣，以避免熱衰竭。

The ideal method of collecting took-mark evidence is to **remove** the mark from the crime scene. 採集工具痕跡證據的理想方法，就是將痕跡從犯罪現場取走。

Usually, firearms' serial number would be **removed**, obliterated, or altered by the smuggling ring to avoid detection. 通常，武器的序號會被走私集團除去、磨掉或變更，以避免被查獲。

vt. 移走，搬開，調動[(+from)]

If there is any disruption during the reading of the verdicts, the bailiffs will have the obligation to **remove** any persons disrupting these proceedings. 如果宣讀判決的時候有任何擾亂，法警會有義務排除任何擾亂程序的人。

A victim was located in a second-floor bedroom and was brought out. Firefighters **removed** several victims from the structure. 消防員說，高熱及濃煙狀況阻礙了搜尋。有一位遇難者在二樓的臥室被找到並被帶出來。消防員從建築物帶出了幾個遇難者。

Firefighters **removed** one trapped patient and that patient was transported to a nearby hospital. 消防員帶出了一位受困的患者，並且該患者被送到附近的一家醫院。

Policer officers and the social workers were on the scene and they jointly determined it was necessary **to remove** the child **from** his home. 員警及社工在現場，並且共同認為有必要將小孩帶離他家。

vt. 【美】遣返

If the immigration officer suspects that an arriving alien may be inadmissible, the immigration officer may order the alien **removed**. The alien, however, may not **be removed to** a country in which his life or freedom would be threaten. 如果移民官懷疑抵達的外國人可能不合於入境，移民官可以命令將該外國人遣返，然而，該外國人不得被遣返到他的生命或自由會遭受威脅的國家。

應用 *to remove allergen* 消除過敏

to remove patient's clothing 脫去患者的衣物

to remove patient to cool area 將患者移到陰涼地區

---

repatriate	*vt.*	把……遣返回國

[ri`petrɪˌet]		Immigration officers said that they are ready to **repatriate** those detainees back to their home countries. 移民官員表示，他們準備將那些被收容人遣返回母國。
repatriation [ripetrɪ`eʃən]	*n.*	遣送回國
repeal [rɪ`pil]	*vt.*	(法令或決議的) 撤銷，廢除，取消
		Adultery is no longer a crime in our country. The law **was repealed** in 2020. 通姦在我國已不再是犯罪，這項法律在 2020 年已被廢除了。
report [rɪ`port]	*n.*	報告
	應用	*arrest report* 逮捕報告
		autopsy report 驗屍報告
		crime lab report 實驗室報告
		crime report 犯罪報告
		crime report 犯罪報案
		daytime reporting 日間報到
		incident report 事件報告
		investigation report 調查報告
		offense report 犯罪報告
		reporting rate 報案率
		to make false report 謊報
		to take a report 受理報案
		to take crime report 受理犯罪報案
		to take one's complaint 受理某人的申訴
	vt.	報告
	應用	*is/am/are under reported* 沒有報案
		is/am/are unreported 沒有報案
		to report back to the agency 報回機關
		to report crime 犯罪報告
		to report for duty 報到服勤
		to report to work 報到勤務
represent [ˌrɛprɪ`zɛnt]	*vt.*	代理，代表
		The defendant chose **to represent himself** in court without a lawyer. But the trial judge instructed the defendant that, in his case, he is entitled to have counsel appointed **to represent him** at every stage of the proceedings. 被告選擇自行出庭應訊，不需要律師。但審理法官告知被告說，就他的案件，他都有資格在訴訟的每一個階段，有指任的律師代理他。
rescue	*vt.*	援救，營救，挽救

[`rɛskju]		Two police officers rushed to the scene of the car crash and **rescued** the driver from the burning car. 兩名員警衝到車禍現場並將駕駛人從燃燒的車子中救出。
	n.	援救，營救，挽救
		Firefighters **came to her rescue** shortly after her call. 她報警後不久，消防員就來救她了。

應用
air rescue cushion 救生氣墊
civilian rescue team 民間搜救隊
climbing rescue 登山搜救
mountain rescue 山難搜救
rescue air cushion 救生氣墊
rescue basket 救生吊籃
rescue boat 搜救艇
rescue litter 救生擔架
rescue net 救生網
rescue operation 救援行動
rescue seat 救生吊座
rescue sling 救生吊索
rescue stretcher 救護擔架
rescue swimmer 游泳救生員
rescue worker 救援人員
search and rescue 搜救
search and rescue dog 搜救犬

rescuer	*n.*	救難人員
[`rɛskjʊɚ]		The driver was trapped in the car for about 30 minutes before **rescuers** could get him out. 該名駕駛被困在車內將近 30 分鐘才被救難人員救了出來。
		Rescuers decided to deploy rescue air cushion as a primary means of rescue or a safety backup. 救難人員決定鋪設救生氣墊做為主要的救援方法或安全備援。
reserved bus lane		公車專用道
reside	*vi.*	住，居住
[rɪ`zaɪd]		Immigration officers may visit the suspect couple at their residence or visit their neighbors to investigate whether they **reside** together. 移民員可以在可疑夫婦的住所訪視他們，或拜訪其鄰居，以調查他們是否有居住在一起。
residence	*n.*	住所，住宅
[`rɛzədəns]		
resident	*n.*	居民，定居者

[ˋrɛzədənt]

residential [ˌrɛzəˋdɛnʃəl]	*adj.* 應用	居住的，住宅的 *residential area* 住宅區 *residential arson* 住宅縱火 *residential burglary* 住宅竊盜 *residential care* 居住照護、社會服務業(指對老弱病殘者提供生活幫助的服務業) *residential fire* 住宅火災
residue [ˋrɛzəˌdju]	*n.* 應用	殘餘 *drug residue* 毒品殘留 *explosive residue* 爆裂物殘留 *gun powder residue* 火藥殘留 *gunshot residue* 火藥殘留
resist [rɪˋzɪst]	*vt.*	抵抗，反抗，抗拒 A person may not use physical force to **resist** an arrest by a police officer or peace officer. 任何人不得使用身體武力，來抗拒員警或治安人員的逮捕。
resistance [ˋrɛzədəns]	*n.*	住所，住宅 An officer is permitted to use the amount of force necessary to overcome the **resistance** or aggression. When the **resistance** or the aggression is reduced, the officers must reduce his or her force correspondingly. 員警被容許使用武力的多寡，僅得在壓制抗拒或侵犯的必要程度內，使用之。當抗拒或侵犯降低時，員警必須相對地降低武力。
resolve [rɪˋzɑlv]	*vt.*	解決 Officers shall not use their police powers to **resolve** personal grievances. 員警不得使用警察權來解決個人的不滿。
resort [rɪˋzɔrt]	*vi.* *n.* 應用	訴諸，求助[(+to)] Criminals frequently **resort to** violence if they perceive a victim is being uncooperative. 罪犯如果感覺被害人不配合時，經常就會訴諸暴力。 訴諸，憑藉，憑藉的手段 All life is precious. Therefore, deadly force must be used only **as a last resort** to protect innocent lives. 所有的生命都是寶貴的，因此，致命的武器必須當成最後手段來使用，以保護無辜的生命。 *as a last resort* 做為最後手段
resuscitate [rɪˋsʌsəˌtet]	*vt.*	（使）恢復，（使）復活，（使）復甦 The two victims were unresponsive when firefighters found

them insides the charred apartment. One **was resuscitated** by firefighters, and the other was declared deat at the hospital. 兩名遇難者被消防員在燒得焦黑的公寓內找到時，都沒有反應了。一人被消防員救出，另一人在醫院被宣告死亡。

respond [rɪ`spand]	*vi.*	作出反應，[(+to)] 對......作出反應，對......作出回答

When the police **respond to** a citizen's report and learn that a crime has been committed, a preliminary investigation will be initiated. 當警方回應民眾報案，並得知有犯罪發生時，就會展開初步偵查。

When the first arriving officer **responds to** a citizen's complaint, he or she shall conduct an assessment of the situation and request specialized resources to **respond to** the scene. 當最早抵達的員警前往現場處理市民的報案時，他(她)應該進行狀況評估，並請求專業的資源前來現場。

Local police **responded to** the shooting, shutting down traffic in the area. Some people were evacuated. 當地警察前往處理此一槍擊案，關閉了這個區域的交通。有些人被撤離了。

Firefighters **responded to** a collapsed building and rescued people trapped in the collapse rubble. 消防員前往處理一處倒塌了的建物，並且救出被困在坍塌瓦礫中的人。

Five fire departments and more than 200 firefighters **responded to** the incident. They **responded to** bring the fire under control. 有5個消防局及超過200位消防員前往處理這個事件。他們前往處理而將火勢控制住。

response [rɪ`spans]	*n.*	反應，應變

Emergency protective order is commonly issued at the request of law enforcement officers **in response to** a domestic violence complaint from a victim who is in immediate danger. 緊急保護令的核發，通常是基於執法人員為回應處在立即危險的被害人的家暴報案，而提出的請求。

responsibility [rɪ,spansə`bɪlətɪ]	*n.*	責任，職責，任務，義務，負擔

The person who commits the crime must **bear the responsibility for** the damage and hurt that he has caused. He cannot evade the responsibility. 犯這個罪的人必須為他所造成的損害及傷害擔起責任，他不可以規避責任。

應用

age of criminal responsibility 刑事責任年齡
criminal responsibility (liability/accountability) 刑事責任
to accept responsibility 接受責任
to bear the responsibility 承擔責任

to deny responsibility 拒絕責任
to evade responsibility 逃避責任
to ssume responsibility 承擔責任
to take responsibility 承擔責任

【補充說明】
按 liability 及 responsibility 的中文翻譯都是「責任，義務」，但略有差別在於 liability 指的比較是法律方面；而 responsibility 指的比較是道德倫理方面。(By definition, liability is a legal issue, and responsibility is a moral and ethical issue)

responsible [rɪˋspɑnsəb!]	adj.	需負責任的，承擔責任的 [(+for/to)] Bailiff **is responsible for** maintaining order during court proceedings. 法警負責在開庭程序中維持秩序。 If stopped by the police while driving a motor vehicle, you **are responsible for** providing your valid driving license, vehicle registration and proof of insurance. 如果開車時被警察攔下來，你有義務提供你的有效駕照、行車執照及保險證明。
	應用	*to hold sb. responsible for* 要某人對……負責 "We will press criminal charges against him, and we will **hold him responsible for** what he did," the captain said. 隊長說，我們會對他提出刑事告訴，並且我們會讓他為他自己的所作所為負起責任。
restore [rɪˋstor]	vt.	恢復，回復，使……復原[(+to)] The forensic scientists returned to the house **to restore the crime scene** to its previous condition. 刑事鑑識科學專家回到那房子，重建犯罪現場回復到當時的狀況。 【補充說明】 按 restore 與 reconstruct 的意思與中文翻譯很接近，就犯罪現場而言，如果是現場已經摧毀的重建，應使用 to reconstruct the crime scene；對於現場不是摧毀，或僅局部毀損的修補或移動回原來樣貌的話，可使用 to restore the crime scene。
restrain [rɪˋstren]	vt.	管束，監禁，控制，限制，約束，阻止 The detained person attempted to attack the witness and **was restrained by** three officers. He **was restrained** in custody. 被拘禁者試圖攻擊證人，而被三位員警制伏。他被管束監禁了。
	應用	*restraining order* 限制令 *protection prder* 保護令 *protective order* 保護令 【補充說明】 「保護令(protection order)」也稱為(protective order) 或「限

制令(restraining order)」，但 protection/protective order 通常是用於刑事案件，禁止家暴及限制某人不得騷擾、威脅、聯絡及接近另一特定人的法院裁定。而 restraining order 大部分用於民事案件。(Protective orders usually apply in criminal cases with criminal charges. It is a court order that prohibits family violence and restricts a person from harassing, threatening, contacting or approaching another specified person. Restraining orders are mostly used in civil cases.)

restrict	vt.	限制，限定，約束
[rɪ`strɪkt]		Interpol urged all countries not **to restrict** police **from** informally exchanging information. 國際刑警組織呼籲所有國家不要限制警方非正式交換資訊。
		Searches incident to arrest **are restricted to** "the arrestee's person and the area 'within his immediate control". 附帶搜索限縮在「被逮捕之人及其立即可控制」的範圍。

restriction	n.	限制，限定，約束，制止，禁止
[rɪ`strɪkʃən]		Although the police power is very broad in concept, it is **not without restriction**. 雖然警察權在概念上非常廣，但是並不是毫無限制。
		Generally speaking, the use of force is subject to the **restriction** that the force used is necessary. 通常而言，武力使用的限制是以該武力的使用有必要性。
		Newspaper said a majority of people want the government **to impose restriction on** the use of facial recognition technology. 新聞說，大部分的人要政府對於人臉辨識科技的使用賦予限制。

result	vi.	結果，導致[(+in)]；發生，產生[(+from)]
[rɪ`zʌlt]		The accident **resulted in** severe injuries. Several motorcyclists sustained serious injuries. 這場意外造成嚴重的受傷，好幾位機車騎士受到嚴重的受傷。
		Investigators believed the homicide **resulted from** a domestic dispute that began earlier in the day. This was not a random incident, the department said. 警方說，偵查員相信這起殺人案是因為當天稍早開始的家庭爭執所造成，這不是一起隨機的事件。
	n.	結果，成果，效果
		He appears to be seriously injured **as a result of** being knocked to the ground. 他被擊倒在地，結果似乎傷得很嚴重。

retain	vt.	聘，僱

[rɪ`ten]		The defendant **retained** a lawyer in the case. At trial, a defendant has the right to be represented by counsel, known as **the right to retain counsel**. 被告在案件中聘請了律師。審判時，被告有權由律師代理，稱為律師權。
	vt.	留下，留有
		Any physician, clinics or hospital must **retain custody of** the abused or maltreated child and notify the appropriate police authorities or the local child protective service to take custody of the child. 任何醫生、診所或醫院必須將受虐待或受不當對待的兒童留置看管，並通知相關警察機關或當地兒童保護機構監護該兒童。
	vt.	保留
		During the execution of the search warrant, officer must prepare an inventory, verify the property seized, and **retain** a copy. 搜索票執行時，員警必須準備一份清冊，核對扣押物，並保留一份正本。
retaliate [rɪ`tælɪ,et]	*vi*	報復，回敬[(+against/on/upon)]
		The gang attempted to use violence **to retaliate against** rival gang members. Police worned the gang members **not to retaliate**. 幫派企圖使用武力報復敵對幫派。警方警告該幫派成員不要進行報復。
retaliation [rɪ,tælɪ`eʃən]	*n.*	報復
		To seek revenge, an arsonist will target the home of someone **in retaliation for** an actual or perceived injustice against him or her. 為了尋求報復，縱火者會鎖定某人的家為目標，以報復一個真正或自我感覺的不公平。
retreat [rɪ`trit]	*vi.*	撤退，退卻，退避，躲避[(+from/to)]
		SWAT team members believed that the gunman **had retreated to** his home and quickly surrounded it. 特殊武器小組成員相信槍手已經退避到房子內，並很快地包圍該房子。
		When the suspect started shooting, officers decided **to retreat from** the scene and called for backup. 當嫌犯開始開槍的時候，員警決定從現場撤退並呼叫支援。
retrieve [rɪ`triv]	*vt.*	重新得到，復得，收回，取回，恢復
		Luckly, fingerprints **were retrieved from** the vehicle and many stolen items **were also retrieved**, police said. 警方說，幸運地指紋被從車上採到了，而且許多失竊地物品也找回了。
		The ship capsized off the coast of Libya, and four migrants drowned. So far three bodies **were retrieved**. 船隻在利比亞外

海翻覆，4 位移民溺斃，目前有 3 位遺體已找到。

return fire		開槍還擊

As the policemen were getting out of their vehicle, several shots were fired from the gunman. The police **returned fire** in self-defence, and killed the gunman on the spot. 當員警步出車輛時，槍手開了好幾槍，警方開槍還擊自衛，並當場擊斃槍手。

reveal [rɪ`vil]	*vt.*	揭示，揭露，暴露，洩露

Shoeprints and footprints may **reveal** a criminal's height. 鞋印及腳印可透露出罪犯的身高。

Investigation **revealed** that the defendants conspired with fellow gang members throughout the country to further the gang's criminal objectives. 調查發現，被告和全國各地的幫派份子共謀，以遂行其幫派的犯罪目的。

Under questioning, he **revealed** the name of the mastermind behind the holdup. 問訊中，他透露了搶案幕後主使者的姓名。

Detectives investigating the death of victim **have revealed** that they cannot rule out the possibility she was murdered. 偵辦這起被害人死亡的偵查員透露，他們不能排除她被謀殺的可能。

revenge [rɪ`vɛndʒ]	*n.*	報仇，報復

Officers must also understand that confidential informants may choose to cooperate with the law enforcement authorities **to seek revenge against** their enemies. 員警也必須了解，線民選擇與執法機關合作，可能是為了報復敵人。

Revenge is the most common motive for a serial arsonist. 報復，是連續縱火犯最常見的動機。

reverse [rɪ`vɝs]	*vt.*	【律】推翻，撤銷

If court finds an error which will affect the result, the higher court will **reverse** the lower court's error in whole or in part. 如果法院發現了會影響結果的錯誤，上級法院將會對下級法的錯誤為全部或局部撤銷。

After the review, the Supreme Court **reversed** and remanded the case to the Court of Appeals for a new trial. 案經審理，最高法院將案件撤銷並發回高等法院重新審理。

reversible lane		調撥車道

review [rɪ`vju]	*vt.*	【法律(上對下的)】審查，覆審，審理

The appellate court **reviewed** the trial court's decision. 上訴法院審理了地方法院的判決。

	n.	【法律(上對下的)】審查，覆審，審理

		After a careful **review** of the record, the Court concludes that the appeal must be denied. 經過仔細審理資料，本院認定該上訴應予駁回。
	應用	*judicial review* 司法審查
		Law Review 法律期刊/評論 (例如：*Harvard Law Review* 哈佛法律評論)

---

revocation	*n.*	吊銷
[ˌrɛvəˋkeʃən]		Under some circumstances, a driver license may be suspended, cancelled or revoked. **Revocation** involuntarily ends your driving privilege. It generally is permanent until you are eligible after the period set by law to apply for a new license. By then, you will have to retake a driver's license examination. 有些情況下，駕照可能會被吊扣、註銷或吊銷。吊銷是非自願地結束你的開車特權，通常是長久性的，直到你過了法律規定的時間，而合於申請新的駕照時為止，到那時候，你必須重新參加考照。
		Revocation aims to discipline the driver and protect the public. **Revocation** involuntarily ends your driving privilege. 吊銷(revocation)的目的是為了訓誡駕駛人及保護公眾，吊銷是非自願地結束你的開車特權。

---

revoke	*n.*	撤銷，撤回，廢除，取消，吊銷
[rɪˋvok]		Under some circumstances, a driver license may be suspended, cancelled or **revoked**. 有些情況下，駕照可能會被吊扣、註銷或吊銷。
	應用	*to revoke visa* 撤銷簽證

---

reward	*n.*	酬金，賞金
[rɪˋwɔrd]		Informants supply information to the police about a crime in exchange for a **reward**. Payment to confidential informants (CIs) can be divided into two categories – awards and **rewards**. Awards may be based on a percentage of the net value of assets seized as a result of information provided by a CI. Unlike awards, **rewards** come directly from an agency's budget. 線民提供犯罪的相關資訊給警方，以換取報酬。付給線民的費用可以分為兩類：獎金(award)與報酬(reward)，獎金可能會是依據線民提供資訊而查扣到的資產淨值的某個比例，報酬則與獎金不同，報酬直接來自於機關的預算。

---

right	*n.*	權利
[raɪt]	應用	*the right of assembly* 集會權
		the right of privacy 隱私權
		the right of self-defense /self-protection 自衛權

the right of speech 言論權

the right of way 路權

the right to appeal 上訴權

the right to assemble 集會權

the right to associate 結社權

the right to confront the witnesses 與證人對質之權

the right to consult with a lawyer 諮詢律師之權

the right to counsel 律師權

the right to petition 請願權

the right to remain silent 緘默權

the right to retain counsel 聘請律師權

the right to silence 緘默權

ring [rɪŋ]	*n.* 應用	(不法)集團，幫派 *crime ring* 犯罪集團 *drug ring* 毒品集團 *firearms smuggling ring* 槍械走私集團 *prostitution ring* 色情應召集團 *ring leader* 集團的首腦
ringleader [ˋrɪŋ,lidɚ]	*n.*	集團的首腦 The drug **ringleader** is on parole for a previous drug conviction. 毒品集團的首腦為先前的一件毒品判決正在假釋中。
riot [ˋraɪət]	*n.* 應用	暴亂，騷亂，大混亂 **Riots** broke out across downtown Baltimore after a 25-year-old black man was fatally injured while in police custody. 就在一名 25 歲黑人在警方拘禁時被傷害而死之後，巴爾的摩市中心即暴動四起。 *prison riot* 監獄暴動 *riot helmet* 鎮暴頭盔 *riot gun* 鎮暴槍 *riot police* 鎮暴警察 *riot shield* 鎮暴盾牌 *riot vehicle* 鎮暴車(又稱 *riot control vehicle*) *to turn into riot* 變成騷亂
rise [raɪz]	*vi.* *n.*	上升，增加，提高，升高，加劇 Chief of Police said that violent crime rates **are rising** nationally. 警察局長說暴力犯罪率在全國都在上升中。 上升，增加，提高，升高，加劇 Police said that violent crimes are **on the rise**. 警方說暴力犯罪正在上升中。

risk	n.	危險，風險
[rɪsk]	應用	*risk analysis* 風險分析
		risk assessment 風險評估
		risk management 風險管理
		at one's own risk 自擔風險(同意不要求賠償損失、損害等)
		at the risk of (one's life) 將(某人的)生命置於險境
		at-risk 有危險，冒風險
		at-risk family 風險家庭
		flood risk 淹水的風險
		to put one's life at risk 將某人的生命置於險境
		to run the risk (of V-ing) 甘冒(做⋯⋯)的風險
		to take risk 冒險

risky	adj.	危險的，冒險的
['rɪskɪ]		The travelers were trapped in the mountains due to typhoon, and the rescue was extremely **risky**. 遊客因為颱風而被困在山上，救援非常冒險。

rival	n.	競爭者，對手，敵手
['raɪv!]	adj.	競爭的；rival gang 敵對幫派

road	n.	街道，馬路
[rod]	應用	*road capacity* 道路容量
		roadblock 路障
		roadside 路邊，路旁地帶
		roadway 道路，路面，車行道
		public roadway 公共道路
		roadworks 道路施工

rob	vt.	搶劫，劫掠，盜取[(+of)]
[rɑb]		The husband and wife **were robbed** at gunpoint. They **were robbed** of their cellphones and a total of five thousand dollars in cash. 這對夫婦被槍抵住而搶劫。他們被搶了手機及總共 5 千元現金。
		The robbers told police they had intended **to rob** the bank. 搶匪告訴警方他們原本打算搶銀行。
	vi.	搶劫
		Officers worned them not **to rob** again. 員警警告他們切勿再行搶。

robbery	n.	強盜
['rɑbərɪ]		*aggravated robbery* 加重強盜
		armed robbery 攜械強盜
		armed bank robbery 攜械銀行搶案

attempted robbery 強盜未遂

round [raʊnd]	*n.*	（子彈）一發 Police recovered one pistol, 35 **rounds of bullet** and some sharp weapons from the spot. 警方從現場找到一把手槍、35 發子彈及一些尖銳武器。 The suspect admitted that he illegally possessed firearms after officers found 5 pistols and **50 rounds of bullets** in his residence. 嫌犯在員警從他住處查獲 5 把手槍及 50 發子彈後，承認他非法持有武器。
round up	*n.*	(罪犯的)圍捕 The **round-up** was carried out by the city police department and many suspects were apprehended in the **roundup**. 此一圍捕由市警局執行，並且許多嫌犯在此一圍捕中被捕。 圍捕(罪犯)
	v.	At least 5 suspects **were rounded up** in raids involving the FBI and the Los Angeles Police Department. 在聯邦調查局與洛杉磯警局的突擊中，至少有 5 名嫌犯被捕。
roundabout [`raʊndə,baʊt]	*n.*	圓環
route [rut]	*n.* 應用	路，路線，路程，航線 *climbing route* (或 *mountain climbing route*) 攀登路線 *escape route* 逃生路線 *evacuation route* 撤離路線 *parade route* 遊行路線
rubber bullet		塑膠子彈
rule [rul]	*vt.* 應用 *n.* 應用	裁決，裁定[O][+that] The court **ruled that** the boy should live with his mother. 法院判決孩童應與母親一起生活。 裁決，裁定 The court **ruled that** Davis was in contempt of court for disobeying the judge's order. 法院判決，戴維斯未遵守法官的命令是藐視法庭。 *rule out* 把……排除在外，排除……的可能性 Detectives revealed that they cannot **rule out** the possibility that the missing person was murdered. 偵查員透露說，他們無法排除這個失蹤者遇害了的可能性。 規範 *to abide by the rule* 遵守規範 *to follow the rule* 遵守規範

> *to obey the rule* 遵守規範
>
> *rule of evidence* 證據規則，證據法則
>
> *traffic rule* 交通規則

| ruling | *n.* | 裁決 |
| ['rulɪŋ] | | |

---

run | *n.* | 跑，逃跑
[rʌn] | |

After the shooting happened, one man is in jail and a second man is **on the run**. 槍擊案發生之後，有一人進了看守所，另一人在逃。

The wanted fugitive was arrested after more than 20 years **on the run**. 這名通緝犯在逃跑超過 20 年之後被捕了。

Any patrol officer who sees the crime of **hit and run** can pursue the suspect and place him into custody. 任何巡邏員警看到肇事逃逸，都可以追捕嫌犯並將其拘禁。

| | *vt.* | (機器)開動，運轉 |

Police said that officers in the patrol car will have an in-car computer that could **run** checks of license plate numbers, driver's license numbers, vehicle identification numbers, and other information. 警方說，巡邏車內的員警會有一部車裝電腦可以清查車牌號碼、駕照號碼、車身號碼及其他資訊。

The forensic analyst and examiner will **run** tests on the evidence brought to the lab, and testify in court as expert witnesses, if necessary. 刑事分析人員與鑑識人員會將帶回實驗室的證據進行檢測，並於必要時，以專家證人的身分在法庭作證。

| | *vt.* | 穿過 |

Do not **run** yellow lights. Always come to a full stop at red lights. 不要闖黃燈，紅燈時要全停。

| runaway | *n.* | 離家出走者，逃跑者 |
| ['rʌnə,we] | | |

---

safeguard | *vt.* | 保護，防衛，為……提供防護措施
['sef,gɑrd] | |

President Barock Obama said: "We're going to do what's necessary to protect the American people, to determine who is behind this potentially deadly act, and to see that justice is done. And I'm going to continue to monitor the situation closely and do what it takes at home and abroad to **safeguard** the security of the American people." 總統歐巴馬說：「我們會做任何必要的事項來保護美國民眾、找出是誰在這個潛在致命行為的幕後，並看到正義獲得伸張，而我將繼續密切地關注情勢，並採取國內及國外的必要作為，來保障美國民眾的安全」。

safety [`sɛftɪ]	*n.*	安全，平安
	應用	*fire safety* 火災安全 *highway safety* 高速公路安全 *household safety* 居家/家戶安全 *pedestrian safety* 行人安全 *physical safety* 人身安全 *public safety* 公共安全 *safety belt* 安全帶（與 *seat belt* 同） safety backup *safety concern* 安全顧慮 *safety cone* 安全錐 *safety precaution* 安全警戒 *safety vest* 安全背心
saliva [sə`laɪvə]	*n.*	涎，唾液
salvage [`sælvɪdʒ]	*n.*	救助，海難救助，營救，搶救，沉船打撈（作業） Firefighting is further broken down into skills which include size-up, extinguishing, ventilation, **salvage** and overhaul. 消防近一步分為一些技術，包括：決斷(size-up)、滅火(extinguishing)、排煙(ventilation)、救援(salvage)與殘火處理 (overhaul 原意為全面檢查)。 Fire investigation is conducted after fire control and salvage activities are completed. 火災調查是在火場控制與救助作為完成後才進行的。
sanction [`sæŋkʃən]	*n.*	制裁
scam [`skæm]	*n.*	【美】【俚】陰謀，騙局
scammer [`skæmɚ]		詐騙犯，詐欺者
scapegoat [`skep‚got]	*n.*	替人頂罪者，代罪羔羊 The suspect was in debt and was used by the syndicate as a **scapegoat.** 嫌犯正負債中，而被犯罪集團當成替罪者。
SCBA	*abbr.*	自給式空氣呼吸器 *self-contained breathing apparatus*
scene [sin]	*n.*	(事件發生的)地點，現場 Criminal will stage a **crime scene** to misdirect investigators so as to get away with the crime. 罪犯會假造一個犯罪現場來誤導偵查人員，以逃避犯罪。 In major crime investigations, one of the priorities of the **crime**

scene investigation (CSI) unit is to seal off the crime scene and conduct a preliminary examination. 在重大犯罪的偵查中，犯罪現場調查小組有一項優先事項，就是封鎖現場並進行初步的鑑識。

Police cordoned off the area with yellow **crime-scene** tape. 警方用黃色的犯罪現場封鎖帶封鎖了該區域。

Police said two weapons were recovered **at the scene**, and the body was recovered from below the bridge. 警方說，有兩把武器在現場被起出，並且屍體在橋下被找到。

An officer **on the scene** said: "We sealed off the road to make sure citizens were safe." 現場有位員警說：「我們封閉了道路，以確保民眾是安全的。」

The first responding officer **at the scene** should secure the **accident scene** and search for the survivors as soon as possible. 最早回應現場的人員應該保全事件現場，並儘快搜尋生還者。

When the first arriving officer responds to a citizen's complaint, he or she shall conduct an assessment of the situation and request specialized resources **to respond to the scene**. 當最早抵達的員警前往現場處理市民的報案時，他(她)應該進行狀況評估，並請求專業的資源前來現場。

There are several steps that need to be taken in order **to process a crime scene**. Some of the steps include: **securing the scene**, a detailed search, documenting the **crime scene**, collecting and preserving evidence, etc. 為了要處理犯罪現場，有些步驟需要採取，一些步驟包括：保全現場、詳細的搜索、現場紀錄、證據採集與保存等等。

The ideal method of collecting took-mark evidence is to remove the mark from the **crime scene**. 採集工具痕跡證據的理想方法，就是將痕跡從犯罪現場取走。

The suspect used a vehicle **to escape crime scene** and avoid being taken into custody by officers. 嫌犯用車輛逃離犯罪現場及避免被執法人員拘禁。

When arson is suspected, firefighters must secure the **fire scene**. 當有懷疑縱火時，消防員應該保全火災現場。

應用
crime scene examination 犯罪現場鑑識
crime scene examiner 犯罪現場鑑識人員
crime scene investigation (CSI) 犯罪現場調查
crime scene reconstruction 犯罪現場重建
crime scene safety tape 犯罪現場封鎖帶

crime scene 犯罪現場

fire scene examination 火災現場鑑識

fire scene examiner 火災現場鑑識人員

fire scene investigation 火場調查

fire scene reconstruction 火場重建

fire scene 火災現場

incident commander at scene 案件的現場指揮官

murder scene 謀殺案現場

on-scene commander 現場指揮官

primary crime scene 第一犯罪現場

secondary crime scene 第二犯罪現場

staged crime scene 故布疑陣的犯罪現場

to conduct a scene reconstruction 進行現場重建

to escape crime scene 逃離犯罪現場

to seal off the crime scene 封鎖犯罪現場

to visit crime scene 查看犯罪現場

schedule [`skɛdʒʊl]	*vt.*	將……列入計畫 (或時間) 表 The trial **is scheduled on** February 10th. 審判時間訂於 2 月 10 日。
scheme [skim]	*n.* 應用	詭計，陰謀 *fraud scheme* 詐欺騙局 *phishing scheme* 假網頁詐騙 *Ponzi scheme* 龐氏騙局，老鼠會 *pyramid scheme* 傳銷，老鼠會，層壓式推銷模式
screen [skrin]	*vt.*	過濾 Each call to the police department should **be** carefully **screened**. 每一通打到警察局的電話都應該小心過濾。
seal off	*v.*	封鎖，封閉 (或稱 cordon off) In major crime investigations, one of the priorities of the crime scene investigation (CSI) unit is to **seal off** the crime scene and conduct a preliminary examination. 在重大犯罪的偵查中，犯罪現場調查小組有一項優先事項，就是封鎖現場並進行初步的鑑識。 An officer on the scene said: "We **sealed off** the road to make sure citizens were safe." 現場有位員警說：「我們封閉了道路，以確保民眾是安全的。」
search [sɝtʃ]	*vt.*	搜索 The court issued the warrant, and police immediately **searched** the premises specified in the warrant. 法院發出令狀，警方立

即搜索了搜索票所載之處所。

vi. 尋找，搜尋 [(+for)]

Officers **are searching for** the fatal hit-and-run suspect. 員警正在尋找該起致命肇事逃逸的嫌犯。

Firefighters at the scene should secure the accident scene and **search for** the survivors as soon as possible. 現場的消防人員應該保全事件現場，並儘快搜尋生還者。

Firefighters should **search** in pairs. If one firefighter becomes lost in smoke, the other firefighter may guide the disoriented firefighter to safety by voice direction. 消防員應該兩人一組搜索，如果一位消防員在煙霧中迷路，另一位消防員可以用聲音導路，導引這個失去方向的消防員到安全(之處)。

n. 搜索

Police obtained his consent and **conducted the search**. 警方取得他的同意然後進行了搜索。

Unless a police officer has probable cause to make an arrest or a reasonable suspicion to conduct a stop and frisk, a person is generally not required to answer an officer's questions or allow an officer to **conduct a search**. 除非員警有相當理由進行逮捕，或有合理懷疑進行攔阻及搜身(stop and frisk) ，否則一般而言，任何人並不需要回答員警的問題，或讓員警進行搜索。

Police executed a **search warrant** at the suspect's house, where they found four loaded firearms. 警方在他家執行搜索票，在那裡警方發現四把裝填彈藥了的武器。

Search warrant authorizes law enforcement officers to **conduct a search** of a specified place and to seize evidence at a specified time and location. Illegally-seized evidence cannot be used as evidence against defendants in a criminal prosecution. 搜索票授權執法人員在特定的時間及處所，對特定地點進行搜索及扣押證據。非法扣押的證據，不得用在刑事起訴中做為不利被告的證據。

應用 *body search* 人身搜索
consensual search 合意而搜索
consent search 同意搜索
emergency search 緊急搜索
exigent search 急迫搜索
illegal search 違法搜索
inventory search 清查搜身
lawful search 合法搜索

protective search 保護性搜索

search and rescue dog 搜救犬

search incident to arrest 逮捕附帶搜索

search lamp 探照燈

search warrant 搜索票

search-and-seizure warrant 搜索扣押票

strip-search 脫光衣物搜索

unlawful search 違法搜索

unreasonable search 不合理搜索

voluntary search 自願搜索

warranted search 有票搜索

warrantless search 無票搜索

seasoned [ˈsiznd]	adj.	經驗豐富的，幹練的 Homicide detectives are often the most **seasoned detectives** within a criminal investigations division. 兇殺案幹員通常是偵查隊之中最幹練的偵查員。
secure [sɪˈkjʊr]	vt.	弄到，獲得，保全 The first responding officer at the scene should **secure** the accident scene and search for the survivors as soon as possible. 最早抵達現場的人員應該保全事件現場，並儘快搜尋生還者。
	adj.	安全的 It is important that a battered woman leaves her abuser and stay at a safe and **secure** place such as a women's shelter. 很重要的是，受暴婦女離開施暴者並留在安全的地方，諸如婦女庇護所。
security [sɪˈkjʊrətɪ]	n. 應用	安全 *national security* 國家安全 *security alarm* 安全警鈴（指系統） *security camera* 監視器 *security check* 安檢 *security guard* 安全警衛 *security measure* 安全措施 *security officer* 警衛人員 *social security* 社會安全
seduce [sɪˈdjus]	vt. 應用	誘惑，引誘，誘使墮落（或犯罪、姦淫） The victim **was seduced by** a man who lured her into his apartment. 被害人被男子誘惑，將她引誘到公寓。 *to seduce sb. into doing sth.* 誘使某人做某事 The man **seduced her into** having sex. 該男子引誘女子發生

關係。

seek [sik]	*vt.*	尋求 Investigators **are seeking** information regarding the identity of the suspects in this case. Reward money is available for any information which leads to an arrest. 偵查人員正在尋求有關本案嫌犯身分的資訊，對於因而導致逮捕的資訊，可以拿到獎金。

應用　*to seek advise* 尋求建議
　　　to seek asylum 尋求庇護
　　　to seek extradition 尋求引渡
　　　to seek fair treatment 尋求公平待遇
　　　to seek information 尋求資訊
　　　to seek protection 尋求保護
　　　to seek refuge 尋求避難收容(如受虐婦女或災害時)
　　　to seek revenge 尋求報復
　　　to seek shelter 尋求避難 (如颱風或天災撤離時)

seize [siz]	*vt.*	沒收，扣押，查封 Search warrant authorizes a law enforcement officer to conduct a search and to **seize** evidence at a specified time and location. **Illegally-seized** evidence cannot be used as evidence against defendants in a criminal prosecution. 搜索票授權執法人員在特定的時間及處所進行搜索及扣押證據。非法扣押的證據，不得用在刑事起訴中做為不利被告的證據。 In general, corrections officers carry no weapons because prisoners might overpower them and use the **seized** weapon. 通常，矯正人員不攜帶武器，這是因為受刑人有可能壓制矯正人員，並使用這些擄獲的武器。

seizure [`sizɚ]	*n.*	扣押 The Constitution protects people against unreasonable searches and **seizures** by law enforcement authorities. 憲法保障人民免於受到執法機關不合理的搜索及扣押。 A major purpose of the exclusionary rule is the deterrence of police misconduct in obtaining evidence and unreasonable searches and **seizures.** 排除法則的主要的目之一，是嚇阻警察在取證時的不當行為及不合理的搜索與扣押。 For any property subject to search or **seizure**, officers must obtain a warrant to execute it. 對於任何應予搜索或扣押之物，員警必須取得令狀執行之。

self	*adj.*	自己的

[sɛlf]	應用	*self defense* 自衛，【律】正當防衛，自衛權 *self-contained breathing apparatus* 自給式空氣呼吸器*(SCBA)* *self-control* 自我控制 *self-defense technique* 防身術 *self-discipline* 自律，自我訓練，自我修養 *self-incrimination* (因證言或供詞而) 陷己入罪，自證己罪 *self-protection* 自我保護 *self-punishment* 自我懲罰 *self-restraint* 自制
sentence [`sɛntəns]	*vt.*	【律】宣判，判刑，判決[(+to)] Those who **are sentenced to** death will be confined in an area of a prison, called death row. 判處死刑的人會被監禁在監獄的某個區域，稱之為死囚區(death row)。 If a person is convicted of robbery and **sentenced to** six years in prison, he or she will be put behind bars and serve the **prison sentence**. 如果某個人被判強盜罪確定，並判刑 6 年監禁，他就會被放到牢裡服刑。
	n.	【律】判決，宣判，課刑 A **life sentence** does not always mean imprisonment for life. After certain years of imprisonment, he may be paroled. 無期徒刑並非都是意味著監禁終生，在監禁一定的年限後，他就可以被假釋了。
separation [ˌsɛpəˋreʃən]	*n.* 應用	分開，分離 *order of legal separation* 分居令 *judgment of separation* 分居判決 *separation agreement* 分居協議
serial [`sɪrɪəl]	*adj.* 應用	連續性的 *serial arsonist* 連續縱火犯 *serial crime* 連續犯罪 *serial killer* 連續殺人犯 *serial murderer* 連續殺人犯 *serial number* 序號 *serial offender* 連續犯罪者 *serial rapist* 連續強姦犯
serve [sɝv]	*vt.*	為……服務 As a law enforcement officer, my fundamental duty is to **serve** the community; to safeguard lives and property. 身為執法人員，我的根本職責是服務社區；保障生命及財產。 It is the mission of the police to safeguard the lives and property

of the people we **serve**. 警察的任務是保障我們所服務的人民的生命與財產。

vt.	(徒刑的)服⋯⋯刑

If a person is convicted of robbery and sentenced to six years in prison, he or she will be put behind bars and **serve** the jail term. 如果某個人被判強盜罪確定，並判刑 6 年監禁，他就會被放到牢裡服刑。

vt.	送達

A summons **is served by** delivering a copy to the defendant personally; or by mailing a copy to the defendant's last known address. 傳喚通知書之送達，可經由對被告親自遞送正本；或郵寄正本到被告最後所知的地址。

---

set
[sɛt]　　*vt.*　　使處於（特定狀態）

According to firefighters, someone threw an ignitable liquid at the house and **set it on fire**, but firefighters have declined to comment on what is in the ignitable liquid. 根據消防員表示，有人將可燃液體丟向房子點燃火災，但消防員不願評論可燃液體是什麼。

Fire investigators believe the man **set fire to** his own apartment. "Accelerant is usually a flammable liquid that will increase the speed of fire. There are indications an accelerant was used to start the fire," fire investigator said. 火災調查員相信，這男子對自己家放火。「觸媒通常是一種可燃性液體，有些跡象顯示，有使用了觸媒來放火」，火災調查員說。

Firefighter said at least two arsonists **set the vehicle on fire** using a flammable liquid. The fire spread quickly. 消防員說，至少兩名縱火犯用可燃液體點火燒車，火勢迅速蔓延。

The arsonist used a car as an incendiary device **to set** buildings **on fire**. 縱火犯使用一輛汽車做為放火裝置，引起建築物發生火災。

Police released a surveillance video of the suspect who **set fire to** a shopping center last week. 警方公布了上星期在賣場縱火嫌犯的監視影帶。

He allegedly **set** his neighbor's home **on fire**. 他涉嫌對鄰居的家放火。

The man was caught on a surveillance camera as he fought with the cashier. Suddenly he **set fire to** a store and then set the car outside ablaze with a lighter. 這名男子跟店員打鬥的時後有被監視器拍到，突然間，他就對店家放火，然後用打火機點火

燒了汽車。

The arsonist confessed that he **set fire to** six businesses. He confessed that he started the fire and killed 3 persons. 縱火犯坦承他對六個商家放火，他坦承放了火，而殺害了三人。

The arsonist is alleged to have **set** the three vehicles **ablaze**. 縱火犯涉嫌對這三輛車子放火。

sexual [`sɛkʃʊəl]	*adj.* 應用	性的，性別的 *sexual abuse* 性侵 *sexual assault* 性攻擊 *sexual contact* 性接觸 *sexual exploitation* 性剝削 *sexual harassment* 性騷擾 *sexual violence* 性暴力

shackle
[`ʃæk!]

n. 腳鐐

vt. 給……戴腳鐐

The court decided **to shackle** the serial murderer for safety and security concerns. 法院基於安全及保全的顧慮，決定對這連續殺人犯戴腳鐐。

Generally speaking, the decision **to shackle** a minor is made on a case-by-case basis. 通常而言，對未成年人是否要上腳鐐，要依個案決定。

sham-marriage
[ʃæm]

n. 假結婚（又稱為婚姻詐騙 fraudulent marriage、或 fake marriage）

shelter
[`ʃɛltɚ]

vt. 藏匿，使……掩蔽，遮蔽，庇護

The defendant was accused of **sheltering** the murderer. 被告被指控藏匿殺人犯。

n. 遮蓋物，躲避處，避難所，庇護所

The mayor said at least 500 people were evacuated, and 300 people had **to take shelter** during the typhoon. 市長說，颱風期間至少有 5 百人被撤離，而有 3 百人必須找地方安置。

應用
animail shelter 動物收容所
emergency shelter 緊急收容所
evacuation shelter 撤離收容所
family shelter 家庭庇護所
homeless shelter 遊民收容所
shelter home 安置機構（處所）
women's shelter 婦女庇護所
youth shelter 青少年庇護所
to seek shelter 尋求收容安置

		to take/find shelter 找尋安置
sheriff [`ʃɛrɪf]	*n.* 應用	【美】(郡)警長 *undersheriff* 副警長(或 *chief deputy*) *deputy sheriff* 郡警(或 *sheriff deputy, sheriff's police, sheriff's officer*)
shield [`ʃild]	*n.* 應用	盾牌，擋板 *ballistic shield* 防彈盾牌 *police tactical shield* 警察戰術盾牌 *riot shield* 鎮暴盾牌 (*police riot shield*)
shift [ʃɪft]	*n.* 應用	輪班，輪班工作時間 *day shift* 日班 *evening shift* 晚班 *midnight shift* 夜班 *8-hour shift* 8 小時班 *shift trade* 交換班，勤務對調 (或稱 *trading of shift*) *shift change* 交接班 *fixed shift* 固定班 *shift rotation* 輪班
shoot [ʃut]	*vt.*	發射，開(槍)，射中 This morning, officers spotted and confronted the murder suspect on 5th street. Suspect opened fire at the officers and **was shot dead by** the police. 今日上午，員警在第五街認出這名謀殺案嫌犯並迎面上前，嫌犯向員警開槍，而被警方開槍擊斃。 The victim **was shot** in the chest and died. His family says all they want is justice and that this crime should not go unpunished. 被害人胸部中彈而死，他的家人說他們所要的是正義，並且這個犯罪不可以就這樣沒受到處罰。 One gunman **was shot** by the SWAT and was pronounced dead at George Washington University Hospital. 一名持槍歹徒被 SWAT(特種武器與戰術部隊)擊中，在喬治華盛頓大學醫院宣告死亡。
shooting [`ʃutɪŋ]	*n.* 應用	槍決，槍戰 *shooting simulation* 模擬射擊 *shooting range* 靶場 (又稱 *firing range*)
shootout [`ʃut,aʊt]	*n.*	槍戰 The gunman was killed after a chase and **shootout** with police. 槍手在與警方進行追逐與槍戰之後被擊斃。
shoplifting	*n.*	商店行竊，順手牽羊

[`ʃɑp,lɪftɪŋ]		Most people who are arrested for **shoplifting** are caught in the department stores or retail stores.大部分因為順手牽羊而被逮捕的人，都是在百貨公司或零售店被逮到的。
shot	*n.*	射擊，開槍
[ʃɑt]		In the shootout, officers fired more than 100 **shots** at the suspect. 槍戰中，員警朝著嫌犯開了超過百發的子彈。
		An investigator's first task at the scene of a shooting is to figure out how many **shots** were fired. 偵查人員在槍擊現場的第一項任務，就是釐清一共開了幾槍。
	應用	*gunshot residue* 火藥殘餘
		gunshot wound 槍傷
	n.	【口】照片；*mug shot* (嫌犯檔案)面部照片
sibling	*n.*	兄弟姊妹
[`sɪblɪŋ]		
sidewalk	*n.*	【美】人行道
[`saɪd,wɔk]		
sin	*n.*	(宗教或道德上的) 罪，罪孽，罪惡；(違反禮節，習俗的) 過錯，過失
[sɪn]		It is not a **sin** to drink alcohol if only you do not drink and drive. 只要你沒酒後開車，喝酒也不是罪惡的事。
single-parent household		單親家庭
siren	*n.*	汽笛，警報器
[`saɪrən]		
sit-in	*n.*	靜坐示威
[`sɪtɪn]		
size up	*v.*	估計……的大小(或多少)，【消防與醫學常用】估計，決斷
[saɪz] [ʌp]		Upon arrival at a fire scene, the Incident Commander must **size up** the situation and choose an attack method to safely and effectively extinguish a fire. 抵達火場之後，事件指揮官必須做狀況的決斷，並選擇滅火方式，來安全地並有效地滅火。
size-up	*n.*	【消防與醫學常用】估計，決斷
		Size-up is a term often mentioned in firefighting. It can be described as an evaluation of problems and conditions that affect the outcome of a fire. **Size-up** should be thought of as an information-gathering process. 「決斷(size-up)」一詞，是消防常用的詞，它可以用來指對於「會影響火災結果的問題與狀況」的評估。「決斷(size up)」應該被當成「資訊蒐集的過程」。
		If we conduct a thorough and accurate **size-up**, we would have

		a successful operation. 如果我們進行完整而正確的決斷，我們就會有成功的行動。
skimming [ˋskɪmɪŋ]	*n.* 應用	撇取，撇去 *ATM skimming* 提款卡側錄 *credit card skimming* 信用卡側錄
slander [ˋslændə]	*n.*	(口頭)誹謗罪 Defamation is a catch-all term for any statement that hurts someone's reputation. Written defamation is called libel, and spoken defamation is called **slander**. 誹謗(defamation)一詞是指傷害他人名聲的言論的通稱，書面的誹謗用 libel 一詞，口頭的誹謗用 slander 一詞。 Police denied the misconduct and filed **slander charges** against him. 警方否認行為失當，並對他提出誹謗告訴。
slave [slev]	*n.*	奴隸，奴隸般工作的人，苦工
slavery [ˋslevərɪ]	*n.*	奴隸身分，奴役
smolder [ˋsmoldə]	*vi.*	（無火苗地）悶燒，燻燒 The fire has been extinguished, but firefighters expect the pile to smolder for days. 火已經被撲滅了，但是消防員預期這建築物會悶燒數日。
smoke [smok]	*vt.* *n.* 應用	抽，吸(煙，毒) 煙 In some countries, **smoking** marijuana is legal. 有些國家，吸大麻是合法的。 煙，煙霧 *smoke alarm* 煙霧警報器 *smoke detector* 煙霧偵測器 *smoke free* 禁菸(區) *smoke grenade* 煙霧彈 *smoke room* 吸菸室
smuggle [ˋsmʌg!]	*vt.*	走私，非法私運 [(+into / out of)] If the **smuggler** sells or brokers the **smuggled** individual into a condition of servitude, or if the **smuggled individual** cannot pay the **smuggler** and is then forced to work that debt off, the crime has now turned form **smuggling** into human trafficking. 如果偷渡者將偷渡客販賣或仲介成為勞役狀態，或如果偷渡客沒錢付給偷渡者，而被迫以工作償債時，這項犯罪就此從偷渡變成人口販運。 【補充說明】

trafficking 與 smuggling 是兩個容易混淆的用字。兩者是不同的犯罪，又分人與物說明如下：

人的方面：有人口販運(human trafficking)與人口走私/偷渡(human smuggling)，兩者主要區別在於有無選擇自由。基本上任何人可以選擇以自願的「人口偷渡(human smuggling)」方式到他國；但若陷入被逼迫、失去自由的剝削狀態時 (例如抵達後時旅行證件被扣、被迫為奴工、娼妓)，就成為「人口販運(human trafficking)」的被害人。

物的方面：如果是是毒品的非法運送、進出口而主要目的是販售圖利時，用詞多為 drug trafficking。

至於走私(smuggling)指的是跨越國界的非法運送物品(illegal transporting of goods)，至於運送的物品本身可能是合法的物品(例如、菸、酒、香菇等等)，也可能是違法的物品(例如槍枝、毒品等) ，此時多用 smuggling 一詞，非法運送的目的可能是為了利潤或避稅，。當然，像是毒品走私(drug smuggling)如果是非法跨越國境、涉及買賣交易，則也是 drug trafficking。

snatch [snætʃ]	*vt.*	(快速地將物或人) 奪走，奪得，奪取，抓住 The man entered the store and **snatched** the wallet of a customer. 男子進入商店，並瞬間奪走顧客的皮夾。 Police have arrested a man who allegedly **natched** a 5-year-old boy from his home yard. Surveillance video shows the man got out of his car, and **snatched** the boy off his home yard. 警方逮到一名涉嫌將五歲男童從他住家院子將他擄走的男子。監視錄影帶顯示該男子從汽車走出，並將男童從他住家院子擄走。
sneak [snik]	*vi.*	偷偷地走，溜 A sex offender **sneaked into** the girl's bedroom and attempted to sexually assault them. 性侵犯潛入該女子的臥室並企圖性侵她。
sniff [snɪf]	*vt.* *vi.*	嗅，聞，發覺[(+out)] 嗅，聞[(+at)] In general, the use of a drug canine to **sniff** property is not considered a search. 一般而言，使用緝毒犬嗅聞物品並不被視為是搜索。
	應用	*drug sniffing dog* 緝毒犬 (又稱 *drug dog* 或 *sniffing dog*)
sniper [`snaɪpɚ]	*n.*	【軍】狙擊手
snitch [snɪtʃ]	*n.*	【口】告密的人，打小報告的人 Students may not report school bullying partly because they are afraid that teacher would tell the bully who told on him or her,

and thinking it was worse to be thought of as a **snitch**. 學生可能不會報告校園霸凌凌林，部分原因是因為害怕老師會告訴惡霸是誰告發的，以及認為被看成一個打小報告的人是更糟的。

snort [snɔrt]	*vt.*	鼻子吸 Ketamine can **be snorted** as powder, dabbed on tongue or injected in liquid form. K 他命可以用粉末由鼻子吸食、撣在舌頭上，或以液態形式注射。
social [`soʃəl]	*adj.* 應用	社會的，社會上的，社交的，交際的 *social activist* 社會運動者 *social background* 社會背景 *social life* 社會生活 *social media* 社群媒體 *social order* 社會秩序 *social phenomenon* 社會現象 *social security* 社會安全 *social wealfare* 社會福利 *social work* 社工 *social worker* 社工人員
solicit [sə`lɪsɪt]	*vt.*	徵求，徵集 [(+from)]，(妓女)拉(客) Officers shall not **solicit** or accept goods, contributions or gratuities without the express consent of their agency. 沒有機關明示同意，員警不得要求或收受物品、酬金或捐助。 New York Penal Law provides that a person is guilty of criminal solicitation when, he **solicits** other person to engage in conduct constituting a crime. 紐約州刑法規定，任何人徵求他人從事構成犯罪之行為時，成立刑事教唆罪。
solicitor [sə`lɪsətə]	*n.*	律師 In the UK, a lawyer who is admitted to plead at the bar and who may argue cases in superior courts is call barrister; a lawyer who consults with clients and prepares legal documents is called **solicitor**. 在英國，允許在法院辯論及可以在上級法院論告案件的律師稱為 barrister；與客戶進行諮詢並準備法律文件的律師稱為 solicitor。
spark [spɑrk]	*n.*	火花，火星 **Sparks** from the wires can ignite fires. 電線產生的火花會引燃火災。
	vt	發動，點燃 Fire investigators are working to determine what **sparked the**

fire. Investigators said there are other components in the room that could **have sparked the fire.** 火災調查員正在進行確認是什麼引發火災。調查員說，房間內有一些可能引發火災的器具設備。

sparkler [ˋspɑrklɚ]	*n.*	煙火

---

speed [spid]   *n.*   速度

應用
high speed police pursuit 高速警察追逐
high speed police chase 高速警察追逐
high-speed pursuit 高速警察追逐
radar speed gun 雷達測速槍 (或 *radar gun; speed gun*)
speed camera 超速照相機
speed camera detector 超速照相偵測器
speed limit 速限
speeding [ˋspidɪŋ]   *n.* 超速

---

spent [spɛnt]   *adj.*   用過的，失去效能的

For firearms examiner, the bullet, **spent** cartridge case, and the burned powder spraying from the barrel are useful and important components. 對於槍枝鑑識人員而言，子彈、已擊發(用過)的彈殼，以及從槍管噴出的燃燒過的火藥灰，都是有用而重要的部分。

---

spot [spɑt]   *n.*   場所，地點

As the policemen were getting out of their vehicle, several shots were fired from the gunman. The police returned fire in self-defence, and killed the gunman **on the spot**. 當員警步出車輛時，槍手開了好幾槍，警方開槍還擊自衛，並當場擊斃槍手。

應用
hot spot 熱區 (或稱 *high-crime area* 高犯罪地區)

---

spousal [ˋspaʊz!]   *adj*   結婚的，配偶的

應用
spousal rape 配偶強姦
spousal support 配偶贍養費
spousal abuse 虐待配偶、配偶暴力

---

spouse [spaʊz]   *n.*   配偶
foreign spouse 外籍配偶

---

spray [spre]   *vt.*   噴，噴灑

When fire crews arrived, smoke was visible and at least two rooms were ablaze. The fire quickly spreaded to the second floor. Firefighters soon **sprayed** water on the house. 當消防同仁抵達時，因誤已經可以看到，並且有兩間著火，火勢很快蔓延至二樓，消防人員迅速地將水灑向房子。

More than 50 firefighters **were sprayed** nearby the buildings to prevent the blaze from burning other structures. 超過五十名消防員分散到建築物的附近，以防止火焰燒到其他建築物。

應用 *pepper spray* 胡椒噴霧

spread [sprɛd]	*vi.*	伸展，延伸，傳開，蔓延

The fire **spreaded to** a number of homes. Flames and black smoke could be seen more than 5 hours after the incident. 火勢蔓延好幾家，火焰及黑煙在事件之後超過五個小時，都還可以看到。

The Incident Commander said the wildfires **spreaded** so quickly and unpredictably that he had to order firefighters withdrawn from the dangerous area. 事件指揮官說，野火蔓延得如此快速而無法預測，因此他必須命令消防人員從危險區域撤回。

Firefighter said at least two arsonists set the vehicle on fire using a flammable liquid. The fire **spreaded** quickly. 消防員說，至少兩名縱火犯用可燃液體點火燒車，火勢迅速蔓延。

Do not attempt to fight a large or **spreading fire** with a fire extinguisher. Make sure you have activated the fire alarm before you use an extinguisher. 不要想用滅火器去撲滅大火或是正在蔓延的火災，要確保你在使用滅火器之前，已經先啟動火災警鈴。

spy [spaɪ]	*n. & vi.*	間諜，密探

Intelligence officer admitted that they used cutting edge technologies to take videos and photos **to spy on** suspicious citizens. 情報人員承認他們用先進的科技錄影及拍照，來監視可疑的市民。

squad [skwɑd]	*n.*	【軍警】班，小隊，小組

【補充說明】實務上，各執法機關會自行成立各式各樣的小隊或小組，例如：毒品及槍械小組(Drug and Firearms Squad)；組織犯罪小組(Organised Crime Squad)；網路犯罪小組(Cybercrime Squad)；命案組(Homicide Squad)；金融犯罪小組(Financial Crimes Squad)；重案小組(Serious Crime Squad)；防爆小組(Bomb Squad)。

stab [stæb]	*vt.*	刺，刺入，戳

The first victim **was fatally stabbed** in the chest. He **was stabbed to death** in his office. The suspect **stabbed** the second victim in the back with a knife. The victim was admitted to the hospital with multiple **stab wounds**. 第一個被害人胸部遭到致命刺入，他被刺死在辦公室內。嫌犯用刀子刺了第二個被

		害人的背部，被害人住進了醫院，有多重刺傷。
stable [`stebɪl]	*adj.*	固定的，安定的 Authorities said the victim was taken to the hospital for smoke inhalation. The man is in **stable** condition. 當局說，被害人因吸入濃煙被送到醫院，該男子狀況穩定。
stage [stedʒ]	*vt.*	把……搬上舞臺，上演(亦即：假造) Sometimes, a criminal would **stage** a crime scene to misdirect investigators so as to get away with the crime. For example, a killer **stages** a crime scene by breaking a window to make it look like a burglar killed the victim. 有時候，罪犯會假造一個犯罪現場來誤導偵查人員，以逃避犯罪，例如，殺手假造一個犯罪現場，藉由將窗戶打破，使得看起來像是入侵者殺了被害人。
	應用	*staged car crash* 假車禍 (或 *staged auto accident; fake accident*) *staged crime scene* 故佈疑陣的犯罪現場 *staging area*【軍、警】集結待命地區
stain [sten]	*n.* 應用	汙點，汙跡，瑕疵 *bloodstain* 血跡
stalk [stɔk]	*vt.*	偷偷靠近，跟蹤 Any person who suspects that he or she **is being stalked** may report incidents to local law enforcement agencies. He or she must learn how to respond to stalker. 任何懷疑自己被尾隨跟蹤的人，可以將案件報告當地執法機關，他(她)也必須學會如何回應跟蹤者。
stalker [`stɔkɚ]	*n.*	跟蹤者 In practice, many stalkers are known to the stalking victims. 實務上，許多跟蹤者是被跟蹤的被害人所認識的。
stand [stænd]	*vt.*	to stand trial 受審 The suspect will **stand trial** on murder charge. He will **stand trial** for the murder of a rival gang member. 嫌犯將會就謀殺案受審，他會就這起敵對幫派分子的謀殺案受審。
standoff [`stænd,ɔf]	*n.*	僵持，(比賽的)平局 Police surrounded the house and there was a **standoff** for about an hour. 警方將房子包圍，對峙了大約一小時。 During the standoff, police attempted **to negotiate with** the hostage taker. 在僵局對峙之時，警方試圖與人質劫持者談判。
start [stɑrt]	*vt.*	使開始，引起 Neighbors said the building was on fire when firefighters **started**

knocking on everyone's apartment doors. 鄰居說房子起火的當時，消防員開始對每戶公寓敲門。

Fire Chief said the arsonist confessed to starting several fires at six locations overnight. He confessed that he **started the fires** and killed 3 persons. "I **started** the blaze," the arsonist said. 消防局長說，縱火犯坦承一夜之間在六個地點放了好幾把火。他坦承放了火，而殺害了三人。「是我放火的」，縱火犯說。

	vi.	開始

The fire **started** at about 4:30 p.m. at the multi-story building on K Street. The Fire Chief confirmed the fire **started** on the third floor. 火災在大約下午 4 點 30 分起於這棟多樓層的建築物。消防局長證實火災起源於三樓。

---

statement	*n.*	陳述
[ˋstetmənt]	應用	*to make false statement* 做不實陳述
		to obtain his statement 取得他的陳述
		to take his statemet 取得他的陳述
		to verify his statement 查證他的陳述
		bank statement 銀行往來明細
		defendant's statement 被告的陳述
		false statement 不實的陳述
		inconsistent statement 不一致的陳述
		Mission Statement(機關的)宗旨
		out-of court statement 法庭外的陳述
		prior inconsistent statement 先前不一致的陳述
		prior statement 先前的陳述
		witness's statement 證人的陳述
		written statement 筆錄

---

statute	*n.*	條例，章程，規則
[ˋstætʃʊt]	應用	*statute of limitation* 時效

---

stimulant	*n.*	興奮劑，興奮飲料，刺激物
[ˋstɪmjələnt]		

---

stipulate	*vt.*	【律】規定，約定[+(that)]
[ˋstɪpjə,let]		

Both parties **stipulated that** the damage to the vehicle was $3,000. **It was stupilated that** the defendant should make the payment within 30 days. 兩造約定車損為 3000 元，約定被告在 30 天內支付。

Chapter 34 of the Texas Penal Code **stipulates that** a person may be charged with money laundering if they acquire, conceal, possess, transfer, or transport the proceeds of criminal activity.

德州刑法第 34 章規定，任何人如果取得、藏匿、持有、移轉或運送犯罪之不法所得，得以洗錢提起控訴。

| stockpile | n. | (應急用的)儲備物資，(供修路的)碎石 |
| [`stɑk,paɪl] | vt. | 儲備，貯存，積累 |

Mayor urged people **to stockpile** sandbags if their home is susceptible to flooding. 市長呼籲人們，如果住家容易淹水的話，要儲備沙包。

| stolen property | | 贓物 |

應用　*to receive stolen goods* 收受贓物

| stop | vt. | 使……停止，阻止，阻擋 |
| [stɑp] | | |

Police set up roadblocks or checkpoints to **stop** and inspect drivers and vehicles passing along a road. 警察設置路障或檢查站以攔檢過路的駕駛人及車輛。

| | n. | 停，停止 |

Police officers must have probable cause to make an arrest or a reasonable suspicion to conduct a **stop and frisk**. 員警必須有相當理由才能進行逮捕，或有合理懷疑才能進行攔阻及搜身。

應用　*pretext stop* 藉故攔檢
stop light 剎車燈
stop sign 停車標誌
traffic stop 交通攔檢

| stowaway | n. | 偷渡客 |
| [`stoə,we] | | |

The Coast Guard officer says there may be **stowaways** inside a shipping container. Investigators are looking into whether **stowaways** are tucked inside a shipping container. 海巡人員說，船隻的貨櫃內可能會有偷渡客，偵查員正在調查是否有偷渡客被塞進船隻的貨櫃內。

| strangle | vt. | 扼死，勒死，絞死，悶住，使……窒息而死 |
| [`stræŋɡ!] | 應用 | *to strangle sb. to death* 把某人掐死 |

Autopsy report shows victim **was strangled to death**. 驗屍報告顯示，被害人是被勒窒息而死。

| stress | n. | 壓力，緊張，壓迫 |
| [strɛs] | | |

Extended interrogation techniques add **stress** and fatigue to the questioning, for example, questioning of 20 hours per day in many consecutive days. 疲勞訊問是將壓迫及疲勞加在問訊中，例如，連續數天每天問訊 20 小時。

stretcher	n.	擔架
[`strɛtʃɚ]	應用	*ambulance stretcher* 救護車擔架
		hospital stretcher 醫院擔架

medical stretcher 救護擔架
rescue stretcher 救援擔架
scoop stretcher 勺型擔架
spine board stretcher 頸椎固定擔架
stretcher straps 擔架綁帶
transport stretcher 運送擔架

---

strike
[straɪk]

A magnitude 3.8 earthquake **struck** the Los Angeles area early this morning. 今天上午，一場震級為 3.8 級的地震襲擊了洛杉磯地區。

n. 罷工，罷課，罷市

Workers **went on strike against** the government's new policy. Thousands of demonstrators rallied at the downtown and then took to the street. 工人罷工抗議政府的新政策，數千名示威者聚集在市中心，並占據街道。

---

strip
[strɪp]

vt. 剝，脫去(衣服)，脫光(衣服) [(+off)]

The drunkard **stripped off** his clothes and shouted, "I will beat you up." 醉漢脫去他的衣服並大叫「我要痛扁你」。

應用 *strip search* (對犯人或嫌疑人的) 裸身檢查，脫衣搜查

The bailiff conducted a **strip search** of the suspect, and found the contraband in his pocket. 法警對嫌犯進行脫衣檢查，並在他的口袋發現違禁品。

---

structure
[`strʌktʃɚ]

n. 構造體，建築物

Structure fire (or structural fire) is a fire in a residential or commercial building. 建物火災 (稱為 structure fire 或 structural fire)是指在住宅或商業建築物的火災。

The Fire Chief said the Department responds to **structural fires,** nonstructural fires, medical emergencies, and other calls, and that the number of structural fires has steadily decreased in the past years. 消防局長說，該局處理的是建物火災、非建物火災、緊急醫療及其他請求，而建物火災在過去這幾年有穩定下降。

Fire officials said the blaze broke out in the basement of a seven-story apartment and soon engulfed the entire **structure.** 消防官員說，這場火災從一棟七層樓公寓的地下室發生，並且很快地將整個建物吞噬。

More 50 firefighters were spraying nearby the buildings to prevent the blaze from burning other **structures**. 超過五十名消防員分到這建築物的附近，以防止火焰燒到其他建築物。

Firefighters removed several victims from the **structure**. 消防

員從建築物救出了幾個遇難者。

stun [stʌn]	*n. vt.* 應用	打昏，昏迷 *stun grenade* 震撼彈 *stun gun* 電擊槍

subpoena [səb`pinə]	*n.*	傳喚通知書(要求證人在通知書指定的時間及地點出席及作證)；傳票 Summonses and **subpoenas** are both legal documents that call a person to the court. A summons is generally used to inform someone that he or she is actually a party to a lawsuit, usually as a defendant. A **subpoena**, on the other hand, is typically used to call witnesses to court. 傳喚通知書 summons 及 subpoena 這兩種都是傳呼某人到法院的法律文件。Summons 這種傳喚通知書，通常用來通知某個人，通知他(她)變成了訴訟的一造，通常是被告。Subpoena 這種傳喚通知書則是用來傳呼證人到法院。 A judge may issue a **subpoena** to command the witness to attend and testify at the spefific time and place the **subpoena** specifies, and order the witness to produce any books, papers, documents, data, or other objects the **subpoena** designates. 法官可以核發傳喚通知書，要求證人在通知書指定的時間及地點出席及作證，並得命令證人提出任何書籍、紙張、文件、資訊，或其他傳喚通知所指定的物品。 傳喚，傳訊，用傳票取得 In the US, law enforcement agencies occasionally **subpoena** telephone records and use them as a source of intelligence or evidence. 在美國，執法機關常會調取電話紀錄，並用之做為情報或證據的來源。
	應用	*to subpoena the witness* 傳喚/傳訊證人

subscriber [səb`skraɪbɚ]	*n.*	裝機者，電話用戶 Basically, toll records can track the calls between a **subscriber** and other phone numbers, and provide reliable information on date, time, and duration. 基本上，通聯可以追蹤裝機者與其他電話號碼之間的電話聯繫，並提供有關日期、時間及期間的可靠資訊。

substance [`sʌbstəns]	*n.* 應用	物質 *controlled substance* 管制物質，管制藥品 (或 *controlled drug*) *substance abuse* 藥物濫用

substantial [səb`stænʃəl]	*adj.*	真實的，實在的，顯著的，重要的 The court of appeal concluded that the decision of the trial court

is supported by **substantial evidence**. 上訴法院認定地方法院的判決是基於有實質證據支持。

sue [su]	*vt.*	控告，對……提起訴訟[(+for)] The innocent person **sued** the police department for false arrest and wrongful imprisonment. 該無辜者控告警察局非法逮捕與錯誤監禁。

suffer [ˋsʌfɚ]	*vt.*	遭受，經歷 Two officers **suffered** minor injuries during the pursuit and arrest and were taken to a hospital for treatment. 兩名員警在追緝與逮捕之際受到輕傷，並被送到醫院治療。 Several residents tried to put out the blaze but **suffered** minor smoke inhalation and had to be rescued. 有好幾位住戶試圖滅火，但是受到輕微的吸入濃煙而必須救出。 One firefighter **suffered** burns to his face and hands while battling the blaze. 有一位消防員在滅火時，受到臉部及手部燒傷。 A total of 170 firefighters battled the blaze. The fire was brought under control around 8:45 p.m. Two firefighters **suffered** minor injuries, officials said. 總共有 170 位消防員在滅火，這場火在晚上 8:45 控制住。有 2 位消防員受到輕傷，官員說。 Jason **suffered** third and fourth degree burns over 70% of his body. 傑生全身百分之 70 受到三度及四度灼傷。 The victim **suffered** smoke inhalation and carbon-monoxide poisoning, and died several days later at the hospital. 被害人受到吸入濃煙及一氧化碳中毒，而數日後在醫院死亡。
	vi.	受苦，患病[(+from)] A patient **suffered from** kidney failure a few days after being exposed to the toxic fumes. 患者暴露在有毒受煙氣數日之後受到腎衰竭。

suicide [ˋsuə,saɪd]	*n.*	自殺，自殺行為 The suspect forged a **suicide note** to make the murder look like a **suicide**. 嫌犯偽造自殺字條，讓這起謀殺看起來像是自殺。 The use of force is justifiable when the actor believes that such force is immediately necessary to prevent the person from **committing suicide**. 當行為人相信，為了防止某人自殺而有使用武力的立即需要時，使用武力是正當的。
	應用	*to commit suicide* 自殺 *assisted suicide* 加工自殺 *suicide attack* 自殺攻擊

suicide attempt 自殺未遂

suicide bomb 自殺炸彈，人肉炸彈

suicide bomber 自殺炸彈客

suicide by cop 透過警察自殺

suicide intervention 自殺防制

suicide jump 跳樓自殺

suicide note 自殺字條

attempted suicide 自殺未遂，意圖自殺

註：自殺而死也可稱為 death by suicide 或是 death by one's own hand.

The woman sait today is the first anniversary of her husband's death by his own hands. 女士說今天是她先生自殺滿一年的日子。

summary [`sʌmərɪ]	*adj.* 應用	即決的，簡易的 *motion for summary judgment* 聲請簡易判決 *summary judgment* 簡易判決 *summary court* 簡易法庭
summon [`sʌmən]	*vt.*	召喚，傳喚，召集 In fact, patrol officers are often the first ones **summoned** to the crime scenes. 事實上，巡邏員警經常是最早被呼叫前往犯罪現場的人。
summons [`sʌmənz]	*n.*	(法院的)傳票 A judge may issue **summons** and requires the defendant to appear at a stated time and place. 法官可以核發傳喚通知書，要求被告在指定的時間及地點到達。
superintendent [,supərɪn`tɛndənt]	*n.*	*Superintendent of Police*【美/芝加哥】警察局長 *Superintendent-General*【東京警視廳】警視總監
support [sə`port]	*n.* 應用	扶養，贍養 *child support* 子女撫養費 *financial support* 金錢輔助 *spousal support* 配偶贍養費
suppress [sə`prɛs]	*vt.*	鎮壓，平定，壓制 Firefighters responded **to suppress** the fire, which had spread to the third floor. 消防員前往壓制火勢，當時該火勢已經蔓延到三樓。
suppression [sə`prɛʃən]	*n.* 應用	抑制，阻止，壓制，鎮壓 *fire suppression system* 滅火系統
surrender [sə`rɛndɚ]	*vt.*	(後接 oneself) 使……投降，使……自首[(+to)] If the offender voluntarily **surrenders himself to** the

authorities, the judge usually will consider a reduction of the penalty. 如果犯罪者自願向機關自首的話，法官通常會考慮減刑。

surround [sə`raʊnd]	*vt.*	包圍，圍困 Police **surrounded** the house and there was a standoff for about an hour. 警方將房子包圍，對峙了大約一小時。

surveillance [sə`veləns]　*n.*　偵查，偵監

應用
covert surveillance 隱密偵查
electronic surveillance 電子監察
physical surveillance 人的跟監
police surveillance 警方的偵監
surveillance equipment 偵監裝備
surveillance technology 偵監科技
surveillance video 監視影帶
technical surveillance 科技偵查
undercover surveillance 臥底偵查
video surveillance camera 錄影監視器

survive [sə`vaɪv]　*vt.*　在……之後仍然生存，從……中逃生

In a serious head-on collision or a multi-vehicle collision, the possibility to **survive** the crash is difficult. 在重大的對撞或連環車禍中，從這種撞擊中生還的可能項不易。

There were dozens of casualties in the train crash. Luckly, most passengers **survived** the crash. 有數十人在那次火車事故中傷亡。幸運地，大多數乘客都生還。

Firefighters said the explosion destroyed the house, and fortunately, all residents **survived** the blast. They all **survived** the fire. 消防員說，這個爆炸摧毀了房子，而幸運地，所有住戶都在火災中生還。他們都在火災中生還。

survivor [sə`vaɪvə]　*n.*　倖存者，生還者

Survivors of a deadly fire told firefighters that many people were being trapped on the stairs. 這場致命火災的生還者告訴消防員說，有很多人正被困在梯間。

suspect [sə`spɛkt]　*vt.*　疑有，察覺，猜想[(+that)]

Officers are allowed to pat the person's outer clothing If they reasonably **suspect** the person to be armed. 如果有合理懷疑某個人攜帶武器，員警即被容許拍搜他的外部衣服。

If you **suspect that** a person is in cardiac arrest, call the local emergency number immediately. 如果你懷疑某人心跳停止，立刻撥打當地的緊急電話。

suspect	n.	嫌疑犯，可疑分子

[`səspɛkt]

Police believe that Johnson is the **prime suspect** and continue to investigate him for years. 警方相信強森是主嫌，並持續對他調查了好幾年。

應用　*criminal suspect* 刑事嫌犯

fleeing suspect 逃逸中的嫌犯

homicide suspect 兇殺案嫌犯

murder suspect 謀殺嫌犯

major suspect 重大嫌犯

prime suspect 主嫌犯，主要嫌犯，頭號嫌犯

to apprehend the suspect 逮捕嫌犯

to arrest the suspect 逮捕嫌犯

to identify the suspect 指認嫌犯

to interrogate the suspect 訊問嫌犯

to locate the suspect 找到嫌犯

to pursue the suspect 追捕嫌犯

to round up the suspect 圍捕

suspected	adj.	

[sə`spɛktɪd]

He was arrested for **suspected** housebreaking and theft. 他因為有侵入住宅行竊的嫌疑而被逮捕。

Officers noticed a **suspected** drug transaction at the scene. 員警注意到現場有一個可疑的毒品交易。

is/am/are suspected of 涉有……之嫌

He **was suspected of** receiving stolen property. 他被懷疑收受贓物。

應用　*suspected arson* 被懷疑的縱火

suspected child abuse 被懷疑的虐童(案件)

suspected fraud 被懷疑的詐騙

suspected murderer 被懷疑涉嫌的殺人犯

suspected offender 被懷疑涉嫌的犯罪者

suspected scammer 被懷疑涉嫌的詐騙者

suspected shooter 被懷疑涉嫌的開槍者

suspected trafficker 被懷疑涉嫌的走私者

suspend	vt.	吊扣

[sə`spɛnd]

Under some circumstances, a driver license may **be suspended**, cancelled or revoked. Suspension involves the temporary withdrawal of your privilege to drive. If you get a traffic ticket and fail to pay the fine, the motor vehicle authorities will **suspend** your driving privilege until you pay the fine. 有些情況下，駕照可能會被吊扣、註銷或吊銷。吊扣(suspension)涉及的是將你

開車的特權暫時撤回，如果你收到罰單而沒有繳交罰鍰的話，監理機關會吊扣你的開車特權，直到你繳交罰鍰為止。

suspicion	n.	懷疑，嫌疑
[sə`spɪʃən]		The man was arrested **on suspicion of** murder. 該男子因涉有謀殺之嫌而被逮捕。
		Officers must have probable cause to make an arrest or a **reasonable suspicion** to conduct a stop and frisk. 員警必須要有相當理由，以進行逮捕，或有合理懷疑，以進行攔阻及搜身。

suspicious	adj.	可疑的
[sə`spɪʃəs]		President Barock Obama: I want to commend the work of the NYPD, the New York Fire Department, and the FBI, which responded swiftly and aggressively to a dangerous situation. And I also want to commend the vigilant citizens who noticed this **suspicious** activity and reported it to the authorities. 總統歐巴馬：我要嘉許紐約市警局、紐約消防局、聯邦調查局，他們迅速而積極地回應危險狀況，同時我也要嘉許有警戒心而注意到這起可疑活動並向當局報案的市民。

應用
suspicious vehicle 可疑車輛
suspicious transaction 可疑交易
suspicious package 可疑包裹
suspicious activity 可疑活動
suspicious behaviour 可疑行為
suspicious call 可疑電話
suspicious death 可疑的死亡

sustain	vt.	遭受，承受，忍受
[sə`sten]		During a high speed chase, two officers **sustained** minor injuries after the marked police vehicle collided with a traffic island. 在高速追逐中，兩名員警在警車擦撞到交通分隔島之後，受到輕傷。
		An officer was assaulted in the line of duty, and **sustained** injuries. 有一位員警在執勤中受到攻擊並且受了傷。

swab	vt.	刮，拭
[swɑb]		Police took his fingerprints and **swabbed** the inside of her cheek to collect a sample of his DNA. 警方採集了他的指紋，並刮取臉頰內部，以採及 DNA 樣本。

SWAT	abbr.	特種武器與戰術部隊/霹靂小組 Special Weapons And Tactics

sweep	n.	掃蕩，肅清，消滅
[swip]		City police department conducted an unannounced **drug**

sweeps of the night pubs using canines trained to detect marijuana and other drugs. 市警局用訓練來偵測大麻與毒品的警犬，進行了無預警的夜店毒品掃蕩。

The FBI has announced that it conducted a three-day **sweep** that resulted in the rescue of several victims who were being held against their wills by the trafficking ring. 聯邦調查局宣布該局進行了三天的掃蕩，結果救出幾名非出於己意而被販運集團拘禁的被害人。

	應用	*to conduct drug sweep* 進行毒品掃蕩
		to conduct gang sweep 進行幫派掃蕩
		to conduct prostitution (hooker) sweep 進行色情掃蕩
symptom [`sɪmptəm]	*n.*	症狀，徵候，徵兆，表徵 The most common warning **symptom** was chest pain, lasting from 20 minutes to several hours before the cardiac arrest. 心臟衰竭之前，最常見的症狀是胸痛，會持續 20 分鐘至數小時之久。
syndicate [`sɪndɪkɪt]	*n.*	【經】企業聯合組織，財團 【犯罪方面】犯罪集團，黑社會組織 Intelligence indicates that the world's most powerful drug **syndicate** continues to operate in this area. 情報顯示，全球最有勢力的毒品犯罪集團仍然繼續在這個地區運作。
tackle [`tæk!]	*vt.*	著手對付 (或處理) The mayor said, "We will do everything we can **to tackle** the crime problems." 市長說，「我們會盡我們所能去對付犯罪問題。」
tactical [`tæktɪk!]	*adj.* 應用	戰術的 *tactical combat* 攻堅 *tactical force* 攻堅武力，攻堅部隊 *tactical gear* 技能操作服 *tactical intervention* 攻堅介入 *tactical operation* 戰術行動 *tactical plan* 戰術計劃 *tactical training* 技能訓練 *tactical unit* 攻堅組
tailgate [`tel,get]	*vi. &* *vt.*	(駕駛時)緊跟著前車行駛 If you **are being tailgated by** an aggressive driver, you must stay calm, get out of their way and avoid flashing your brake lights. 如果你被咄咄逼人的駕駛人緊跟，你必須保持冷靜，離開他們的車道，並且避免閃煞車燈。

taint [tent]	*vt.*	污染，使……感染，使……腐壞，沾染，汙染 Evidence derived from an illegal search, arrest, or interrogation is inadmissible because the evidence **was tainted by** the illegality. 非法搜索、逮捕或訊問所取得的證據，無證據能力，因為，證據已經被不法所污染了。
take [tek]	*vt.* 應用	拿，取 *to take (sb) hostage* 拿(人)當作人質 *to take a person into custody* 拘禁某個人 *to take a report* 製做報案 *to take charge of* 負責 *to take control of* 掌管 *to take his life* 結束他的生命 *to take his statement* 取得他的陳述 *to take his testimony* 取得他的證詞 *to take police action* 待採取適當作為 *to take step* 採取做為 *to take the initiative* 取得先機，首創 *to take the necessary measure* 採取必要的措施 *to take his fingerprint* 取得他的指紋
tamper [`tæmpɚ]	*vi.* 應用	損害，瞎搞，(用不正當手段)影響 He was charged with **tampering with** evidence. 他被指控竄改證據。 *to tamper with* 干涉，用非法的手段影響，竄改
tattoo [tæ`tu]	*n.*	刺青
tear gas 	 應用	催淚瓦斯 *tear gas grenade* 催淚瓦斯手榴彈
telephone [`tɛlə,fon]	*n.* 應用	電話 *telephone analysis* 通聯分析 *telephone tapping* 電話監聽(或稱 *wire-tapping*) *telephone toll (record) analysis* 通聯(紀錄)分析 *voice telephone interception* 語音電話攔
telephone toll (record) analysis		通聯(紀錄)分析
tension [`tɛnʃən]	*n.*	拉緊，繃緊，(精神上的)緊張，緊張狀況 Although he remained silent during the interrogation, his expression revealed his **tension**. 雖然他在偵訊時保持緘默，但他的表情顯露出他的緊張不安。
terrify	*vt.*	使……害怕，使……恐懼，使……驚嚇

[`tɛrə,faɪ]		Residents **were terrified by** the gunfire. 居民都被槍響驚嚇到。
terrifying	*adj.*	可怕的
[`tɛrə,faɪɪŋ]		Residents said that the shootout **was terrifying**. 居民說槍戰令人驚嚇害怕。
term	*n.*	期，期限
[tɝm]		He was convicted of robbery and sentenced to six years in prison. He will be put behind bars and serve the **jail term**, which is the 6 year prison sentence. 他被判強盜罪確定，並處 6 年監禁，他將會被放到牢裡服刑，亦即該 6 年徒刑。
		He will be released after his **term of imprisonment** is completed. 他的刑期完成之後，就會被釋放。
	n.	名稱，術語
		Officers should avoid using the **legal terms** or law enforcement jargon to talk with the citizens. 員警應該避免使用法律術語或執法的行話來與民眾交談。
terrorism	*n.*	恐怖主義
[`tɛrə,rɪzəm]		
terrorist	*n.*	恐怖主義者，恐怖分子
[`tɛrərɪst]		
test	*vt.*	試驗，檢驗，測驗，化驗，分析[(+for)]
[tɛst]		Corrections officers said that all inmates **were tested** for drug. 矯正官員說，全部的受行人都要進行毒品檢測。
	vi.	測得結果
		Some inmates **tested positive** for marijuana. The other inmates tested negative. 有些受刑人化驗結果為大麻陽性，其他受刑人化驗呈陰性。
	n.	試驗，測試，化驗
		The forensic analyst and examiner will **run tests on** the evidence brought to the lab. 刑事分析人員與鑑識人員會將帶回實驗室的證據進行檢測。
		Police said Jason was willing to **take a** polygraph **test** to prove his innocence. 警方說，傑生願意接受測謊證明他是無辜的。
	應用	*alcohol test* 酒精檢測
		annual test 年度測試
		blood alcohol test 血液酒精檢測
		blood test 血液檢測
		breath test 呼吸檢測
		breathalyzer test (酒精)呼吸器檢測

DNA test DNA 檢測
driving test 路考
Field sobriety tests 清醒程度測試
functional test 功能測試
lie detector test 測謊器測謊
periodic inspection and test 定期檢查
periodic testing 定期測試
polygraph test 測謊
roadside check 路邊臨檢
urine test 尿液檢測

testify [`tɛstə,faɪ]	*vi.*	作證[(+for/against/to)] The suspect agreed to **testify against** his drug dealer. 嫌犯同意對他的毒品交易者為不利的作證。 The forensic analyst and examiner will have to **testify** in court as expert witnesses, if necessary. 必要時，刑事分析人員與鑑識人員將必須以專家證人的身分在法庭作證。 A witness is ordinarily presumed to have the mental capacity to **testify**. 證人通常推定有作證的精神能力。
testimony [`tɛstə,monɪ]	*n.* 應用	【律】證詞，證言 *expert testimony* 專家證詞 *eyewitness testimony* 目擊證人證詞 *false testimony* 不實的證詞 *opinion testimony* 意見證詞 *oral testimony* 口頭證詞 *out-of-court testimony* 法庭外的證詞 *written testimony* 書面證詞
thief [θif]	*n.*	小偷 The NYPD is asking for the public's help in finding the **thief** who snatched a purse right off a women's arm in Brooklyn. 紐約市警局請求大眾協尋在布魯克林區行竊一名婦人手臂皮包的小偷。
threat [θrɛt]	*n.*	威脅，恐嚇 The suspect poses a **threat** to the police officer, who was compelled to use deadly force to take his life in such a life-threatening situation. 嫌犯對員警作勢威脅，迫使員警在這樣的生命威脅情況下，使用致命武器結束他的生命。
threaten	*vt.*	威脅，恐嚇 In order to control victims, traffickers often **threaten** victims with arrest or deportation, and **threaten** to harm or kill family in the

victim's homeland, 為了控制被害人，販運分子常會以逮捕及遣送來威脅被害人，並且威脅要傷害或殺害被害人在家鄉的家人。

thrownaway [ˋθronəˏwe]	*n.*	被趕出家門的人
thumbcuff	*n.*	姆指銬
tip [tɪp]	*n.*	內部情報，祕密消息

應用 *anonymous tip* 匿名線報

	vt.	洩露，暗示

To urge people **to tip off** police about crime, police will set up an anonymous tip line for people to give a clue. 為了呼籲民眾向警方通報犯罪，警方會設置匿名報案專線，讓民眾提供線索。

應用 *to tip off* 向……洩漏消息

tolerate [ˋtɑləˏret]	*vt.*	忍受，容忍，寬恕

At the press conference, the Chief of Police sent strong message to the gang members that their violence will no longer **be tolerated**. 在記者會上，警察局長向幫派份子發出強烈的訊息表示，他們的暴力將不再被容忍。

tool mark		工具痕跡
torture [ˋtɔrtʃə]	*vt.* *n.*	拷打，拷問 拷打，酷刑，拷問
tow [to]	*vt.*	拖吊

To keep traffic moving, police may **tow** the vehicle left in a **tow-away zone** or other area that causes safety concerns, and use **tow truck** or wrecker to transport the vehicles to the vehicle storage facility. 為了讓交通保持行進，警察得拖吊停放在拖吊區域或其他會造成安全疑慮的地區內的車輛，並用拖吊車將這些車輛運送到保管場的車子。

toxicologist [ˏtɑksɪˋkɑlədʒɪst]	*n.*	毒物學家，毒理學家
trace [tres]	*n.*	痕跡，遺跡

Police are searching for the old man who disappeared **without a trace** last week. Officers are seeking the public's assistance in finding the man who vanished **without a trace** last week. 警方正在尋找這名上星期消失無蹤的老人，員警請求大眾協尋這名上星期失蹤的老人。

Edmund Locard, a French criminologist, stated that every contact leaves a **trace**, known as the Locard Exchange Principle. 法國犯

罪學家 Edmund Locard 曾說，凡接觸必留下痕跡，此即為熟知的羅卡交換定律。

	應用	*trace evidence* 微物證據
		trace analysis 微物分析
	vt.	追溯　[(+back/to)]

Police **traced** a fingerprint and matched to her. 警方追蹤指紋並比對與被害人相符。

He was arrested at his home after the police **traced** him through his license-plate number. 警方從他的車盤追蹤，並在他家將他逮捕。

Police **traced** the call to an address in Taipei. 警方從電話追蹤到台北的一個地址。

The police **traced** the number to an apartment in New York. 警方追蹤電話號碼查到紐約的一個公寓。

The chain of custody is intended to **trace** the item of evidence from its discovery to court. 物證管制流程是用來進行證據物件從發現直到法院的追蹤。

---

track	*vt.*	跟蹤，追蹤
[træk]		

Officers said that they would **track down** the escaped suspect. 員警說他們會追蹤這個脫逃的嫌犯。

應用　*to track the movement of offender* 追蹤犯罪者的動向
to track someone's phone calls 追蹤某人的電話

n.　行蹤，足跡

Radio dispatcher must **keep track of** all field officers and their status. 無線電派遣員必須對所有的轄區員警及他們的狀態保持追蹤。

The police are **on the track of** the gang. 警方正在追蹤這個幫派。

應用　*to keep track of* 持續追蹤
to lose track of 失去……蹤影，失去……線索
tire track 輪胎軌跡

---

traffic	*vt.*	買賣，非法交易
[ˋtræfɪk]		

Each year, many women were **trafficked** abroad for purposes of sexual exploitation. 每年，許多婦女基於性剝削的目的而被販運到國外。

n.　交通

Traffic backed up significantly on highway near the St. Francis off ramp. All surrounding roads are jam-packed with traffic. The St. Francis northbound off-ramp will require a full closure for 5 days.

Drivers are asked to plan their drive time accordingly, expect delays, watch for construction personnel working the area, observe temporary construction signing, and reduce speed to the posted speed limit. 高速公路靠近「聖法蘭西斯」閘道出口的交通嚴重回堵，所有的周遭道路都被交通給堵塞。「聖法蘭西斯」北向出口將會需要完全封閉 5 天，駕駛人請盤算開車時間，要預期會有延誤，小心該區域工作的施工人員，注意臨時的施工號誌，並將速度降低到公告的速限。

應用　*traffic accident reconstruction* 交通事故重建

traffic barricade 交通路障（或稱 *roadblock; road block*)

traffic cone 交通錐

traffic congestion 交通阻塞

traffic fine 交通罰鍰

traffic island 交通分隔島

traffic jam 交通阻塞

traffic lane 交通線道

traffic light 交通號誌

traffic noise 交通噪音

traffic regulation 交通規則

traffic rule 交通規則

traffic signal 交通號誌

traffic sign 交通標誌

traffic speed 行車速度

traffic stop 交通攔檢

traffic violator 交通違規者

traffic volume 交通流量

| trafficking | *n.* | 販運、走私 |
| [ˋtræfɪkɪŋ] | | |

應用　*drug trafficking* 毒品走私

firearms trafficking 槍械走私

human trafficking 人口販運

trafficking investigation 走私案調查

trafficking route 走私路徑

weapons trafficking 武器走私

【補充說明】

trafficking 與 smuggling 是兩個容易混淆的用字。兩者是不同的犯罪，又分人與物說明如下：

　　人的方面：有人口販運(human trafficking)與人口走私/偷渡(human smuggling)，兩者主要區別在於有無選擇自由。基本上任何人可以選擇以自願的「人口偷渡(human smuggling)」

方式到他國；但若陷入被逼迫、失去自由的剝削狀態時 (例如抵達後時旅行證件被扣、被迫為奴工、娼妓)，就成為「人口販運(human trafficking)」的被害人。

　　物的方面：如果是是毒品的非法運送、進出口而主要目的是販售圖利時，用詞多為 drug trafficking。

至於走私(smuggling)指的是跨越國界的非法運送物品(illegal transporting of goods)，至於運送的物品本身可能是合法的物品(例如、菸、酒、香菇等等)，也可能是違法的物品(例如槍枝、毒品等) ，此時多用 smuggling 一詞，非法運送的目的可能是為了利潤或避稅，。當然，像是毒品走私(drug smuggling)如果是非法跨越國境、涉及買賣交易，則也是 drug trafficking。

trafficker [ˋtræfɪkɚ]	n.	走私者
tragedy [ˋtrædʒədɪ]	n.	悲劇性事件，慘案，災難
tragic [ˋtrædʒɪk]	adj.	悲劇性的，悲慘的，不幸的 The **tragic** fire at the warehouse has claimed at 4 lives. Investigations are underway to determine the cause of the blaze in this **tragic** incident. 這場不幸的倉庫火災奪走了 4 條寶貴的生命，調查正在進行，以確定這場不幸事件中造成大火的原因。
training [ˋtrenɪŋ]	n. 應用	訓練，執法機關的各式訓練如下： *baton technique* 警棍技巧 *command level training* 指揮層級訓練 *edged weapons defense* 銳器防禦 *firearms training* 武器訓練 *frisking technique* 搜身技巧 *grappling technique* 擒拿術 *handcuffing technique* 手銬技巧 *in-service training* 在職訓練 *leadership training* 領導統御訓練 *physical training* 體能訓練 *promotional training* 升遷訓練 *recruit training* 新進人員訓練 *self-defense technique* 防身術 *shooting simulation* 模擬射擊 *tactical training* 技能訓練
transfer [træns`fɚ]	vt.	轉換，調動 The prisoner **has been transferred to** a prison in another city

for mental health treatment. 該名囚犯已經被轉送到另一個城市的監獄做精神治療。

| | *vt.* | 搬遷，轉移 |

This morning, EMS responded to a residence near Holidays Inn for a person in cardiac arrest. The patient **was transferred to** a regional emergency department for continued care. 今天早上，緊急救護技術員回應靠近假日飯店的一處住家，有人心跳停止，患者被送一家區域急診部做後續照護。

| | *n.* | (人的) 解送，遞送 (ICTY 及 ICTR 刑事法庭) |
| | 應用 | *transfer of sentenced person* 受刑人解送、移交 (或 *transfer of prisoner*) |

| transmit | |]傳播，傳染(疾病)，傳送，傳達 |
| [træns`mɪt | | |

Cold and flu are caused by viruses and are easily transmitted to other people. 一般感冒與流行感冒是病毒所引起的，並且容易傳給其他人。

| transport | *n.* | 運輸，運送 |
| [`træns,pɔrt] | | |

EMTs gave immediate care to the critically injured driver and provided **transport** to the hospital. 緊急救護技術員給予這個傷重的駕駛立即的照護，並且運送到醫院。

| transport | *vt.* | 運輸，運送 |
| [træns`pɔrt] | | |

The offenders **were transported** via the jail bus to the Jail. 犯罪者被用監獄巴士送到看守所。

All the injured **were transported** to local hospitals. 所有的傷者都被送到了當地醫院。

Many drug traffickers use postal and package delivery services **to transport** illicit drugs. 許多毒品販運者使用郵政及包裹快遞服務公司來運送非法毒品。

The use of postal services affords drug traffickers the ability **to covertly transport** large quantities of drugs. 利用郵政服務讓毒品販運者能夠隱密地運送大量的毒品。

| | 應用 | *to transport patient* 運送傷患 |

| transportation | *n.* | 運輸，輸送 |
| [,trænspɚ`teʃən] | 應用 | *drug transportation network* 毒品運送網絡 |

drug transportation route 毒品運送路線
illegal transportation of alien 非法運送外國人
illegal transportation of migrant 非法運送移民
illegal transportation of drug 非法運送毒品 (或非法運送 *cigarette* 香菸 / *alcoho* 酒類 / *intoxicating liquor* 酒精飲料 / *animal* 動物)

trap [træp]	*n.*	陷阱 The suspect alleged that police illegally set **trap** to catch him. 嫌犯指控警方非法設陷阱抓他。 He was lured into a **trap**. 他被引入陷阱。
	vt.	設陷阱補抓……，使……落入困境 The driver **was trapped** in the car for about 30 minutes before rescuers could get him out.駕駛人被困在車內將近 30 分鐘才被救難人員救了出來。 The travelers **were trapped** in the mountains due to typhoon. 遊客因為颱風而被困在山上。 A raging fire swept over several houses in downtown, and luckly no victim **was trapped**. 一場熊熊燃燒的大火橫掃過市區的幾間房子，幸運地，沒有人受困。 Firefighter extricated two victims **trapped** inside the voids. 消防員拖救出兩位困在空際內的遇難者。 Firefighters crawled down the hallway beneath the smoke and saved the boy who **was trapped in** the room. 消防員緩慢爬行在煙霧之下，並救了困在房間內的男孩。 Firefighters responded to a collapsed building and rescued people who **were trapped in** the collapse rubble. 消防員前往處理一處倒塌了的建物，並且救出被困在坍塌瓦礫中的人。 The patient inside the car **was trapped** very badly and was in bad condition. 車內的傷患被困得很慘，狀況很糟。
trauma [`trɔmə]	*n.*	【醫】外傷，傷口；(感情、情緒等方面的) 創傷
traumatic [trɔ`mætɪk]	*adj.*	【醫】外傷的，創傷的，令人痛苦的 Line of duth injury or death is traumatic. 值勤中的傷亡是令人痛苦的。 A police officer or firefighter's death in the line of duty **is traumatic** and tragic for both the relatives and fellow officers. 員警或消防員在執勤中死亡，對於家屬及同僚而言是感到創痛而不幸的。 Many first responders, including police, firefighters, fire rescue personnel, and EMTs said they had experienced **Post Traumatic Stress Disorder (PTSD)** symptoms at some point in their lives. 許多第一線處理人員包括警察、消防員、火警救援人員及、緊急救護人員(EMT)說，他們在一生中會有一些時候會經歷過創傷後壓力症候群。
treat	*vt.*	醫療，治療

[trit]

The EMT testified he has properly assessed and **treated** the patient. 緊急救護技術員作證說，他有適當地對患者評估及治療。

Three firefighters got sick at the scene. They **were** all **treated** and then released from the hospital. 三名消防員覺得作嘔，他們都受到治療，然後從醫院出院。

Many residents were affected by the fire and heavy smoke and had **been treated** in the hospital. Some of them **were treated** for minor burns. 大部分居民受到這場火勢及濃煙的影響，而必須在醫院接受治療，其中有一些因輕微燒傷接受治療。

treatment	n.	對待，待遇，勒戒，治療

[`tritmənt]

Correctional officers estimated that more than 200 inmates in the prison needed **drug treatment**. 矯正人員估計監獄內有超過 200 名囚犯需要毒品勒戒治療。

應用

alcohol treatment 酒精勒戒

drug treatment 毒品勒戒

medical treatment 醫學治療

pre-hospital treatment 到院前的救護

inhuman or degrading treatment (國際人權相關方面法規的) 不仁道或貶抑對待

trespass	vi.	【律】擅自進入，非法侵入，侵害行為

[`trɛspəs]

The suspect allegedly **trespassed into** the hotel and stole the baggages of hotel guests. 該嫌犯涉嫌非法侵入飯店並偷取飯店房客的行李。

trespasser	n.	侵害者，違反者，入侵者

[`trɛspəsɚ]

The **trespasser** was arrested by the police. 侵入者被警方逮捕。

triage	n.	分類，已分類的事物，【醫】檢傷分類

[`traɪɪdʒ]

Triage is the job of deciding which patients get treated first if there are too many injuries for resources to handle – also known as Mass Casualty Incident (MCI). 「檢傷分類(triage)」的工作是在決定當有太多需要處理的傷者----亦即所稱的「大量傷患事件(MCI) 」的時候，哪些患者應該優先予以治療。

In the U.S., Simple Triage And Rapid Treatment (START) is a **triage method** used by first responders to quickly classify victims during a mass casualty incident (MCI) based on the severity of their injury. 在美國，START 是最初期應變者在「大量傷患事件(MCI) 」中，用來快速將受害者分類的檢傷方式，依據的是傷害的嚴重性。

First responders must evaluate victims and assign them to one of the following four categories: (1) walking wounded/minor (green); (2) delayed (yellow); (3) immediate (red), or (4) deceased/(black).

初期應變者必須隊受害者進行評估，並將他們指定為以下四個分類的一類：(1)能走動的傷者/輕微(綠色)；(2)延後治療(黃色)；(3)立即治療(紅色)；(4)死亡(黑色)。

| trial | *n.* | 審問，審判 |
| [ˋtraɪəl] | | |

The suspect **went on trial** on murder charges las week. Prosecutors said DNA on the cartridge connects him to the crime. 嫌犯上星期為謀殺案出庭，檢察官說，彈殼上的 DNA 將他與這起犯罪連在一起。

The defendant **is on trial** for burglary. 被告因竊盜案受審。

At trial, the judge may decide to dismiss the complaint and discharge the defendant; or to admit the defendant to bail. 審判時，法官可以決定駁回訴狀並釋回被告，或准予被告交保。

The judge will review evidence presented by the prosecutor and decides whether there is sufficient evidence to require a defendant **to stand trial**. 法官會審視檢察官提出的證據，並決定是否有充分的證據要求被告受審。

應用　*criminal trial* 刑事審判

fair/unfair trial 公平/不公平審判

trial court 審理法院，地方法院 (或稱 *court of first instance; court of instance; instance court*)

trial judge 審理法官

| trigger | *vt.* | 觸發，引起 |
| [ˋtrɪgɚ] | | |

The incident **was triggered by** arguments about the child custody. 這起事件是因為兒童監護爭論所引起。

(槍砲的) 扣扳機

At trial, the defendant admitted that he was the one who **pulled the trigger**. 審判時，被告承認他就是扣板機開槍的人。

| trooper | *n.* | 【美】州警 |
| [ˋtrupɚ] | | |

| trump up | *v.* | 捏造要，編造(謊言、罪名等) |

Investigators said that the crime scene was trumped up. There were signs that the crime scene was staged to mislead investigators. 偵查人員說，犯罪現場被捏造了。有跡象顯示，犯罪現場被故佈疑陣，以誤導偵查人員。

| true | *adj.* | 真實的，確實的 |
| [tru] | | |

I hereby declare that the above made statements **are true** to the best of my knowledge and belief, and that I understand it is made for use as evidence in court and is subject to penalty for perjury.

本人謹此聲明，就本人所知及認知，以上所做的陳述都是真實無誤。我也了解它將在法院作為證據之用，並且會受到偽證罪的處罰。

應用	*true copy of the original document* 核與正本相符

trustworthy [`trʌst,wɝðɪ]	*adj.*	值得信賴的，可信的，可靠的 The trial court concluded that witness statement **was trustworthy**. 地方法院認定證人的陳述是可信的。
truth [truθ]	*n.*	實話，事實，實情 The judge believed the defendant did not **tell the truth**, and rejected his statement. 法官相信被告並未吐實，而將他的陳述予以排除。 The defendant kept harassing and intimidating victims' families **to hide the truth**. 被告不斷騷擾及恫嚇被害人的家人去隱瞞事實。
truthful [`truθfəl]	*adj.*	誠實的，坦承的，講真話的 The President testified that Ms. Lewinsky's affidavit, in which she stated she had never had a sexual relationship with the President, was accurate. The President further testified that he believed this testimony **to be truthful**. 總統作證說，陸文思基的證詞，其中她提到她從未與總統有性關係，是正確的。總統進一步作證說，他相信這份證詞所言實在。
try [traɪ]	*vt.*	審理，審判 Cases of the district court **are tried by** one judge alone. 地方法院的案件是由法官一人獨任審判。 In the United States, criminal case **is tried to** a judge or jury. In many civil law countries, it **is** always **tried** to a judge. 在美國，刑事案件是由法官或陪審團審理，在許多大陸法系國家，案件向來是由法官審理。
turf [tɝf]	*n.*	地盤，勢力範圍 Gang members often intimidate people who live and work within their **turf**, and are prepared for the deadly encounters with law enforcement officers and rival gangs. 幫派成員常恐嚇在他們地盤內生活及工作的人，並準備著與執法人員及敵對幫派做致命衝突。
turmoil [`tɝmɔɪl]	*n.*	騷動，混亂 The city **is in turmoil**. Roving gangsters are attacking citizens and tourists. 城市陷入一片混亂，流竄的幫派分子正攻擊著市民與遊客。
turn	*vi.*	轉

[tɚn]	應用	*turn into riot* 變成暴動
	vt.	把(注意力等)轉向

Many people complain that police often **turn a blind eye to** people who cross the street on a red light. 許多人抱怨警方常常對於闖紅燈的人閉一隻眼。

	應用	自首 to turn himself in to

Suspect's family persuaded him to **turn himself in to** authorities. 嫌犯的家人說服他向當局自首。

	應用	*turn in* 自首

turn oneself in (向警方) 自首 [(+to police)] (或稱 *surrender*)

	n.	轉向
	應用	*to make a left turn* 左轉

to make a right turn (on red) (紅燈)右轉

to make a U-turn 迴轉

turn signal 方向燈

turn light 方向燈

turnout lane (高速公路的) 避車道，爬坡道

---

unattended	*adj.*	沒人照顧的；未被注意的
[ˌʌnəˈtɛndɪd]		

Always keep in mind that it is illegal to **leave** a child **unattended** in a motor vehicle. 要隨時記得，將小孩單獨留在汽車裡，是違法的。

Sometimes, the undercover agent would **leaves** a car **unattended** in a high crime area, with the door unlocked, and then round up the suspect while he is committing the car theft. 有時候，臥底幹員會把車子留在高犯罪地區，讓車門沒上鎖，然後等嫌犯進行竊車時圍捕他。

If you are involved in a collision with an **unattended** vehicle, you must provide contact information either in person or by leaving a note. 如果你與無人車輛發生擦撞，你必須提供聯絡資訊，不管是親自或留下字條的方式。

---

unconscious	*adj.*	不省人事的，失去知覺的
[ʌnˈkɑnʃəs]		

The patient was found **unconscious**. EMTs arrived at the scene and performed chess compression on him, since he had stopped breathing. 患者被發現失去意識，緊急救護技術員抵達了現場並對她進行胸部按壓，因為她的呼吸停止了。

---

uncover	*vt.*	揭開，揭露，發現，起出
[ʌnˈkʌvɚ]		

The suspect has been arrested after detectives **uncovered** the alleged **plot** to shoot the drug dealer. 偵查幹員發現這個槍殺毒販的密謀，之後以經將嫌犯逮捕了。

While checking the inmate's cell, prison officers found the notes and several pieces of metal, and **uncovered** the escape plot. 監獄人員在檢查受刑人囚房之時，發現了字條以及幾片金屬片，而揭發了這起脫逃陰謀。

Airport authorities **uncovered** a plot to blow up an airplane. Suspect was arrested after the port authorities **uncovered** the bomb plot. 機場當局發現了這起炸掉飛機的陰謀。在機場當局揭發炸彈策畫之後，嫌犯被予以逮捕。

Police **uncovered** an illicit drug factory in the small town. During the search, they also **uncoverd** many weapons. These weapons **were uncovered** in the basement. 警方在這個小鎮發現了一個非法毒品工廠，在搜索中，他們也起出了許多武器，這些武器是在地下室被找到的。

undercover [ˌʌndɚˋkʌvɚ]	*adj.*	臥底的，從事秘密工作的

The young police officer volunteers **to go undercover** to infiltrate the crime ring. 這名年輕的員警自願臥底，來滲透這個犯罪組織。

Sometimes, narcotic officers may **work undercover** to earn the trust of the drug dealer and thus obtain drug intelligence from them. 有時候，毒品幹員可能會從事臥底工作，來取得毒販的信任，而從他們獲得毒品情報。

應用 *undercover agent* 臥底幹員（或稱 *undercover police officer; undercover operative*）
undercover investigation 臥底偵查
undercover operation 臥底行動
undercover surveillance 臥底偵監

uniform [ˋjunəˌfɔrm]	*n.*	制服
	應用	*police uniform* 警察制服

unlawful [ʌnˋlɔfəl]	*adj.*	不合法的，法律上不正當的
	應用	*unlawful act* 非法行為

unlawful arrest 非法逮捕
unlawful assembly 非法集會
unlawful conduct 非法的行為
unlawful detention 非法拘禁
unlawful employment of alien 非法雇用外國人
unlawful entry 非法進入
unlawful gathering of evidence 非法蒐集證據
unlawful gathering 非法聚集
unlawful imprisonment 非法拘禁

unlawful killing 行兇殺人

unlawful order 非法的命令

unlawful possession of a firearm 非法持槍

unlawful possession of controlled substance 非法持有管制物質 (毒品)

unlawful possession of weapon 非法持有武器

unlawful search and seizure 非法搜索及扣押

unlawful surveillance 非法偵查

unlawful use of force /weapon 非法使用武力/武器

unmarked police vehicle	應用	一般警車
		marked police vehicle 制式警車

unpunished [ʌn`pʌnɪʃt]	*adj.*	未受處罰的
		The victim was shot in the chest and died. His family says all they want is justice and that this crime should not **go unpunished**. 被害人胸部中彈而死,他的家人說他們所要的是正義,並且這個犯罪不可以就這樣沒受到處罰。

unreported [ˌʌnrɪ`pɔ:tɪd]		沒有報案的
		For some reason, many sexual harassment cases **go unreported**. 因為某種原因,很多騷擾案件沒有被報案。

unsolved [ʌn`salvd]	*adj.*	未偵破的,未解決的
		Chief of Police said the mission of Cold Case Unit is to investigate unsolved cases. With the help of cutting-edge technologies, investigators will be able to reopen **unsolved cases**. 警察局長說,「冷案組(Cold Case Unit)」的任務是調查未偵破案件。在尖端科技的幫助下,偵查人員將能夠重新開啟未偵破的案件。 In the US, the clearance rate for arsons is low. Statistics show that many arson cases often **go unsolved**. 在美國,縱火的破案率是低的,統計顯示,許多縱火案件常常沒有偵破。

unresponsive [ˌʌnrɪ`spansɪv]	*adj.*	無反應的
		James was discovered **unresponsive** in his room. He **was unresponsive** when firefighters found him insides the charred apartment. 詹姆士被發現在他房間沒了反應,他被消防員在燒得焦黑的公寓內找到時,他已經沒反應了。

unwitting [ʌn`wɪtɪŋ]	*adj.*	不知情的
		The suspect said he had used **unwitting** taxi drivers to deliver the durg packages to the buyers. 嫌犯說他是利用不知情的計程車司機將毒品包裹送去給買主。

uphold [ʌp`hold]	*vt.*	維持原判
		According to New York Times, South Korean's Supreme Court

upheld a lifetime sentence for the captain of the ferry that sank 2014, killing more than 300 people. 根據紐約時報，南韓最高法院對於 2014 年沉沒而造成 300 人死亡的渡輪船長，維持無期徒刑的判決。

【請參看 affirm, vacate, remand】

urine [`jʊrɪn]	*n.*	尿，尿液
vacate [`veket]	*vt.*	廢棄，撤銷，使⋯⋯無效 The Court of Appeals **vacated** in full the lower court's judgment and remanded the case to a new trial. 上訴法院全部撤銷下級法院的判決，並將案件發回重新審理。 【請參看 affirm, uphold, remand】
vagrant [`vegrənt]	*n.*	流浪漢，漂泊者，無業遊民
valid [`vælɪd]	*adj.*	合法的，有效的 If the driver license is later suspended, cancelled or revoked, it is not **valid**. 駕照如果之後被吊扣、註銷或吊銷，就變成無效。
vandalism [`vændlɪzəm]	*n.*	故意破壞公物(或文化、藝術)的行為
verdict [`vɝdɪkt]	*n.*	【律】(陪審團的)裁決，裁定 Ladies and gentlemen of the jury, have you **reached a verdict**? 陪審團先生及女士，你們已經做成判決了嗎？ Yes, we have. Your honor. 是的，庭上。 What is your verdict? 你們的判決為何？ We find the defendant guilty. 我們認定被告有罪。
verify [`vɛrə,faɪ]	*vt.*	證明，證實，核對，查實，查清 CCTV is a surveillance technology. CCTV images can used **to verify** a witness's or suspect's account. 閉路監視器(CCTV)是一項監視科技，閉路監視器的影像可以用來查證證人或嫌犯的說法。
victim [`vɪktɪm]	*n.*	犧牲者，遇難者，受害者，受騙者，受災者 The first officer at the scene should secure the accident scene as soon as possible, search for the survivors, if any, locate and identify the **victims** and recover the bodies of all the **victims**. 最早在現場的人員應該儘快保全事件現場、搜尋生還者——如果有的話，找到及確認被害人，並找出所有被害人的遺體。
	應用	*accident victim* 意外事件被害人 *crime victim* 犯罪被害人 *innocent victim* 無辜的被害人

potential victim 潛在的被害人

rape victim 性侵害之被害人

victim advocate 被害人權益促進倡議者

VIN	*abbr.*	車身號碼 Vehicle Identification Number
vindicate [ˈvɪndɪkeɪt]	*vt.*	證明……無辜，證明……清白 After maintaining his innocence for 20 years, Jame was finally vindicated by DNA evidence. He was vindicated by the court of appeal. 經過了 20 年的堅持無辜，詹姆士終於經由 DNA 證據證明了清白。他被上訴法院證明是清白的。
violate [ˈvaɪə,let]	*vt.*	違反 If the defendant **violates** the condition of probation at any time prior to the expiration or termination of the term of probation, the court may revoke the sentence of probation and resentence the defendant. 如果被告在緩刑期間到期或結束之前違反緩刑條件的話，法院得撤銷緩刑判決，並對被告重為判決。
violator [ˈvaɪə,letɚ]	*n.*	違犯者，違規者 Once a traffic **violator** is legally stopped, the officer may require the driver to get out of the vehicle and may require identification. 一旦交通違規者被合法攔下，員警得要求駕駛人下車並得要求出示身分。
violation [,vaɪəˈleʃən]	*n.*	違反，違背，違犯 The jury found the Defendant, Orenthal James Simpson, not guilty of the crime of murder in **violation of** penal code section 187(A). 陪審團認定被告辛普森不成立違反刑法第 187(A)條的謀殺罪。 Evidence obtained in **violation of** an accused person's constitutional rights is not admissible. 違反被告憲法權利所取得的證據，無證據能力。
	應用	*criminal violation* 刑事違法 *moving violation* 動態違規 *non-moving violation* 靜態違規 *parole violation* 違反假釋 *probation violation* 違反緩刑 *traffic violation* 交通違規 *parking violation* 停車違規
violator [ˈvaɪə,letɚ]	*n.*	違法者，違反者，侵犯者
violence [ˈvaɪələns]	*n.* 應用	暴力 *domestic violence* 家暴(或稱 *family violence*)

gang violence 幫派暴力

gun violence 槍枝暴力

marital violence 婚姻暴力

physical violence 身體暴力

street violence 街頭暴力

workplace violence 職場暴力

violent	adj.	由暴力引起的，暴力的
[`vaɪələnt]	應用	*violent behavior* 暴力行為
		violent crime 暴力犯罪
		violent criminal 暴力罪犯
		violent encounter 暴力對峙
		violent gang 暴力幫派
		violent protest 暴力抗爭

visa	n.	(護照等上的)簽證
[`vizə]		Some **visas** can be granted on arrival. A visa granted at a port of entry is called **visa on arrival**. 有些簽證可以在抵達時核發，在入境港埠核發的簽證稱為落地簽證。

visibility	n.	能見度
[,vɪzə`bɪlətɪ]		You must turn on your headlights in case of low **visibility**. 萬一能見度低，你必須打開車前燈。

visitation	n.	探視，探視權
[,vɪzə`teʃən]		The **visitation order** shall specify the time, day, place, and manner of transfer of the child for **visitation** to limit the child's exposure to potential domestic conflict or violence and to ensure the safety of all family members. 探視裁定應指定時間、日期、處所及兒童送交探視的方式，以減少兒童暴露在可能的家庭衝突或暴力，並確保所有家庭成員的安全。
	應用	*attorney visit* 律師會見
		Inmate visitation 受刑人探視
		visitation right 探視權
		visiting hours 探視時間

vital [`vaɪt!]	adj.	生命的，維持生命所必需的
		The patient's **vital signs** have returned to normal levels, doctor said. 醫生說，病人的生命跡象回復到正常水準。
		In general, there are four primary **vital signs**: body temperature, blood pressure, pause (heart rate), and breathing rate (respiratory rate). 生命跡象也是重要的，大致而言，主要有四大生命跡象：體溫、血壓、脈搏(心跳率)，以及呼吸頻率。
	應用	*vital sign* 生命跡象

vital evidence 關鍵證據

to assess the patient's vital signs 評估患者的生命跡象

voiceprint [ˋvɔɪsˏprɪnt]	*n.*	聲紋

void [vɔɪd]	*vt.*	使無效，把……作廢，(簽證的)註銷

If you overstay your visa, the visa can **be voided** and cancelled. In the U.S. overstaying just for one day will **void** your existing visa. 如果你逾期停留，簽證會無效及取消。在美國，逾期即使只有一天，也會讓你的既有簽證無效。

voluntary [ˋvɑlənˏtɛrɪ]	*adj.* 應用	自願的，志願的

voluntary departure 自願離境

voluntary confession 自願自白

voluntary consent 己意同意

volunteer [ˏvɑlənˋtɪr]	*n.* *adj.* 應用	自願參加者，志願者，義工 自願參加的，自願的

volunteer firefighter 義消

volunteer rescuer 救援志工

rescue volunteer 救援志工

volunteer worker 志工

volunteer police 義警

vulnerable [ˋvʌlnərəbḷ]	*adj.*	易受責難的，有弱點的，容易受害的

The elderly may be as **vulnerable** to violence as children are. 老年人可能會像小孩一樣容易受害。

Research has shown that illegal immigrants are extremely **vulnerable** to crime and that many immigrant crimes are under reported. 研究顯示，非法移民極容易成為犯罪受害，並且很多移民犯罪都沒有報案。

waive [wev]	*vt.*	放棄，撤回

If you choose to **waive** your right to counsel, the police can question you at the police station without a lawyer present to represent your interests. 如果你選擇放棄律師權，警方可以在沒有律師代表你的利益的情況下，在警局裡對你問話。

wanted [ˋwɑntɪd]	*adj.*	被通緝的

Any alien who **is wanted by** the Interpol or foreign judicial authorities is inadmissible and shall be taken into custody for deportation. 任何受國際刑警組織或外國司法機關通緝的外國人，不得許可入境，並應予拘禁，以便遣送。

He **is wanted in** the US **on a charge of** drug smuggling. 他因毒品販運的告訴，受美國通緝。

	應用	*wanted fugitive* 通緝犯
		wanted person 通緝犯
war crime		戰爭罪
warden	*n.*	【美】典獄長
[ˋwɔrdn]	應用	*prison warden* 典獄長
		jail warden 看守所所長
warning triangle		警示三角錐
warrant	*n.*	令狀
[ˋwɔrənt]	應用	*to execute a warrant* 執行令狀
		to issue a warrant 核發令狀
		to obtain a warrant 取得令狀
		arrest warrant 逮捕令
		death warrant 死刑執行令
		outstanding warrant 未結案的令狀
		search warrant 搜索令狀
		search-and-seizure warrant 搜索扣押令狀
		warrant for Mr. Simpson's arrest 逮捕 Simpson 的令狀
		warrantless arrest 無令狀逮捕
		warrantless search 無令狀搜索
		warrantless seizure 無令狀扣押
water cannon		噴水車
weapon	*n.*	武器，兵器，兇器
[ˋwɛpən]	應用	*dangerous weapon* 危險武器
		deadly weapon 致命武力
		edged weapon 銳器
		high-power(ed) weapon 高性能武器
		lethal weapon 致命性武器
		nonlethal weapon 非致命的武器
whereabouts	*n.*	行蹤，下落
[ˋhwɛrəˋbaʊts]		

The FBI and law enforcement officials are seeking the public's assistance in locating the person believed to be connected to the abduction of Paul Smith. The suspect is described as a white male, approximately 5'10" tall, 180 pounds, with long hair and eyeglasses. If you have any information as to the identity or **whereabouts** of the suspect, who is featured in the surveillance video above, please contact authorities. 聯邦調查局及執法人員正尋求大眾的協助，找尋這位據相信與 Paul Smith 綁架案有關的人，嫌犯的特徵為白人男子、身高約 5 呎 10 吋、180 磅、蓄留長髮、戴眼鏡。如果你有任何關於上述監視影帶中

的嫌犯的身分及下落的資訊，請與當局聯絡。

willfully	adv.	蓄意地
[`wɪlfəlɪ]		

The suspect **willfully** injured innocent people without warning as he fired more than 20 rounds from a semi-automatic rifle. 嫌犯毫無預警蓄意地傷害無辜者，當時他從半自動步槍發射了超過 20 發子彈

wiretap	vi. vt.	監聽
[`waɪr,tæp]	應用	

wiretapping 監聽(wire-tapping)

telephone tapping 電話監聽

lawful interception 合法監察

voice telephone interception 語音電話攔截

withdraw	vt.	(法律上的) 撤回，撤銷
[wɪð`drɔ]		

The plaintiff decided **to withdraw** the charge against the defendant. 原告決定撤回對被告的告訴。

	vi.	(犯罪的) 中止，退出 [(+from)]

The defendant was acquitted because he **withdrew from** the conspiracy and participation in the offense prior to the commission and made a substantial effort to prevent the commission. 被告被無罪釋放，因為他在該犯罪進行之前，即退出犯罪的共謀及參與，並做實質的努力，防止其進行。

	vi.	撤退，撤離，使退出[(+from)]

IThe Incident Commander said the wildfires spreaded so quickly and unpredictably that he had to order firefighters **withdrawn from** the dangerous area. 事件指揮官說，野火蔓延得如此快速而無法預測，因此他必須命令消防人員從危險區域撤回。

witness	n.	證人
[`wɪtnɪs]	應用	

accomplice witness 共犯證人

adverse witnesse 敵性證人

alibi witness 不在場證人

character witness 品格證人

competent witness 適格的證人

expert witness 專家證人

eyewitness 目擊證人

hostile witness 敵意證人

lay witness 一般證人

prosecuting witness 起訴證人

reliable witness 可信 (靠) 的證人

to cross-examine witness 詰問證人

unavailable witness 無法出庭的證人

witness protection 證人保護

wound	*vt.*	使……受傷

[wund]

Police returned fire and fatally **wounded** the suspect. 警方開將還擊並且嫌犯受傷不治。

Authorities say two police officers **were wounded** and three suspects were killed in the gun fight. 當局說，在這場槍戰中，有兩名員警受傷，並且有三名嫌犯被擊斃。

n. 傷，傷口

應用 *bullet wound* 槍傷
burn wound 燒傷
fake wound 假的傷
gunshot wound 槍傷
stab wound 刺傷

wrecker	*n.*	拖吊車(或稱 tow truck)，搶修車，救難船

[`rɛkɚ]

wrongdoer	*n.*	做壞事的人，違法犯罪者

[`rɔŋ`duɚ]

It took the detective a long time to figure out who the **wrongdoer** was. 偵查員用了很長時間弄清楚了誰是做壞事的人。

wrongful	*adj.*	非法的，違法的，不正當的

[`rɔŋfəl]

Wrongful incarceration means that you are incorrectly arrested, prosecuted, and found guilty and ordered to serve a prison term. 非法的監禁是指你被錯誤地逮捕、起訴並且被判有罪，並且被命令服刑。

應用 *wrongful act* 不法行為
wrongful arrest 非法逮捕 (或稱 *false arrest*)
wrongful conviction 不當的有罪判決
wrongful punishment 不當處罰
wrongful death 不當致死
wrongful accusation 不當指控
wrongful imprisonment 不當監禁 (或稱 *false imprisonment*)
wrongful incarceration 不當監禁

yield	*vi.*	讓路

[jild]

Vehicles entering or exiting the roundabout must use your turn signals and **yield to** all traffic including pedestrians. 進出圓環的車輛必須打方向燈，並禮讓所有交通，包括行人在內。

vt. 讓

Everyone must **yield** the right-of-way to any police vehicle, fire engine, and ambulance. 每個人都必須禮讓路權給警車、消防

車及救護車。

應用 *yield sign* 禮讓標誌

海巡執法英文字彙

A.B.	*abbr.*	幹練水手 Able Seaman
aboard	*adv.*	在船(或飛機，車)上，上船(或飛機，車)
[əˋbord]	*prep.*	在(船，飛機，車)上，進入，上(船，飛機，車)

The boat is ready to leave. **All aboard**! 船就要開了，請大家上船。

The coast guard said that there were more than 100 migrants **aboard** the ship. 海巡說，船上有超過 100 名移民者。

They were the last two to **go aboard** the ship. 他們是最後兩位上船的人。

adrift	*adj.*	漂浮著的，漂流著的
[əˋdrɪft]		

The two missing boaters were later found **adrift** in a life raft. 這兩名失蹤的乘船者後來被發現在救生筏內漂流著。

aeronautical	*adj.*	航空的
[ˌɛrəˋnɔtɪk!]		

Every country recognizes the importance of saving lives and the need to be directly involved in rendering maritime and **aeronautical** search and rescue. Coast Guard is usually designated as the maritime and **aeronautical** SAR Coordinator for the waters. 每一個國家都認同拯救生命的重要，以及有直接加入提供海空搜救的必要，海巡通常被指定為海域上的海空搜救協調者。

afloat	*adj.*	飄浮著的，漂流著的，浸滿著水的
[əˋflot]		

The ship master was unable to keep the boat **afloat**, so he made a distress call to the Coast Guard before abandoning their vessel. 船長無法讓船浮著，所以棄船之前，向海巡發出了海難訊號。

The lower deck is afloat. 下層甲板浸滿了水。

	adv.	飄浮著，在船上，在海上，漂流著，浸滿著水
aground	*adv.*	在地上，擱淺，船(觸礁)
[əˋɡraʊnd]		

When a ship runs **aground**, it is important to know: Is the ship taking on water? How fast is the flooding? Are there any other vessels in the area? Are there any pumps onboard? Can they keep up with the flooding? Where and why is the vessel flooding? Are there any injuries or people in the water? Is there any pollution as a result of the grounding? What is the type of fuel and quantity of fuel?

當船隻擱淺時，取得以下有關問題的相關資訊是很重要的：船正在進水嗎？淹水的速度多快？該地區有其他船隻嗎？船上有幫浦嗎？幫浦能跟上淹水的速度嗎？船隻的何處淹水及為何淹水？有無受傷或任何人在水裡嗎？有沒有因為擱淺而有任何汙染？燃料的種類及燃料的量為何？

aid to navigation		助航
airway	*n.*	(肺的)氣道，航空路線
AIS	*abbr.*	船舶自動識別系統 Automatic Identification System
anchor	*n.*	錨
[`æŋkɚ]		The master decided to drop **anchor** in the bay to escape the storm. 船長決定拋錨將船停泊在港灣中，以躲避暴
	vt.	風雨。
	vi.	拋錨使(船)停泊，使固定，繫住
		拋錨泊船，固定
		The master attempted to **anchor** but the surf was too rough and the anchors would not hold. 船長決定拋錨將船固定，但是海浪波濤洶湧，船錨無法固定。
archipelagic	*adj.*	群島的
[ˌɑrkɪpə`lædʒɪk]		Hot pursuit must be commenced when the foreign ship is within the internal waters, the **archipelagic** waters, the territorial sea or the contiguous zone of the pursuing State. 緊追(hot pursuit)必須是在該外國船隻在追逐國的內水、群島水域、領海或鄰接區內的時候開始。
armed robbery against ships		武裝劫船
		Coast states must work with each others to suppress piracy and **armed robbery against ships**. 沿海國必須相互合作，以壓制武裝搶劫。
ashore	*adv.*	向岸，上岸，在岸上，向陸地，上陸地，在陸地
[ə`ʃor]		According to the Coast Guard, some of the passengers swam **ashore** after the boat capsized. 依據海巡署，船隻翻覆之後，有些乘客游泳上岸。
assistance entry		救援進入
		The international law recognizes the duty to save lives in danger or distress, even when they are within a coastal State's territorial sea. In the United States, such entry is called **assistance entry**. 國際法認可對於陷入危險或困境的生命負有救助的這項義務，即使當這些人是在某沿海國的領海之內。在美國，這種進入稱為「救援進入」。

at-sea	*adv.* & *adj.*	在海上 The illegal activities **at sea** may include offenses such as homicide, marine pollution, poaching, illegal transshipment **at sea**, human trafficking, smuggling of migrant, etc. 海上的非法活動可能包括的犯罪例如：殺人、海洋汙染，越界偷捕、非法海上轉載、人口販運、移民偷渡等等。 Piracy means robbery, kidnapping, or other criminal violence committed **at sea**. 海盜罪是指在海上所犯的強盜、綁架或其它犯罪暴力。 不知所措，茫然，糊塗 I am all **at sea**. I have no idea how to do it. 我手足無措，我不知道怎樣做。
baseline [ˋbeslaɪn]	*n.*	基線 The contiguous zone may not extend beyond 24 nautical miles from the **baselines**. 鄰接區不得超過基線起 24 海浬。
bay [be]	*n.*	(海或湖泊的)灣
boarding and inspection		登船及檢查 In general, ships without nationality are subject to **boarding and inspection**. The inspecting State shall ensure that **boarding and inspection** is not conducted in a manner that would constitute harassment of any fishing vessel. 一般而言，無國籍船隻應受登船及檢查。檢查國應確保登船及檢查的進行，方式上不會構成對漁船騷擾的樣子。
boatswain [ˋbot,swen]	*n.*	水手長
buoy [bɔɪ]	*n.*	浮標，浮筒，救生圈，救生衣 After the boat capsized, the three boaters swam to a **buoy marker**, where they stayed afloat for nearly a day and were rescued. 船隻翻覆之後，這3個船上的人游到一個浮筒，在那裡浮了將近 1 天而被救起。 *lifebuoy* n. 救生圈，救生帶
call sign		船舶呼號
capsize [kæpˋsaɪz]	*vi.*	傾覆，翻 Two men have died and one man has been rescued after their small fishing boat hit rocks and **capsized** in rough

seas off Botany Bay on Sunday afternoon. 星期日下午，一艘小船在 Botany 灣外洶湧的海面撞到岩石而翻覆之後，其上的兩名男子死亡，一人被救起。

According to the Coast Guard, some of the passengers swam ashore after the boat **capsized**. 依據海巡署，船隻翻覆之後，有些乘客游泳上岸。

captain ['kæptɪn]	*n.*	船長 (或稱 master)
car & passenger ferry		汽車旅客渡輪
cargo ship		貨輪
catcher boat		漁船
chemical tanker		化學液體船
chief engineer		輪機長(或通稱 Chief)
chief officer		大副 first mate, chief mate
Coast Guard		海巡 (或 Coastguard)
cold shock		冷休克
		Response to sudden immersion in cold water includes **cold shock** (0-2 minutes), functional disability (2-15 minutes), and Hypothermia (15-30 minutes). **Cold shock** response occurs immediately upon entry, it may last up to 2 minutes. 突然泡在冷水中的反應包括冷休克(0 至 2 分鐘)、功能殘疾(2 至 15 分鐘)，及失溫(15 至 30 分鐘)，冷休克反應在入水時立刻發生，那會持續至 2 分鐘。
consignment [kən'saɪnmənt]	*n.*	委託，交付，運送託付物，託賣品，遞運的，委託貨物 Transshipment means the unloading of fishery products on board a fishing vessel to another fishing vessel. It is the transfer of **consignments** from a fishing vessel to another vessel. 轉載(transshipment)是指將某艘漁船上的漁獲卸到另一艘漁船，那是將委託貨物從某艘漁船移轉到另一艘漁船。
container ship		貨櫃船
contiguous zone		鄰接區
		Jurisdictional limits of a State over and under the sea include: territorial sea, **contiguous zone**, exclusive economic zone, continental shelf, and high seas.國家對於海上及海底的管轄界限的五個地帶包括：領海、鄰接區、專屬經濟海域、大陸棚及公海。
continental shelf		大陸棚，大陸架

course [kors]	n.	路線，方向 The Vessel Monitoring System (VMS) provides data to the fisheries authorities about the vessels' location, **course** and speed. 「漁船船位監控系統(VMS)」提供了關於船隻的位置、路線與速度的資料給漁業機關。
CPR	abbr.	【醫】心肺復甦法 cardiopulmonary resuscitation
crew member	n.	機務(或船務)人員 The U.S. Coast Guard has seized a Mexican fishing boat and detained its five **crew members** in a poaching investigation off the Gulf Coast waters of South Texas. 美國海巡在德州南部的墨西哥灣水域進行的一件越界捕魚調查案中，查扣一艘墨西哥漁船，並留置該船的 5 名船員。
cruise [kruz]	n.	巡航，航遊 應用 *cruise ship* 郵輪
current [`kɝ·ənt]	n.	海流 Wind and **current** in the marine environment will cause ships to move or drift over time unless they are moored, anchored or aground. 海上環境的風與海流會導致船隻隨著時間而移動或漂流，除非是有纜繩固定、下錨停泊或擱淺。
cutter [`kʌtɚ]	n.	巡邏艇，緝私巡邏艇，(美國海巡長度在 65 英呎以上的)船艇 The U.S. Coast Guard uses **cutters**, boats, aircrafts and helicopters to conduct its daily business. **Cutter** is basically any Coast Guard vessel 65 feet in length or greater, having adequate accommodations for crew to live on board. 美國海巡使用船舶(分為 cutter 與 boat【註：兩字意思皆為船、艇】)飛機及直升機從事日常業務，稱 cutter 的基本上是指長度在 65 英呎以上而讓船員有足夠膳宿在船上生活的船艇。
D/C	abbr.	駕駛(甲板)實習生 Deck Cadet
deck [dɛk]	n.	(船的)艙面，甲板，(公車，汽車等的)底板，層 All personnel on **deck** must wear personal flotation device (PFD). 所有在甲板上的人必須穿著個人漂浮設備(PFD)。 *Deck Cadet (D/C)* 駕駛(甲板)實習生 *deck crew* 甲板組員 *deck department* 甲板部門
depletion	n.	消耗，用盡

[dɪˋpliʃən]		IUU fishing will result in overfishing and rapid **depletion** of fish stocks. 「非法、未報告及未受規範捕魚(IUU fishing)」會導致過度捕撈及讓漁業資源快速枯竭。
disembark [͵dɪsɪmˋbɑrk]	*vi. &* *vt.*	下車，下飛機，下船，下火車，登陸，上岸 Because of mechanical problem, the master decided to **disembark** the passengers via the lifeboats. 由於機械問題，船長決定用救生筏讓乘客下船。
disputed waters		爭議水域
distress [dɪˋstrɛs]	*n.*	悲痛，苦惱，憂傷貧困，窮苦危難，不幸 Emergency phase comprise three phrases: i.e. uncertainty phase, alert phase and **distress phase**. 緊急階段包括三個階段，即「不確定階段」、「警示階段」及「海難階段」。 Under long-standing traditions of the sea and various provisions of international law, ship masters are obliged to assist others **in distress** at sea whenever they can safely do so. 在長久建立的海上傳統及國際法條款之下，船長在可以安全進行的情況下，有義務協助其他海上的遇難者。 Coastal states must ensure that persons **in distress** will be assisted without regard to locations, nationality, or circumstances. 沿海國必須確保受到海難的人會受到協助，不論其地點、國籍或情況為何。
distressed [dɪˋstrɛst]	*adj.*	痛苦的，憂傷的 The responsibilities to render assistance to a **distressed vessel** or aircraft are based on humanitarian considerations. 提供協助給遇難船隻或飛機，這個責任依據的是人道考量。
drift [drɪft]	*vi.*	漂，漂流 Wind and current in the marine environment will cause ships to move or **drift** over time unless they are moored, anchored or aground. 海上環境的風與海流會導致船隻隨著時間而移動或漂流，除非是有纜繩固定、下錨停泊或擱淺。
driftnet	*n.*	流刺網
drown [draʊn]	*vi.*	溺死，沉沒，浸沒 Police said that most passengers had **drowned** when their vessel overturned. It was also reported that many of them on board had **drowned** because they were trapped on the

boat's lower levels. 警方說，大部分乘客在船隻翻覆時溺
斃了，同時據報其中許多人溺斃，是因為被困在船隻的
下幾層。

dry suit		乾式潛水衣
encroachment [ɪnˋkrotʃmənt]	*n.*	侵入，侵佔，侵蝕 [(+on/upon)]
		It is one of the objectives of Coast Guard to prevent illegal foreign fishing vessels **encroachment** of the EEZ (exclusive economic zone). 防止外國漁船非法入侵專屬經濟海域，是海巡的目標之一。
enforcement craft		執法船
enforcement vessel		執法船
EPIRB	*abbr.*	應急指位無線電示標 *Emergency Position Indicating Radio Beacon*
escort vessel		護艦船
exclusive economic zone		專屬經濟區，專屬經濟海域
First Assistant Engineer		大管輪(或 *Second Engineer*)
fisher [ˋfɪʃɚ]	*n.*	漁工，漁人，漁夫
fishery observer		漁業觀察員
fishing [ˋfɪʃɪŋ]	*n.* 應用	釣魚，捕魚 *freedom of fishing* 捕魚自由 *fishing license* 捕魚許可 *IUU fishing* 非法、未報告及未受規範捕魚 (*illegal, unreported, unregulated fishing*) *overfishing* 過度捕撈 *fishing gear* 漁具 *fishing ground* 漁場 *fishing vessel* 釣魚船，漁船 *fishing boat* 釣魚船，漁船 *fishing vessel incursion* 漁船侵入 *fishing resource* 漁業資源
flag [flæg]	*n.*	旗
		Researches indicate that many illegal fishing vessels are flying **flags of convenience** to avoid detection and penalty for wrongdoing. 研究指出，許多非法漁船是權宜船(懸掛方便旗)，以逃避查緝及違法行為的處罰。
float	*vi.*	浮，漂浮

[flot]		The two men were found **floating** in the water. 這兩人被發現浮在水中。
fly	*vt.*	懸掛(旗)，升(旗) flying (country's) flag
[flaɪ]		Researches indicate that many illegal fishing vessels **are flying** flags of convenience to avoid detection and penalty for wrongdoing. 研究指出，許多非法漁船是權宜船(懸掛方便旗)，以逃避查緝及違法行為的處罰。
freedom of navigation		航行自由
freedom of the high seas		公海自由原則
go-fast vessel		快艇
gross tonnage		(船舶的)淨噸位
grounding	*n.*	(船的)擱淺
[`graʊndɪŋ]		**Ship grounding** is a type of marine accident. Disasters at sea caused by **groundings** may cause serious problems for the environment, human lives, and property. 船隻擱淺是海上意外事件的一種型態，擱淺造成的海上災難可能會對環境、性命及財產造成嚴重的問題。
harbor police		港警(也稱 port police)
high sea		公海
		If there are reasonable grounds for suspecting that a fishing vessel on the **high seas** is without nationality, any State may board and inspect the vessel. 如果有合理事由懷疑公海上的某一漁船為無國籍，則任何國家都可以登船及檢查。
		All nations have recognized the right of hot pursuit as an essential exception to the principal of freedom of the **high seas**. 所有國家都承認緊追權是公海自由原則的一項重要例外。
hoist	*vt.*	(用繩索，起重機等)吊起，提起，舉起，升起
[hɔɪst]		Coast Guard officials said that their patrol vessels **hoisted** the survivors from the drifting liferaft after the cruise sank 150 miles offshore. 海巡官員表示，郵輪在海外 150 英里處翻覆之後，海巡的巡邏艇從漂流的救生筏拉上了生還者。
	n.	起吊裝置，起重機，絞車
		Each year, Coast Guard will perform a number of rescue and **hoist operations** at sea. 每年，海巡都會執行許多的海

上吊掛行動。

hover craft		氣墊船
huddle [`hʌd!]	*vi.*	蜷縮，縮成一團[(+up)]，偎依[(+against)]，擠作一團，聚在一起[(+together)] In cold water, if everyone is wearing a life vest, to **huddle** closely with each other is a good way to conserve heat. 在冷水中，如果每個人都有穿救生衣，則彼此緊緊偎依是一個保持溫度的好方法。
hull [hʌl]	*n.*	船身，船殼
hydrofoil craft		水上飛船
hypothermia [ˌhaɪpəˈθɝmɪə]	*n.*	低體溫症 Response to sudden immersion in cold water includes cold shock (0-2 minutes), functional disability (2-15 minutes), and **hypothermia** (15-30 minutes). Immersion suit can assist in prevention of **hypothermia**. 突然泡在冷水中的反應包括冷休克(0 至 2 分鐘)、功能殘疾(2 至 15 分鐘)，及失溫(15 至 30 分鐘)，保溫救生衣可以幫助預防失溫。
ICAO	*abbr.*	國際民航組織 *International Civil Aviation Organization*
ice breaker		破冰船
immersion [ɪˈmɝʃən]	*n.*	泡在水中(還能將頭保持在水面上) **Immersion** is different from submersion. Submersion means a state of being completely in the water, including one's head. **Immersion** means that the person is still able to keep his or her head out of water. 泡在水中(immersion)與沉入水中(submersion)是完全不同的，沉入水中(submersion)是指一個完全在水中的狀態，包括頭部；泡在水中(immersion)是指該人還能將頭保持在水面上。
	應用	*immersion suit* 保溫救生衣 (*survival suit, immersion survival suit*)
IMO	*abbr.*	國際海事組織 *International Maritime Organization*
IMRF	*abbr.*	國際海上救援聯盟 *International maritime Rescue Federation*
incursion [ɪnˈkɝʃən]	*n.*	進入，流入，侵入，入侵 Foreign **fishing vessel incursions** occur frequently, especially in disputed waters or the overlapping economic zone. 外國漁船侵入經常發生，特別是在爭議水域或重疊的經濟區域。

To counteract the threat of foreign encroachment, the Coast Guard will interdict **illegal incursion** into the territorial waters by foreign fishing vessels. 為了反制外國入侵的威脅，海巡會制止外國漁船非法侵入領海。

inflatable life raft		充氣橡皮製救生艇
innocent passage		無害通過

Ships of all States enjoy the right of **innocent passage** through the territorial sea. 所有國家的船隻都享有無害通過領海的權利。

intercept [ˌɪntəˈsɛpt]	*vt.*	攔截，截住，截擊

Coast Guard frequently spots and **intercepts** fishing vessels suspected of poaching fish within its waters or offshore inside the exclusive economic zone. 海巡經常會在海域內或外海在經濟海域內發現與攔截到疑似越界捕魚的漁船。

interdict [ˌɪntəˈdɪkt]	*vt.*	禁止，制止，封鎖，阻斷

To counteract the threat of foreign encroachment, the Coast Guard will **interdict** illegal incursion into the territorial waters by foreign fishing vessels. 為了反制外國入侵的威脅，海巡會制止外國漁船非法侵入領海。

Coast Guard will use high-speed surface enforcement vessels to **interdict** drug trafficking ships. 海巡會使用高速海上執法船來攔截毒品販運船。

interdiction [ˌɪntəˈdɪkʃən]	*n.*	禁止，制止，封鎖，阻斷

The purpose of shiprider agreements is to strengthen maritime surveillance and **interdiction**. Such operations are specifically called **maritime interdiction**. 登船執法協定(shiprider agreement)的目的是強化海洋偵查及攔阻，這種行動特別稱為海上攔阻(maritime interdiction)。

應用 *drug interdiction* 毒品查禁
illegal migrant interdiction 非法移民查禁

internal waters		內水

Hot pursuit must be commenced when the foreign ship is within the **internal waters**, the archipelagic waters, the territorial sea or the contiguous zone of the pursuing State. 緊追(hot pursuit)必須是在該外國船隻在追逐國的內水、群島水域、領海或鄰接區內的時候開始。

IUU fishing		非法、未報告及未受規範捕魚 (*illegal, unreported, unregulated fishing*)

junior officer		見習三副(見習船副)
landlocked [ˋlænd‚lɑkt]	*adj.*	為陸地所包圍的，內陸的 In the exclusive economic zone, all States, whether coastal or **land-locked**, enjoy the freedoms of navigation. 在專屬經濟區內，所有國家不論是沿海國或內陸國，都享有航行自由。
latitude [ˋlætə‚tjud]	*n.*	緯度
lifeboat [ˋlaɪf‚bot]	*n.*	救生艇，救生船(又稱 *survival craft*)
lifebuoy [ˋlaɪfbɔɪ]	*n.*	救生圈，救生帶
lifejacket [ˋlaɪfdʒækɪt]	*n.*	救生衣
lifeline [ˋlaɪf‚laɪn]	*n.*	救生索
liferaft [ˋlaɪf‚ræft]	*n.*	橡皮製救生艇
lifesaving [ˋlaɪf‚sevɪŋ]	*adj.*	救命(用)的 The laws and regulations require vessels to carry **lifesaving** equipment and rescue equipment on board. 法規要求船隻要攜帶船上救生設備及救援設備。
	n.	救生(術)
line throwing apparatus		拋繩設備
litter [ˋlɪtə]	*n.*	擔架
LKP	*abbr.*	最後所知地點 *Last Know Position* The Coast Guard was requested to proceed to the **LKP** (Lat 30° 42.95 N Lo 081° 28.75 W.) to find the PIW. 海巡受請求前往最後所知地點尋找落水者。 *PIW* 落水者(*People In Water*)
longitude [ˋlɑndʒə‚tjud]	*n.*	經度
low-water line		低潮線
marine [məˋrin]	*n.* *adj.*	海軍陸戰隊隊員 海的，海生的，船舶的，航海的，海運的，海事的 應用 *marine accident* 海上意外事件 *marine firefighter* 海上消防員

marine patrol 海上巡邏
marine police 海上警察
marine pollutant 海洋汙染源，海洋汙染物
marine pollution 海洋汙染
marine safety 海上安全

---

mariner [ˋmærənɚ]	*n.*	水手，船員

---

maritime [ˋmærə,taɪm]	*adj.* 應用	海的，海事的，航海的，與船舶有關的 *illegal maritime activity* 非法海上活動 *International Maritime Organization* 國際海事組織 *International maritime Rescue Federation* 國際海上救援聯盟 *maritime crime* 海上犯罪 *maritime drug smuggling* 海上毒品走私 *maritime drug trafficking* 海上毒品非法交易 *maritime human trafficking* 海上人口販運 *maritime interdiction* 海上攔阻 *maritime kidnapping for ransom* 海上綁架勒贖 *maritime law enforcement agency* 海洋執法機關 *maritime law* 海洋法 *maritime navigation* 海上航行 *maritime piracy* 海上強盜 *maritime rescue organization* 海上救援組織 *maritime search and rescue* 海上搜救 *maritime smuggling of migrant* 海上移民偷渡 *maritime surveillance* 海上偵查 *maritime traffic* 海上交通 *maritime zone* 海洋地帶(即：*territorial sea* 領海、*contiguous zone* 鄰接區、*exclusive economic zone* 專屬經濟海域、*continental shelf* 大陸棚及 *high seas* 公海)

---

master [ˋmæstɚ]	*n.*	船長 (或稱 *captain*) The **master** decided to drop anchor in the bay to escape the storm. 船長決定拋錨將船停泊在港灣中，以躲避暴風雨。 The **master** attempted to anchor but the surf was too rough and the anchors would not hold. 船長決定拋錨將船固定，但是海浪波濤洶湧，船錨無法固定。 The **master** was unable to keep the boat afloat, so he made

a distress call to the Coast Guard before abandoning their vessel. 船長無法讓船浮著，所以棄船之前，向海巡發出了海難訊號。

mayday [`me,de]	*n.*	【無線電】救難信號，緊急求救 **MAYDAY** (three times) 「緊急求救(MAYDAY 三次) This is SWAMPER (three times). I am a 46 foot cabin cruiser, white hull – MMSI 366123456. 這是 SWAMPER 號(三次)----我是一艘 46 呎有艙房的汽艇，白色船殼—MMSI 366123456。 My position is Lat 30˚ 42.95 N Lo81˚ 28.75 W. 我的位置是緯度 30、北 42.95、經度 81、西 28.75。 Three persons on board. I lost power and the seas are getting rough. Request assistance – Over. 船上有三人，我失去動力，而海浪愈來愈洶湧，請求協助，結束。
moor [mʊr]	*vt.*	使停泊，繫泊，(用纜、索等)固定，繫住 Wind and current in the marine environment will cause ships to move or drift over time unless they **are moored**, anchored or aground. 海上環境的風與海流會導致船隻隨著時間而移動或漂流，除非是有纜繩固定、下錨停泊或擱淺。
multi-purpose ship		多功能船
nautical [`nɔtək!]	*adj.*	海上的，船員的，船舶的，航海的 Every State has the right to establish the breadth of its territorial sea up to a limit not exceeding 12 **nautical miles**. 每一個國家有權確定其領海的寬度，直至低潮基線量起不超過 12 海里的界限為止。 The contiguous zone may not extend beyond 24 **nautical miles** from the baselines. 鄰接區不得超過從測算領海寬度的基線量起 24 海浬。 The exclusive economic zone shall not extend beyond 200 **nautical miles** from the baselines. 專屬經濟區從測算領海寬度的基線量起，不應超過 200 海里。
navigation [,nævə`geʃən]	*n.*	航海，航空，航行，航運，水上運輸
O.S.	*abbr.*	水手 ordinary seaman
offshore [`ɔf`ʃor]	*adj.*	離岸的，向海的 Many traffickers shipped their drugs to other countries. To avoid detection and arrest, a number of **offshore island**

	adv.	have been used by smugglers to operate their illegal business. 許多私梟將毒品用船運到別的國家。為了避免被查獲，許多外島被走私者用來進行他們的非法生意。 離岸，向海面 Coast Guard officials said that their patrol vessels hoisted the survivors from the drifting liferaft after the cruise sank 150 nautical miles **offshore**. 海巡官員表示，郵輪在離岸 150 海里翻覆之後，海巡的巡邏艇從漂流的救生筏拉上了生還者。
oil tanker		油輪
on board		上船，上飛機，上火車，在船上，在飛機上，在火車上 In general, officers of a coastal State may at any time **go on board of** any vessel subject to the jurisdiction. 通常，沿海國的官員得於任何時間登上其管轄內的任何船隻。 On the high seas, or in any other place outside the jurisdiction of any State, every State may seize a pirate ship or aircraft, or a ship or aircraft taken by piracy and under the control of pirates, and arrest the persons and seize the property **on board**. 在公海上或在任何國家管轄範圍以外的任何其他地方，每個國家得扣押海盜船舶或飛機或為海盜所奪取並在海盜控制下的船舶或飛機，並逮捕其上人員並扣押其上財物。 Transshipment means the unloading of fishery products **on board** a fishing vessel to another fishing vessel. 轉載 (transshipment)是指將某艘漁船上的漁獲卸到另一艘漁船。
overboard [`ovɚ,bord]	*adv.*	向船外，(自船上)落水 If you fall **overboard**, it is suggested that you should get out of the water no matter what the weather condition is. 如果你跌到船外，建議你應開離水裡，不管天氣狀況如何。
overdue [`ovɚ`dju]	*adj.*	過期的，遲到的，未兌的 Emergency phase comprise three phrases: i.e. uncertainty phase, alert phase and distress phase. An UNCERTAINTY phase exists when a vessel has been reported **overdue** at its destination 緊急階段包括三個階段，即「不確定階段」、「警示階段」及「海難階段」。「不確定階段」的存在，是當船隻據報超過時間仍未抵達目的地。
overfishing	*n.*	(魚的)過度捕撈，漁撈過度

[ˌovəˈfɪʃɪŋ]		IUU fishing will result in **overfishing** and rapid depletion of fish stocks. 「非法、未報告及未受規範捕魚(IUU fishing)」會導致過度捕撈及讓漁業資源快速枯竭。
overflight	*n.*	(飛機的)飛越領空
[ˋovɚˌflaɪt]		In the exclusive economic zone, all States, whether coastal or land-locked, enjoy the freedoms of navigation and **overflight**. 在專屬經濟區內,所有國家不論為沿海國或內陸國,都享有航行和飛越的自由。
PFD	*abbr.*	個人漂浮(救生)裝置 *personal flotation device*
pilot	*n.*	(船舶的)領航員,舵手,(飛機等的)駕駛員,飛行員
[ˋpaɪlət]		*pilot ladder* 引水人領港梯
piracy		海盜行為,剽竊,著作權侵害,盜印
[ˋpaɪrəsɪ]		
pirate ship		海盜船
PIW	*abbr.*	落水者 People In Water
		The Coast Guard was requested to proceed to the LKP (Lat 30° 42.95 N Lo 081° 28.75 W.) to find the **PIW**. 海巡受請求前往最後所知地點尋找落水者。
		LKP 最後所知地點(*Last Know Position*)
pleasure craft		休閒船
plunge	*vt.*	使投入,將……插入,將……刺進,使突然前傾
[plʌndʒ]	*vi.*	投(入),跳(入),陷(入) *plunge into*
		Coast Guard's Dive Team soon **plunged into** the waters to search for the missing swimmer. 海巡的潛水隊很快地跳入海中尋找這名失蹤的泳客。
poach	*vt.*	(侵入他人地界)偷獵(或偷捕),偷獵,偷捕[(+from)]
[potʃ]	*vi.*	侵入他人地界,偷獵,偷捕[(+on)]
		Coast Guard frequently spots and intercepts fishing vessels suspected of **poaching** fish within its waters or offshore inside the exclusive economic zone. 海巡經常會在海域內或外海在經濟海域內,發現與攔截到疑似越界捕魚的漁船。
		The U.S. Coast Guard has seized a Mexican fishing boat and detained its five crewmembers in a **poaching investigation** off the Gulf Coast waters of South Texas. 美國海巡在德州南部的墨西哥灣水域進行的一件越界捕魚調查案中,查扣一艘墨西哥漁船,並留置該船的 5 名船員。
POC	*abbr.*	涵蓋機率 *probability of containment*

POD	*abbr.*	偵測機率 probability of detection
pollutant [pə`lutənt]	*n.*	汙染物，汙染源
port [port]	*n.* 應用	港，港市，口岸機場，航空站避風港，避難場所 *port side* 左舷 (*starboard side* 右舷；*the bow* 船頭；*the stern* 船尾)
Port Police		港警(也稱 Harbor Police)
portside [`port,saɪd]	*n.* *adj.*	左舷，港口地區 左邊的，碼頭區的
POS	*abbr.*	成功機率 probability of success
public vessel		公務船
quartermaster [`kwɔrtɚ,mæstɚ]	*n.*	舵手，舵工 The captain ordered the **quartermaster** to send out a signal. 船長命令舵手發出信號。
rescue		*rescue basket* 救生吊籃 *Rescue Coordination Center* 搜救協調中心 *rescue litter* 救生擔架 *rescue net* 救生網 *rescue seat* 救生吊座 *rescue sling* 救生吊索 *rescue swimmer* 游泳救生員
right of visit		登臨權
rough [rʌf]	*adj.*	暴風雨的，狂暴的，劇烈的 The ship sailed in **rough seas**. 這艘船在波濤洶湧的海面行駛。 Two men have died and one man has been rescued after their small fishing boat hit rocks and capsized in **rough seas** off Botany Bay on Sunday afternoon. 星期日下午，一艘小船在 Botany 灣外洶湧的海面撞到岩石而翻覆之後，其上的兩名男子死亡，另一人被救起。
rowboat [`ro,bot]	*n.*	划艇
SAR	*abbr.*	搜救(search and rescue；海巡常用之縮寫) Coast Guard is usually designated as the maritime and aeronautical **SAR** Coordinator for the waters. Rescue Coordination Center (RCC) is internationally recognized as the center with the responsibility to promote efficient organization of SAR services and to coordinate the conduct of SAR operations within a **search and rescue** region. 海

巡通常被指定為海域上的海空搜救協調者，搜救協調中心(RCC)是國際認可的中心，負有責任促進搜救服務的有效組成，並協調搜救區域內的搜救行動之進行。

sea [si]	n.	海

The ship sailed in **rough seas**. 這艘船在波濤洶湧的海面行駛。

On the **high seas**, every State may seize a pirate ship and arrest the persons on board. 在公海上，每一個國家都可以扣押海盜船舶並逮捕船上的人員。

Piracy means robbery, kidnapping, or other criminal violence committed **at sea**. 海盜罪是指在海上所犯的強盜、綁架或其它犯罪暴力。

I am **all at sea**. I have no idea how to do it. 我茫然不知所措，我不知道怎樣做。

應用　*freedom of the high sea*s 公海自由原則
high seas 公海
sea law 海事法(或 *admiralty law*)
territorial sea 領海
go to sea 做水手

seabed [`si,bɛd]	n.	海底，海床
seafarer [`si,fɛrɚ]	n.	船員，航海家
seaward [`siwɚd]	adv.	朝海，向海

Coast Guard is empowered to stop, board, and search vessels located **seaward** of 12 miles from shore. 海巡被授權對於位在海岸向外 12 海里的船隻進行攔停、登船及蒐查。

Second Assistant Engineer	二管輪(或 *Third Engineer*)
second officer	二副 *second mate*
set sail	啟航

The fishing boat **set sail** from the port of Miami. 這艘漁船從邁阿密港出航。

Shiprider Agreement	登船執法人員協定

The United States has successful **shiprider agreements** with many Pacific Island nations. Such agreements provide authorization to stop, board, and search vessels suspected of illegal activities. 美國與許多太平洋島國有成功的「登

		船執法人員協定」，此種協定提供了攔阻、登上及搜索可疑有非法活動的船隻的權限。
shipyard [`ʃɪp,jɑrd]	n.	造船廠，修船廠，船塢
shoreline [`ʃorlaɪn]	n.	海岸線，岸線地帶
starboard [`stɑrbord]	n. adj.	(船、飛機的)右舷 右舷的 應用 (port side 左舷；starboard side 右舷；the bow 船頭；the stern 船尾)
stateless vessel		無國籍船隻
stern [stɜn]	n.	船尾，(物體的)尾部 應用 末端 (port side 左舷；starboard side 右舷； the stern 船尾)
strand [strænd]	vt.	使……擱淺，使……受困 Coast Guard said that these migrants **were stranded** at sea for nearly a month. They **were stranded** at sea for 4 weeks without water and food. 海巡說，這些移民受困在海上已經將近一個月，她們困在海上四個星期沒有飲水與食物。
submerge [səb`mɝdʒ]	vi.	潛入水中，淹沒 Records show that a sinking, even in the worst cases, usually requires at least 15 to 30 minutes for the vessel to fully **submerge**. 紀錄顯示，船隻沉沒即使是最慘的情況，至少也要 15 至 30 分鐘船才會完全淹沒。
submersion [səb`mɝːʃn]	n.	沉入水中(完全在水中的狀態) **Submersion** is different from immersion. **Submersion** means a state of being completely in the water, including one's head. Immersion means that the person is still able to keep his or her head out of water. 沉入水中(submersion)與泡在水中(immersion) 是完全不同的，沉入水中(submersion)是指一個完全在水中的狀態，包括頭部；泡在水中(immersion)是指該人還能將頭保持在水面上。
subsoil [`sʌb,sɔɪl]	n.	下層土，底土
surf [sɝf]	n.	(沖擊岩石、海岸的)碎浪，海浪，浪花 The master attempted to anchor but the **surf** was too rough and the anchors would not hold. 船長決定拋錨將

船固定，但是海浪波濤洶湧，船錨無法固定。

In summer, many people **are surfing** at the beach. 夏天時，很多人在海邊衝浪。

surface enforcement vessel		執法船
tanker [`tæŋkɚ]	*n.*	運輸船
territorial sea		領海
Third Assistant Engineer		三管輪(或 *Fourth Engineer*)
third officer		三副(資淺船副)
tide [taɪd]	*n.*	潮，潮汐，潮水
transship [træns`ʃɪp]	*vt.*	把……轉載於另一船(或另一運輸工具)，換船，換運輸工具

Reports indicate that reefers are also used to **transship** illegal and profitable items at sea (include lost/stolen vehicles and outboard engines, cigarettes, timber, oil, fish, gravel, agricultural products, etc.) 研究顯示，冷凍船同時也被用來在海上轉載非法及有利潤的項目(包括失竊的車輛及船外引擎、香菸、木材、油品、漁獲、砂礫，農產品等)。

transshipment [træns`ʃɪpmənt]	*n.*	轉載，中轉，轉運，轉車

Because **transshipments** often take place in remote locations, it is difficult to monitor **transshipment at sea**. 因為轉載經常發生在遙遠的地方，要監控海上轉載是困難的。

Many costal states are experiencing increased use of their maritime zones for the **transshipment** of drugs. 許多沿海國家遇到越來越多利用海上作為毒品轉載。

應用 *illegal transshipment at sea* 非法海上轉載

trawler [`trɔlɚ]	*n.*	拖網漁船
tugboat [`tʌg,bot]	*n.*	拖船 (或稱 tug)
UNCLOS	*abbr.*	聯合國海洋法公約 United Nations Convention on the Law of the Sea
unload [ʌn`lod]	*vt.*	從……卸下貨物，卸(貨)，卸(客)

Sometimes, pirate fishing vessels would transship their

catches to reefers. The reefers then return to port to **unload** their catches. 有時，偷捕的漁船會將魚獲轉載到冷凍船，然後冷凍船回到港口卸下魚獲。

Vice Admiral		副司令
vital sign		生命跡象
VMS	*abbr.*	漁船船位監控系統 *Vessel Monitoring System*
voyage [`vɔɪɪdʒ]	*n.*	航海，航行，乘船旅遊
warship [`wɔr,ʃɪp]	*n.*	軍艦，艦艇
water craft		船隻
water police		水上警察
waterfront [`wɔtɚ,frʌnt]	*n.* *adj.*	水邊，灘，(城市中的)濱水區 濱水區的
waters [`wɔtɚs]	*n.* 應用	海域 *adjacent waters* 緊鄰的水域 *archipelagic waters* 群島水域 *disputed waters* 爭議水域 *internal waters* 內水 *international waters* 國際水域 *territorial waters* 領海
waterway [`wɔtɚ,we]	*n.*	水路，航道
wave [wev]	*n.* 應用	浪 *freak waves* 瘋狗浪(或稱 *rogue waves*)
WCPFC	*abbr.*	中西太平洋漁業委員會 *Western and Central Pacific Fisheries Commission*

通訊用詞	
ACKNOWLEDGE	【海上通訊用語】讓我知道你已經收到訊息並且了解
AFFIRM	【海上通訊用語】是的/確認
CLEARED	【海上通訊用語】已清除/准予依據指定條件進行
CONFIRM	【海上通訊用語】確認(有無收到訊息)
CORRECTION	【海上通訊用語】更正
DISREGARD	【海上通訊用語】當作通訊沒傳，勿予理會
GO AHEAD	【海上通訊用語】請說
I READ BACK	【海上通訊用語】我覆誦

MAYDAY	【無線電救難信號】求救求救，緊急求救
OUT	【海上通訊用語】(通訊中，不需對方回覆的)結束
OVER	【海上通訊用語】(通訊中，期待對方回覆)結束
PAN-PAN	【海上通訊用語】緊急情況
READ BACK	【海上通訊用語】請覆誦
ROGER	【海上通訊用語】收到
STANDBY	【海上通訊用語】請稍候

消防相關英文字彙

宗旨與任務

Mission Statement FEMA

FEMA's mission is to support our citizens and first responders to ensure that as a nation we work together to build, sustain and improve our capability to prepare for, protect against, respond to, recover from and mitigate all hazards.

「美國聯邦緊急應變總署(FEMA)」任務宗旨

「美國聯邦緊急應變總署(FEMA)」旨在援助民眾及初期應變者，確保我們作為一個國家，將會共同打拼，來建立、承擔，及增進我們對於所有災害在整備、對抗、回應、復原及減輕的能力。

Mission Statement FEMA

Mission Statement USFA

As an entity of the U.S. Department of Homeland Security's Federal Emergency Management Agency, the mission of the U.S. Fire Administration is to provide national leadership to foster a solid foundation for our fire and emergency services stakeholders in prevention, preparedness and response.

「美國聯邦消防署(USFA)」任務宗旨

作為美國國土安全部「美國聯邦緊急應變總署(FEMA)」的一個實體，「美國聯邦消防署(USFA)」旨在提供全國性的領導地位，以強化我們的消防及緊急應變之利害相關機構在預防、整備及回應方面的穩固基礎。

Mission Statement USFA

Mission Statement FDNY

As first responders to fires, public safety and medical emergencies, disasters and terrorist acts, FDNY protects the lives and property of New York City residents and visitors. The Department advances public safety through its fire prevention, investigation and education programs. The timely delivery of these services enables the FDNY to make significant contributions to the safety of New York City.

紐約市消防局任務宗旨

Mission Statement FDNY

身為火災、公共安全以及醫療急救、災難與恐怖行動的初期應變者，紐約市消防局將會保護紐約市民及訪客的生命與財產。本局透過火災的預防、調查及教育課程，來提升公共安全，這些服務的即時傳遞，讓紐約市消防局能對紐約市的安全，做出有意義的貢獻。

Mission Statement LAFD

Mission Statement LAFD

The Los Angeles Fire Department preserves life and property, promotes public safety and fosters economic growth through a commitment to prevention, preparedness, response and recovery as an all risk life safety response provider.

洛杉磯市消防局任務宗旨

洛杉磯市消防局以身為處理所有生命安全的應變者，承諾預防、整備、應變及復原，而保障生命與財產，提升公共安全，並促進經濟成長。

Emergency Management

Emergency management is also known as disaster management. According to U.S. FEMA, emergency management generally refers to activities associated with avoiding and responding to natural and human-caused hazards. Emergency management functions are grouped into four phases: Mitigation, Preparedness, Response, and Recovery.

應急管理

應急管理 (emergency management) 也稱災難管理 (disaster management)，依據「美國聯邦緊急應變總署 (FEMA)」，應急管理通常指與避免或處理天然及人為造成的災害有關的行動。應急管理的功能分為四個階段：減災 (Mitigation)、整備 (Preparedness)、應變 (Response) 及復原 (Recovery)。

Mitigation activities entail identifying risks and hazards to either substantially reduce or eliminate the impact of an incident through structural measures.

「減災」的作為需確認風險及危害，透過組織性的措施，去實質地降低或排除事件的衝擊。

Preparedness is distinct from mitigation because rather

Emergency Management

than focusing on eliminating or reducing risks, the general focus of preparedness is to enhance the capacity to respond to an incident by taking steps to ensure personnel and entities are capable of responding to a wide range of potential incidents. Preparedness activities may include: training; planning; procuring resources such as food, water and medication stockpiles; intelligence and surveillance activities to identify potential threats; and exercising to assure the adequacy of planning efforts and the use of after-action reports to improve emergency response plans.

「整備」有別於減災，因為，整備的主要重點在於，經由採取一些確保人員及機關有能力回應各式各樣可能事件的步驟，來提升回應事件的能力，而非著重於排除或降低風險。整備作為包括：訓練；計畫；取得資源，例如食物、飲水及醫療儲備物資；情資與偵監作為，以確認潛在的威脅；以及進行操練以確保計畫的充分性，並使用「事後報告」來改進緊急應變計畫。

Response activities are comprised of the immediate actions to save lives, protect property and the environment, and meet basic human needs. Response involves the execution of emergency plans and related actions, and may include: evacuating victims; establishment of incident command operations; and deployment of response teams, medical stockpiles, and other assets.

「應變」作為包括拯救性命、保護財產與環境，以及滿足基本人性需求之立即行動。應變涉及緊急計畫與相關行動的執行，並可能包括：撤離受害人、建立事件指揮行動，以及布署應變小組、醫療儲備物資及其他財物。

Recovery activities are intended to restore essential services and repair damages caused by the event. Recovery activities may include: the reconstitution of government operations and services (e.g., emergency services, public safety, and schools); housing and services for displaced families and individuals; and replenishment of stockpiles.

「復原」作為的目的是要重建必要的服務，及修復事

件所造成的損害，復原作為包括：恢復政府的運作及服務(例如緊急服務、公共安全及學校)；安置及服務被迫遷離的家庭及個人；以及重新補足儲備物資。

Natural disaster 天然災害	
autoignition	[ɔto ɪg`nɪʃən]自燃
backdraft	[`bæk,dræft]爆燃
backfire	[`bæk`faɪr]逆火
bonfire	[`bɑn,faɪr]營火
cyclone	[`saɪklon] 【氣】氣旋[U]，旋風，暴風 【說明】Cyclone, tropical cyclone and typhoon are different names for the same phenomenon. In the Atlantic and Northeast Pacific, the term "hurricane" is used; in the Northwest Pacific it is referred to as a "typhoon" and "cyclones" occur in the South Pacific and Indian Ocean. 氣旋、熱帶氣旋及颱風是相同現象的不同名稱。在大西洋及東北太平洋，使用的是 hurricane 這個字，在西北太平洋，用的是 typhoon 這個字，而 cyclone 則是發生在南太平洋及印度洋。
debris	[də`bri]殘骸，破瓦殘礫，【地】岩層【地】岩層
debris flow	[də`bri] [flo] 【地】岩屑流動，土石流
drought	[draʊt] 乾旱，旱災
earthquake	[`ɝθ,kwek] 地震
flashover	[`flæʃ,ovɚ]閃燃【電】閃絡
flood	[flʌd]洪水，水災，漲潮，滿潮 / flash floods 豪雨成災 / floodwater 洪水
fooding	[`flʌdɪŋ] 洪水，水災，漲潮，滿潮 / flash floods 豪雨成災 / flash flooding 豪雨成災 / river flooding 河流泛濫
emission	[ɪ`mɪʃən]放射，散發 / gas emission 氣體外洩
global warming	[`globl] [`wɔrmɪŋ] 地球暖化
hail	[hel] 雹，冰雹[U]
heatwave	[`hitwev] 【氣】熱浪，奇熱時期
hurricane	[`hɝɪ,ken] 颶風，暴風雨
landslide	[`lænd,slaɪd] 山崩，滑坡
lightening	[`laɪtnɪŋ] 閃電，電光
magnitude	[`mægnə,tjud]【地】震級 / a magnitude 5.0 earthquake 震級為 5 級的地震 / magnitude scale (surface magnitude) 震級規模/ magnitude 7.2 on the Richter scale 芮式規模 7.2

mudslide	[`mʌd,slaɪd]	土石流，塌方，山崩
overflow	[,ovə`flo]	泛濫，滿水溢出
rainfall	[`ren,fɔl]	降雨，下雨，降雨量
sinkhole	[`sɪŋk,hol]	天坑，沉洞
storm	[stɔrm] 暴風雨 / thunderstorm [`θʌndə,stɔrm] 大雷雨 [C] / indstorm [`wɪnd,stɔrm] 暴風 / firestorm [`faɪr,stɔrm] 風暴性大火 / dust storm 沙塵暴 / water shortage 缺水	
tornado	[tɔr`nedo]	龍捲風，旋風，颶風
tsunami	[tsu`nɑmi]	（源自日語）海嘯，地震海嘯
typhoon	[taɪ`fun]	颱風[C]
wildfire	[`waɪld,faɪr]	大火災，不易撲滅的野火
Bee sting	[bi stɪŋ]	蜂螫

常見化學與氣體		
acetone	[`æsə,ton]	丙酮
alcohol	[`ælkə,hɔl]	酒精，醇
ammonia	[ə`monjə]	氨
benzene	[`bɛnzin]	苯
butane	[bju`ten]	丁烷
carbon dioxide	[`kɑrbən] [daɪ`ɑksaɪd]	二氧化碳
carbon monoxide	[`kɑrbən][mɑn`ɑksaɪd]	一氧化碳
carbon tetrachloride	[`kɑrbən][,tɛtrə`klɔraɪd]	四氯化碳
chlorine	[`klorin]	氯氣
esetylene	[ə`sɛtəlin]	乙炔
ethane	[`ɛθen]	乙烷
formaldehyde	[fɔr`mældə,haɪd]	甲醛
gas	[gæs]	氣體【軍】毒氣，毒瓦斯【美】【口】汽油
gasoline	[`gæsə,lin]	汽油
hydrocarbon	[,haɪdrə`kɑrbən]	碳氫化合物
hydrogen	[`haɪdrədʒən]	氫氣
hydrogen chloride	[`haɪdrədʒən] [`klɔraɪd]	氯化氫
hydrogen cyanide	[`haɪdrədʒən] [`saɪə,naɪd]	氰化氫
mercury	[`mɝkjərɪ]	汞
methane	[`mɛθen]	甲烷
methanol	[`mɛθə,nol]	甲醇
oxygen	[`ɑksədʒən]	氧，氧氣

petroleum	[pə`trolɪəm] 石油
propane	[`propen] 丙烷
toluene	[`tɑljʊ,in] 甲苯
fume	[fjum]（有害，濃烈，或難聞的）煙，氣，汽 / poisonous fumes 有毒煙氣 / noxious fumes 有毒煙氣
toxic	[`tɑksɪk]毒(性)的，有毒的 / toxic gases 有害氣體
noxious	[`nɑkʃəs]有害的，有毒的 / noxious gas 有毒氣體
lithium battery	[lɪθiəm]鋰電池
Hydrofluoric acid	[ˌhaɪdrəfluˈɒrɪk] 氫氟酸

消防相關設備	
axe	[æks] 斧 / flat-head axe 消防斧
Halligan bar	三用撬棒
boot	[but] （長筒）靴
bulldozer	[`bʊl,dozə] 推土機
circuit	[`sɚkɪt]電路，回路，線路圖 / short circuit 短路 / circuit breaker 斷路器
combustible	[kəm`bʌstəb!] 可燃的 / combustible materials 可燃物 / combustible liquid 可燃液體
combustion	[kəm`bʌstʃən]燃燒 / smoldering combustion 悶燒 / combustion rate 燃燒率
compass	[`kʌmpəs] 羅盤，指南針[C]
crane	[kren] 起重機，吊車
cushion	[`kʊʃən] 墊子，墊狀物，緩衝器，減震墊 / rescue air cushion 救生氣墊
cutter	[`kʌtɚ] 刀具，切割機，裁剪機 / acetylene cutter 乙炔切割器 / disk cutter 圓盤切割器
dry suit	[draɪ] [sut] 乾式潛水衣
dump truck	[dʌmp] [trʌk] 傾卸大卡車
engine	[`ɛndʒən] 消防車，救火車
excavator	[`ɛkskə,vetɚ] 挖掘機
fireboat	[`faɪr,bot] 救火船，消防船
firehouse	[`faɪr,haʊs] 消防站(屋) / engine house 消防站(屋) / fire station 消防站 / fire hall 消防站(屋)
fireproof	[`faɪr`pruf] 防火的，耐火的
flashlight	[`flæʃ,laɪt] 照明燈，【美】手電筒
footwear	[`fʊt,wɛr] （總稱）鞋類

fork	[fɔrk] 叉，耙
fuel	[`fjʊəl]燃料[C][U]
glove	[glʌv] 手套
handsaw	[`hænd,sɔ] 手鋸
headlight	[`hɛd,laɪt]（消防，醫生等用的）頭燈，額燈
helicopter	[`hɛlɪkɑptə]直升飛機
helmet	[`hɛlmɪt] 盔，頭盔，鋼盔，帽盔，安全帽
hose	[hoz]軟管，水龍帶[C] / fire hose 消防水帶
hovercraft	[`hʌvə,kræft]（水陸兩用）氣墊船
hydrant	[`haɪdrənt] 消防栓
ladder	[`lædə] 梯子 / aerial ladder 雲梯 / A-frame ladder　A 型梯 / escape ladder 逃生梯 / extension ladder 伸縮梯 / folding ladder 摺疊梯 / hook ladder 掛鉤梯
lifeboat	[`laɪf,bot]救生艇，救生船(又稱 survival craft)
lifebuoy	[`laɪfbɔɪ] 救生圈，救生帶
lifejacket	[`laɪfdʒækɪt] 救生衣
lifeline	[`laɪf,laɪn] 救生索
liferaft	[`laɪf,ræft] 橡皮製救生艇
rope gun	[roʊp gʌn] 拋繩槍
stretcher	[`stretʃ.ə] 擔架
loader	[`lodə] 山貓，堆高機 (front end loader)
maul	[mɔl] 大木槌，楔頭大錘[C]
nozzle	[`nɑz!] 瞄子，嘴，管嘴，噴嘴
outfit	[`aʊt,fɪt] 全套裝備，
pike pole	[paɪk] [pol] 消防勾
pipeline	[`paɪp,laɪn] 輸送導管
pumper	[`pʌmpə] 抽水機，消防車
rope	[rop] 繩，索[C][U] / guide rope 導向繩
sandbag	[`sænd,bæg]沙袋，沙包
saw	[sɔ] 鋸子，鋸條 / chain saw 鏈鋸 / handsaw 手鋸 / power saw 電鋸
shelter	[`ʃɛltə] 躲避處，避難所，庇護
shovel	[`ʃʌv!] 鏟子，鐵鍬
siren	[`saɪrən] 汽笛，警報器
strap	[stræp]帶子，皮帶，用帶捆綁（或束住），繃帶包紮
system	automatic dry standpipe system　自動乾式立管系統 automatic wet standpipe system　自動濕式立管系統 automatic sprinkler system　自動灑水系統

emergency power system 緊急電力系統

fire alarm system 火災警報系統

fire detection system 火災偵測系統

fire hydrant system 消防栓系統

fire protection system 防火系統

sprinkler system 灑水系統

standpipe system 給水立管系統

tow truck	[to] [trʌk] 【美】拖吊車
ventilation	[ˌvɛntl̩ˋeʃən] (消防) 排煙
ventilator	[ˋvɛntl̩ˌetɚ] (消防) 排煙器
voltage	[ˋvoltɪdʒ]電壓，伏特數[U][C]
wire	[waɪr]電纜，電線，電話線[C][U]

EMT 裝備、急救常見物品、用品	
adhesive bandage	有黏性繃帶 / non-adhesive bandage 無黏性繃帶
side effect	副作用
alcohol	[ˋælkəˌhɔl]酒精，【化】醇
anti-bacterial ointment	[ˌæntɪbækˋtɪrɪəl] [ˋɔɪntmənt] 抗細菌藥膏
bandage	[ˋbændɪdʒ] 繃帶[C]
bed sheet	被單
blanket	[ˋblæŋkɪt]毛毯，毯子
blood pressure meter	[blʌd preʃ.ɚ miţɚ] 血壓計
cap	[kæp] 帽，罩，套
catheter	[ˋkæθɪtɚ]導管【醫】導尿管，尿液管，導管
cervical	[ˋsɝvɪkl̩]頸部的，子宮頸的 / cervical collar 頸椎頸圈 / cervical spine 頸椎，脊柱頸段
cold pack	【醫】冰袋，冷毛巾，冷裹用品
collar	[ˋkɑlɚ]頸圈，項圈，護肩
cutting blade	刀片
disinfection	[ˌdɪsɪnˋfɛkʃən]消毒
dressing	[ˋdrɛsɪŋ] 紗布，包紮用品 / sterile dressing 消毒紗布
drugstore	[ˋdrʌgˌstor]藥房
forceps	[ˋfɔrsəps] （醫用）鑷子，鉗子
gauze	[gɔz] 薄紗，網紗，（醫用）紗布
glove	[glʌv] 手套

gown	[gaʊn]（醫生等穿的）手術衣
Heimlich	[`haɪmlɪk]哈姆立克急救法(Heimlich maneuver)
hydrogen peroxide	[`haɪdrədʒən][pə`rɑksaɪd]過氧化氫(俗稱雙氧水)
incubator	[`ɪnkjə,betə]早產兒保育器 infant incubator 嬰兒保溫箱
infant	infant incubator 嬰兒保溫箱 / infant warmer 嬰兒保溫台(器) (如剛出生嬰兒照光用 / infant[`ɪnfənt]嬰兒
infusion	[ɪn`fjuʒən]注入，灌入
injection	[ɪn`dʒɛkʃən]注射[C][U]，注射劑，注射液[C]
intravenous	[,ɪntrə`vinəs]注入靜脈的（簡稱 IV）； IV fluid 靜脈點滴輸液；IV injection 靜脈注射；IV pump 靜脈輸注幫浦； /IV pump 靜脈輸注幫浦
iodine	[`aɪə,daɪn] 碘，碘酒 / iodine swab 碘酒棉花棒
irrigation	[,ɪrə`geʃən] 沖洗 / water irrigation 用水沖洗
medical tape	醫用膠帶
medication	[,mɛdɪ`keʃən]藥物，藥物治療
oxygen	[`ɑksədʒən] 氧，氧氣
paper towel	紙巾
patch	[pætʃ]（護傷用的）膏藥，裹傷布，(保護病傷眼睛用的）眼罩
pharmacist	[`farməsɪst]製藥者，藥劑師，藥商
pharmacy	[`farməsɪ]藥房，配藥學
Pregnant	[`prɛgnənt] 懷孕的，懷胎的
prescription	[prɪ`skrɪpʃən]處方，藥方，處方上開的藥 / prescription drug 處方藥
pump	[pʌmp]泵，唧筒
respirator	[`rɛspə,retə]人工呼吸機，口罩
scissors	[`sɪzəz] 剪刀
solution	[sə`luʃən]溶液，溶劑[C][U]
splint	[splɪnt]【醫】夾板
sponge	[spʌndʒ]消毒紗布，藥棉[C][U]
steroid	[`stɪrɔɪd] 類固醇
stethoscope	[`stɛθə,skop] 聽診器
symptom	[`sɪmptəm]症狀，徵候，徵兆，表徵
tablet	[`tæblɪt] (藥)片，(藥)錠
temperature	[`tɛmprətʃə]溫度，氣溫[C][U] 體溫[C][U]
thermometer	[θə`mɑmətə]溫度計，寒暑表 / Centigrade [`sɛntə,gred] 攝氏溫度/ Fahrenheit [`færən,haɪt]華氏溫度計，華氏溫標
tourniquet	[`tʊrnɪ,kɛt] 【醫】止血帶，壓脈器，壓血帶
towelette	[,taʊə`lɛt] 濕巾紙

untrasound	[`ʌltrə,saʊnd]超音波
urine	[`jʊrɪn]尿[U]
vitamin	[`vaɪtəmɪn]維他命，維生素
wheelchair	[`hwil`tʃɛr] 輪椅
wound pad	(貼傷口用的) 繃帶
paramedic	[,pærə`mɛdɪk]醫務輔助人員

In the U.S, paramedics provide advanced life support (ALS) in a pre-hospital setting to individuals during medical emergencies. Paramedics receive more advanced training and can perform some invasive procedures and give some medications under the supervision of a physician. 在美國，「醫務輔助人員(paramedic)」是緊急情況中，提供「高級救命術(ALS) 」給到院前的人。「醫務輔助人員(paramedic)」接受了更進階的訓練，並且，在醫生監督之下，可以執行侵入性的程序並給予藥物。

EMT 常見藥品	
acetaminophen	解熱鎮痛劑
amiodarone	心臟血管系統用藥／抗心律不整劑
aspirin	[`æspərɪn]阿斯匹靈，阿斯匹靈藥片，中樞神經系統用藥／解熱鎮痛劑
atropine	[`ætrəpin]末稍神經系統用藥／副交感神經抑制劑
dopamine	[`dopə,min]【生化】多巴胺，心臟血管系統用藥／低血壓及休克治療
epinephrine	[,ɛpə`nɛfrɪn]腎上腺素，心臟血管系統用藥／低血壓及休克治療
flumazenil	代謝性藥物／解毒劑
glucagon	[`glukə,gɑn]胰高血糖激素，高血糖因子
glucose	[`glukos]葡萄糖
heparin	[`hɛpərɪn]肝素，肝磷脂（肝臟中防止血液凝固的物質）血液系統用藥／抗凝血劑血栓溶解劑
insulin	[`ɪnsəlɪn]胰島素，代謝性藥物／降血糖劑
morphine	[`mɔrfin]嗎啡
nicotine	[`nɪkə,tin]菸鹼，尼古丁
nitroglycerin	[`naɪtrə`glɪsərɪn]硝化甘油，心臟血管系統用藥／抗狹心症藥物
norepinephrine	[,nɔrɛpə`nɛfrɪn]正腎上腺素，末稍神經系統用藥／擬交感神經劑
normal saline	[`nɔrml] [`selaɪn]生理食鹽水
steroid	[`stɪrɔɪd] 類固醇
transfusion	[træns`fjuʒən]輸血，輸液

virus	[`vaɪrəs]病毒，病毒感染

身體部位	
abdomen	[`æbdəmən] 腹部
ankle	[`æŋk!] 踝，足踝，踝關節
arm	[ɑrm] 手臂
back	[bæk] 背脊，背部
brain	[bren] 腦，腦袋，智力，頭腦
calf	[kæf] 小腿
cervical	[`sɝvɪk!] 頸部的，子宮頸的 / cervica l spine 頸椎，脊柱頸段
cheek	[tʃik] 面頰，臉頰，腮幫子
chest	[tʃɛst] 胸 / chest pain 心口痛，胸痛
chin	[tʃɪn] 下巴
elbow	[`ɛlbo] 肘 elbow joint 肘關節
extremity	[ɪk`strɛmətɪ] 手足，四肢[P] / extremity injuries 四肢傷害 / lower extremities 下肢 / upper extremities 上肢 / extremity fracture 四肢骨折
finger	[`fɪŋgɚ] 手指 nail 指甲 / thumb 大拇指 / index finger 食指 / middle finger 中指 / ring finger 無名指 / little finger 小指
foot	[fʊt] 腳，足
forehead	[`fɔr,hɛd] 額，前額
groin	[grɔɪn] 鼠蹊部，腹股溝
head	[hɛd] 頭
heel	[hil] 腳後跟
hip	[hɪp] 部臀部，屁股，髖部，髖關節
Joint	[dʒɔɪnt] 關節
knee	[ni] 膝蓋
kneecap	[`ni,kæp] 膝蓋骨
knuckle	[`nʌk!] 指（根）關節
leg	[lɛg] 腿，足，小腿
lip	[lɪp] 嘴唇
mouth	[maʊθ] 口，嘴
muscle	[`mʌs!] 肌，肌肉 / muscle cramps 肌肉痙攣 / muscle strain 肌肉拉傷
neck	[nɛk] 頸，脖子
nose	[noz] 鼻子 / nosebleeding [`noz,blid] 鼻出血
palm	[pɑm] 手掌，手心

pulse	[pʌls] 脈搏，脈的一次跳動
pulseless	[pʌlslɪs] 無脈動的
pelvis	[`pɛlvɪs] 骨盆
pupil	[`pjupl] 瞳孔 / dilated pupils 瞳孔放大
rib	[rɪb] 肋，肋骨
scar	[skɑr] 疤，傷痕
skeleton	[`skɛlətn] 骨骼，骸骨，【口】骨瘦如柴的人
sklin	[skɪn] 皮膚，皮
skull	[skʌl] 頭蓋骨，頭骨
temple	[`tɛmpl] 太陽穴
thigh	[θaɪ] 大腿
throat	[θrot] 喉嚨
toe	[to] 腳趾，足尖
tongue	[tʌŋ] 舌，舌頭
tooth	[tuθ] 牙齒
waist	[west] 腰，腰部

常見疼痛與症狀	
abdominal	[æb`dɑmənl]腹部的 / abdominal pain 腹痛
abortion	[ə`bɔrʃən] 流產，墮胎
abrasion	[ə`breʒən] 擦傷
acute	[ə`kjut] 嚴重的，尖銳的，敏銳的，劇烈的，激烈的，【醫】急性的 / acute myocardial infarction 急性心肌梗塞 / acute renal failure 急性腎衰竭
AIDS	愛滋病
allergen	[`ælə,dʒɛn]過敏原
allergic	[ə`lɜdʒɪk]過敏的 / allergic reaction 過敏反應
Alzheimer	[`ɑlts,haɪmə] 阿茲海默症，老年痴呆症
altitude sickness	高山症，又稱 acute mountain sickness (AMS)
Amnesia	[æm`niʒɪə] 記憶缺失，健忘（症）
Anemia	[ə`nimɪə] 貧血（症）
anesthesia	[,ænəs`θiʒə] 麻醉
anorexia	[,ænə`rɛksɪə] 食慾缺乏（症），厭食
anxiety	[æŋ`zaɪətɪ] 焦慮(壓力反應)
appendicitis	[ə,pɛndə`saɪtɪs] 闌尾炎，盲腸炎
arrest	[ə`rɛst] cardiac arrest 心跳停止，心臟停跳

arrhythmia	[ə`rɪθmɪə] 心律不整
asphyxiation	[æs,fɪksɪ`eʃən] 窒息
asthma	[`æzmə] 氣喘（病），哮喘
bacteria	[bæk`tɪərɪə] 細菌
bite	[baɪt] 咬，啃，叮，蜇，刺 / animal bite 動物咬傷 / ant bite 螞蟻咬傷 / dog bite 狗咬傷 / insect bite 昆蟲咬傷 / mosquito bite 蚊子叮咬 / snake bite 蛇咬傷
bleeding	[`blidɪŋ] 流血的，出血的 / Internal bleeding 內出血
blood	[blʌd] 血，血液 / blood glucose 血糖 / blood group 血型 / blood pressure 血壓 / blood serum 血清 / blood sugar 血糖 / red blood cell 紅血球 / white blood cell 白血球
breathing	[`briðɪŋ]呼吸 / breathing difficulty 呼吸困難
cancer	[`kænsɚ]癌，惡性腫瘤，癌症 / breast cancer 乳房癌 / cancer of the esophagus 食道癌 / cancer of the womb 子宮癌 / gastric cancer 胰臟癌 (cancer of the stomach) / liver cancer 肝癌 / lung cancer 肺癌 / oral cancer 口腔癌
cardiac	[`kɑrdɪ,æk]心臟的，心臟病的 / cardiac arrest 心跳停止 / cardiac disease 心臟疾病 / cardiac arrhythmia 心律不整 / cardiac dysrhythmia 心律不整 / irregular heartbeat 心律不整
cardiopulmonary	[,kɑrdɪo`pʌlmənərɪ]與心肺有關的 / cardiopulmonary arrest 心跳呼吸驟停 / cardiopulmonary resuscitation (心搏停止後的)心肺復甦術，簡稱 CPR
chest	chest pain 胸痛 / chest compression 胸部按壓
choke	[tʃok] 窒息，噎
chronic	[`krɑnɪk] （病）慢性的，（人）久病的 / chronic hepatitis 慢性肝炎
cold	[kold]傷風，感冒 / common cold 感冒 / Influenza 流行性感冒
coma	[`komə] 昏睡（狀態），昏迷
complication	[,kɑmplə`keʃən]併發症 / complication of diabetes 糖尿病併發症
concussion	[kən`kʌʃən] 腦震盪
congelation	[,kɑndʒə`leʃən] 凍傷，凍瘡
congenital	[kən`dʒɛnət!] 天生的，先天的 / congenital heart disease 先天性心臟疾病
conscious	[`kɑnʃəs]神志清醒的，有知覺的
consciousness	[`kɑnʃəsnɪs]意識，知覺
contagious	[kən`tedʒəs]接觸傳染性的 / contagious disease 傳染性疾病
convulsion	[kən`vʌlʃən]抽搐，驚厥
coordination	[ko`ɔrdn,eʃən] 協調 / loss of coordination 失去平衡

cough	[kɔf]咳嗽
Cramp	[kræmp]抽筋，痙攣，（腹部）絞痛 / muscle cramp 肌肉痛性痙攣
decompression sickness	[ˌdikəm`prɛʃən]減壓病，潛水伏病
dehydration	[ˌdihaɪ`dreʃən]脫水，乾燥，極度口渴
dementia	[dɪ`mɛnʃɪə] 失智症
Dengue fever	登革熱
depression	[dɪ`preʃn] 憂鬱症
diabetes	[ˌdaɪə`bitiz] 糖尿病
diabetic	[ˌdaɪə`bɛtɪk] 糖尿病患者，患糖尿病的
diarrhea	[ˌdaɪə`riə] 腹瀉
disease	[dɪ`ziz] 病，疾病 / infectious disease 傳染性疾病
dislocation	[ˌdɪslo`keʃən] 脫臼
disorder	[dɪs`ɔrdə]失調
dizziness	[`dɪzənɪs] 暈眩
dizzy	[`dɪzɪ] 頭暈目眩的
drowsiness	[`draʊzɪnɪs] 欲睡，睡意，困倦
drowsy	[`draʊzɪ] 昏昏欲睡的，困倦的
dyspenia	[dɪsp`niə] 呼吸困難
ecchymosis	[ˌɛkə`mosɪs] 瘀血
edema	[i`dimə] 浮腫，水腫
electric shock	觸電
seizure	[`ɛpəlɛpsɪ] 癲癇，（俗稱）羊癲瘋
failure	[`feljə] 衰退 / heart failure 心臟衰竭，心臟麻痺，心臟停跳 / respiratory failure 呼吸衰竭 / renal failure 腎衰竭
fatigue	[fə`tig] 疲勞，勞累
fever	[`fivə] 發燒
flu	[flu]【口】流行性感冒 / bird flu 禽流感
fracture	[`fræktʃə] 骨折，斷裂 / extremity fracture 四肢骨折 / pelvic fracture 骨盆骨折 / open fracture 開放性骨折
frostbite	[`frɔst,baɪt] 凍傷，凍瘡
gout	[gaʊt] 痛風
headache	[`hɛd,ek] 頭痛
heart	[hɑrt] 心臟/ heart attack 心臟病發作 / heartbeat 心跳 / heart stroke 心臟病發作 / heart disease 心臟病 / heart failure 心臟衰竭，心臟麻痺
heat	[hit] 熱度，溫度[U] 暑熱，高溫 / heat exhaustion 熱衰竭 /

	heat cramp 熱痙攣 / heat stroke 熱中暑
hemorrhage	[`hɛmərɪdʒ]出血
hyperlipidemia	[ˌhaɪpəˈglaɪˈsimɪə] 血糖過高症，高血糖症
hypertension	[ˌhaɪpəˈtɛnʃən] 高血壓
hyperventilation	[ˌhaɪpəˌvɛntɪˈleʃən]（肺的）換氣過度
hypoglycemia	[ˌhaɪpoglaɪˈsimɪə] 血糖過低
hypotension	[ˌhaɪpəˈtɛnʃən]低血壓
hypothermia	[ˌhaɪpəˈθɜˈmɪə]低體溫症
hypoxemia	[ˌhaɪpakˈsimɪə]血氧過少
hypoxia	[haɪˈpaksɪə] 組織缺氧
hysteria	[hɪsˈtɪrɪə] 歇斯底里
indigestion	[ˌɪndəˈdʒɛstʃən]消化不良
infection	[ɪnˈfɛkʃən]傳染，侵染
inflammation	[ˌɪnfləˈmeʃən]發炎
influenza	[ˌɪnfluˈɛnzə]流行性感冒
insomnia	[ɪnˈsamnɪə]失眠，不眠症
intubation	[ˌɪntjuˈbeʃən] 插管
laceration	[ˌlæsəˈreʃən] 撕裂傷
malnutrition	[ˌmælnjuˈtrɪʃən] 營養不良，營養失調
miscarriage	[mɪsˈkærɪdʒ] 流產
myocardial infarction	[ˌmaɪəˈkardɪəl] [ɪnˈfrækʃən]心肌梗塞
nausea	[`nɔʃɪə] 噁心，作嘔
obesity	[oˈbisətɪ]肥胖，過胖
pain	[pen]痛，疼痛，痛苦
abdominal pain	腹痛 / back pain 背痛 / low back pain 下背痛
pale	[pel] (膚色)蒼白的
panic	[`pænɪk]恐慌，驚慌，恐慌的
paralysis	[pəˈræləsɪs] 麻痺，癱瘓
Parkinson's disease	帕金森氏病，震顫性麻痺
patient	[`peʃənt]病人
psychosis	[saɪˈkosɪs] 精神病，精神變態
pulmonary	[`pʌlməˌnɛrɪ] 肺的，肺病的 / pulmonary Edema 肺水腫
puncture	[`pʌŋktʃə]刺，刺穿，戳破 / puncture pound 穿刺傷
reflex	[`riflɛks]【生理】反射（作用），本能的反應 / light reflex 對光反應
shivering	[`ʃɪvərɪŋ]顫抖，發抖；顫抖的
shock	[ʃak] 休克，中風

sprain	[spren] 扭傷	
sting	[stɪŋ]刺，螫，叮 / bee sting 蜜蜂刺(螫)	
strain	[stren] 扭傷	
stroke	[strok]（病）突然發作，中風 / heat stroke 熱中暑	
sweat	[swɛt] 汗，汗水	
syndrome	[`sɪn,drom]併發症狀	
tachycardia	[,tækɪ`kɑrdɪə] 心跳過速	
therapy	[`θɛrəpɪ]治療，療法	
thermal	[`θɝm!]熱的，熱量的 / thermal wound 燙傷	
toothache	[`tuθ,ek] 牙痛	
trauma	[`trɔmə] 外傷，傷口，（感情等方面的）創傷	
tremor	[`trɛmɚ]震顫，顫抖	
unconsciousness	[ʌn`kɑnʃəsnɪs]無意識，失去知覺，神志不清	
virus	[`vaɪrəs] 病毒	
vomit	[`vɑmɪt] 嘔吐，使嘔吐，嘔吐，嘔吐物	

片語動詞與執法應用

back up	支持，支援
	Detective said that he is on call for 24 hours, and part of his job is **to back up** the patrol officers. 偵查員說他是 24 小時待命，並且他的工作有一部分是支援巡邏員警。
	The officer began the pursuit and called for **backup**. 員警開始追逐，並呼叫支援。
back up	後退，向後移動，倒退回去，倒(車)
	Police have been called to multiple accidents on the westbound lanes. Four lanes are closed at the moment. Vehicles are getting by on the shoulder of the road. Traffic **is backing up**, please try to avoid the area and use an alternate route. 警方被呼叫前往西向車道的連環車禍，四線車道目前被封閉，車輛目前是由路肩經過，交通正在回堵中，請盡量避開這個區域並且使用替代路線。
	Traffic **backed up** for miles after the accident. 車禍之後，交通回堵了好幾英里。
	An accident has caused traffic **to back up** on the highway. Eastbound traffic is backed up for miles. 車禍造成在高速公路上交通回堵，往東的交通回堵了好幾英里。
bail out	(用錢) 保釋
	The judge set the bail at 1 million. But the detainee's family cannot gather enough funds **to bail him out of jail**. 法官訂出壹百萬元保釋金，然而，被拘禁者的家屬無法湊足資金將他保出來。
be fed up with	對……厭煩或不滿
	People who live in this district **are fed up with** the violence in their community and said police must take action. 住這一區的人受夠了社區的暴力，並且說警方必須採取做為。
bear on	與……有關，對……有影響
	The proficiency of the dispatchers directly **bears upon** the safety of every officer in the field. 派遣官的專業直接攸關轄內每一位員警的安全。
beat up	痛毆，毒打
	The gangsters have been charged with murder as they allegedly **beat up** the victim and left him for dead in the park. 幫派分子

被指控謀殺，因為他們涉嫌毒打被害人，並將他遺棄在公園而死亡。

"My husband beat me up", the battered woman said. 受暴的婦女說，「我的丈夫狠狠地打了我」。

block off	封鎖，封閉，阻斷
	The police **blocked off** the road after the murder. They **blocked off** the area and searched for the suspect. 交通事故之後，警方將道路封鎖了。他們將這個地區封鎖並搜尋嫌犯。
break down	拋錨
	The driver was arrested after his vehicle **broke down** during the pursuit, police said. 警方說，駕駛在追逐之際車輛拋錨之後被捕。
break in	(尤指為了竊盜而) 闖入
	Burglars **broke in** and took everything. 竊賊闖了進去並拿走所有東西。
break into	(尤指為了竊盜而) 闖入
	"Burglars **broke into** the house last night when we were away," homeowner said. 「昨天晚上我們外出的時候，竊賊闖進了房子」，屋主說。
break out	暴發，發生，(激烈事件)突然發生
	Police say an argument **broke out** and the victim was shot multiple times. The shooting **broke out** after a group of men started to fight outside the night club. 警方說有爭執發生，然後被害人被開了好幾槍。這個槍擊是在一群人於夜店外面打鬥之後爆發的。
	Fire officials said the blaze broke out in the basement of a seven-story apartment and soon engulfed the entire structure. 消防官員說，這場火從一棟七層樓公寓的地下室發生，並且很快地將整個建物吞噬。
break out of	(強行)逃出，脫逃
	Three inmates **broke out of** prison last week and are still at large. 三名受刑人上星期越獄，而目前仍逍遙法外。
break through	突破(障礙)，強行穿過(某事物)
	Although the crowds **broke through** police lines, the Police Chief said, "Protesters are citizens, not suspects. Our job as police is to keep them safe while they exercise their rights." 雖然群眾突破警戒線，但警察局長說，「抗議者是市民，不是嫌犯，我們身為警察的工作是在他們行使權利之際，保持他們

	的安全。」
break up	瓦解，解散
	The demonstration turned violent. Police used tear gas, water cannon, rubber bullets, and pepper spray **to break up** the crowd of protesters. 示威轉變為暴力，警方使用了催淚瓦斯、水柱、塑膠子彈及胡椒噴霧器來驅散抗議群眾。
bring (sb) in	(指警察)將某人抓去盤問，逮捕某人
	Commander of the 1st Precinct said the suspect **was brought in** for questioning. 第一分局分局長說，嫌犯已被帶回問訊。
bring (sb) to justice	使(人)歸案受審
	Police continue to search for the suspect in the building, hoping to be able to track him down and **bring him to justice**. 警方持續在建築物內搜尋嫌犯，希望能追蹤到他並將他歸案受審。
bring about	引起，導致
	When the girl learned that her boyfriend had brought about the murder of the victim, she let him. 當這個女孩知道他的男朋友引起了被害人被謀殺之後，她就離開他了。
bring into effect	生效
	Patrol officers said that new DUI laws will **be brought into effect** in the near future. 巡邏員警說，新的酒駕法律將在最近生效。
bring on	引起
	Investigators are looking into the case to know what **brought on** the fight. 偵查人員正在調查本案，以了解是甚麼引起了這場打鬥。
bring to an end	結束，終止
	The pursuit lasted almost 20 minutes and was finally **brought to an end** when officers fired several shots at the tires of the vehicle. 這場追逐持續了將近二十分鐘，在員警對車輪開了數槍之後才結束。
bring under	控制，制服
	Firefighter said the fire was **brought under** control before midnight. It **was brought under** control in 50 minutes. No one was injured. 消防員說，火災在半夜之前被控制住，火災在 50 分鐘內被控制住，沒有人受傷。
bring up	養育
	She **is brought up** by a single mother who suffered from domestic violence. 她被一個受過家暴的單親媽媽養育長大。

call for	呼籲 President Obama **called for** stronger gun laws. He also **called for** better funding for police. 歐巴馬總統呼籲更有力的槍枝法律，他同時也呼籲給警察更多的經費。 呼叫 Officers began the pursuit and **called for** backup. 員警開始追逐，並且呼叫支援。
call in	請來 "The unmarked police car was assisting other officers pursuing a shooting suspect. Backup officers **were called in** to help go after the shooter's car," an officer said. 員警說，「偵防車協助了其他員警追逐槍擊嫌犯。支援員警被呼叫進來協助追緝槍擊犯的車子。」
chase down	找出，追蹤 The detective has used warrants issued by the judge **to chase down** suspects as far away as Virginia and New York. 偵查員用法官核發的令狀，一路追到維吉尼亞及紐約之遙。
cheat (sb) out of	騙取 (財物) The plaintiff alleged that the defendant **cheated him out of** two million dollars. 原告指控被告騙取他兩百萬元。
cheat on	不忠於 (妻子、丈夫等) He **cheated on** his wife and often got violent with her. 他對他妻子不忠，並且經常對他暴力相向。
come about	發生 "We are working hard to establish exactly how this accident **came about**," police said. 「我們正努力在確認這場車禍是如何發生的」，警方說。
come across	(偶然)碰見 "We **came across** the suspect in a vehicle, and he tried to run us over", captain said. 「我們遇到這名歹徒在車內，而他試圖輾過我們」，隊長說。
come before	比……重要 Drug abuse is not good for you. Your physical and mental health comes before anything. 濫用毒品對你是不好的，身心健康重於一切。
come clean about	【口】全盤托出，招供 Victim's family called on the police **to come clean about** the circumstances of the fatal shooting on Monday evening. Police soon arrested the suspect. "We are going to give you one chance

to come clean about what you know," detectives said. Suspect said he had killed Jennifer because she threatened **to come clean about** what happened that night. The suspect wouldn't **come clean about** his relationship with the victim, but agreed to **come clean about** several other crimes. 被害人去找警察，全盤托出星期一晚上的致命槍擊案的情況，警方很快地逮捕嫌犯。「我們給你一個機會招供你所知道的」，偵查員說。嫌犯說她殺了珍妮佛，因為她威脅要供出那天晚上所發生的事。嫌犯不願意供出他與被害人的關係，但同意供出其他幾個案件。

come down (up)on	(口)責罰

Tom Cruise had a rough childhood with an abusive father who often **came down on** him when something went wrong or his grades were poor. He had a difficult time in school and went through fifteen schools in twelve years. 湯姆克魯斯有一個艱困的童年，他有一個漫罵的父親，每當他有出錯或是成績差的時候常常罵他。校園日子難捱，12 年當中歷經 15 個學校。

come forward	站出來，自告奮勇，挺身而出

Police have arrested the suspect and called for potential victims and witnesses **to come forward** and provide evidence and information to the police. 警方逮捕了嫌犯，並呼籲可能的被害人及證人挺身而出，並提供證據及資訊給警方。

come into effect	生效

Patrol Officer said the speed limit change will **come into effect** next year. 巡邏員警說，變更速限會在明年生效。

come over	從遠方過來

The male came up behind him and fired several shots at him. "The victim fell to the ground, and the suspect **came over** and shot him again multiple times as he lay on the ground," witness said. 該男子從他後面上來，並對他開了數槍。「被害人倒地，而嫌犯在他人躺在地上時，上前再開了幾槍。」

come to	The vehicle struck the victim and **came to a stop** on the sidewalk. 該車撞到被害人，並在人行道上停了下來。

The detectives **came to the conclusion** that it was a homicide and not a suicide. The police **came to believe** that the murder was a robbery-homicide. 偵查員做出結論那是他殺而不是自殺，警方後來相信這場謀殺是強盜殺人。

come to oneself	甦醒，恢復知覺

The intoxicated driver **passed out** while driving. After he sobered-up and came to himself, he said he could not remember anything. 爛醉的駕駛在開車時昏睡過去,在他酒醒及清醒之後,他說他甚麼都不記得。

comply with	(對要求、命令等)依從,順從,遵從

When offenders are released from prison on parole, parole officers will supervise them to ensure that they **comply with** the conditions of their parole. 當犯罪者被假釋出獄時,假釋官會監控他們,以確保他們遵守假釋條件。

confess to	坦白,供認,承認,交代

The murder suspect said that he had been forced **to confess to** crime. 殺人嫌犯說他被強迫承認犯罪。

The suspect **confessed to** beating her to death and dumping her body in a river. 嫌犯坦承將她毆打至死,並將屍體扔進到河裡。

conspire with	與……勾結

It is difficult to decide if the alien **conspires with** the citizen to enter into a marriage for the purpose of evading the immigration laws. 外國人是否為了逃避移民法,而與公民共謀締結婚姻,是很難判斷的。

cover up	掩蓋,掩飾

Usually, suspects tend to give false alibi to the police **to cover up** their crimes, unless they are caught red-handed. 通常,嫌犯傾向會給警方假的不在場證明,來掩蓋他們的犯罪,除非他們被當場逮獲。

crack down on	(對某人、某事)嚴加取締或限制

City Police Department will conduct a week-long operation **to crack down** on speeding and aggressive drivers. 市警局將會進行為期一周的行動,取締超速及咄咄逼人的駕駛人。

cut across	逕直穿過

School Board said that it is dangerous that kids across the street to catch the bus. 學校委員會說,孩童直接穿過馬路去搭車是危險的。

The suspects cut across the east-west traffic lanes. Then, they cut across, again, as the driver turned right and headed south. 嫌犯直接穿過東西向的線道,然後隨著駕駛向左轉,他們又一次直接穿過,並朝著南邊而去。

cut at	猛砍

While committing the crime of robbery, the suspect pulled a

	knife and **cut at** the victim's arm. 犯該起強盜罪之際，嫌犯拔出刀子並猛砍被害人的手臂。
cut down on	削減
	The mayor praised police officers' successful effort **to cut down on** crime, and urged the city council **not to cut down on** the overtime budget. 市長嘉勉員警們的努力成功降低了犯罪，並且呼籲市議會不要砍超勤預算。
cut in	切入，超車
	He told highway patrol officer that he was being tailgated by the truck. Suddenly, the aggressive truck driver pulled ahead and **cut in**. 他告訴高速公路巡邏員警說，他被大卡車尾隨跟車，強勢的卡車司機開到前面然後切入。
cut in and out	進進出出切入
	His car rolled several times into the westbound lanes and he was ejected. Police said he was driving fast when he **cut in and out** of traffic. 他的車子翻了好幾圈到西向的車道，然後他被彈出。警方說他開快車，那時進進出出切入。
cut loose from	使擺脫束縛，分開
	Firefighter said that the trapped driver has a broken arm and had to **be cut loose from** his seat belt as soon as possible. 消防員說，受困的駕駛一隻手臂斷掉，必須盡速將他從安全帶上解開。
cut off	切斷
	"The kidnappers threatened **to cut off** his fingers and kill him, and punched him in the face and body," police said. 警方說，「綁匪威脅要切斷他的手指並且殺他，並且揍了他的臉與身體。」
	The suspect became angry and cut off the negotiation. 嫌犯變得生氣，並切斷了談判。
cut through	切穿，超近路
	Firefighter **cut through** the door and got everyone out of the house. 消防員將門切穿，並把所有人救出房子。
	The officers put on the siren **to cut through** the cars. 員警放上警報器，從車陣中穿了過去。
do away with	廢除，停止
	According to a poll, a majority of people support death penalty while on a few people said the country should **do away with** death penalty. 根據一項民調，大部分的人支持死刑，而只有少部分人說國家應該廢除死刑。

do justice to	公平地對待(某人)
	He believes that the jury will **do him justice**. 他相信陪審團會公平地對待他。
	People expect the court to fairly try the case and **do justice to** the victim. 人們期待法院公平審理案件,給被害人一個公道。
end up (in/with)	結果成為,以……終結,以……結束,最後
	The protest turned into a riot that **ended up** injuring 30 people and 3 police officers. Investigator said police **ended up** catching 5 suspects. 抗議變成了暴動,結果有 30 人及 3 位員警受傷。偵查人員說,警方結果抓到了 5 個嫌犯。
	The Ford hit a curb, overturned, and struck a pole, before it **ended up in** the river. The driver was drunk that he **ended up** spending 30 days in prison and was sentenced to 100 hours of community service. 這輛福特撞到了路邊護欄、翻覆、並撞到桿子,最後掉進河裡。駕駛酒醉,最後被關 30 天並被處 1 百小時社區服務。
	Officer said it started as a simple traffic stop but **ended up with** a crash. 員警說,那一開始只是一個單純的交通攔檢,但結果變成車禍。
fall back on	依賴,求助於
	Because many abusers seek to isolate victims from friends and family, often times, domestic violence survivors have few people **to fall back on** for support. 由於許多施暴者會孤立被害人於朋友及家人之外,因此,經常地,家暴的倖存者幾乎沒有朋友可以求救協助。
fall in with	偶然遇到
	Jack was just 19 years old when he **fell in with** the wrong crowd and was sentenced to three years for robbery. 傑克結交到不好的這群人並且因強盜罪被判刑 3 年的時候,只有 19 歲。
fall into	陷入(某種狀態)
	Police said the victim **fell into** a coma after the accident, and was taken to hospital. 警方說,被害人在車禍之後陷入了昏迷,並被送到了醫院。
fall off	落下,減少,下降
	Police responded to a report of a dead body. They were investigating whether the person jumped or **fell off** the fifteen-story building. 警方前往處理屍體報案,他們正在調查這個人是從這 15 層樓高的建築物跳樓還是墜落。
	Police Chief said the property crime rate **fell** 4% last year,

Juvenile arrests **fell off** dramatically. The overall crime rate **fell off** by 3%. 警察局長說，財產犯罪下降了百分之 4，青少年的逮捕急遽下降，整體犯罪下降了百分之 3。

fall out with	與(人)爭吵

Jennifer testified she **fell out with** her boyfriend after she discovered he had been lying about his marriage status. So she hired someone to kill him. 珍妮佛作證她發現他男朋友對於婚姻狀況一直在撒謊之後，與她吵了一架，所以就雇人殺他。

fall over	倒下

Officers say the driver sped off and ran a red light before hitting a taxi cab. The taxi cab then hit two people on the sidewalk and a pole. The pole **fell over** and hit one of the victims, who was riding a bike. 員警說，該駕駛在撞到計程車之前是超速疾駛並闖紅燈，計程車又撞到人行道上的兩個人及桿子，桿子倒下來擊中正在騎自行車的被害人。

fall under	列入……項下

The judge said DUI and substance abuse **fall under** the criminal law category, and in general, most criminal cases **fall under** the jurisdiction of the district court. 法官說，酒駕及藥物濫用是屬於刑法項下，並且，通常而言，大部分的刑事案件是屬於地方法院管轄。

feel for	同情

Officers attempted to pull the car over, but the suspect fled and was killed in the crash. "I **feel for** the juvenile's family but at the same time he should be accountable for his actions," officer said. 員警試圖把車子攔下，但是嫌犯逃逸並且在車禍中喪命。「我對青少年感到同情，但同時他應該要為自己的行為負責」，員警說。

fill out	填寫(表格、申請等)

Please notice that all inmate visitors are required **to fill out** a Visitor Application on-line. All information must **be filled out** completely and truthfully or your application will be denied. All visitors 18 and older must **fill out** an application. Minors under the age of 18 do not need **to fill out** an application. 請注意，所有受刑人訪客都需要上線填寫「訪客申請表(Visitor Application)」，所有資料必須完整而如實填寫，否則你的申請將會被拒絕，所有 18 歲以上的訪客都必須填寫申請表，18 歲以下的未成年人不需填寫申請表。

find for	裁決，判決(+人)，做出對(某人)有利的裁決 Defendant's dogs killed plaintiff's cat. The trial court **found for** the plaintiffs. The trial court found that defendant was negligent. 被告的狗弄死了原告的狗，審理法院做出有利原告的判決，審理法院認定被告有過失。 In a civil case, the verdict is usually "We the jury **find for** the plaintiff" or "We the jury **find for** the defendant." 在民事案件中，裁決通常是：「本陪審團認定有利原告」，或「本陪審團認定有利被告」。
get across	解釋清晰明白，使人了解 The police chief wanted **to get across** the message that drug use can only hurt. "I hope **to get across to** the young people that drug abuse can ruin your life." 局長想要傳達的訊息是，毒品只會有害。「我希望傳達給年輕人了解，濫用毒品會毀了你的人生。」
get ahead	獲得成功，能存些錢，償清債務 Police say the male struggled to get by on the minimum wage, so he decided to commit the robbery **to get ahead** in lives. 警方說，該男子靠著最低工資勉強度日，所以他決定犯該起強盜讓生活有起色。 We know that to get ahead we need to work hard. But the criminals believe that cheating is the easiest way to get ahead. 我們知道，為了成功我們必須努力工作，但是罪犯相信，欺騙是最容易的成功方法。
get along with	相處 To survive in prison, the offenders must try **to get along with** other inmates. 為了在監獄中生存，人犯必須試著與其他囚犯相處。
get around	避開，逃避 The accused argued the substances are legal, but authorities said they were trying to find ways **to get around** the law. 被告主張該藥物是合法的，但當局說他們只是試著想找到方法避開法律。
get away	逃脫 The suspects held up the store at gunpoint and **got away** before police got to the scene. The suspects **got away** for a short time but were eventually found. 嫌犯用槍行搶商店，並且在警方抵達現場之前逃逸了。嫌犯只逃逸了短暫的時間，但最後還是被發現了。

get away with	受到(較輕的處罰)，不因某事受到處罰，攜帶……逃走
	The bank robber **got away with** a small amount of cash after handing a teller a note that said he had a gun. 銀行搶匪給行員看一張字條寫著他有槍，然後夾帶少許的現金逃走了。
	The suspect staged a crime scene to misdirect investigators so as **to get away with** the crime. 嫌犯假造了一個犯罪現場來誤導偵查人員，以逃避犯罪。
get back at (sb)	報復
	The offender said that he was trying **to get back at** the gangster that shot him many years ago. 犯罪者說他是想要報復多年前槍擊他的那個幫派分子。
get behind the wheel	駕車
	The drunk driver **got behind the wheel** of his SUV and collided with another vehicle. "You have to think about the consequences if you do decide **to get behind the wheel** after drinking," police said. 喝醉的駕駛開了他的休旅車，並與其他車輛發生擦撞。「如果你酒後決定開車，你必須要想想後果」，警方說。
get by	勉強度日
	Many people struggled **to get by** on the minimum wage. Police say more and more homeless people are resorting to burglary **to get by.**
	很多人靠著最低工資勉強度日，警方說，越來越多的遊民訴諸行竊勉強度日。
get in	進入
	The male waved down the cab, **got in** and pointed a gun at the driver demanding money. 該男子揮手攔下計程車，進到裡面並用槍對著駕駛要求拿錢。
	The officer was on foot patrol when he and a partner spotted a gun inside a sport utility vehicle. They followed the vehicle after three men **got in** and drove away. 員警正在步巡的時後，和他的夥伴瞥見休旅車內有一把槍，他們等到 3 個人進入並開走之後，跟蹤了該車。
	Police deployed one flash bang around 5 a.m. Police finally **got in** the home. 警方大約清晨 5 點佈署了震撼彈，警方最後進入了該房子。
get into	開始(某事)
	The incident first started at around 6:00 p.m. on Tuesday night, when the suspect **got into** an argument with his wife. Then he

got into a fight with other people there. 這個事件先是在星期二晚上大約下午 6 點開始，嫌犯與他的妻子發生爭吵，之後她與那裡的人發生了打鬥。

get off with	以⋯⋯而避免(處罰、損失)

Police said if he pleaded guilty, he might **get off with** a lighter (or reduced) sentence. The defendant hoped that he could **get off with** a fine or probation. 警方說，如果他認罪，他可能會受到較輕的刑期，被告希望他能夠受到罰金或緩刑的較輕處罰。

get out of	從⋯⋯中出來

The defendant **got out of** the jail after his family posted the bond. 被告在家人繳納保金之後就出獄了。

This case was so brutal I couldn't **get it out of** my mind. 這個案子太殘暴了以至於我無法將它從我的腦海抹去。

get over	克服

"You can never make the incident disappear, but you can help the victim **to get over** it." His wife tells him to **get over** it. But he said he was still working **to get over**. "I will never **get over** what happened to me. It can take a while **to get over** the pain," he said. 「你沒辦法讓事件消失，但是你可以幫忙被害人克服渡過。」他的太太告訴他要克服渡過，但他說他還在努力克服中。「我永遠也無法克服在我身上發生的事，要克服這個痛苦是需要好一陣子的。」他說。

get rid of	去除

People that are addicted to drugs need to get the treatment they require **to get rid of** drug addiction. 吸毒成癮的人須要取得他們需要的治療，以便去除毒癮。

get through	經過，經過(周折之後到達目的地)

Firstly, they have **to get through** all the tests and interviews. At the police academy, the police cadets must **get through** the physical fitness exams and police training. They **get through** the tough times before they become a police officer. 首先，他們必須通過所有的測驗與面試，在警察學校時，警校生必須通過體能考試及警察訓練，成為一名員警之前，他們通過了艱困的日子。

get to	到達

The suspects held up the store at gunpoint and got away before police **got to** the scene. 嫌犯用槍行搶商店，並且在警方抵達現場之前逃逸了。

give in	屈服，投降，退讓
	Residents gathered at the city hall to remember the young girl killed by a gunman last year. "We will not **give in** to violence," the police chief said. 居民聚集在市政府以紀念去年被槍手殺害的年輕女子。「我們不會屈服於暴力」，警察局長說。
	Police negotiated with Ramon to try to get him to surrender for more than two hours, but he **refused to give in.** 警方與雷猛談判並試圖讓他投降，時間超過 2 小時，但是他拒絕投降。
give off	發出，散發
	Drug chemists said the production of amphetamines usually **give off** toxic gases. 毒品化學專家，安非他命的製造通常會散發有毒氣體。
	Firefighter says those chemicals give off gases that not only contaminate the air, but also pose major public health risks. 消防員說，那些化學品散發出了不僅汙染空氣，也對公眾的健康造成危害的氣體。
	to give off smoke 發出煙霧
	to give off smell 發出味道
give rise to	引起
	If the traffic stop **gives rise to** probable cause to believe that the suspect has committed a crime, then the police shall be empowered to make a formal arrest of the person. 如果交通攔檢引起相當理由足以相信嫌犯已經犯罪時，則警察應被賦予權力去進行正式的逮捕。
go after	追求，追逐，追蹤
	Patrol officer **went after** the burglar, and found him in the house. 巡邏員警追緝竊嫌，並在屋子內發現了他。
go against	違背
	The drug ringleader threatened to kill people who dare **go against** him. 毒品集團首腦威脅要殺掉膽敢違背他的人。
go off	響起
	Baker said he had just returned home when an alarm went off. 貝克說他才剛回家時，警報器就響起。
	Police got a call from a woman saying that a man was threatening her with a gun. While she was on the phone, officers heard the gun go off. 警方接獲一個婦人的電話說，有一名男子用槍威脅著她。當她正在講電話的同時，員警聽到槍聲響起。
go off	離開
	A car traveling northbound went off the road and struck a tree

this morning. Police say they were called to the scene of the crash at around 2 a.m. 今晨，一輛往北的車子岔出道路並撞到一棵樹，警方說他們大約在清晨兩點被呼叫前往現場。

go through	經過，穿過

A witness told police that just before the crash, the driver cut in and out of lanes several times and **went through** a red light. 證人告訴警方，就在車禍事故前，該駕駛在車道上進進出出切了好幾次，並闖過紅燈。

The victim may **go through** a wide range of emotions, such as vulnerability, shame, hopelessness, helplessness, fear, guilt, and anger. 被害人會經歷許多的情緒，例如軟弱、羞恥、沒有希望、無助、恐懼、罪惡及生氣。

go under	沉沒

Coast guard said it remains unclear how many people were on the boat when it **went under**. 海巡說，還不清楚當船隻翻覆的時候，有幾個人在船上。

go without	放棄, 不用

"As drug use increases, it becomes increasingly difficult **to go without** the drug," doctor said. 醫生說，隨著毒品使用的增加，要放棄毒品也逐漸變得困難。

hand oneself in	自首

Suspect's brother asked him **to hand himself in** to police, so he turned himself in to authorities and pleaded guilty. 嫌犯的哥哥要他向警方自首，所以他就向當局自首並且認罪。

hand over	(把權利或物品)交出

Police Chief said the investigation **was handed over to** the FBI. The suspect **was also handed over to** the FBI. 警察局長說，這項調查移轉給 FBI 了，嫌犯也移轉給 FBI 了。

hang out	(待在某處，或與某人待在一起)閒逛

Do not allow your children **to hang out with** gang members or to attend parties where gang members might be present. 不要讓你的小孩與幫派分子出去閒晃，或參加幫派分子可能出現的派對。

head for	前往

On Wednesday, authorities successfully apprehended two men suspected of stealing a car in San Francisco and driving it to Los Angeles, where they stole another vehicle and **headed for** Las Vegas. 星期三，當局成功地逮捕到涉嫌在舊金山偷車並開到洛杉磯，並且在當地又偷了另外一輛車而前往拉斯維加斯的

	兩名男子。
hear about	聽說，知道
	The witness said he was worried that something was wrong, so he came forward to tell police when he **heard about** the murder. 證人說他擔心有事情不對勁，所以當她聽到謀殺案時，他就前往告訴警察。
hear from	從……得到消息，收到……的訊息
	The fugitive went missing around 10 years ago. He disappeared without a trace and nobody has ever **heard from** him since. 逃犯消失了將近 10 年，他消失無蹤並且從此沒人聽過他的消息。
hear of	聽說過
	Officer set out to visit the suspect's neighbors but was told they had never interacted with or **heard of** the suspect. 員警出去拜訪嫌犯的鄰居，但被告知說他們從來沒有與該嫌互動或是聽說過該嫌。
hold (sb) down	壓制，壓抑
	Patrol officers used the baton **to hold down** the break-in suspect. Officers **held him down** with the baton. 巡邏員警使用警棍壓制了非法闖入的嫌犯。員警用警棍將他壓制。
hold on	不掛電話，緊握
	"**Hold on**, please. I will transfer you." Then you may **put the person on hold**. When you come back on the line after holding, say "Thanks for holding." 「請不要掛電話，我為您轉接。」然後你可以讓該人等候。當你之後回到線上時，說：「謝謝等待」。
keep abreast of	跟上，保持與……並駕齊驅
	Dispatchers or duty officer must monitor police radio communication and radio channels **to keep abreast of** police activities. 派遣官或是值日人員必須監控警察無線電通訊及無線電頻道，以對警察的做為保持瞭解。
keep away	使遠離
	The judge issued a protection order, ordering the violent partner **to keep away from** the victim's residence or work. 法官核發了保護令，命令暴力的一方遠離被害人的住所或是工作。
keep back	阻擋，阻止(某人)靠近
	The fire started in the basement of the building. Police blockaded off the street **to keep back** a large crowd of onlookers. 火災從建築物的地下室開始，警方封鎖了街道，阻止大群圍觀群眾

	靠近。
keep down	躲好，躺低
	SWAT team blocked off the area and told residents **to keep down** and stay away from the building. 「特種武器與戰術部隊/霹靂小組 (SWAT)」封鎖了這個區域，並告訴居民躲好並遠離該建築物。
keep from	阻止，避免
	An officer pulled the keys from the van **to keep the suspect from** leaving. 一位員警從休旅車拔掉鑰匙，阻止嫌犯離開。
keep out of	避免捲入其中
	Officer wanted **to keep him out of** trouble. "I don't want to him roaming around the streets and selling drugs," officer said. 員警要他避免捲入麻煩。「我不想要他在街上晃來晃去販賣毒品」，員警說。
keep to	遵守
	The judge wanted him **to keep to** his promise and not to take drugs again. 法官要他遵守諾言而不再吸毒。
keep to oneself	不讓人知道，不表現，不說出
	Neighbors told police that the suspect was a loner and tended to **keep to himself.** 鄰居告訴警方說，該嫌犯是一個獨來獨往的人，傾向不與人來往。
keep up with	保持，跟上
	Officers complained that they are struggling **to keep up with** the increasing caseloads. 員警訴苦說他們苦撐著跟上逐漸增加的案件量。
	Police chief said the Department will add 500 police officers **to keep up with** the population growth and rising crimes. 警察局長說，警局將增加 500 名員警，以跟上人口增加及上升的犯罪。
knock down	擊倒，撞倒
	It took firefighters only about 10 minutes to knock down the blaze. 這場火勢只花了消防員十分鐘的時間就撲滅。
	It took 50 firefighters more than two hours to knock down the blaze. 撤場火勢共有五十位消防員花了超過兩小時才撲滅。
know about	知道關於......的情形
	At this point, police don't **know much about** the suspect except that he is a male with short hair and eyeglasses. 目前，

	警方除了(知道)是蓄留短髮及戴眼鏡的男性之外，還不太知道關於嫌犯的情況。
know of	聽說過
	If you **know of** his whereabouts or if you think you may have seen him, please contact investigator (02) 2766-1919. 如果你聽過他的下落或如果你認為你有看過他，敬請聯絡偵查人員，電話：(02)1766-1919。
let (sb) off	不加以嚴厲懲罰
	Brown requested the Judge **to let him off** because he had a sick wife and four children. Eventually, he **was let off** with a fine of 5000 dollars. 布朗請求法官輕放他，因為他有一個生病的妻子與4個小孩，後來他被罰5000元輕放。
let out	放出去
	The prisoner has been released from the prison as the Parole Board decided that he should **be let out.** 該囚犯以經釋放了，因為保釋委員會決定應該要讓他出來。
	He was let out of prison after serving five years of an eight-year sentence. 他在8年的刑期服了5年之後，被釋放出獄了。
live on	以……為食物，活下來
	Defendant's lawyer said his client had no choice but to commit burglary as she needed money **to live on.** The lawyer also asked the Judge to let him off as he did not threaten the victim with any weapon. 被告的律師說，她的委託人別無選擇犯下竊盜，因為他需要錢活下去，律師也請求法官輕放他，因為他沒有使用任何武器威脅被害人。
live through	經歷過
	The suspect took his own life during the standoff and was taken to the intensive care unit of the hospital. Police said he was not expected **to live through** the night. 嫌犯在僵持之際自我了斷，並被送到醫院的加護病房。警方說，預計他活不過今晚。
live up to	實踐，遵守，堅持，無愧於
	Some children feel they cannot **live up to** their families' expectations. They might turn to drugs or alcohol as a relief. 有些小孩覺得他們無法達到家人的期待，他們可能會尋求毒品或酒精當成慰藉。
live with	與……住在一起，接受或容忍某現象
	The abused woman said she continued **to live with** the violence

	in order to protect their children. 受虐婦女說，她繼續容忍暴力是為了保護他們的小孩。
lock (sb) up	將某人監禁起來
	The accused allegedly **locked the girl up** in the basement and raped her. She was raped and **kept locked up** for several days. 被告涉嫌將該女子鎖在地下室並姦淫她，她被姦淫並監禁了好幾天。
look about	到處搜查
	When she noticed her front door was ajar, she **looked about** and noticed that her purse was missing and no doubt stolen by a suspect who entered her home through the unlocked door. 當她查覺到前門半開半關時，她四處查看並發現她的皮包不見了，無疑地是被從該未上鎖的門進入房子的嫌犯給偷走。
look around	四下環顧，仔細察看
	Officers marked the location of shell casings, and used flashlights **to look around** for evidence. 員警標記彈殼的位置，並使用手電筒仔細查看尋找證據。
look for	尋找
	Police blocked off the area **to look for** shell casings and other evidence. 警方封鎖該區，以尋找彈殼及其他證據。
look for trouble	行為輕率，挑釁，由於自己的行為及表現而自找麻煩或困難
	The ringleader told the rival gang "We don't look for trouble, but we don't back away from it." 集團首腦告訴敵對幫派說，「我們不找麻煩，但我們也不退縮。」
look forward to	期待，盼望
	I have worked as a beat officer for this area since last week. I **look forward to** working with the community to ensure that our citizens feel safe and respected in the neighborhood. Please feel free to stop me if you see me on patrol. 我從上星期開始擔任這一區的勤區員警，我盼望與社區合作以確保我們的市民在社區內感到安全與被尊重，如果你看到我在社區巡邏，請隨時找我。
look in	往裡面看，迅速一瞥
	A legal stop gives the officer an opportunity **to look in** and smell the vehicle's interior and to get as close as a few inches from the car's occupants. 合法的攔檢讓員警有機會往裡面看並嗅聞車子的內部，並靠近乘客到幾公分之近。
look into	調查，研究 (問題，罪行等)
	Police **are looking into** the murder and the death of the gang

member. 警方正在調查這件謀殺案以及這個幫派分子的死因。

Investigators **are looking into** whether stowaways are tucked inside a shipping container. 偵查員正在調查偷渡客是否有被塞進船隻的貨櫃內。

look on as	將某人(某事物)看作他人(他事物)
	The gangsters **looked on him as** their big brother and protector. 幫派分子將他視為大哥以及保護者。
look out	【口】小心，注意；向外看
	According to investigators, a resident was awakened by dogs barking. She went to her window **to look out** and saw someone inside her neighbor's vehicle. She called the police at once. 根據偵查人員說，有位居民被狗叫聲吵醒，她到窗戶邊向外面看，並看到有人在她鄰居的車子內，她立刻報警。
	The traffic signs worn: Danger! Look Out For Truck. 交通號誌警告：危險！小心卡車。
look out for	留意找，設法得到
	Patrol officers were told **to look out for** the suspect and the vehicle. 巡邏員警接獲告知，要注意該嫌犯及該輛車子。
look over	檢查
	Police **are looking over** surveillance video to find the driver who ran the red light and hit the victim. 警方正在看著監視錄影帶要找到那個闖紅燈並撞到被害人的駕駛。
look through	快速檢查某事物，快速閱讀某物
	Officers responded to his home, **looked through** a window and saw a person lying in a pool of blood in the kitchen. 員警前往他家，從窗子看進去並看到廚房內有一個人倒臥血泊中。
	The arresting officers seized his phone, **looked through** it and found incriminating evidence. In addition, officers also **looked through** the crime scene photos. 進行逮捕的員警查扣了他的手機，快速瀏覽並發現足以入罪的證據，此外，員警也快速瀏覽了刑案現場照片。
look to (sb) for	依賴，指望
	Because of his expertise in criminal justice, other detectives usually **looked to him for** advice. 由於他在刑事司法方面的經驗，其他的幹探通常都會仰賴他的建議。
look up	敬佩，尊敬
	Detective Wong will retire next month. He is well respected within the community, and officers have always **looked up** to

	him. 王偵查員將於下個月退休，他在社區非常受到尊敬，員警向來敬佩他。
make away	急忙離開 The burglar **made away** before the police arrived. 竊嫌在警方抵達之前就急忙逃走了。
make away with	挾帶……潛逃，偷走 The thief **made away with** some expensive jewelry with a total value reported at 2 million. 該竊賊偷走貴重珠寶潛逃，總價值據報在 2 百萬元。
make off	【口】匆匆離開，(尤指)逃走 The suspects had **made off** before officers arrived. Investigating officers say the suspects made off in a red Ford following the theft. 嫌犯在警方抵達之前就急忙逃走了。偵查人員說，嫌犯在行竊之後，乘一輛紅色的福特逃走了。
make off with	偷走 Burglars smashed the glass door of the jewelry store and **made off with** 25,000 worth of jewelry, according to the police. 根據警方，竊嫌搗毀珠寶店的玻璃門，並偷走價值 25000 元的珠寶。
make out	寫出，填寫 Patrol officers then returned to the patrol car and began to **make out** an arrest report. 巡邏員警於是回到巡邏車，並開始寫逮捕報告。
make up for	彌補 The judge ordered the defendant to pay money **to make up for** the harm that the defendant caused in the traffic accident. 法官命令被告支付金錢，以彌補被告在這場交通事故所造成的傷害。
make up of	由……組成 Police Chief said the SWAT team **is made up of** 30 officers, who are on call 24 hours a day, seven days a week. It **is made up of** snipers, negotiators, K9, Fire Rescue, etc. 警察局長說，「特種武器與戰術部隊/霹靂小組 (SWAT)」是由 30 位員警組成，他們是一星期 7 天，全天 24 小時待命。該組是由狙擊手、談判官、警犬隊、消防等等組合而成。
pass (sb) off as	冒充，把……充做 Authorities say she **passed herself off as** an 18 year-old girl on Facebook in order to attract potential customers. 當局說，她在 FB 上假充自己是 18 歲的女孩，以吸引潛在的「人客」。

pass away	(委婉語)去世 The victim in yesterday's crash **has passed away**. "Wilson **passed away from** her injuries yesterday. He was struck and killed by a truck," police said. 昨天車禍的被害人去世了。「威爾森因為昨天的受傷而去世，他被卡車撞到而喪命」，警察說。
pass by	經過，過去 The first victim was attacked from behind after the suspect **passed by**. The second victim was robbed from behind while the suspect **passed by** on motorcycle. Authorities are seeking a male between the ages of 18-25 with a crew cut. 第一個被害人是被嫌犯經過時從後面攻擊，第二個被害人是嫌犯騎摩托車經過時從後面被搶，當局正在找尋這名年約 18 至 25 歲留平頭的男子。
pass out	【俚】昏倒，失去知覺，酒醉 He only intended to rob her and then she **passed out** in the course of the mugging. He said he didn't even know she had died, and that if he had known, he would have stopped attacking women. 他只是想對她行搶，而她在行搶過程中昏了過去，他說他根本不知道她死了，如果他早知道，他那時早就停止對她的攻擊。 A California Highway Patrol officer rescued an intoxicated driver, who appeared **to be passed out** in the driver's seat while on a busy freeway. 加州高速公路巡邏員警救了一名爛醉如泥的駕駛，該駕駛在繁忙的高速公路上，顯然在駕駛座上昏睡過去。 A male **was passed out** in a vehicle. Officers discovered he **had passed out** behind the wheel of his vehicle while in an intersection. He was charged with driving under the influence. 一名男子在車子內失去知覺。員警發現他行經十字路口時，昏在自己車內的駕駛座。他被控告酒駕。
pick (sb) out	挑選出 The detective said, "We are bringing some pictures and we want to see if you can **pick someone out**." Then he further asked, "Do you think you could **pick him out of** a lineup?" 偵查員說，「我們拿一些照片，我們要看看你是否可以把某個人挑出來。」然後他又問，「你認為你可以從指認中將他挑出來嗎？」
pick on	【口】找……的碴，盯上，對……嘮叨，指責 The victim told the officers that he had been targeted by a bully,

who had **picked on him** at school. He got tired of the bullying and decided to fight the bully. 被害人告訴員警說，他一直被一個霸凌者當成目標，在學校時都找他麻煩，他對霸凌感到厭倦，並決定反抗霸凌者。

pull (sb) in	【口】把某人帶(到警察局)去問話，拘留某人 Police **pulled him in** for questioning about the murder, but he had an alibi and the police had to let him go. His lawyer said, "the police didn't have enough evidence at that point **to pull him in** and talk to him about this crime." 警方將他帶去問訊有關謀殺一案，但他有不在場證明，所以警方讓他走了。他的律師說，「警方當下沒有足夠的證據將他帶去並談論此案。」 (帶去問話：was taken in for questioning/ was brought in for questioning/ was pulled in for questioning)
pull ahead	領先、超前 He told highway patrol officer that was being tailgated by the truck. Suddenly, the aggressive truck driver **pulled ahead** and cut in. 他告訴高速公路巡邏警察說，他被那輛卡車跟車，突然間，那個咄咄逼人的卡車駕駛就搶到前面然後切進。
pull out	退出，駛出 The driver reduced his speed prior to passing the hiding officers but, to his dismay, police **pulled out** and turned its lights on and pulled the car over, even though he had slowed to 100 km/h. 該駕駛在經過躲著的警察之前就減下速度，但令他沮喪的是，警察將車子開了出來，打開警示燈把車子攔下來，即便他的車子已經慢到時速 100 公里了。
pull over	把……開到路邊 Officers spotted the stolen Nissan and pulled it over. He **pulled the car over** to the side of the road and stopped. 員警瞥見這輛失竊的日產汽車，並把該車攔下。他把車開到路邊，停了下來。 The driver reduced his speed prior to passing the speed camera, but, police pulled out and turned its lights on and **pulled the car over.** When the officer approached his car, the driver asked why he **was being pulled over.** 該駕駛在經過超速照像之前就減下速度，但警察將車子開了出來，打開警示燈把車子攔下來。當員警上前時，該名駕駛問說為何他被攔。
pull up	(使)停下來 Officer turned on his flashing lights and **pulled up** behind the suspicious vehicle. 員警打開他的閃燈，然後在這輛可疑的車

	子後面停了下來。
put out	撲滅
	Firefighter said there were several people in the building when the fire alarm went off. They attempted **to put out** the flames. 消防員說，當消防警報響的時候，有很多人在這建築物內，他們試圖滅火。
	Several houses had been burnt to the ground when the blaze **was put out**. 大火撲滅時，好幾間房子已全部燒毀。
	There was a lot of smoke, a lot of flames. Residents attempted **to put out** the flames. Minutes later, the house was fully engulfed in flames. 有很大的煙，很大的火，住戶試圖滅火。幾分鐘之後，這個房子就全部被吞噬在火焰中了。
	Don't attempt **to put out** the fire yourself, unless you can do so quickly and safely. 不要想自己去撲滅火勢，除非你可以很快而安全的這麼做。
put (sb) through	使某人經受(苦難、考驗等)
	In a letter he wrote to the victim after his arrest, he said, "I'm truly sorry for the pain I've **put you through**. I'm not a bad person. I am truly sorry for the misery in which you have endured. 在一封他被逮捕之後寫給被害人的信件中，他說，「我對於我讓你受到的痛苦真的感到抱歉，我不是一個壞人，我對於你忍受的苦難真的感到抱歉。」
put behind bars	【口】被關押，坐牢，在監獄服刑
	If a person is convicted of robbery and sentenced to six years in prison, he or she will **be put behind bar**s and serve the jail term. 如果某個人被判強盜罪確定，並判刑 6 年監禁，他就會放被到牢裡服刑。
put off	推遲，拖延
	The defendant moved **to put off** the trial until the next court on account of the absence of the witness. 由於證人缺席，被告聲請延後審理到下一次庭。
put on	穿(戴)上(服裝)
	The suspect **put on** a mask and went into the bank. After a short, he pointed his gun at employees and ordered them to the ground. 嫌犯戴上口罩並進入銀行，過一會兒之後，他用槍對著員工並命令他們趴到地上。
put out	撲滅
	Don't attempt **to put out** the fire yourself, unless you can do so quickly and safely. 不要想自己去撲滅火勢，除非你可以很快

	而安全的這麼做。
put up with	忍受、忍耐
	"I would never **put up with** that abuse," the abused victim said. 受虐的被害人說，「我不願意再忍耐那種暴力了。」
round up	圍捕
	Officer purposely left a car unattended in a high crime area, with the door unlocked, and then **rounded up** the suspect while he was committing the car theft. 臥底幹員故意把車子留在高犯罪地區，讓車門沒上鎖，然後等嫌犯進行竊車時圍捕他。
rule out	把......排除在外，排除......的可能性
	Detectives investigating the death of victim have revealed that they cannot **rule out** the possibility she was murdered. 偵辦這起被害人死亡的偵查員透露，他們不能排除她是被謀殺的可能。
run (sb) in	【口】逮捕某人, 拘留某人
	About two minutes later, officer arrived, and the witness said he was able to point out the suspect. As a result, officer quickly stopped the suspect, handcuffed him and **ran him in**. 大約 2 分鐘之後，警方抵達。證人說他可以指出嫌犯，結果，員警很快的攔到嫌犯，將他上銬並逮捕。
run across	穿過道路；意外找到，偶然遇見
	Police say the victim suddenly **ran across** the street and was struck by a vehicle that was travelling southbound. 警方說，被害人突然穿過馬路，並被一輛往南行駛的車子撞到。
run after	追趕，追蹤，追逐（對象等）
	An officer in a patrol car spotted the suspect walking on Lincoln Avenue, near Central Park, and the officer got out of his car and **ran after** the suspect. He called for backup while he **ran after** him on foot. 一位員警在巡邏車內瞥見嫌犯走在靠近中央公園的林肯大道上，然後該員警就出了他的車子並追逐該嫌犯，他用跑的追逐之際，呼叫了支援。
run away	逃跑，離家
	Officer said the burglar **ran away** and was tracked by police to an abandoned building. 員警說，竊嫌逃走了並且被警方追蹤至一間荒廢的建築物。
run away with	與......一起跑掉，偷走，與......私奔
	The two robbers **ran away with** the cash and drove off in an unknown vehicle. Surveillance image shows they demanded cash from the teller. The teller complied and the

suspect **ran away with** the cash. 兩名搶匪偷走現金並開一輛不詳的車子跑掉，監視畫面顯示，他們向櫃員要現金，櫃員照著意思，並且嫌犯就帶著現金跑掉了。

The judge decided to award full custody to the boy's father. The mother **ran away with** her son after the court ruled the boy should live with his father. 法官決定把全部的監護判給男孩的父親。母親就在法院判決孩童應與父親一起生活之後，帶著她的這個兒子走掉了。

run down	撞倒
	Police say a vehicle **has run down** pedestrians on the main street. After the crash, the driver called the police and reported that her car had run into pedestrians. She ran up to the sidewalk and ran over a young man. 警方說，一輛車子在大道上撞倒行人，車禍之後，駕駛打電話給警方報案說，他撞到了行人，他撞到人行道上並輾過一位年輕人。
run into	撞上；偶然碰到
	The drunk driver wasn't able to stop in time, and **ran into** the BMW from behind. The car also **ran into** the crowd. 酒醉的駕駛無法即時停下，並從後面撞上 BMW，車子也撞進了人群中。
run off	跑掉，逃走，離開
	Officers said they were searching for a suspect who **ran off** earlier. The suspect **ran off** but was found nearby with a gunshot wound in the leg. 員警說，他們正在搜尋稍早跑掉的嫌犯，該嫌犯跑掉，但在附近被找到，而腿部受到槍傷。
run off with	挾……而逃，與……一起走人
	Sally married him in 2014, but two years later she **ran off with** someone she met on the internet. 莎莉在 2014 年嫁給他，但是兩年之後，她與一位網路認識的人跑了。
run out of	用完，耗盡
	A motorcycle rider is behind bars after leading police on a high speed chase. Police pursued the biker until he **ran out of** gas and surrendered to the police. 機車騎士在導致警方高速追逐之後，被關了起來。警方追逐該騎士直到他耗盡汽油並向警方投降。
run over	壓過，輾過
	Police say a vehicle has run down pedestrians on the main street. After the crash, the driver called the police and reported that her car had run into pedestrians. She ran up to the sidewalk and **ran**

	over a young man. 警方說，一輛車子在大道上撞到行人，車禍之後，駕駛打電話給警方報案說，他撞到了行人，他撞到人行道上並輾過一位年輕人。
seal off	封鎖，封閉 (或稱 *cordon off*)
	Firefighter **sealed off** the area around the gas leak. 消防員將氣體外洩附近的區域封閉了。
	The crime scene investigation (CSI) unit **sealed off** the crime scene and conducted a preliminary examination. 犯罪現場調查小組封鎖了現場並進行初步的鑑識。
see for oneself	親自求證，親眼去看
	Detectives said that Chief of Police and the medical examiner had visited the crime scene to **see for himself** the circumstances surrounding the incident. 偵查員說，警察局長及法醫已經到過犯罪現場親自看了案件的相關情況。
see off	為……送行，向……告別
	He gave an alibi, saying that he had the platform ticket because he had accompanied Jennifer to the station to **see her off**. His alibi was checked and found to be correct, and they were both released. 他提供了一項不在場證明，說他有月台票，因為他陪珍妮佛去車站送她，他的不在場證明清查之後證實是正確，然後他們就被釋放了。
see through	透過(透明物)看，不為……所蒙蔽
	After the shooting, the suspect ran to a local store in an attempt to establish an alibi. The police **saw through** his alibi and arrested him for the murder. 槍擊案發生後，嫌犯跑到當地的一家商店想要建立一個不在場證明，警方看穿他的不在場證明，並將他依謀殺罪逮捕。
see through (sb)	滿足某人的需要，幫助或支持某人(尤指困難時)
	The woman is isolated and away from her family. She needs friends to stand beside her and help **see her through**. "We need to **see her through** this tough time," officer said. 該婦女被孤立並遠離家庭，她需要朋友在她的身邊並幫助她渡過。「我們必須幫助她渡過這個艱困的時刻」，警方說。
see to it	一定留意到，務必
	SWAT captain said he will **see to it** that safety equipment is inspected and being used before the raid is conducted. 「特種武器與戰術部隊/霹靂小組 (SWAT)」隊長說，他一定會注意，在掃蕩進行之前，安全裝備都有檢查以及使用。
set aside	駁回，撤銷

	The Court granted the defendant's motion **to set aside** the sentence. 該法院同意被告有關撤銷判決的聲請。
set forth	列舉，提出
	In general, crimes and penalties **are set forth** in the Criminal Code. Criminal proceedings and standards **are set forth** in the Criminal Procedure Code. 通常，犯罪與處罰是規定在刑法，刑事程序與標準是規定在刑事訴訟法。
	To become a police officer, police cadets must first ensure they meet the minimum requirements set forth by the police academy. 要成為一位員警，警校生首先必須確保達到警察學校規定的最低要求。
set off	使爆發，出發，動身
	Police is offering a $100,000 reward for the arrest of a man believed **to have set off** explosives near the Central Hospital. The blast **was set off by** a bomber at about 8p.m. last night. 警方提供 10 萬元獎金，以逮捕該名據信在中央醫院附近引燃爆裂物的男子，該爆炸是一個炸彈客大約昨天晚上 8 點引爆的。
	The suspect set off an explosion that nearly blew off the car. Some people assumed it was a firework. 嫌犯引爆了炸彈，幾乎炸掉整台車，有些人誤以為是鞭炮。
set out	動身，開始
	Dispatchers received a call from a woman who was yelling and screaming for help. The woman was unable to tell police where she was and what had happened, so police **set out** to find her. 派遣官接獲一名喊叫救命的婦女，因為該婦女能夠告訴警方她在哪裡以及發生了什麼事，所以警方動身前往找她。
Set sb. up	設局陷害
	Richard contacted the defendant Ramon and said he had set up a buy for amphetamine. At trial, Ramon claimed that that Richard set him up because Richard wanted to seek revenge on him. 理查聯絡了被告雷猛，並說他以經安排一次安非他命的買賣，審判時，雷猛聲稱，理查設局陷害他，因為理查想要報復他。
set up	設置
	To urge people to tip off police about crime, police will **set up** an anonymous tip line for people to give a clue. 為了呼籲民眾向警方通報犯罪，警方會設置匿名報案專線，讓民眾提供線索。

He turned to the police for help. The police decided **to set up** a controlled delivery of the marijuana to catch him. 他向警方求助，警方決定安排大麻的控制下交付來抓他。

shut down	(使)關閉，停工，使暫停營業，使停業

A crash on Roosevelt Road backed up traffic for hours this morning. Police shut down two lanes of traffic on the westbound side and closed the left lane on the eastbound route. 今天早上在羅斯福路的一場車禍讓交通回堵數小時，警方封閉了西向的兩個線道，並關閉了東向的左線道。

(使)關閉

The house fire shut down five streets near downtown as firefighters battled the blaze. 這場住家火災在消防員在進行滅火時，讓市中心的 5 條街道給封閉了。

shut off	關掉，切斷，使隔絕，停止供應(煤氣、水等等)

The SWAT unit was called to the scene and they spent several hours trying to negotiate with the suspect. Around 3:00 a.m. SWAT **shut off** the power to the house to try to force the suspect out. 「特種武器與戰術部隊/霹靂小組 (SWAT)」被呼叫到現場，並且他們花了數小時試圖與嫌犯談判，大約清晨 3 點鐘的時候，SWAT 關掉了該房子的電源試圖迫使該嫌出來。

In case of a disaster of any type, it is necessary to learn how to shut off utilities to avoid further damage to your family or your home. 萬一有任何種類的災害發生，學會如何切掉關掉各項設施來避免進一步的災害發生在你家人或你的家，是必要的。

It's important to know where the shutoff valve of gas meter is located. 知道瓦斯表的關閉閥在何處，是重要的

stand against	反對，對抗

"We are angry that this kind of violence is still happening. I hope that we can come together **to stand against** violence. We should come together to stop it," police said. 「我們很生氣這種暴力仍然在發生，我希望我們能夠團結一起對抗暴力，我們應該團結一起對抗它，」警方說。

stand aside	袖手旁觀

"I will not **stand aside** or back down. This isn't about me. This is about helping our citizens," the DIstrict Commander said. 「我不會袖手旁觀或退縮，這不是關乎我個人，這是關乎幫助我們的民眾」，分局長說。

stand back	退後

	When the protest turned into violence, officers immediately drew their baton and ordered the crowd **to stand back**. 當抗議演變成暴力時，員警立即拔出了警棍並命令群眾後退。
stand by	待命，準備行動；袖手旁觀
	During the standoff, police chief asked SWAT team **to stand by** in case the crisis cannot be resolved peacefully. 在對峙之際，警察局長要求「特種武器與戰術部隊/霹靂小組 (SWAT)」待命，以備萬一危機無法和平解決。
	Victim's family felt upset that people who witnessed the attack just **stood by** and watched without calling the police. 被害者的家人感到沮喪，那些目睹攻擊的人只是袖手旁觀並且看著，而沒有打電話報警。
stand for	代表；容忍
	The acronym CI **stands for** "confidential informant." The acronym CD stands for "Controlled Delivery". CI 這個縮寫代表「秘密線民(confidential informant)」，CD 這個縮寫代表「控制下交付(control delivery)」。
	The victim said she could not **stand for** the violence anymore. 被害人說她在野無法忍受暴力了。
stand up against	反對，抵抗
	At the conference, Unit Chief of the Domestic Violence Unit encouraged people **to stand up against** domestic violence. "We have to come together as a community, a group, to stop it," Unit Chief said. 會議上，家暴組組長鼓勵人們抵抗家暴，「我們必須社區必須團結一起來阻止它」，組長說。
stand up for	支持，捍衛，挺身而出
	Sometimes our children need **to stand up for** themselves to get bullies to stop. "They just need to have someone **stand up for** them physically to get the bullies to stop picking on them," experts say. 有時候，我們的孩子必須挺身而出讓霸凌者停止。「他們就是需要有人親身支持他們，讓霸凌者停止找他們麻煩」，專家說。
stay away from	(與某人/某事物)保持距離，不打擾
	The judge ordered the defendant to stay away from the victim. The judge also asked him to stay away from drugs and those who take drugs. 法官命令被告遠離被害人，法官同時也命令他遠離毒品及那些吸毒之人。
stay out	外出，不在家
	Do not allow your children **to stay out** late and hang out with

gang members or to attend parties where gang members might be present. 不要讓你的孩子在外面太晚並且跟幫派份子出去閒晃，或參加幫派分子可能出現的派對。

stay out of	避開，在……之外
	He said the gangster threatened him "You had to be in a gang if you wanted **to stay out of** big trouble." 他說幫派份子威脅他「如果你要避開大麻煩，就得加入幫派。」
stay put	【口】停在原地不動，保持原狀
	According to the police, the suspect barricaded himself inside his home and fired at the officers. Nearby businesses and homes in the area were all told **to stay put** during the shootout. 根據警方，嫌犯把自己阻絕在家裡，並對員警開槍，槍戰時，該地區附近的商家及住家都被告知停在原地不動不要動。
step in	插手干預，介入
	Because of the unusual circumstances of the victim's disappearance, the Major Crimes Unit **stepped in** and took over the investigation. 因為被害人特殊的失蹤情況，因此重案組介入並接手該項調查。
take account of	考慮到，體諒
	Correctional officials should **take account of** a prisoner's criminal history, and assesses the prisoner's special needs. 矯正官員應考慮受刑人的犯罪紀錄，並評估受刑人的特殊需要。
take down	取下，記下，寫下
	The witness **took down** the number plate and gave it to police. He was able to provide the police with the suspect's physical description and a description of the get-away vehicle. On the scene, police **took down** the name of the witness and his description of the suspect. 證人記下了車牌號碼並給了警方，他能夠向警方提供嫌犯的身體特徵以及逃逸車輛的特徵。在現場，警方記下證人的姓名及他對於嫌犯的描述。
take on	承擔，接受(挑戰)
	Homicide Division **took on** the investigation and arrested the prime suspect after a year-long investigation. 兇殺組接下該案偵查，並且在長達一年的調查之後，逮捕了主嫌。
take over	接管，接收，接任
	Because of the unusual circumstances of the victim's disappearance, the Major Crimes Unit was notified and **took over** the investigation. When the Major Crime Unit **took over** the investigation last Monday, the district police turned over

their evidence. Later, the suspect was also handed over to the Unit. 因為被害人特殊的失蹤情況，因此重案組被通知接手該項調查。當重案組接手該項調查時，分局就把證據移轉了，後來嫌犯也移轉給該組了。

take to the streets	走向街頭

Rioters **took to the streets** to protest the foreign dignitary's visit. 暴動者走上街頭抗議該位外國政要的訪問。

tell about	講述

Jack was apprehended and made a statement to the police, in which he **told about** his plan to evade apprehension. 傑克被捕並向警方做了陳述，其中他有講到他逃避逮捕的計畫。

tell on	告發，打小報告

Some students do not report bullying to teachers or parents partly because they are afraid that the bully would know who **told on** him.
有些學生不向老師或家長報告霸凌事件，有一部分是因為害怕老師會告訴惡霸是誰告發的。

think much of	想太多

"I heard a gunshot, but I didn't **think much of** it because it wasn't very loud, and I thought it was a firecracker," the witness said. 「我聽到槍響，但是我沒有想太多，因為那時很吵，而我以為那是鞭炮聲，」證人說。

think of	想到，考慮

The victim owed some money to the killer. The witness replied that he could not **think of** any other motive for the killing. "Other than that, I could not **think of** any reason why he would have killed the victim." 被害者欠殺人犯一些錢，證人回答說，他無法想到這件殺人案的其他動機。「除了那之外，我無法想到任何原因它會殺了被害者。」

think of...as	認為……是……

Domestic violence **is often thought of as** a family problem or private matter. It **is commonly thought of as** something that happens only to women. 家暴常被認為是家庭問題或私事，那經常被認為是只發生在婦女的事。

think over	考慮，仔細考慮

The court advised defendant that he could accept the plea bargain that day, and also offered defendant some time to **think it over.** 法院告知被告可以接受認罪協商，並且也給了他一段時間考慮。

tip off	向……洩漏消息
	To urge people **to tip off** police about crime, police will set up an anonymous tip line for people to give a clue. 為了呼籲民眾向警方通報犯罪，警方會設置匿名報案專線，讓民眾提供線索。
turn (oneself) in	自首
	Prosecutor recommended a reduction in his offense because he **had turned himself in** to authorities and pleaded guilty. 檢察官建請減輕其刑，因為他向當局自首並且認罪。
turn against	與……為敵
	The ringleader was arrested and lost the support. Some of his followers **turned against** him while he was incarcerated. They tried to remove him from power. 集團首腦被逮捕並失去支持，在他被關的時候，他的一些擁護者轉而與他為敵，他們想將他去除權力核心。
turn away from	轉身離去
	Nicole claimed that she **turned away from** Michael after an argument, and when she turned her back on Michael, Michael was angry and knocked her to the floor. 妮可聲稱吵架之後，她就轉身離開了麥可，並且當他轉身不理麥可時，麥可生氣並把他打到地上。
turn in	交上，歸還，投案
	The officer was suspended for taking bribes. The officer has been told **to turn in** his gun and badge. 該員警因為收受賄賂被停職，該員警已經被告知繳回他的槍與徽章。
	The Task Force was flooded with tips. Over 100 tips **were turned in**. 專案小組湧入了線索，有超過一百條的線索進來。
	Sam broke into a neighbor's house and stole the money. The police showed up at their house a few days later. Later on, Sam's mother found his son and called the police **to turn him in**. 山姆闖入鄰居家裡偷錢，幾天後警方上門到他家，後來，山姆的媽媽找到他兒子並打電話給警方投案。
turn into	變成
	The protest **turned into** a riot that ended up injuring 30 people and 3 police officers. Investigator said police ended up catching 5 suspects. 抗議變成了暴動，結果有 30 人及 3 位員警受傷。偵查人員說，警方結果抓到了 5 個嫌犯。
	When the protest **turned into** violence, officers immediately drew their batons and ordered the crowd to stand back. 當抗

議演變成暴力時，員警立即拔出了警棍並命令群眾後退。

turn one's back on	轉身不理，避開，拒絕接受
	Nicole claimed that she turned away from Michael after an argument, and when she **turned her back on** Michael, Michael was angry and knocked her to the floor. 妮可聲稱吵架之後，她就轉身離開了麥可，並且當他轉身不理麥可時，麥可生氣並把他打到地上。
turn out	結果是，證明是
	Police rushed to solve the crime under intense pressure. It **turned out** that the suspect was not a criminal. The suspect **turned out to be** innocent thanks to DNA testing. 警方在強烈壓力下急著結案，結果該嫌犯不是罪犯，因為 DNA 測試，該嫌犯結果證明是無辜的。
turn over	翻倒，傾覆；移交
	The driver was driving on the westbound expressway just before Exit 16 at 8:30 p.m. when he lost control of his vehicles, went off road and **turned over.** 該名駕駛下午 8 時 30 分的時候正開在西向的快速道路上 16 號出口前方，那時他車子失去控制、岔出道路並翻覆了。
	Police have completed their investigation into the death of Freddie Gray and **turned over** their findings to prosecutors. 警方完成了 Freddie Gray 死亡案的調查，並將調查結果移轉給了檢察官。
turn to (sb) for help	求助於
	Some studies showed that foreign spouses who are abused by their partners are less likely **to turn to police for help** because they feel that they'll be treated unfairly. 有些研究顯示，被施暴的外國配偶比較不可能向警察求助，因為他們覺得他們不會被公平對待。
walk into	走進
	Investigators said the unwitting victim **walked into** a trap set by her ex-boyfriend and was stabbed in the back. 偵查人員說，這個不知情的被害者走進了她前男友設下的圈套，背部遇刺。
walk off with	拿走，偷走
	The homeowner told officers someone had broken into his house and **walked off with** his 42-inch TV and some cash. 屋主告訴員警說，有人侵入了他的房子，並偷走他的 42 吋電視及一些現金。
	Susan told police that the stranger came up to her and offered

help, and then she attempted **to walk off with** her daughter. 蘇珊告訴警方說，該陌生人向他走來並表示要幫忙，然後該陌生人企圖要帶著她女兒走人。

walk out on	遺棄

The two children were left without a mother because she **walked out on** them after an argument with their father. She **walked out on** her family and returned to her country. 這兩個小孩被丟下沒了媽媽，因為媽媽與爸爸爭吵後丟下他們一走了之，她丟下家庭回去她的國家。

walk up to	走近

The suspect **walked up to** him, held a gun to his head and told him to give him his money or he would shoot him. 嫌犯走向他，握著槍對著他的頭，並告訴他把錢給他，否則會對他開槍。

watch out for	留意，防備

Watch out for cars when you cross the road. Pedestrians should **watch out for** driver when crossing a street although they have the right-of-way in crosswalks. 過馬路時當心車輛。雖然行人在行人穿越道有路權，但在穿越街道時，應留意駕駛人。

watch over	照看; 監視

The suspect was taken into custody for questioning. Captain said four officers **watched over** the suspect who was in handcuff. 嫌犯被拘禁問訊，隊長說，四位員警在看著這名上手銬的嫌犯。

work for	為……工作，為……做事 (work for...as... 為……工作而擔任……)

Raymond acknowledged that he **had worked for** the drug lord for five years. But he argued that he can't be prosecuted because even as he **worked for** Raymond, he also worked for the police a confidential informant. 雷猛承認他替這個毒梟工作了五年，但他主張不可以起訴他，因為即使他替雷猛做事，他也為警方工作擔任秘密線民。

work off	償清，還完

Traffickers confiscated their passports and used debt to force the victim **to work off** a debt. The Asian victims said they were willing **to work off** their checks by working in the restaurants. 販運者沒收了他們的護照，並用債務來強迫被害者以工償債，亞裔被害人說他們願意在餐廳做工，以工償還支票。

work on	從事

Detectives **are working on** leads that patrol officers have been receiving. The investigation is ongoing and detectives **are working on** a motive for the murder. Detectives **are working on** the theory that the suspect shot the six persons before turning the gun on himself. Meanwhile, police **are working on** notifying next of kin. 偵查員正在處理巡邏員警接獲的線索，調查仍在進行，並且偵查員正在進行有關謀殺的動機，偵查員在研究一項推論是，嫌犯在舉槍自盡之前先槍殺了這六人，同時，警方正在進行通知家屬。

| work over | 【俚】痛打某人(如為逼出情報) |

He'd **been worked over by** the gang for giving information to the police. 他向警方提供情報而遭到那幫人毒打。

Defendant alleged that he confessed to the crime after **being worked over by** police. 被告指稱他被警察動手而坦承犯罪。

相關縮寫 abbr.	
AED	自動體外心臟去顫器 automated external defibrillator
ACLS	高即心臟救命術 Advanced Cardiac Life Support
ALS	高級救命術 advanced life support
ATLS	高級外傷救命術 Advanced Trauma Life Support
BLS	基本救命術 Basic Life Support
BSA	身體面積區域 body surface area
SCBA	自給式空氣呼吸器 self-contained breathing apparatus
CAD	電腦輔助派遣系統 computer-aided dispatch
CS	昏迷指數 coma scale Glasgow coma scale (GCS) 葛氏昏迷指數
DOA	到院前死亡 Death On Arrival，目前多用 OHCA，即：「到院前心肺功能停止(Out of the Hospital Cardiac Arrest)」
DOS	於現場死亡 Death On Scene
DNR	放棄心肺復甦術 Do not resuscitation
EKG	心電圖 electrocardiogram [ɪ,lɛktroˋkɑrdɪə,græm]
EMS	急救醫療服務 Emergency Medical Services
EMT	緊急救護技術員 emergency medical technician
EOC	緊急應變中心 Emergency Operations Center
ER	急診室 Emergency Room
ETOA	預計到達時間 Estimated Time of Arrival (ETOA 或 ETA)
GCS	葛氏昏迷指數 Glasgow Coma Scale
HAZMAT	有害物質 hazardous materials(美國常用)
ICU	加護中心 intensive care unit
MCI	大量傷患事件 Mass Casualty Incident
NS	生理食鹽水 normal saline
OHCA	到院前心肺功能停止(Out of the Hospital Cardiac Arrest)，同「到院前死亡 Death On Arrival (DOA)」
PALS	高級小兒救命術 Pediatric Advanced Life Support
PHTLS	院前創傷生命救援術 Pre-hospital Trauma Life Support

國家圖書館出版品預行編目資料

執法英文字彙手冊／柯慶忠著. -三版.-臺中
市：白象文化事業有限公司，2024.2
　　面；　公分
ISBN 978-626-364-227-0（平裝）

1.CST: 法學英語 2.CST: 詞彙

805.12　　　　　　　　　　　112021769

執法英文字彙手冊（三版）

作　　者　柯慶忠
校　　對　柯慶忠
發 行 人　張輝潭
出版發行　白象文化事業有限公司
　　　　　412台中市大里區科技路1號8樓之2（台中軟體園區）
　　　　　出版專線：（04）2496-5995　　傳眞：（04）2496-9901
　　　　　401台中市東區和平街228巷44號（經銷部）
　　　　　購書專線：（04）2220-8589　　傳眞：（04）2220-8505
專案主編　林榮威
出版編印　林榮威、陳逸儒、黃麗穎、水邊、陳婷婷、李婕、林金郎
設計創意　張禮南、何佳誼
經紀企劃　張輝潭、徐錦淳、林尉儒
經銷推廣　李莉吟、莊博亞、劉育姍、林政泓
行銷宣傳　黃姿虹、沈若瑜
營運管理　曾千熏、羅禎琳
印　　刷　基盛印刷工場
初版一刷　2016 年 1 月
二版一刷　2016 年 9 月
三版一刷　2024 年 2 月
定　　價　400 元